I realized, looking around for the first time, that we weren't in Dusty Acres anymore. But where were we?

On the side of the pit on which I stood, a vast field of decaying grass stretched into the distance. It was gray and patchy and sickly, with the faintest tinge of blue. On the far side of the pit was a dark, sinister-looking forest, black and deep. Everything around here seemed to have that tint to it, actually. The air, the clouds, even the sun, which was shining bright, all had a faded, washed-out quality to them. There was something dead about all of it. When I looked closely, I saw that tiny blue dust particles were floating everywhere, like the wispy floating petals of a dandelion—except that they were glittering, giving everything a glowing, unreal feeling.

But not everything was blue. Underneath the boy's feet, yellow bricks, as vivid as a box of new crayons, were almost glowing in stark contrast to the blown-out, postapocalyptic monochrome of the landscape.

The golden path led all the way up to the ravine and then dropped off into nothingness. In the other direction, it wound its way through the field and spiraled off into the horizon.

It was a road.

DOROTHY MUST

DANIELLE PAIGE

HARPER

An Imprint of HarperCollinsPublishers

Library of Congress Control Number: 2014930869

ISBN 978-0-06-228068-8

Typography by Ray Shappell

Hand lettering by Erin Fitzsimmons

21   PC/LSCC   40 39 38 37 36 35 34

❖

First paperback edition, 2015

For Mom, Dad, Andrea, Sienna & Fiona

ONE

I first discovered I was trash three days before my ninth birthday—one year after my father lost his job and moved to Secaucus to live with a woman named Crystal and four years before my mother had the car accident, started taking pills, and began exclusively wearing bedroom slippers instead of normal shoes.

I was informed of my trashiness on the playground by Madison Pendleton, a girl in a pink Target sweat suit who thought she was all that because her house had one and a half bathrooms.

"Salvation Amy's trailer trash," she told the other girls on the monkey bars while I was dangling upside down by my knees and minding my own business, my pigtails scraping the sand. "That means she doesn't have any money and all her clothes are dirty. You shouldn't go to her birthday party or you'll be dirty, too."

When my birthday party rolled around that weekend, it turned out everyone had listened to Madison. My mom and I were sitting at the picnic table in the Dusty Acres Mobile Community

Recreation Area wearing our sad little party hats, our sheet cake gathering dust. It was just the two of us, same as always. After an hour of hoping someone would finally show up, Mom sighed, poured me another big cup of Sprite, and gave me a hug.

She told me that, whatever anyone at school said, a trailer was where I lived, not who I was. She told me that it was the best home in the world because it could go anywhere.

Even as a little kid, I was smart enough to point out that our house was on blocks, not wheels. Its mobility was severely over-sold. Mom didn't have much of a comeback for that.

It took her until around Christmas of that year when we were watching *The Wizard of Oz* on the big flat-screen television—the only physical thing that was a leftover from our old life with Dad—to come up with a better answer for me. "See?" she said, pointing at the screen. "You don't need wheels on your house to get somewhere better. All you need is something to give you that extra push."

I don't think she believed it even then, but at least in those days she still cared enough to lie. And even though I never believed in a place like Oz, I did believe in her.

That was a long time ago. A lot had changed since then. My mom was hardly the same person at all anymore. Then again, neither was I.

I didn't bother trying to make Madison like me anymore, and I wasn't going to cry over cake. I wasn't going to cry, period. These days, my mom was too lost in her own little world to bother cheering me up. I was on my own, and crying wasn't worth the effort.

Tears or no tears, though, Madison Pendleton still found ways of making my life miserable. The day of the tornado— although I didn't know the tornado was coming yet—she was slouching against her locker after fifth period, rubbing her enormous pregnant belly and whispering with her best friend, Amber Boudreaux.

I'd figured out a long time ago that it was best to just ignore her when I could, but Madison was the type of person it was pretty impossible to ignore even under normal circumstances. Now that she was eight and a half months pregnant it was really impossible.

Today, Madison was wearing a tiny T-shirt that barely covered her midriff. It read Who's Your Mommy across her boobs in pink cursive glitter. I did my best not to stare as I slunk by her on my way to Spanish, but somehow I felt my eyes gliding upward, past her belly to her chest and then to her face. Sometimes you just can't help it.

She was already staring at me. Our gazes met for a tiny instant. I froze.

Madison glared. "What are you looking at, Trailer Trash?"

"Oh, I'm sorry. Was I staring? I was just wondering if *you* were the Teen Mom I saw on the cover of *Star* this week."

It wasn't like I tried to go after Madison, but sometimes my sarcasm took on a life of its own. The words just came out.

Madison gave me a blank look. She snorted.

"I didn't know you could afford a copy of *Star*." She turned to Amber Boudreaux and stopped rubbing her stomach just long enough to give it a tender pat. "Salvation Amy's jealous. She's had a crush on Dustin forever. She wishes this were her baby."

I didn't have a crush on Dustin, I definitely didn't want a baby, and I absolutely did not want Dustin's baby. But that didn't stop my cheeks from going red.

Amber popped her gum and smirked an evil smirk. "You know, I saw her talking to Dustin in third period," she said. "She was being all flirty." Amber puckered her lips and pushed her chest forward. "Oh, Dustin, I'll help you with your algebra."

I knew I was blushing, but I wasn't sure if it was from embarrassment or anger. It was true that I'd let Dustin copy my math homework earlier that day. But as cute as Dustin was, I wasn't stupid enough to think I'd ever have a shot with him. I was Salvation Amy, the flat-chested trailer-trash girl whose clothes were always a little too big and a lot too thrift store. Who hadn't had a real friend since third grade.

I wasn't the type of girl Dustin would go for, with or without the existence of Madison Pendleton. He had been "borrowing" my algebra almost every day for the entire year. But Dustin would never look at me like that. Even at forty-pounds pregnant, Madison sparkled like the words on her oversize chest. There was glitter embedded in her eye shadow, in her lip gloss, in her nail polish, hanging from her ears in shoulder-grazing hoops, dangling from her wrists in blingy bracelets. If the lights went out in the hallway, she could light it up like a human disco ball.

Like human bling. Meanwhile, the only color I had to offer was in my hair, which I'd dyed pink just a few days ago.

I was all sharp edges and angles—words that came out too fast and at the wrong times. And I slouched. If Dustin was into shiny things like Madison, he would never be interested in me.

I don't know if I was exactly interested in Dustin, either, but we did have one thing in common: we both wanted out of Flat Hill, Kansas.

For a while, it had almost looked like Dustin was going to make it, too. All you need is a little push sometimes. Sometimes it's a tornado; sometimes it's the kind of right arm that gets you a football scholarship. He had been set to go. Until eight and a half months ago, that is.

I didn't know what was worse: to have your shot and screw it up, or to never have had a shot in the first place.

"I wasn't . . . ," I protested. Before I could finish, Madison was all up in my face.

"Listen, Dumb Gumm," she said. I felt a drop of her spit hit my cheek and resisted the urge to wipe it away. I didn't want to give her the satisfaction. "Dustin's mine. We're getting married as soon as the baby comes and I can fit into my aunt Robin's wedding dress. So you'd better stay away from him—not that he'd ever be interested in someone like you anyway."

By this point, everyone in the hallway had stopped looking into their lockers, and they were looking at us instead. Madison was used to eyes on her—but this was new to me.

"Listen," I mumbled back at her, wanting this to be over.

"It was just homework." I felt my temper rising. I'd just been trying to help him. Not because I had a crush on him. Just because
he deserved a break.

"She thinks Dustin needs her help," Amber chimed in. "Taffy
told me she heard Amy offered to *tutor* him after school. Just a
little one-on-one academic counseling." She cackled loudly. She
said "tutor" like I'd done a lap dance for Dustin in front of the
whole fourth period.

I hadn't offered anyway. He had asked. Not that it mattered.
Madison was already steaming.

"Oh, she did, did she? Well why don't I give this bitch a little
tutoring of my own?"

I turned to walk away, but Madison grabbed me by the wrist
and jerked me back around to face her. She was so close to me
that her nose was almost touching mine. Her breath smelled like
Sour Patch Kids and kiwi-strawberry lip gloss.

"Who the hell do you think you are, trying to steal my boyfriend? Not to mention my baby's dad?"

"He asked me," I said quietly so that only Madison could hear.

"What?"

I knew I should shut up. But it wasn't fair. All I'd tried to do
was something good.

"I didn't talk to him. He asked me for help," I said, louder
this time.

"And what could he find so interesting about you?" she snapped
back, as if Dustin and I belonged to entirely different species.

It was a good question. The kind that gets you where it hurts.
But an answer popped into my head, right on time, not two

seconds after Madison wobbled away down the hall. I knew it was mean, but it flew out of my mouth before I had a chance to even think about it.

"Maybe he just wanted to talk to someone his own size."

Madison's mouth opened and closed without anything coming out. I took a step back, ready to walk away with my tiny victory. And then she rolled into her heels, wound up, and—before I could duck—punched me square in the jaw. I felt my head throbbing as I stumbled back and landed on my butt.

It was my turn to be surprised, looking up at her in dazed, fuzzy-headed confusion. Had that just happened? Madison had always been a complete bitch, but—aside from the occasional shoulder check in the girls' locker room—she wasn't usually the violent type. Until now.

Maybe it was the pregnancy hormones.

"Take it back," she demanded as I began to get to my feet.

Out of the corner of my eye, I saw Amber a second too late. Always one to take a cue from her best friend, she yanked me by the hair and pushed me back down to the ground.

The chant of "Fight! Fight! Fight!" boomed in my ears. I checked for blood, relieved to find my skull intact. Madison stepped forward and towered over me, ready for the next round. Behind her, I could see that a huge crowd had gathered around us.

"Take it back. I'm not fat," Madison insisted. But her lip quivered a tiny bit at the f-word. "I may be pregnant, but I'm still a size two."

"Kick her!" Amber hissed.

I scooted away from her rhinestone-studded sandal and

stood up just as the assistant principal, Mr. Strachan, appeared, flanked by a pair of security guards. The crowd began to disperse, grumbling that the show was over.

Madison quickly dropped her punching arm and went back to rubbing her belly and cooing. She scrunched her face up into a pained grimace, like she was fighting back tears. I rolled my eyes. I wondered if she would actually manage to produce tears.

Mr. Strachan looked from me to Madison and back again through his wire rims.

"Mr. Strachan," Madison said shakily. "She just came at me! At us!" She patted her belly protectively, making it clear that she was speaking for two these days.

He folded his arms across his chest and lowered his glare to where I still crouched. Madison had him at "us." "Really, Amy? Fighting with a pregnant girl? You've always had a hard time keeping your mouth shut when it's good for you, but this is low, even for you."

"She threw the first punch!" I yelled. It didn't matter. Mr. Strachan was already pulling me to my feet to haul me off to the principal's office.

"I thought you could be the bigger person at a time like this. I guess I overestimated you. As usual."

As I walked away, I looked over my shoulder. Madison lifted her hand from her belly to give me a smug little wave. Like she knew I wouldn't be coming back.

***

When I'd left for school that morning, Mom had been sitting on the couch for three days straight. In those three days, my mother had taken zero showers, had said almost nothing, and—as far as I knew—had consumed only half a carton of cigarettes and a few handfuls of Bugles. Oh, and whatever pills she was on. I'm not even sure when she got up to pee. She'd just been sitting there watching TV.

It used to be that I always tried to figure out what was wrong with her when she got like this. Was it the weather? Was she thinking about my father? Was it just the pills? Or was there something else that had turned her into a human slug?

By now, though, I was used to it enough to know that it wasn't any of that. She just got like this sometimes. It was her version of waking up on the wrong side of the bed, and when it happened, you just had to let her ride it out. Whenever it happened, I wondered if this time she'd be *stuck* like this.

So when I pushed the door to our trailer open an hour after my meeting with the principal, carrying all the books from my locker in a black Hefty bag—I'd been suspended for the rest of the week—I was surprised to see that the couch was empty except for one of those blankets with the sleeves that Mom had ordered off TV with money we didn't have.

In the bathroom, I could hear her rustling around: the faucet running, the clatter of drugstore makeup on a tiny counter. I guess she'd ridden it out again after all. Not that that was always a good thing.

"Mom?" I asked.

"Shit!" she yelped, followed by the sound of something falling into the sink. She didn't come out of the bathroom, and she didn't ask what I was doing home so early.

I dropped my backpack and my Hefty bag on the floor, slid off my sneakers, and looked over at the screen. Al Roker was pointing to my hometown on one of those big fake maps. He was frowning.

I didn't think I'd ever seen America's Weatherman frown before. Wasn't he supposed to be reassuring? Wasn't it, like, his job to make us feel like everything, including the weather, would be better soon? If not tomorrow then at some point during the extended ten-day forecast?

"Hey," Mom said. "Did you hear? There's a tornado coming!"

I wasn't too worried about it. They were always predicting disaster around here, but although nearby towns had been hit a few times, Dusty Acres had always been spared. It was like we had cliché to shield us—Tornado Sweeps Through Trailer Park, Leaves Only an Overturned Barbecue. That's something that happens in a movie, not in real life.

My mom emerged from the bathroom, fussing with her hair. I was glad to see her vertical again, freshly scrubbed with her face all done up, but I had to wince at the length of her skirt. It was shorter than anything I owned. It was shorter than anything Madison Pendleton owned. That could only mean one thing.

"Where are you going?" I asked, even though I knew the answer. "For three days, you're one step away from a coma and now you're heading to the bar?"

It was no surprise. In my mother's world, there were only two pieces of scenery: the couch and the bar. If she wasn't on one, she was in the other.

She let out an accusatory sigh. "Don't start. I thought you'd be happy that I'm back on my feet again. Would you rather I just lie on the couch? Well, you might be content to mope around the house all day, but *some* of us have a life." She fluffed up her already teased hair and began looking for her purse.

There were so many things wrong with everything she'd just said that I couldn't even begin to process all the ways it was infuriating. Instead, I decided to try the sensible argument. "You're the one who just told me there's a tornado on the way. It's dangerous. You could get hit by a tree or something. Won't Tawny understand?"

"It's a *tornado* party, Miss Smarty-Pants," Mom said, as if that explained things. Her bloodshot eyes lit up as she spotted her purse lying on the floor next to the refrigerator and slung it over her shoulder.

I knew there was no point arguing when she got this way. "You need to sign this," I demanded, holding out the slip of paper Strachan had given me. It was to show that she understood what I'd supposedly done today, and what the consequences were.

"I got suspended," I told her.

It took her a few seconds to react, but when she did, her face registered not surprise or anger, but pure annoyance. "Suspended? What did you do?" Mom pushed past me again to get to her keys. Like I was just a thing that was in the way of something she wanted.

If we lived in a regular house, with one and a half bathrooms, I wondered, would she still hate me this much? Was resentment something that grew better in small spaces, like those flowers that Mom used to force to bloom inside in little vases?

"I got in a fight," I said evenly. Mom kept staring. "With a pregnant girl."

At that, Mom let out a long, whistling sigh and looked up at the ceiling.

"That's just great," Mom said, her voice dripping with something other than motherly concern.

I could have explained it to her. I could have told her exactly what happened; that it wasn't my fault. That I hadn't even hit anyone.

But the thing is, at that moment, I kind of liked having her think I'd done something wrong. If I was the kind of girl who got in fights with pregnant girls, it meant it was on her. And her stellar lack of parenting skills.

"Who was it?" Mom demanded, her plastic purse slamming into the counter.

"Madison Pendleton."

She narrowed her eyes but not at me. She was remembering Madison. "Of course. That little pink bitch who ruined your birthday party."

Mom paused and bit her lip. "You don't see it, do you? She's already getting hers. You don't need to help it along."

"What are you talking about? I'm the one who was suspended."

Mom flung her hand out and gripped the air, mimicking a pregnant belly. "I give her a year. Two tops before she's got a trailer of her own around the corner. That boy she's with won't stay. And she'll be left with a little bundle of karma."

I shook my head. "She's walking around like she's God's gift. Like she and Dustin are still going to be prom king and queen."

"Ha!" Mom hooted. "Now. But the second that kid comes, her life is over." There was a pause I could drive a truck through.

For a split second, I thought of how things used to be. My *before* Mom. The one who'd dried my tears and challenged me to a cake-eating contest at that fateful birthday party. "More cake for us," she'd said. That was when I was nine. After Dad left, but before the accident and the pills. It was the last time she'd even bothered remembering my birthday.

I didn't know what to do when she acted like this. When we were almost having a normal conversation. When she almost seemed like she cared. When I almost saw some glimmer of who she used to be. I knew better but I leaned into the kitchenette counter anyway.

"One second, you have everything, your whole life ahead of you," she said, fluffing her hair in the reflection from the stove. "And then, boom. They just suck it all out of you like little vampires till there's nothing left of you."

It was clear she wasn't talking about Madison anymore. She was talking about me. I was her little vampire.

Anger pricked in my chest. Leave it to my mother to turn any situation into another excuse to feel sorry for herself. To blame me.

"Thanks, Mom," I said. "You're right. I'm the one who

ruined your life. Not you. Not Dad. The fact that I've been taking care of you every day since I was thirteen—that was just my evil scheme to ruin everything for you."

"Don't be so sensitive, Amy," she huffed. "It's not all about you."

"All about me? How could it be, when it's always about you?"

Mom glared at me, and then there was a honk from outside. "I don't have to stand here and listen to this. Tawny's waiting." She stormed to the door.

"You're just going to leave me in the middle of a tornado?"

It wasn't that I cared about the weather. I wasn't expecting it to be a big deal. But I wanted her to care; I wanted her to be running around gathering up batteries for flashlights and making sure we had enough water to last through the week. I wanted her to take care of me. Because that's what mothers do.

Just because I'd learned how to take care of myself didn't mean I didn't still feel panic setting in every time she left me like this—all alone, with no clue when she'd be back, or if she'd ever be back at all. Even without a tornado on the way, it was always an open question.

"It's better out there than in here," she snapped.

Before I could think of a good enough retort, she was gone.

I opened the door as she slid into the front seat of Tawny's Camaro; I watched as Mom adjusted the mirror to look at herself and saw her catch a glimpse of me instead, just before the car vroomed away.

Before I could have the satisfaction of slamming the door

myself, the wind did it for me. So maybe this tornado was coming after all.

I thought of Dustin and his wasted scholarship, and about my father, who'd left me behind just to get out of here. I thought of what this place did to people. Tornado or no tornado, I wasn't Dorothy, and a stupid little storm wasn't going to change anything for me.

I walked to my dresser, pushed up flush against the kitchen stove, and opened the top drawer, feeling around for the red-and-white gym sock that was fat with cash—the stash of money I'd been saving for an emergency for years: $347. Once the storm cleared, that could get me bus tickets. That could get me a lot farther than Topeka, which was the farthest I had ever gone. I could let my mother fend for herself. She didn't want me. School didn't want me. What was I waiting for?

My hand hit the back of the drawer. All I found were socks.

I pulled the drawer out and rifled through it. Nothing.

The money was gone. Everything I'd spent my life saving up for. Gone.

It was no mystery who'd taken it. It was less of a mystery what she'd spent it on. With no cash, no car, and no one to wave a magic wand, I was stuck where I was.

It didn't matter anyway. Leaving was just a fantasy.

In the living room, Al Roker was back on TV. His frown was gone, sort of, but even though his face was now plastered with a giant grin, his jaw was quivering and he looked like he might start crying at any second. He kept chattering away, going on and on about isotopes and pressure systems and hiding in the basement.

Too bad they don't have basements in trailer parks, I thought.

And then I thought: Bring it on. There's no place like anywhere but here.

TWO

I had to admit it looked a little scary outside: the darkening sky stretched out over the empty, flat plain—a muddy, pinkish brown I'd never seen before—and the air seemed eerily still.

Usually on a day like today, even with bad weather, the old guy next door would be out in the yard, blasting old-fashioned country songs—the kind about losing your car, losing your wife, losing your dog—from his ancient boom box while the gang of older kids I never talked to would be drinking neon-colored sodas from little plastic jugs as they sprawled out on the rusty green lawn furniture and old, ratty sofa that made up their outdoor living room. But today, they were all gone. There was no movement at all. No kids. No music. No nothing. The only color for miles was in the yellowed tops of the dried-out patches of grass that dotted the dirt.

The highway at the edge of the trailer park, where cars normally whizzed by at ninety miles an hour, was suddenly empty.

Mom and Tawny had been the last car out.

As the light shifted, I caught a glimpse of myself in the reflection in the window and I saw my face, framed by my new pink hair. I'd dyed it myself and the change was still a shock to me. I don't even know why I'd done it. Maybe I just wanted some color in my stupid, boring gray life. Maybe I just wanted to be a little bit more like Madison Pendleton.

No. I didn't want to be anything like her. Did I?

I was still studying my face when I heard squeaking and rustling, and turned around to see my mom's beloved pet rat, Star, going crazy in her cage on top of the microwave. Star has got to be the world's laziest rat—I don't think I've seen her use her wheel a single time in the last two years. But now she was racing frantically, screaming her gross little rat screams and throwing herself against the sides of her home like she was going to die if she didn't get out.

This was new.

"Guess she abandoned both of us, huh?" I tried to ignore the twinge of triumph I felt at this. I'd always had the sneaking suspicion that Mom loved Star more than me. Now she couldn't be bothered with either of us.

The rat stared right at me, paused, and then opened her mouth to reply with a piercing squeal.

"Shut up, Star," I said.

I thought she'd stop after a second, but the squeal just kept coming.

Star didn't stop.

"Fine," I said when I couldn't take it anymore. "You wanna come out? Fine." I unlatched the top of her cage and reached in to free her, but as I wrapped my hand around her body, she thanked me by sinking her tiny teeth into my wrist.

"Ow!" I yelped, dropping her to the floor. "What's wrong with you?" Star didn't answer—she just scurried off under the couch. Hopefully, never to be seen again. Who even keeps a rat as a pet?

Suddenly the door of the trailer swung open.

"Mom!" I called, running to the open door. For a split second, I thought maybe she'd come back for me. Or, if not for me, then at least for Star.

But it had just been the wind. For the first time, it occurred to me that the impending tornado might not be a joke.

When I was twelve, when it all first started, I didn't get it at first. I thought Mom was actually changing for the better. She let me skip school so we could have a pajama day. She took me to the carnival in the middle of the school day. She jumped on the bed. She let us eat pizza for breakfast. But pretty soon she wasn't making breakfast at all, she was forgetting to take me to school, and she wasn't even getting out of her pajamas. Before long, I was the one making breakfast. And lunch. And dinner.

The mom I'd once known was gone. She was never coming back. Still—whoever she was now—I didn't want her out there on her own. I couldn't trust Tawny to take care of her in a disaster. More than that, I didn't want to be alone. So I picked up my phone and punched in her name. No service. I hung up.

I went to the door, still open and creaking back and forth on its hinges, and took a step outside to scan the horizon, hoping I'd see the red Camaro zooming back down the highway. A change of heart.

As soon as I put my foot on the first stair outside the trailer, I heard a whooshing noise as a plastic lawn chair flew through the air toward me. I hit the ground just in time to avoid getting beaned in the face.

Then, for a moment, everything was still. The lawn chair was resting on its side a few feet away in the dirt like it had been there all along. It began to drizzle. I thought I even heard a bird chirping.

But as I hesitantly got to my feet, the wind started back up. Dust swirled and stung my eyes. The drizzle turned into a sheet of rain.

The sky just overhead was almost black and the horizon was a washed-out, cloudy white, and I saw it, just like in the movies: a thin, dark funnel was jittering across the landscape and getting bigger. Closer. A low humming sound, like an approaching train, thrummed in my ears and in my chest. The lawn chair shot up into the air again. This time, it didn't come back down.

Slowly, I stepped backward into the trailer and yanked the door closed, feeling panic rising in my chest. I turned the deadbolt and then, for good measure, pulled the chain tight, knowing none of it would do any good.

I pressed my back to the wall, trying to keep calm.

The whole trailer shook as something crashed against it.

I had been so stupid to think this might be a joke. Everyone else was gone—how hadn't I seen this coming?

It was too late now. Too late to get out of town—even if I'd had the money to do it. I had no car to get to a shelter. Mom hadn't even thought to ask Tawny to drop me off somewhere. I was trapped here, and whichever way you sliced it, it was my mother's fault.

I couldn't even lie down in the bathtub. We didn't have a bathtub any more than we had a basement.

Al Roker's voice on the TV had been replaced by the buzz of static. I was alone.

"Star?" I squeaked. My voice barely made it out of my chest. "Star?"

It was the first time in my life that I'd been desperate for the company of my mother's rat. I didn't have anyone else.

As I sank onto the couch, I couldn't tell if I was shaking, or if it was the trailer itself. Or both.

My mom's stupid Snuggie was rancid with the stench of her Newports, but I pulled it over my face anyway, closing my eyes and imagining that she was here with me.

A minute later, when something snapped on the right side of the trailer, everything pitched to the side. I gripped the cushions hard to keep from falling off the couch. Then, there was another snap, and a lurch, and I knew that we'd come loose from our foundation.

My stomach dropped and kept dropping. I felt my body getting heavier, my back plastered to the cushions now, and suddenly—with a mix of horror and wonder—I knew that I was airborne.

The trailer was flying. I could feel it.

Dreading what I would see, I peered out from under the blanket and toward the window, squinting my eyes open just a crack to discover my suspicion had been right: Pink light danced through swirling clouds. A rusted-out car door floated by as if it were weightless.

I had never been on a plane. I had never been higher than the observatory, the tallest building in Flat Hill. And here I was now flying for the first time in a rusty old double-wide.

The trailer bounced and swayed and creaked and surfed, and then I felt something wet on my face. Then a squeak.

It was Star. She had made it onto the couch and was licking me tenderly. As her soft squeaks filled my ear, I let out a breath of something like relief just to have her here with me. It wasn't much, but it was something.

Mom was probably on her third drink by now, or maybe huddled with Tawny in the basement of the bar, a stack of kegs to keep them happy for as long as necessary. I wondered what she would do when she got back—when she saw that the trailer was gone, and me along with it. Like we were never here. Would her life be better without me in it?

Well, I had wanted to be gone. I'd wanted it for as long as I'd known there was anywhere to go. I wanted other places, other people. Another me. I wanted to leave everything and everyone behind.

But not like this.

I scratched my index finger against Star's furry spine and waited for the falling part. For the crash. I braced myself against the cushions, knowing that my tin-can house wasn't going to protect me when we hit the earth. But the crash didn't come.

Up and up and up we went. More white-pink light, more pink clouds, and every kind of junk you could imagine all swirling around in the surreal air blender: an unbothered-looking Guernsey cow. An ancient, beat-up Trans Am. An old neon service-station sign. A tricycle.

It was like I was on the world's most insane amusement park ride. I've never liked roller coasters. Going up would be fun if you didn't have to think about what always came next.

THREE

When I came to, the first thing I saw was the spongy gray floor of the trailer above me. Star was scampering around my achy body like it was a racetrack, trying frantically to wake me. It took me a second to realize that I was lying on the ceiling.

Light streaked through the dirty windows—normal, bright, white light again, not the blushy pink I'd seen during the tornado or the watercolor brown just before it.

I was alive. And someone was talking to me.

"Grab my hand," he was saying. "Step lightly." I turned my head and looked up to see a torso leaning in through the open door, half-in, half-out, and an arm reaching for me. It was a he, silhouetted by light pouring in from behind. I couldn't make out his face.

"Who are you?" I asked.

"Just take my hand. Try not to make any sudden movements."

From my side, Star squeaked and scrambled into the pocket of my hoodie.

I rose slowly to my feet and dusted myself off. Nothing seemed to be broken. But everything hurt like I was a rag doll that'd been thrown around in a giant tin can. When I took a step, the double-wide lurched beneath me. I rolled back on my heels, trying to get my balance, and it rocked with even more menace. I stopped.

"Just two steps and you're home. Hurry," he said. The distance between his hand and me seemed farther than two steps. I wanted to move again. But I didn't.

"It's okay," he said. "Don't panic. Just move."

I took another step, careful not to upset the equilibrium, and then another. I put my hand in his.

As my skin touched his, I saw his face, and I felt electricity shooting through my body. His eyes were the first thing I noticed: They were emerald green with flecks of something I couldn't even describe to myself, and they seemed to be glowing, almost floating in front of his face. There was something about them that seemed almost alien.

Was he a rescue worker? And if so, how far from home was I, exactly?

"Am I dead?" I asked. It certainly seemed possible. Likely, even. It was hard to believe that I had survived any crash.

"Of course not. If you were dead, would we be having this conversation?"

With that, he gave my arm a sharp, strong yank and pulled me through the tipped doorway. We fell backward, tumbling onto the ground outside.

I scrambled quickly to my feet and turned around to see that

I was standing on the edge of a deep ravine. My poor little trailer was barely holding on, teetering on the precipice.

The chasm was more like a canyon: it was as wide as a river and stretched on for as far as I could see in either direction. The bottom was all blackness.

"What the . . . ?" I whispered.

My trailer heaved, and then, with a final, aching creak, it lurched backward, letting go.

"No!" I screamed, but it was too late. The home that had once been mine was spinning down and down and down into the hole.

I kept expecting to see it crash and shatter into a million pieces, but it just kept on falling as I stood there watching it disappear into the abyss.

It was gone without even a sound. I had almost gone with it.

Everything I owned was in there. Every piece of ugly clothing. Every bad memory.

I was free of all of it.

"I'm sorry about your house," my rescuer said. His voice was soft, but it startled me anyway. I jumped and looked up to find that he was standing at my side. "It's a miracle you made it out. A few inches to the left and you'd have gone straight into the pit. Lucky, I guess." The way he said it made it sound like he thought it had been something more than luck.

"Did the tornado do that?" I asked. I stared back into the pit, wondering how far down it went. Wondering what was down there. "I didn't know tornadoes made giant holes in the ground."

"Ha. No." He laughed, but he didn't seem to think it was all that funny. "The pit's been here for a long time now." He didn't elaborate.

I turned to face him, and when I saw him standing there in the pale, blue-gray sunlight, my breath caught somewhere beneath my ribs. The boy was probably my age, and about my height, too. He was slim and sinewy and compact, with a face framed by dark, shaggy hair that managed to be both strong and delicate at the same time.

His skin was paler than pale, like he'd never left home without sunscreen or like he'd never left home period. He was part rock star, part something else. I couldn't put my finger on what the something else was, but I knew that it was somehow important.

And those eyes. They were glittering even brighter than before, and there was something about them that made me uneasy. It was like he had whole worlds behind his eyes.

He was beautiful. He was too beautiful. It was the kind of beautiful that can almost seem ugly; the kind of beautiful you don't want to touch, because you know it might burn. I wasn't used to talking to people who looked like him. I wasn't used to being *near* people who looked like him.

But he had saved my life.

"I won't miss it," I said, not sure if I meant it or not. "The house, I mean."

I could tell he didn't believe me, but he didn't argue. "I've never seen anything like it. Your tin farm. It must be very precious. A house made out of metal."

I guess they didn't have trailers where he was from. Lucky him.

I realized, looking around for the first time, that we weren't in Dusty Acres anymore. But where were we?

On the side of the pit on which I stood, a vast field of decaying grass stretched into the distance. It was gray and patchy and sickly, with the faintest tinge of blue. On the far side of the pit was a dark, sinister-looking forest, black and deep. Everything around here seemed to have that tint to it, actually. The air, the clouds, even the sun, which was shining bright, all had a faded, washed-out quality to them. There was something dead about all of it. When I looked closely, I saw that tiny blue dust particles were floating everywhere, like the wispy floating petals of a dandelion—except that they were glittering, giving everything a glowing, unreal feeling.

But not everything was blue. Underneath the boy's feet, yellow bricks, as vivid as a box of new crayons, were almost glowing in stark contrast to the blown-out, postapocalyptic monochrome of the landscape.

The golden path led all the way up to the ravine and then dropped off into nothingness. In the other direction, it wound its way through the field and spiraled off into the horizon.

It was a road.

"You've got to be kidding me." I was so astonished that I wasn't even sure if I had said it out loud or not.

I had been dropped here by a tornado, and now I was standing on something that looked remarkably like a road of yellow bricks.

This had to be some big mix-up. Maybe Kansas had finally cashed in on the whole Dorothy thing with a theme park and the tornado had just happened to drop me there. In which case, this guy was just a really hot park guide. I stared at him, waiting for him to explain.

"Welcome to Oz," the boy said, nodding, like he expected I'd figured that out already. It came out sounding almost apologetic, like, *Hate to break the bad news.*

Oz.

I touched my head, looking for a bump or something. I must have gotten knocked out and was having a particularly crazy hallucination.

At that, I let out a hoot of laughter. Good! With the way things had been lately, I figured I could use a fantastical hallucination right about now. It seemed like it had done Dorothy some good in the movie—and in Dorothy's fantasy, she'd been greeted by a bunch of Munchkins. A beautiful boy beat that any day.

"Aren't you supposed to bow down for me or something?" I asked, still laughing.

Instead of laughing along with me, concern washed over the boy's face, like he was worried I was going a little bit crazy.

Was I crazy? My head was swimming. If this was a fantasy, it was a strange one: this wasn't the Oz that I had read about or seen in the movie. It was as if someone had drained out some of the Technicolor and introduced some serious darkness.

Where were the good witches, the fields of enormous

poppies? Where were the jolly Munchkins? I guess even in my concussion-induced fantasies, I'm not creative—or cheerful—enough to come up with all that. Instead, I'd conjured up something that looked suspiciously like Dusty Acres right after a nuclear explosion.

I spun around to take it all in—a little too quickly in my excitement—and began to wobble at the edge of the cliff. My rescuer was there with a hand on my wrist, pulling me onto the brick road just in time to save me, yet again, from plunging to my death.

It took me a second, but I recovered my balance and stepped forward, getting my bearings. As I set one foot and then another onto the road, the bricks themselves seemed to almost pulse under me. Like there was a current running through them. "It feels like there's something under there," I said, looking down at my sneakers.

"The road wants you to go to the city."

"The road? Wants . . . me?" I rubbed my head in confusion.

"It wants everyone. That's what it's for. The road's been here longer than any of us. There's deep magic in there—magic even she doesn't understand. Some people think it has a mind of its own. It wants you to go to the city, but it doesn't like to make the trip easy."

It figured. Nothing was ever easy, in my experience.

"Who's 'she'?" I asked.

The boy reached out and tugged at a lock of my hair. The way he did it wasn't romantic, but more curious really. It was tender, too, but it was a sad kind of tenderness. No one ever touched me, anyway, and I flinched automatically. "There is so much you don't know. So much you have to learn. I wish you didn't."

Learn what? I wanted to ask. Or maybe I didn't want to know.

Then I felt a wriggling at my hip and looked down to see that Star was poking her head out of the pocket of my hoodie and was sniffing the air, looking just as confused as I felt. I pulled her out and placed her on the bricks, and she jolted. I guess the road had given her the same feeling it had given me.

"Easy, girl," I said. "You'll get used to it in a second." I looked back up at the boy. "If this is Oz . . . ," I trailed off, searching for the question that was on the tip of my tongue. Then I found it. "What happened here?" I asked.

I was waiting for him to answer when, out of nowhere, a look of panic crossed his face. For a moment, he looked disoriented, like he'd forgotten who he was. Something around the edges of his body seemed to flicker.

"Are you okay?" I asked. He didn't answer. He hadn't moved; now he seemed to be looking right through me.

I reached out and touched him on the shoulder.

"I have to go," he said.

"Go?" I didn't understand. He just got here. I just got here. What the hell was happening? "Where are you going?"

He shook his head. "Sorry," he said. "It's getting late. I've never left for this long. I have to get back before . . ."

"Don't," I said, maybe a little too desperately. Maybe this was a dream and maybe it wasn't, but either way, I didn't want to be left here, in the middle of nowhere, all alone. "Before what? What are you talking about? Who are you?"

"I'm no one," he said, turning away and walking toward the pit.

"Please," I begged.

He turned back to me one more time.

"This is where it all began for her, you know. I don't know why you're here or who brought you, Pink Hair, but if you're here, it means it's all beginning for you, too. You're like her in so many ways, but I can tell you're different. I can't help you. I'm not powerful enough. But you can help yourself. Prove me right. Don't make the same mistakes she made."

"But . . ."

"Be brave," he said. "Be angry. Don't trust anyone. I'll see you soon."

He stepped to the edge of the road, to right where the bricks crumbled away into the black. Then he jumped.

"No!" I screamed, lunging forward, catching myself just in time before I followed him. Below me, the darkness looked relentless and unforgiving. The road wanted something, he had told me, and now I knew the pit did, too. It was hungry. It was already infinite and still it wanted more.

There was no sign of him. The boy was gone.

I looked down at Star, who was perched on her haunches at my feet. "So what do we do now?" I asked, half expecting her to say something back.

She didn't need to. I knew the answer already: what I was going to do next was the same thing I'd been doing my whole life.

I turned back. Just put one foot in front of the other. Nothing had changed except the color of the road.

FOUR

Star and I walked, following the road, and when she seemed to get tired, I took her and placed her on my shoulder, where she perched patiently and looked out into the distance. She knew just as well as I did that we were very far from home.

Despite my crash landing in Oz, my body was surprisingly free of bruises, aches, and pains. Actually, I felt pretty good. The headache I'd had when I'd first landed had subsided, and now I felt full of energy.

I was hoping that the place would cheer up as I got farther away from the pit. I was still hoping for a tree that grew lollipops or a welcome committee of cheerful Munchkins—or *anything* cheerful, really. But as I walked down the road, the countryside remained as grim and desolate as before, everything cast in the eerie blue light that reminded me of the glow of a television from underneath the crack of a closed door.

There were no singing birds. The only signs of life were the giant ravens that occasionally swooped overhead, startling me every time they crowed. There were no trees to be seen, but the air smelled vaguely of burning leaves.

After a while, the bedraggled fields by the side of the road turned into huge cornfields on either side, with stalks as tall as my body. I was used to cornfields back in Kansas, obviously, but these were different: every ear was as black and shiny as oil. It looked like each one had been dipped in tar. Or like all the life had been sucked out of them and had something dead and evil pumped back in their place.

Curious, I reached out to pull one of them from its stalk. Before I could even touch it, a black vine sprung up from the ground and curled around my arm like a whip, squeezing tight. It burned. I yelped and pulled away, managing to twist myself free, and retreated to a spot in the center of the road that I hoped was safely out of reach. I made a note not to go poking around at anything else here. This wasn't Dorothy's Oz.

It was Oz, wasn't it? The boy had called it that, and the fact that I was walking along a road made of yellow bricks was enough to convince me I wasn't in Canada or Argentina. I just had no idea what *this* Oz had to do with the story I knew. It would have been nice if he'd given me a little more information.

Or maybe he had: Suddenly I remembered what he'd said to me before he'd disappeared into the pit. "Don't make the same mistakes she made."

Could he have been talking about Dorothy? "This is where it all began for her," he'd said. Who else could he have meant?

And what "mistakes" had she made?

I thought about it some more. What if Dorothy had been here, just like the book said, but she had somehow gotten it wrong? Like, what if the witch had killed *her* instead of the other way around? If so, this depressing version of fairyland definitely felt wicked enough to be the result.

It was a weird idea—so weird that I felt my headache coming back as I tried to wrap my head around it—but what if Dorothy had screwed everything up and someone had decided to bring over another girl from Kansas as some kind of do-over?

I shuddered to myself. I had enough problems of my own back in Kansas. Why couldn't I have been swept away to an imaginary kingdom where nothing was wrong at all—where I could just kick my legs up and enjoy a nice, relaxing vacation? I racked my brain, trying to remember if there were any books or movies like *that*, and realized there weren't any.

Well, one thing was for sure—I didn't have any magical shoes to take me home. Even if I *could* click my heels together and be right back in Kansas where I'd started, I wouldn't. This place was dark and scary and a little evil seeming, but it was something new and different. Now I just needed to find someone to tell me what was going on here.

So I felt my heart leap when the road dipped down into a shallow valley and curved to the right, heading right toward a cluster of buildings that was sprawled at the foot of the hill.

A town. There *had* to be people living there. This time, I would make them give me some answers.

As I made my way toward it, though, I began to see that my hopes for human contact might need to wait a little longer. The buildings, which were arranged around a decrepit stone plaza, were all cracked and crumbling and grown over with ivy that looked like it had never been tended. The facades of some of the houses had been spray-painted with some kind of graffiti tag: an angry, green frowny face.

The whole area had the distinct look of a place that had slowly been deserted, kind of like the town a few miles away from Flat Hill that everyone had abandoned when the plastic flower factory had shut down.

"Hello?" I called out when I had reached the ring of buildings encircling the town square. There was no response.

From up close, it was clear that this place had actually been nice, once. Even abandoned like this, there was something cheerful and quaint about the way the houses—all of various heights—were built so close together that they were practically stacked on top of one another, as if personal space wasn't something they cared about around here. And although they were falling apart now, each house was beautifully crafted, with domed roofs and round windows and ornate wooden shutters with fancy iron hardware.

I had to hunch a little to peer inside the nearest window, which barely reached my chin. Inside, there was a table set for five with moldy food on each plate, like whoever had once lived there had left in the middle of dinner.

"They could really use some Munchkins around here, huh?"

I said to Star, who hadn't moved from her perch on my shoulder. She just stared back at me balefully and didn't bother squeaking a response.

I jumped back in surprise when I stepped into the square. Someone was smiling down at me triumphantly. Then I realized it wasn't a *person* at all. It was a statue cast in marble, and it was the first thing I'd seen in the whole town that wasn't dirty and crumbling. In fact, it was so white that it was glowing—all except for the pair of glittering silver shoes on its feet.

Of course, I recognized it immediately. With her kind, smiling face, her jaunty gingham dress, and her neatly curled pigtails, there was no mistaking her: it was Dorothy. The silver plaque on the pedestal confirmed it:

Here Stands Dorothy Gale, it read. She Who Arrived on the Wind, Slayed the Wicked, and Freed the Munchkins.

By now, I'd given up on the idea that I was dreaming—my body felt too heavy and solid, and as bizarre as everything was, none of it had the sticky, underwater quality of a dream. Even so, it was kind of unreal to confirm the alternative with my own two eyes: that I had been thrown into a fairy tale.

"Dorothy likes her statues," a voice said, from out of nowhere. Startled, I looked around to see where it was coming from, and saw a face peering down at me from the second-story window of a house a few paces off. "Me, I have to say, I'm pretty sick of them."

There was a thud as a small black knapsack landed next to me. Unthinkingly, I reached down for it.

"Don't touch that!" the voice growled. I jumped back and saw her scrambling out the window. She dangled by her fingers before dropping to the ground, landing softly as if the height were no big thing. It was a girl. She looked up at me with a mixture of suspicion and curiosity, and when she sprung to her feet, I saw that there was no way she was more than four feet tall, even in her platform boots.

Now *this* was more like it. I was face-to-face with a real, live Munchkin.

At least, I was pretty sure that's what she was. Her hair was inky blue-black and her eyes were caked in thick eyeliner with triple fake lashes. She was wearing a vampy eggplant-hued lipstick and a leather skirt. Her T-shirt revealed arms covered in complicated tattoo sleeves.

But she was short, and she moved with a springiness and agility that was something more than just plain old human. Anyway, I'd already been here long enough that I wasn't shocked to find out that there was such a thing as a goth Munchkin.

"Excuse me?" the girl barked as I looked her up and down curiously. "Do you have a problem?"

Heat rose to my face as my mind flashed to Madison Pendleton.

"Nope. Do you?" I snapped right back at her. I couldn't even look at a *Munchkin* without starting trouble. Was she going to punch me now, too?

She didn't. Instead, she let out a wry cackle and rolled her eyes. "Let's see," she said. "Do I have a problem? How about, do I have *five thousand*?" She marched right over to where I

stood and grabbed her bag from where it lay at my feet. It was
stuffed to the seams with what I figured must be an entire leather
wardrobe. "The answer's yes, by the way."

"I'm Amy," I said, hoping this was what passed for friendly
in Munchkin Country. I reached out a hand, which she ignored.

"Indigo," she replied. She eyed my shoulder. "Cool rat, by the
way. I love rats. Does it talk?"

I glanced at Star, still hoping she would decide that the answer
was yes. She didn't respond.

"Nope." I shrugged.

"Too bad." Her eyes traced up to my head. "But I don't know
about the hair. *She's* not going to like it."

I put a hand to my scalp and brushed a pink lock from my eyes.

"Why would my pet rat care what my hair looks like?"

Again, Indigo hooted. "Not your rat, dumbass. *Her.*"

"Who's *she*?"

Indigo scrunched her face up and swiveled her neck like I was
a complete moron. "Oh yeah, *who's she*? she asks. Please."

"No, seriously," I said. "I'm new around here. Tell me who
you're talking about."

"*I'm new around here,*" Indigo mocked me in a squeaky fal-
setto, slipping her backpack on. But as she did it, she looked at
me. Really looked at me.

"Wait, you're not kidding, are you? You really *aren't* from
around here." She was staring at my clothes. I guessed that jeans
and a hoodie were not what the kids were wearing in Oz.

"No," I said simply. "I'm not."

Her jaw dropped open in slow motion as it dawned on her. "Holy *shit*," she said. "You're from the Other Place, aren't you?" She looked over one shoulder and then the other, then asked quietly: "How did you get here?" I couldn't tell if her tone was one of excitement or fear.

"It was a tor—" I began, but before I could finish, I was cut off by a loud, metallic clanking sound from somewhere off in the distance.

Indigo took a step backward. "You know what?" she said, her eyes darting nervously from building to building. "Never mind. It's better if I don't know. In fact, it's better if I don't talk to you at all."

"What? Why?"

She busied herself with her backpack, her tiny face scrunched up with worry.

"Like I said, I've already got about five thousand problems, give or take a thousand. Getting caught conspiring with an outlander would be five thousand and one. I'd love to hear your story, but it's not worth it. Good luck. You'll need it." With that, she hoisted her pack on her shoulders and began to walk away.

"No way!" I yelled. "Just let me ask you some questions. I have *no* idea what's going on."

"If you're lucky, you'll never find out," she said, not slowing her pace or bothering to look back.

I wasn't going to let this happen again. She was speeding along, heading off the road, but my legs were longer. I raced after her and grabbed her by the elbow.

"Hey!" she said, whirling around to face me. "Don't touch me!" She yanked her arm away, but I yanked right back. And I was stronger.

"Let me come with you," I whispered urgently. I didn't know where she was going, but she was the best hope I had. Hope of what, I wasn't sure, but I would figure that out later. "I promise— I'll do whatever you want. I swear I won't get you in trouble. But I'm alone here, and I have no idea what I'm doing."

She bit her lip. The thing is, I could tell she was as curious about me as I was about her. I could tell part of her wanted to relent.

But then we heard that clanging noise again. This time it was louder.

"You seem like a nice person," Indigo hissed. "And I love rats. But get your fucking hands off me and get the hell away from me. The best thing you can do right now is get your ass back to wherever it is you came from and hope you never wind up in this sorry place again."

"I don't know *how* to go home," I said. But I let her elbow go. This wasn't getting me anywhere.

"It looks like you've got problems, too, then." Indigo folded her arms across her chest, planting her stocky body firmly in place. "See ya," she said.

Honestly, I was starting to think this girl was kind of an asshole. But if she wasn't going to help me, I couldn't think of any good way to force her. All I could do was keep following the road and hope it led me somewhere better than this.

So I walked away, back to the famous road paved with yellow

bricks. At least I had a general sense of where that would take me. When I looked back over my shoulder, the angry little Munchkin was watching me go.

As I passed the statue of Dorothy, I changed my mind one more time. "Just tell me one thing," I asked her, spinning around. She shrugged, noncommittal. She hadn't budged from the spot where I'd left her. "They talk about Oz where I'm from. I've heard about it my whole life. But this is messed up. What happened here?"

Indigo's impassive face twisted into a snarl. "*Dorothy* happened," she said.

FIVE

Dorothy happened. I'd tried to ask Indigo what she'd meant, but her eyes had gone from blue to black and she'd threatened to punch me in the face if I came one step closer or asked her another goddamn question. I had already been punched in the face once today—that had been today, hadn't it?—so I did what she wanted and kept on moving.

It was only a few minutes before I put the tiny little town behind me. Now I was back on the road. Ahead, it led up a steep hill that was completely devoid of any grass at all, the raw dirt interrupted only by a few stunted, sickly shrubs here and there.

Dorothy had been here, I reminded myself. She had walked this very same path. *You're like her in so many ways*, the boy had said.

Kansas, tornado, blah, blah, blah. I mean, the similarities were pretty obvious, right? But there were plenty of differences between us, too. First off, from what I remembered it hadn't taken her long at all to make friends. It was like everyone she'd run into—witches not included—had wanted to jump on the Dorothy Express.

As for me, I'd come across two people so far, and exactly both of them had wanted nothing to do with me. It was kind of depressing to think that I could travel all the way to Oz and still be just as unpopular as I was back in Flat Hill, Kansas.

I didn't know where to go next, but the Emerald City seemed as good a place to start as any. That's where Dorothy had gone for help. The road would take me there. It *wanted* to take me there.

So I trudged up the hill, and as I did, the banging sound I'd heard back in the village continued. It was still intermittent— there were a few minutes of welcome silence for every thirty seconds of racket. It was getting louder with every step I took, though, and soon it was so loud that I had to cover my ears every time it started.

When I finally reached the top of the incline I saw where it was coming from.

In the distance, across a periwinkle field of dust and dirt and beyond a tangled maze of gnarled, thorny trees, stood a towering seesaw contraption that was attached by a mess of pipes and wires to something that looked like a cross between an oil rig and a windmill.

When I squinted, I saw at least twenty people of less-than-average height piled on either end of the seesaw thing. Every few minutes, the Munchkins would start bouncing up and down in place, and as they did, the taller machine would begin spinning and clanging, jackhammering into the earth.

Above all of the action a statuesque figure in a glittering ball gown floated serenely in midair, just watching them at work. I tried to see what was holding her up but as far as I could tell she was just . . . floating.

Wait, a *ball gown*?

I couldn't make up my mind which part I was more curious about: the fact that she was levitating or the fact that she was doing it above a field of dirt, dressed like she was on her way to the prom.

I stared at her with rapt curiosity. Even from here, I could tell that she was no Munchkin. Not just because she was too tall to be one either. There was just something *different* about her. Something familiar that I couldn't place. She had to be at least a couple of hundred feet away, but it was like her image was burning right through all that distance and imprinting itself right onto my retinas.

She was the most beautiful creature I'd ever seen. Her hair was red, and her skin was glowing, and her body was radiating a shower of glittering pink sparks.

I smacked my head as it came to me.

Duh. It must be Glinda. She was supposed to be the Good Witch of the South, right?

I felt my face light up at the sheer insanity of it all. When I'd watched *The Wizard of Oz* with my mother, Glinda had always been my favorite character—because who wouldn't want to travel around in a flying soap bubble wearing an awesome dress? She'd been my mom's favorite character, too, but for a different reason.

"She's a witch, but she's *Good*," Mom always said. "Now that's what I call the best of both worlds."

Finally, Oz was living up to its name. I had to see her up close.

As I stepped off the road and began to push my way through the thick mass of gnarled and twisted trees, I saw that they had sickly pale blue bark. They were thorny, too, and I had to gingerly push the branches aside, being careful not to cut myself. The whole time, I stared into the sky, mesmerized by the sight of Glinda. I couldn't wait to meet her. I didn't even care about the fact that my skull was vibrating from the noise the machine was making.

As I wound my way toward her, Star began to get uneasy. She clawed and fidgeted at my shoulder. There was something about all this that she didn't like.

"Will you stop it?" I whispered to her. "It's *Glinda*. Jeez."

I could somehow hear Glinda's voice echoing over the deafening noise, like she was speaking through a megaphone.

"There is no crying, little ones," I heard Glinda call out, her lilting voice full of kind, gentle encouragement.

The Munchkin boy she was talking to couldn't have been older than seven or eight. He was sitting in a little chair near the top of the seesaw, and from his red cheeks and puffy eyes, it was clear he'd just finished one major sob session and was working himself up for another. Glinda was talking him down from it. "What we do, we do for the good of Oz," she cooed. "You do love Oz, don't you?"

The kid nodded, sniffing up his tears and wiping the snot from his nose, and then he threw himself back into the motion of the seesaw.

The clanging began again. My skull was vibrating so hard

that I thought it might explode. My hands flew to cover my ears, but that did virtually nothing.

I was close enough to really see her now. Her dress was even more extraordinary from this vantage than it had appeared in the distance. Instead of the beautiful, flowing dress that the character had worn in the book, this gown was more like armor: thin metallic petals made up the voluminous skirt while magenta jewels dipped and curved across her chest in a tight, plunging bodice. It wasn't my style, okay, but it was still pretty amazing.

She seemed perfect. And yet, as I approached, an uneasy feeling prevented me from calling out her name.

Something wasn't right. From far off, she looked beautiful, ethereal, otherworldly. But up close, there was something ugly about her. Something was wrong with her *face*.

Yes, she was delicate-featured with exquisite bone structure, her perfect strawberry-blonde curls escaping from underneath a blinged-out golden crown as she smiled benevolently down at her loyal subjects. But that smile. It was—I don't know how else to put it—kind of super-gross.

It stretched unnaturally wide, spreading out maniacally all the way across her jaw from one cheekbone to the other, and it was twitching at the corners like her lips had been pinned into place.

Other than the twitching, it didn't move. At all. Even when she talked.

"What's with her mouth?" I asked Star under my breath, after the machine had halted its banging once again.

I jumped when an actual voice answered in a hoarse whisper from behind me.

"(A) it's PermaSmile, and (B) are you out of your dumbass *mind*?"

I whirled around to see Indigo's bright, aquamarine eyes staring out at me from somewhere within the shadowy web of the tree branches.

"Have *you* been following *me*?" I whispered back at my stalker, and then—my curiosity winning out over my annoyance—added, "And what's PermaSmile?"

"I wasn't *following* you," Indigo replied with a petulant scowl. "I was just going in the same direction you were going in." She paused. "Besides, I couldn't let you just wander up to Glinda like she's going to give you a kiss and a cookie. I'm a softer touch than you think. And *this* is PermaSmile."

She pulled out a small tube and held it up. "I never wear it, but it comes in handy to have around," she said, uncapping the top and smearing it across her mouth like lipstick. As she did, her scowling lips stretched like putty into a wide, maniacal grin and stayed that way.

"Ew," I said, unable to help myself.

"I know," she said. "I hate it." Her huge grin barely moved as she spoke. It was like Botox in a tube. Then she drew it across her face again, in the opposite direction this time, and, just like that, her mouth returned to its customary half scowl. "Everyone wears it in the city, and since that's where I'm going, I'll need it."

"The Emerald City?"

"Yes, the Emerald City," she mimicked. "Where else? Now come *on*. We can't just hang around down here. She could smell us at any second."

"*Smell* us?" I asked, genuinely confused. "What is she, a hunting dog? Besides, isn't she supposed to be a *good* witch?"

"Sure," Indigo snorted. "*Good*. Like that means anything around here. I hate to break it to you, but just because someone has pretty hair and good skin tone and a crown instead of a pointy hat doesn't mean she's not the baddest bitch this side of the Emerald City. Seriously. I can't believe I'm risking my own neck to help you out."

"But—" I said.

"No buts," Indigo said. "Look, I'm giving you a chance. If you want to stay here and hope she takes a liking to you, be my guest. If you'd rather not get killed, follow me."

Then she was scampering back toward the road, effortlessly weaving through the thorns and branches like they weren't even there.

I paused for a moment. Glinda and Dorothy the bad guys? It was all so upside down—and yet, something about what Indigo was saying seemed right. I didn't want to believe her, but I knew all too well that you can't always get what you want. So I followed.

By the time I made it back to the road I was a scratched-up mess, my shirt torn and my arms crisscrossed with tiny cuts. Indigo was waiting for me, looking typically sour.

"Don't get too excited," she grumbled, but I could tell that somewhere underneath all that, she was happy I was joining her. "You can come with me as far as the city and then you're on your own. And you do what I say, got it? You've already proven you have no survival instincts."

"Deal," I said.

I craned my neck back up at the so-called good witch, who was still floating eerily in the sky. How could I come all the way to Oz and pass up a chance to meet the one and only sorceress herself? It was like going to Disney World and not getting your picture taken with Cinderella.

I don't think I have to tell you that my mom never took me to Disney World.

I was still wavering when Star hissed at me angrily. I knew what she was trying to tell me. With a twinge of regret, I chased after Indigo.

Sometimes you just have to trust your pet rat's instincts.

SIX

"Now, can you tell me what was going on back there?" I asked when we were back on our way.

"She's magic mining," Indigo explained, with the tone of someone explaining why the sky is blue to a toddler for the five hundredth time.

I half understood. Maybe. "Magic mining? But she's a witch. Doesn't she already *have* magic?"

Indigo gave a loud, angry snort. "It's never enough. Never enough for her, and sure as hell never enough for Dorothy. They're digging holes from here to the capital and sucking it right up out of the land. Why do you think all of Munchkin Country's such a dump? Oz needs magic to survive. Without it, it just dries up."

"So magic is like—in the ground?"

I thought of the dark, gaping pit that had swallowed my trailer. Was that one of Glinda's excavation sites? If so, Greenpeace would have a few bones to pick with the Witch of the South if they ever made it to Oz.

"Yup." Indigo nodded. "Well, it's everywhere, but it starts in the ground and seeps out from there. Dig it all up and take it for your royal self, though? No more magic. The end; unhappily ever after."

I'd never thought of myself as someone who was slow on the uptake, but this was all very confusing.

"Okay," I said eventually. "Back up. You keep talking about Dorothy like she's still here. But she went back to Kansas. That's, like, the whole point of the story. *There's no place like home* and all that."

Really, it was the one part of *The Wizard of Oz* that I'd never liked. Girl gets whisked away to fairyland and all she can think about is *going home*? Sure, she missed her auntie Em. But you'd think her aunt would be happy for her to have gotten out of Kansas. Personally, I'd always thought Dorothy should have knocked her heels together and wished for something better than a trip back to Nowheresville.

"You only heard half the story. She *did* go home," Indigo said. "Turns out home wasn't so great after all. So Glinda brought her back here. Or, at least, most people think it was Glinda who brought her back. That's like, how the legend goes. One way or another, when Dorothy got here, that's when the problems all started."

"What do you mean?"

Indigo shrugged and waved her hand over the landscape.

"See for yourself. She was okay at first—I guess—but then they gave her a crown and made her a princess. And somewhere along the way she got a taste for magic. Pretty soon nothing was enough for her. The more she got, the more she wanted."

"So the magic made her go off the deep end and start digging pits? Why is Glinda even helping her?"

"Think of it this way," Indigo said. "You've got your Witch of the East. Dorothy crushes her with a house. The Witch of the West—Dorothy melts *her* with a bucket of water. Glinda's the Witch of the South. Notice that she's the one who's still standing? Glinda knows what's good for her. She knows that the worst thing you can do around here is get in Dorothy's way."

"What about North?" I asked.

Indigo gave me a puzzled look.

"East, West, South," I said. "What about the Witch of the North?" I asked.

Indigo just looked away. "You ask too many questions," she said.

The world had been changing color while we'd talked. The closer we got to the Emerald City and away from Glinda and her machine, the more the chilly blue glow of the sky melted into something sunnier and pleasant. The grass grew greener and thicker on the ground, too, and every now and then I noticed a few crocuses poking their heads out of the earth.

I wasn't positive, but as I listened carefully I was pretty sure I even heard some birds singing a tentative song. On the other hand, maybe it was just the residual sound of the drill ringing in my ears.

"Why do the Munchkins cooperate?" I asked. "If it's ruining their home, it seems like they wouldn't go along with it."

Indigo leveled me with a cool stare.

"How about you stop asking about things you'll never understand," she said. "We're going to get you to the Emerald City and you're going to find some nice witch who will know how to send you right back to Kansas where you and your pink hair belong."

After that, we walked in silence. Every time I tried to find another avenue for conversation, she shot me right down.

I thought about what she'd said about Dorothy. The explanation that she'd given me was barely any explanation at all: it was one thing to believe that Oz had been corrupted by someone truly evil, but Dorothy had been good once. She had fought the Wicked Witch of the West and freed Oz. How had things gone so wrong for her?

Suddenly my mother's face flashed into my head, and I remembered what it had been like for her.

It hadn't happened overnight. She'd been in a lot of pain after the car accident, and at first the pills just made her happy again. In some ways, it was happier than I'd seen her since my dad had left and we'd sold the house. Which made *me* happy, too.

It always wore off, though, and then it started wearing off faster and faster. She always wanted more. When she got more, she wanted more than that. And that was the end of life as we knew it. Every time I came home to find her sprawled out on the couch, or on the floor, the orange bottle still in her hands, I found myself amazed that something so tiny could hold so much power over her.

If what Indigo said was true, Dorothy had gotten a taste of magic, and when it was gone, it had left her hollow. How much magic did she have now?

It wasn't a question worth asking. To someone like her, or someone like my mom, it wasn't a matter of how much she had. It was how much she *didn't* have.

All of this was making me wonder where my mom was. I hoped she was okay.

It felt like we'd been walking for hours. My feet were shooting with pain but the sun showed no signs of waning. Although our surroundings had brightened up considerably, it was monotonous and unchanging. The novelty was wearing off. I was too bored to even be creeped out anymore.

I kept waiting to come across a unicorn or a talking scarecrow or a river of lemonade, or some other magical Oz thing. I would have settled for a regular tree or a river made out of water. Or even, maybe, a monster.

So far, there was nothing.

"I have to sit," I said finally. Indigo twisted her lips and then nodded.

"Fine," she said, plopping herself down onto a rock by the side of the road. I sat down next to her. I took Star off my shoulder and placed her on the ground, and she took the opportunity to scamper away into a patch of weeds. I knew she'd be back.

"How far is the city?" I asked. "We've been walking forever."

"Dunno," Indigo said. "I've never been."

So we sat in silence. I wished I could pull my phone out just to have something to do, but my phone, along with everything else I'd ever owned, was at the bottom of the pit. If the pit even had a bottom. Instead, I found myself studying the Munchkin's tattooed arms, trying to untangle the elaborate, inky swirls that were etched into them, but it was weird—the more I stared at the designs, the more they seemed to be a blur. It was like they didn't want me to understand them; like they were hiding their true meaning from me.

Indigo noticed me staring, and she rolled up her T-shirt sleeves to let me take a better look. "It's Oz. The *real* Oz," she said. "I wanted to remember how it used to be. So I got it inked. They'll have to skin me if they want me to forget now."

As she spoke, the tattoos began to form themselves into a picture before my eyes and I saw what she was talking about: her arms were a history. It was a beautiful, picturesque panorama, filled with flowers and animals—some of which I didn't even recognize—and happy, smiling people. The craziest part was that the picture was moving. Just barely, but moving for sure. The Munchkins on Indigo's biceps were dancing a jig. The animals were frolicking; the flowers were rustling in the breeze. There was even a witch, green and wicked with a pointy black hat, cheerfully dancing something like a hula.

"Magic ink," she said. "Cool, right?" She said it like it was no big deal, like she was talking about the new shoes she'd just bought at the outlet mall. She waved her hand in the air, gesturing at the landscape around us. "It's better here since we're farther away from the mines, but nothing's what it used to be. It'll just be one big pit soon."

She looked so sad. It was the worst kind of sad, too—the kind where you're sad about something that you know will never change. The kind of sad you can't even bother getting angry about anymore.

Did all of Oz feel this way? If so, it must be a terrible place to live.

I stood up and brushed myself off. "Come on," I said. "We're going to the Emerald City."

Indigo stared up at the sky like she was looking for a clue. I was beginning to wonder when the sun was going to go down. The sky was just as light as it had been when we'd started walking. It didn't even feel like it was the same *day*, much less the same afternoon.

"I don't know," she said after a while of just looking. It sounded more like she was talking to herself than to me. "I don't actually really know anything. I don't even really know why I want to go. We'll probably get caught before we make it there anyway. She has spies everywhere." She sighed a long sigh. But she followed me back onto the road.

"You asked why they work for her," she said. "You asked why the Munchkins don't just tell Glinda to fuck off and take her machine somewhere else."

"Yeah. I was wondering that. Maybe it was stupid of me."

"It was," Indigo said, shooting me an annoyed look. "Do you think they have a choice? I was one of those kids bouncing up and down on a seesaw for hours, you know. But I got away. Now my family's gone, my house is empty, and I have no idea what I'm going to do with myself. If I get caught, they'll kill me. So. That's why they do it, okay?"

"I didn't know," I said. "I'm sorry." And I was.

"When we get to the Emerald City, we're going to find someone to send you home. And when we do, they're going to send me along with you. Anything's better than this."

She saw it before I did.

"What the hell?" she said, stopping dead in her tracks in the middle of the road.

Ahead of us, we heard a screechy, unearthly caterwaul. Star squealed in response. I sped up to see what was going on. Then I wished I hadn't seen it at all.

A few paces off, something was tied to a post at the edge of the road. The something was furry. It screeched again.

"One of the monkeys," Indigo said, almost in a whisper. The creature was dangling upside down from the post, a thick rope binding his ankles in place. This wasn't your normal monkey, though: he was dressed like a little preppy in khaki pants with jaunty red suspenders and leather Top-Siders on his feet.

Despite his outfit, he looked a long way from Nantucket. He

appeared to be in so much pain: his eyes were half closed, blood-crusted, and unfocused. His mouth was dry and cracked; his fur was dirty and matted. He didn't look at us—I was pretty sure he couldn't even tell we were there.

But he was conscious enough to express his anguish, and he let out yet another earsplitting scream. Indigo raced forward and when I caught up with her, she was kneeling, reading a sign that was nailed just below where the monkey's head swayed inches from the ground.

For the Crime of Sass, This Monkey Is Hereby Sentenced to Official Attitude Adjustment. Do Not Tamper. By Royal Order of Princess Dorothy.

"The crime of *sass*?" I whispered angrily. They'd made that a crime?

Indigo seemed paralyzed. She didn't respond.

Well, at least *I* was here to help him. "Poor little monkey," I said. "Let's get you down from there." I made a move to untie him, but Indigo grabbed my wrist. She was almost shaking.

"No," she said. "We can't."

"What are you talking about? You can't just leave a defense-less animal tied up by the side of the road. Look at him. I'm surprised he's still alive. And what the hell? This is what she calls an *attitude adjustment*? What's wrong with this place?"

Indigo shook her head sadly. "We have to leave him. If we don't, we'll be considered just as guilty as he is. I've seen it before." She looked up at me with tears in her eyes, and I some-how understood that this had already happened to someone she loved. "Welcome to Oz," she said. Her voice caught, and then she stood and dusted herself off. Her face, which had just a moment ago looked close to crumpling, hardened back into her typical scowl.

"Come on. Let's keep moving. Forget we even saw it."

I shook my head at her. *It* was wearing pants. *It* had dried blood all over it. *It* was in eardrum-busting pain.

"You saved me from talking to Glinda."

"That was different. You hadn't been convicted of anything."

I looked at her and then back at the monkey. I couldn't leave him. There was just no way. So without hesitating—without thinking, really—I reached up and began to untie the ropes that held him to the post.

"No!" Indigo cried. But she didn't try to stop me. Within seconds I'd gotten him free. I caught him in my arms—he was heavier than he looked—and as I laid him carefully down on the yellow bricks, I felt two rough, bald little stumps on his shoulder blades.

It took me a second to realize what they were, and when I did, I felt sick to my stomach. This monkey had once had wings.

"Shit," Indigo said, running her fingers through her hair in panic. "Shit, shit, shit shit." She had scampered to the middle of the road and was looking up and down in either direction like she thought they would be coming for us at any moment. But no alarm bells started ringing. No gunshots rang out; no flare was sent up. Nothing happened at all.

"What do you think is coming?"

"You don't understand. They have their ways. They know everything. They see everything."

"How? Who?"

"They just do."

"If *they* knew everything that went on around here, they'd have already caught us. Come on—you must have some water somewhere in that giant pack of yours, right?"

Reluctantly, Indigo dug around in her bag and came back with a canteen. She handed it to me, and I poured the water over the animal's cracked lips and waited. After a moment, his eyes fluttered open. He gurgled and sputtered for a moment before registering our presence.

"There you are . . . ," I said, leaning over to give him another sip.

"Thank you," he said in a weak, hoarse voice.

"Oh my God!" I exclaimed, jumping back. "He can talk!"

"Of course I can talk," he croaked. Even in his weakened state, he managed to sound offended. "I'm an educated monkey. My name is Ollie."

Although I was still freaked out, I bent down to help him sit up. My fingers brushed against the jagged, stumpy nubbins poking out of his shoulder blades.

"Don't mind those," he explained, seeing the look of confusion on my face. "That's just where my wings used to be. Before I cut them off."

SEVEN

"We need to move," Indigo said. "That post he was tied to was probably enchanted. They'll know that we freed him."

"Maybe we should leave the road," I said. "We're too exposed. If they're looking for us . . ."

Indigo was shaking her head emphatically. "No," she said. "The road leads to the Emerald City. That's where we're going."

Ollie agreed. "We're in the wildest part of Munchkin Country," he said. "Once we step off the road of yellow bricks, things get turned around. Directions stop making sense. We'll be lost in no time."

"You're going to the city, too?" I asked.

Ollie nodded. "They say that the entrance to an underground tunnel is hidden somewhere in the city walls. The tunnel leads north, to where the rest of the Wingless Ones live. I'm going to find it."

"There are others like you? Without wings?"

"Dorothy wanted to harness them," Indigo snapped, her face suddenly red. "Make them her slaves. She wanted a thousand of them pulling her sicko flying monkey chariot. What else were they supposed to do?"

It was good to see her mad, actually. At least anger can get you somewhere. I liked this Indigo better than the Indigo I'd been sitting with on the rock an hour ago, the Indigo who seemed like she'd just given up. I liked this Indigo better than the one who had been so terrified that she'd wanted to leave Ollie strung up by the side of the road.

I just didn't know what she was talking about. I looked at Ollie quizzically.

"My people have always been used by those who are more powerful," he began to explain. "Even before Dorothy rose to power, we were slaves to others. It's part of our enchantment. The wings are vulnerable to magic; they make us easy to control. When we were freed from the witches we thought we would never have to serve anyone again. But then Dorothy came back. This time, some of us decided that the price of freedom was worth paying."

"So you cut off your wings," I said. I couldn't imagine that kind of sacrifice. I thought I understood it, though.

"I would rather be free than fly," Ollie said firmly. "Not all of my people agreed." A look of pure disgust crested his face. "The ones who would be free went north, into hiding."

"Why are you here, then?" I asked. "Why aren't you up north with them?"

"I couldn't leave them."

"Who?" I asked.

He looked at the ground. "My parents," he said. "My sister. They thought their wings were what made them special. So they stayed behind. Now they pull Dorothy's chariot. I thought I could help them. I thought I could convince them. . . ." He faltered, his voice breaking.

"I guess Dorothy must not have liked that plan," I said.

Indigo was getting antsy. "We need to go," she snapped. "We don't have time for Oz History 101."

There was still so much more I wanted to ask Ollie, but Indigo was right. If everything they were telling me about Dorothy was true, we were asking for trouble just sitting around like this.

"Can you make it?" I asked Ollie. "You still look pretty weak."

But Indigo was already marching ahead of us, her boots stomping against the brick road. Ollie shrugged and he and I followed a few paces behind, moving as quickly as we could.

I was starting to get tired, not to mention hot. The sun, which had had an eerie, icy-blue tint to it back in Munchkin Country where I'd landed, was now a bright, fiery yellow, beating down on my skin. I could feel a bead of sweat forming at the base of my scalp.

The sun had changed colors; it had gotten hotter. But it hadn't actually *moved*: it was still hanging in exactly the same place, dead center in the sky, that it had been when I'd set out on my way. It didn't show any signs of budging.

"Is it just me, or has this day been really long?" I asked Ollie.

He groaned. "The day's as long as Dorothy wants it to be," he said. "She controls the time around here. Sometimes it's ages before she remembers to turn the hands on the Great Clock and make it night again. The princess gets distracted easily."

I shuddered. In addition to everything else, Dorothy controlled time itself. We kept walking.

The girl took us all by surprise when she appeared in the middle of the road out of nowhere, blocking our way. She had dark hair and flawless, ivory skin, and was dressed in a silk sheath dress in emerald green, setting off huge green eyes. She must have been about my age, and she was more beautiful than any girl I'd ever seen before. She also had way more bling: strapped to her head was a tall gold crown that burned in the endless afternoon sunlight. Her ears were covered by giant, jewel-encrusted poppies that looked like really fancy earmuffs.

As soon as they saw her, Indigo and Ollie dropped instantly to one knee. Indigo grabbed my arm and pulled me down with her.

"Dearest people of Munchkin Country!" The girl was talking to us as if she were addressing a huge audience, except there was no one else here. "I am pleased to announce this auspicious day for all of Oz! A day when sadness bids its final farewell and joy begins its eternal reign! By royal order, under punishment of death, I hereby declare Happiness henceforth!"

Indigo sighed in disgust and rose to her feet just as the girl was starting her speech all over again. It was like someone had set her on repeat. "Dearest people of Munchkin Country!" the girl cried again.

"It gets me every time," Indigo muttered. "Just ignore her," she said, noticing my confused expression. "Come on."

"It's not real," Ollie explained, standing, too. "Just a recording. You come across them every now and then, to keep us in line. I bet it means we're getting closer to the Emerald City, though."

"Who is she?" I asked. "That's not Dorothy. Is it?"

"It's Ozma. Oz's true ruler," Indigo said. "She's still technically in charge, but no one's seen the real Ozma outside the palace in ages. It's always just these illusion things. Look."

She wound her arm up like a pitcher and went to slap the girl. Her hand passed easily through the princess's head.

"See? Fake. The *real* Ozma doesn't care about us anymore."

"I am pleased to announce this auspicious day for all the people of Oz!" Ozma kept babbling.

Ollie looked away from the hologram like it hurt him to stare at her even a second longer, and then Indigo stepped right through her and we all just kept on walking. Ozma's canned speech faded slowly away into the distance.

"We waited a long time for a ruler like her." Ollie sighed. "She was supposed to be in charge all along—she's descended from the fairy who gave Oz its magic. But she was just a baby when the Wizard came here, and he didn't want her getting in his way. So he sent her off somewhere. Then, when *he* left, he made the Scarecrow the king. That didn't go well."

"The Scarecrow was evil, too? Like Dorothy?" I asked. I was having a hard time keeping track of all this, but something about it seemed important.

"No," he said, and then chuckled ruefully to himself. "Not *then* at least. He just wasn't a very good king."

"He wanted to sit around the palace thinking all day," Indigo cut in. "If you ask me, brains aren't all they're cracked up to be. Anyway, everything went to hell, until Ozma came back."

"Where was she that whole time?"

"No one knows," Ollie said. "She would never talk about it. But she has fairy blood, which meant she had a right to the crown. It's deep magic—since she was finally of age, no one could do anything to take it away from her."

"Dorothy did," I pointed out.

"Not exactly," Ollie said.

"Ozma was in charge for a long time," Indigo said. "Things were good with her. The best. The sun rose and set on time. There was magic everywhere. . . ."

"The monkeys flew wherever they wanted while Ozma reigned," Ollie interjected.

"It was what Oz was supposed to be all along," Indigo said. "The funny part is that when Dorothy came back, everyone was happy at first. She was a hero, you know. And nothing changed for a while, except that she moved into the palace. She and Ozma became friends. They did *everything* together. No one even minded when Ozma made her a princess, too. It seemed like she deserved it."

"And then?"

"Then came the Happiness Decree. After that, we stopped seeing so much of Ozma. It was, like, all Dorothy all the time. Ozma was just . . . gone."

"You think Dorothy did something to her."

Indigo nodded. "I don't know *what*," she said. "But Ozma would never let this happen to Oz. She must have been tricked . . . or . . ."

"Or she's dead," Ollie said.

"No!" Indigo nearly shouted. "She can't be dead. Dorothy's not powerful enough. *No one's* powerful enough. Once Ozma had the crown, nothing could take it away from her. It's fairy magic—that's the strongest there is. Nothing can break it. Nothing can kill her."

Ollie didn't look so sure. "What if the magic's gone?" he asked. Indigo didn't answer him.

The whole time they'd been giving me a primer on Oz's history—which I still wasn't sure I understood—we'd been walking, and now we had come to a wide, stagnant river. The water was mossy and still and rotten-smelling, and had a toxic green tint to it. At the muddy bank, a tangle of thick black vines twisted like snakes.

Luckily, we didn't have to swim through that muck: as it neared the water, the yellow bricks began to ascend, stretching up and out into the air in a meandering path. There was nothing supporting them—no cables or columns or beams—and the whole road swayed and fluttered back and forth like a ribbon in the wind.

I gulped. "Are we supposed to cross that?" I asked. Heights weren't exactly my favorite thing.

But the height was the least of our problems.

"Monkeys," Ollie breathed, pointing at the tiny silhouettes

that swooped and dove against the newsprint-gray of an end-less cloud that hovered just above the road. "They're patrolling the bridge."

I laughed nervously. "Time to turn back, I guess." But I knew we couldn't. Where would we go? We had seen what there was to see back there. The only direction was straight ahead.

Indigo looked up at the monkeys in thought. "I think we can make it past them," she said. "I know a spell that might work."

"Wait," I said. "You can do magic? You didn't tell me that."

Indigo cocked her head and raised her eyebrows like she was offended. "My grandmother was a sorceress," she said. "She may not have been as powerful as Glinda, but she taught me a thing or two. She would have taught me more, if Dorothy hadn't banned it. But the Winged Ones are more susceptible to magic than almost anyone. I think a misdirection charm will get us past them."

She closed her eyes and raised her hands, moving her fingers in front of her in rapid, fluttery movements. I looked down at myself, waiting to see what would happen—was I going to turn invisible or something? But nothing changed.

After a minute, Indigo opened her eyes. "I think we're good to go," she said. "Just don't talk. Don't do anything that will attract attention."

"I don't think it worked," I said.

"It worked. Misdirection's not that powerful, but it will do the job. It won't hide us from them totally; it just makes us easy to overlook. They'll simply be distracted every time they look in our direction. Trust me."

The thing is, I was having a really hard time concentrating on what she was saying. But I got the idea.

Crossing the flying road was like trying to walk on a breeze. It rippled and dipped and swayed back and forth, and every time you lifted your foot you had to wonder if there would be anything under it when you put it back down.

Ollie was fine: he went scampering on ahead on all fours as easily as if we were still on solid ground. Indigo didn't have too much trouble either. She was so squat and compact that it would take a wrecking ball to knock her over. But I was neither a monkey nor a Munchkin and I had to stretch my arms out at my sides and consider each step carefully.

I didn't look down. I just kept my eyes on the road; the bricks yellower than ever against the dull gray of the sky.

Well, I tried to. Unfortunately, it's hard to keep your eye trained on a moving target. Every time the narrow swath of road shifted, it revealed the water a million feet below us and still as menacing as ever. I didn't know which would be worse: the fall, or what would be waiting for me underneath the surface of the nasty, slimy river.

With every step, I wanted to panic. I wanted to sit down in the middle of the road and hug my legs to my knees and give up. But I didn't do any of those things.

Tornado or no tornado, a girl from Kansas doesn't let much get to her. So I set my fear aside, put one foot in front of the other, and as the road carried me high into the sky, I felt myself becoming less and less afraid. I wasn't going to let anything as stupid as a breeze or a few wobbly bricks knock me off my feet.

That's what it means to be from the prairie. It was something I had in common with Dorothy.

I knew exactly how high up I was when I felt my fingertips scraping clouds.

After my dad left, my mom and I would watch *Wheel of Fortune* every night after dinner. I wasn't very good at it, but my mom always guessed the answer before the contestants. At the end of each episode, Pat would thank their sponsors, and as he reminded us about the joys of Flying the Friendly Skies, an airplane would drift across the screen, bound for Sunny Aruba or Fabulous Orlando or wherever, floating in slow motion across a sunset-pink landscape of fluffy clouds.

I didn't like the idea of airplanes, and I didn't really want to go to Orlando anyway. But I'd always wondered what it would be like to touch a cloud.

Now I knew the answer to that, at least when it came to Oz clouds. It turned out they were just as soft and fluffy as they looked on *Wheel of Fortune*, as solid as cotton balls, but they were nothing you'd want to curl up and take a nap on. Every time my fingers grazed one, it sent an icy shock up my arm and down my spine into my toes. Some of them were as small as party balloons and others were as big as couch cushions, and soon they were so thick in the air that I had to swat them out of my path in order to keep moving.

Meanwhile, I could hear monkeys screeching, getting louder and louder. They were so close that I could feel their wings flapping just inches above my head. Every now and then I'd hear a scream so loud it straightened my spine. The sour smell of monkey breath filled my nostrils.

But Indigo's spell had worked. They were close enough to touch, but the monkeys were ignoring me, acting like I wasn't even there.

Finally the road began to curl in on itself, rising up in a steep, tight coil until I came to the top and stepped onto a small, circular platform twice as wide around as a hula hoop. This was the top. I was so high up that even the monkeys were beneath me now. It was all downhill from here. Literally: on the far edge of the platform, the yellow road plunged back toward the ground at a steep, straight incline, the rough texture of the bricks suddenly slick and smooth. It was a Yellow Brick Slide.

But that was nothing in comparison to the sight on the horizon. The Emerald City had come into view. Nothing I'd seen so far had prepared me for it. It seemed to have come out of nowhere, just when I was least expecting it, and now that I was looking at it, it was hard to understand how it hadn't been visible all along, with its swooping skyline that was so green it colored in the sky around it, and the palace with towers so high that they disappeared beyond the clouds.

From up here, looking down on the city in the distance, you could almost forget everything that had gone wrong here. From up here, you could almost pretend that this was the Oz that should have been.

But as much as I would have liked to have stayed up here

forever with that fantasy, I knew the monkeys would spot me eventually if I didn't keep moving. I gulped, looking down. *Just pretend you're going down a waterslide at AquaLand*, I told myself. It might have made me feel a little better if I'd ever actually *been* to AquaLand. My mom had never taken me.

So I just took a deep breath, dropped to my butt, and reassured myself that going down had to be easier than coming up. If nothing else, it would be faster. I closed my eyes and pushed off.

My stomach dropped as I hurtled downward, the wind whipping across my face and gaining speed every second. At first I was terrified, but after a minute, I inched my eyes open and saw the clouds whipping by as the ground approached at high velocity. Feeling a rush of exhilaration, I opened my mouth to whoop with joy and caught myself just in time to remember that the monkeys would hear me. Instead, I let out a quiet little squeal, grinning from ear to ear.

I landed with a thump on solid ground, where Indigo and Ollie were waiting for me, both looking a little shaky.

"That was actually sort of fun," I said, scooping myself to my feet and dusting myself off.

Indigo glared at me. Ollie looked away, and I instantly realized my mistake. He wasn't thinking about the slide or the thrill of survival. He was thinking about the monkeys.

I wondered how it had felt for him to be so close to his people and to not even be able to look at them. The monkeys weren't evil: they were slaves, and some of them had probably been his friends once. Were his parents and his sister up there some-where? Had he recognized any of the voices that had cackled in his ears?

"Ollie," I said. "I'm sorry."

He shook his head like it was no big deal, but when he finally spoke, it was through gritted teeth and I could tell he was angry. Maybe not at me, but it didn't really matter.

"I would do anything to get them back," he said quietly. "Is there anyone in your life like that? Anyone you'd do anything to help? No matter what?"

"I . . ." I bit my lip and hesitated. There was a time when I would have said my mother. Now I wasn't sure. I had tried to help her so many times, had done everything I could possibly think of, and none of it had worked. Not even a little. Now she was probably dead. "I don't know," I finally said, feeling my face flush with shame.

He cocked his head like he didn't believe me. It wasn't the answer he had expected.

Indigo just rolled her eyes. "I feel sorry for you," she said. "I really do."

We didn't say anything after that. We just trudged on ahead.

But I couldn't stop thinking about the question Ollie had asked me. I made a decision. A promise to myself. I couldn't help my mother anymore. If I'd ever had a chance, it was long gone now. But if I ever had a chance to help the monkeys, I would take it. No matter what it cost me. It was the least I could do. Not for him, but for myself. Just to say I had someone.

When the road turned a few minutes later we found ourselves in an apple orchard. The trees were lush and green in contrast to the icky cornfields. Huge, red apples dangled temptingly from their branches, shiny and juicy-looking.

I stepped off the road, the grumbling in my stomach outweighing what I'd seen with the mutant corn.

Star, still in my pocket, knew what was up, too. She poked her nose out and chirped hungrily as I reached for a piece of fruit.

For a split second I thought I saw the tree blink. I snatched my hand back.

I looked at the talking monkey next to me, remembering that anything was possible here. "Did that tree just move?"

"They talk, too, but they've taken a vow of silence."

"Voluntarily?"

"The princess felt that their conversation ruined the apple-eating experience and was therefore a violation of the Happiness Decree."

"What about their happiness? The trees, I mean?"

"I think we all realized a little too late that the only happiness that matters is Dorothy's," Indigo chimed in.

Ollie looked at me. "I know you want to, but you can't."

"Is it poison? Or is it forbidden?"

"It's against the Happiness Decree. It's not worth the risk," Indigo said.

"But we need to eat. And Ollie needs his strength. No one is around."

I plucked two apples and nodded at the tree, meeting its sad eyes. "Thanks," I said. I handed one to Ollie, who took it and examined it, unsure.

The first bite melted in my mouth. It tasted like pie. Apple pie. Apple and cinnamon and sugar and butter all mosh-pitted around in my mouth. It was a magically delicious apple! Finally, something in Oz that was actually as cool as advertised.

It was too good to last. I'd just taken another satisfying bite when I saw Indigo's face go white. She pointed behind me and opened her mouth to say something. No sound came out.

And then.

It started to get dark. But it wasn't the sun setting. The sky was as sunny as ever. Instead, it was like the world around us was being covered in shadows, starting with the yellow road. Then the shadows began to rise up from the ground, curling and inflating and twisting into forms. They were taking on shapes. Shapes that looked oddly, eerily familiar to me.

It was the Tin Woodman. He wasn't alone.

EIGHT

I knew we were really in trouble when I saw that Indigo was too scared to even mutter an *I told you so*. She was just a little wall of fear with wide eyes. The color seemed to drain from her tattoos until they were just gray impressions on her skin. Ollie was shaking right down to the tip of his tail, the uneaten apple still in his hand.

This Tin Woodman was not the Tin Woodman I remembered. By now I shouldn't have expected anything different—nothing was the way it was supposed to be in Dorothy's remade Oz. Still. I wasn't prepared for what I was looking at now.

He looked more like a machine that had been cobbled together out of spare parts, a hodgepodge of scrap metal and springs and machinery pieces all held together by screws and bolts. His long, spindly legs were a complex construction of rods and springs and joints, and bent backward at his ankles like a horse's legs; his face was pinched and mean, with beady, flashing metal eyes and a thin, cylindrical nose that jutted out several inches from his face and ended in a nasty little point. His oversize jaw jutted out from the rest of his face in a nasty underbite, revealing a mess of little blades where his teeth should have been.

I half remembered the Tin Woodman's story. He had been a flesh-and-blood man until a witch had enchanted his ax to make him chop off pieces of his body one by one, and one by one he had replaced them with metal parts until that was all that was left of him. From what it looked like, he had been making improvements ever since. The only thing that was really familiar about him was the funnel-shaped hat he wore. I guess some things never change.

Behind the Tin Woodman, four people in black suits materialized out of the shadows a moment after he did. They weren't made of tin, but they weren't exactly people either. Each of them was mostly flesh—with a few mechanical modifications.

One of them had a silver plate bolted to his face where his mouth should have been; another was round and squat with huge copper ears the size of his entire head. The third was a girl, probably about my age, with a glinting sword in place of an arm. But it was the last one who was the creepiest: He was just a disembodied head grafted to the body of a bicycle, with two robotic arms where the handlebars should have been, the knuckles of his mechanized hands scraping the bricks on the road.

"Run," I said. It came out as more of a breath than a word. But no one moved. There was nowhere to run to, and anyway, I was so scared that my knees felt like they were made of jelly.

I tried to smile my widest, most ass-kissing smile—the one I usually used on Dr. Strachan at school. When I remembered that it had never worked with him, I made it even wider. If anyone noticed, they didn't mention it.

"In the name of Ozma of Oz," the Tin Woodman said grimly, his voice robotic and scratchy, "by order of Princess Dorothy, I—the Tin Woodman of Oz, Grand Inquisitor of the Emerald Police and commander of the Tin Soldiers—hereby arrest you for crimes of treason."

He held out a piece of paper with a gold seal on it, and for the first time I got a look at his hands. A chill ran through my entire body.

He had fingers like knives and needles, each one of them twisted into a slightly different shape. Like dentist tools.

I had avoided cavities my entire life exactly because I'm not good with pain. My body tensed up, anticipating one of those sharp things pressing into my skin.

"Treason?" I squeaked.

At the Tin Woodman's words, Ollie, who had been frozen at my side, suddenly came to his senses. He began to screech his ear-shaking monkey wail and he sprung into the air like he'd been shot from a slingshot. Hooking his tail onto the branch of the nearest apple tree, he used it to pull himself up into its leafy boughs.

It all happened in an instant. I got one last glimpse of his tail as he swung into the next tree and then disappeared into the orchard completely.

As he went, Bicycle-body reared on his hind wheel to chase after him but the Tin Woodman put up a calm hand. "Let him go," he said. "The Lion knows the movements of all the beasts. He will take care of him. He won't make it beyond the forest."

Ollie had gotten away. He had abandoned us, if you wanted to be technical about it, but I didn't blame him. For a second, I almost wanted to cheer. I hoped he made it far, far away.

I was happy about it, but Indigo and I didn't have that option. And we were in big, big trouble.

She had been right all along. There were consequences in Oz. Supersized consequences that didn't fit the crime. If Ollie had been tied to a post for "sass," then what would *our* punishment be?

I wanted to tell her I was sorry. She had warned me—begged me, even—and I had ignored her. But was I sorry? Should I *not* have freed him? I didn't think so. What else could I have done?

It had been right to free Ollie. But was that what we were *really* being punished for? Her frozen face broke, and she collapsed to her knees, sobbing.

"P-p-please," she sputtered through her tears. "I was trying to help Dorothy. I was bringing the traitor to be interrogated! I swear! I just wanted to help! I can give you information!"

She was betraying me. She had to, of course, and I didn't blame her. This was on me, and if her pleading helped her then at least one of us would get out of this.

I knew that, but still, it stung to listen to her selling me out.

"Is that so, little one?" the Tin Woodman asked coldly. "You were delivering the outlander to your princess?"

"Of course!" Indigo pleaded. "I love Dorothy more than words. Why would I ever betray her when she's made me so happy?"

I had to help her. Since I wasn't from Oz and didn't know all of Dorothy's rules, maybe they'd be more lenient on me. I stepped forward. "She's right. She had nothing to do with any of this."

Indigo glanced at me now. I think she seemed grateful, but it was hard to tell.

The Tin Woodman looked her up and down for a second and then nodded to the man with the plate over his mouth. The plate slid open to reveal a spigot-like device that telescoped outward in Indigo's direction.

"What are you doing? I was the one who took the apple. I was the one who freed the monkey." The words tumbled out wildly. Whatever the *thing* was that they were pointing at Indigo, it looked like it was going to hurt.

He grumbled to himself, as if he didn't owe me any explanation. "Save your confession for Dorothy, outlander. Loyalty is very important in Oz. The Munchkin must be punished for her cravenness."

"She just told you she's been loyal to Dorothy."

"Perhaps. But she was not loyal to you. Either way, she is guilty of the crime."

"What are you talking about? You can't have it both ways—either she's guilty of being disloyal to Dorothy or she's guilty of being disloyal to me."

"Indeed." The Tin Woodman's metal face somehow managed to look smug. "Now. For her punishment."

The gunlike nozzle extended from the Tin Soldier's lips. It twisted and pivoted, adjusting itself as he put Indigo in his sights. She was heaving and shaking on her knees.

"Run," I said again. "Run!" I cried, willing her to get up. She didn't listen. She didn't even open her eyes.

The Tin Soldier fired and the device made a popping sound.

A tiny sigh of desperate relief escaped my lips when I saw what came shooting out of his mouth: a stream of iridescent bubbles. That was it? I wanted to laugh as the innocent-looking bubbles floated toward Indigo, zipping forward in a happy little stream. They began to swarm her like bees on honey.

But instead of popping when they touched her, they clung to her clothes and skin. She swatted at them frantically but it was no use. They didn't budge. My eyes widened in horror as the bubbles began to melt into her flesh.

I made a move forward to help her—to do anything—but before I could get to her, Sword-Arm's blade snapped out at me. She pressed it tight against my jugular.

"I'm sorry!" I told Indigo. "I'm sorry."

She looked at me then. "No. You were right. Please help us," she said. "You're from the Other Place. You're like her. You can do something."

A calm look came across her face—too calm. Like, good-bye calm. Then the bubbles covered her face, too.

As they merged with her body, her tattoos separated from her skin and slipped off her, the ink puddling in a shiny, mercurial mass. Indigo was melting.

She was barely recognizable now. She was just a big lump of

sticky, pinkish flesh, her arms and legs only barely discernible as limbs, her features only little misshapen blots where her face should have been.

"Make it stop," I begged, still crying. "Please. I didn't mean to—I didn't know. She shouldn't pay for what I did. Please."

"I hate to burst your bubble," the Tin Woodman said with a sly grin, "but ignorance is no excuse. You can tell the whole story to Dorothy. The princess is . . . curious about you."

Pop!

All I could see of what had been Indigo was a red splatter of bone and blood where she had knelt just a few seconds ago. I felt myself gagging, but nothing came up. I leaned over, hands on my knees, trying to get a breath.

She had painstakingly written the history of the world on her body so that it would live on. And the Tin Woodman and his goons had just erased her with the push of a button.

"It's very messy, but we find it's a deterrent," the Tin Woodman said.

This place was insane. He was insane. I thought they'd given him a heart—how had he become *this*?

"Now as for you," I heard him saying. It sounded like he was talking to me from the end of a long tunnel. "The princess is *very* interested to meet the girl who dropped out of the sky.

"Take her," he told his men. I didn't resist as they grabbed me. I didn't say anything. I *couldn't* say anything.

Everything went black. I became a shadow, like them.

NINE

We were standing in the middle of the road and then we weren't. The world blurred before me for a second in a swirl of colors. I blinked hard, trying to keep from getting dizzy, and when I opened my eyes again, I was standing on a glossy marble floor.

I looked up. The Tin Woodman and his metallic backup band were standing beside me. We must have traveled by magic.

The room we were in was the biggest I'd ever been in. It was bigger than my high school auditorium that doubled as a gym, and, where there should have been a ceiling, an ever-shifting kaleidoscope of rainbows formed a majestic dome, casting a shower of vivid colors down upon the pair of gold-and-emerald thrones that sat majestically on a raised dais.

On every wall, stained-glass windows seemed to tell a story. I knew most of it already: it was the story of Dorothy.

There was Dorothy's house in the cyclone. Dorothy walking down the road of yellow bricks, arm in arm with her famous friends. Dorothy facing off with the Wicked Witch of the West. They all went on like that. The last panel showed Dorothy kneeling, as a girl I recognized as Ozma placed a crown on her head.

But where was the one that explained what happened after that?

"Don't speak until spoken to," the Tin Woodman was saying brusquely, and I realized that he was talking to me. "And don't look Her Highness directly in the eye."

I felt nauseous. He had just killed my friend, and now he was giving me an etiquette lesson.

I had never seen anyone die before. I'd thought it would leave me scared, but now all I wanted to do was fight. More than anything I wished to put my fist through the Tin Woodman's face. Or worse.

But I was no match for him, let alone him and his whole death squad. If I tried to lift a finger against any of them, I knew that the last thing I would see was one of Dorothy's sick, sad, phony rainbows. It wasn't worth it.

The Tin Woodman either didn't notice my anger or didn't care. He was too busy lecturing me: "And for heaven's sake, stand up straight. The princess deserves respect." With that, he overcorrected his own already perfect posture and frowned at something on his metallic arm.

It was bubble splatter. Indigo splatter. I swallowed hard, fighting my gag reflex as he used a little blade from his Swiss Army fingertip to scrape it away with a look of private satisfaction.

Just then, a flourish of trumpets began to play out of nowhere. The Tin Woodman and his men bowed down awkwardly—all except the one on wheels who just bowed his head. Their metal limbs creaked as they kneeled. I rushed to kneel along with them. I kept my eyes trained steadily on the ground.

With a few clicks, her shoes appeared right under my nose.

They were bright-red high heels, at least six inches tall and made from the shiniest leather I'd ever seen. Or maybe they weren't *shiny*, exactly. They didn't reflect the light as much as they seemed to shine from within.

I heard a thumping sound beside me. It was coming from the metal shell that was the Tin Woodman.

"Well, look who we have here," a sharp voice said. "Go ahead. Stand up."

I took a breath and rose slowly to my feet to face the owner of the shoes. She was both exactly and nothing like I could have imagined.

This was not the same girl I'd read about. She was wearing the dress, but it wasn't *the* dress exactly—it was as if someone had cut her familiar blue-checked jumper into a million little pieces and then put it back together again, only better. Better and, okay, a little bit more revealing. Actually, more than a little bit. Not that I was judging.

Instead of farm-girl cotton it was silk and chiffon. The cut was somewhere between haute couture and French hooker. The bodice nipped, tucked, and lifted. There was cleavage.

Lots of cleavage.

Dorothy's boobs were out to *here*, her legs up to *there*. Her face was smooth and unblemished and perfect: her mouth shellacked in plasticky crimson, her eyes impeccably lined in silver and gold. Her eyelashes were so long and full that they probably created a breeze when she blinked. It was hard to tell how old she was. She looked like she could have been my age or years older. She looked immortal.

She had her hair pulled into two deep chestnut waves that cascaded down her shoulders, each one tied with red ribbon. Her piercing blue eyes were trained right on me. I knew I was supposed to look down, like the Tin Woodman had instructed. Instead, I found myself falling into her gaze. I couldn't help it.

Her eyes didn't look evil. They looked curious and almost kind. Like she was just trying to figure me out. She was so pretty that it was hard to imagine she was responsible for Indigo's death or any of the other atrocities I'd been told were her fault.

As we stood there, face-to-face, the Tin Woodman creaked back up from his bow and began to speak.

"In the name of Ozma of Oz," he said. "By order of Princess Dorothy, I, the Tin Woodman of Oz, Grand Inquisitor of the Emerald Police, present—"

Without looking away from me, Dorothy flicked a flawlessly manicured hand at him and he shut right up. She cut him off in a bored voice. "Let me get a look at her. What is your name?"

"Amy Gumm." My voice came out louder than I had expected. It sounded like it belonged to someone else.

I tried to inhale as shallowly as possible as she walked in a slow circle around me, the heels of her shoes *clack-clack-clacking* against the green marble floor.

As she examined me, I noticed out of the corner of my eye that while I'd been focused on Dorothy, two more people had entered the room.

I knew them both instantly. In one of the thrones—the larger one—sat the girl I recognized from the hologram—or whatever it was—back on the road. It was Ozma, looking dazed and vacant. Her eyes were open but no one was home. I wondered if this was really her or if she was just another illusion.

At Ozma's side stood a tall thin man dressed in a baby-blue, one-size-too-small suit. Beneath a small hat, bits of straw and yarn stuck out in every direction. His face was a skein of tightly pulled burlap with two unnervingly lifelike buttons sewn on in place of eyes. His lips were thin lines of embroidery stitched in pinkish-brown yarn underneath a painted on red triangle for a nose. His buttons were fixed right on me.

A chill shot through my body. It was the Scarecrow. Like the Tin Woodman, he had been twisted and warped into something I hardly recognized.

"Now, Amy," Dorothy was saying. "This is very, very important—and I need you to be completely honest with me." She casually began to amble over to the empty throne next to Ozma's, where she sat, tossed her head, and crossed her legs.

If I hadn't read the story, I wouldn't believe that she had ever lived on a farm. She had shed that girl long ago and replaced it with a poised, haughty princess. Her neck stretched upward as if she were searching for the perfect light. Her voice was perky, but there was a threat lurking somewhere in there, too.

I steeled myself for whatever she was going to ask, getting the distinct impression that she would be able to see through any lie.

"What do you think of my hair?" she demanded. She ran a long red nail through one of her curls.

She had to be kidding.

"Well?" she asked.

She wasn't kidding. My life was about to be judged by how sincerely I delivered a trivial compliment.

Luckily, I had a lot of practice with humoring popular girls. Madison Pendleton had taught me well.

"It's *so* pretty," I said sweetly. "And so *shiny*!" I added for good measure when she looked unconvinced.

Dorothy smiled and clapped her hands together and leaned over to Ozma with an expression of deep confidentiality. "Ozma likes my hair, too," she said in a stage whisper. Ozma just stared straight ahead with an unchanging expression.

Feeling like I was on a roll, I decided to keep going. Maybe flattery would get me somewhere—for instance, *the hell out of here*. "I've read tons about you. I saw the movie like a million times."

Dorothy beamed. "Really? What do you mean?"

"Oh, you know," I replied shakily. "You're, like, an icon where I come from."

Suddenly she narrowed her eyes at me. "And where, exactly, is that?" she asked.

"Kansas," I said. "The United States."

Her face instantly darkened. "Kansas," she said slowly. "You're from Kansas."

"You've heard of it?" I asked, a hint of unwise sarcasm creeping into my voice. I knew it was the wrong thing to say, but I couldn't help myself. It's my greatest weakness: I never can.

"And how did you *get* here from Kansas, Miss Gumm?" she said sharply.

"Well . . ."

She arched an overplucked eyebrow and cocked her head, waiting for my answer. In my pocket, I felt Star wriggling, and I squeezed her tightly, hoping that she would get the message to calm down. I had a pretty good feeling the princess wouldn't take kindly to the fact that I had brought a rodent into her royal court.

Star cooled it, thank goodness, but she had momentarily distracted me and now Dorothy was waiting for her answer. She cleared her throat testily. "What *brought* you here, Miss Gumm. Don't make me repeat myself."

I knew I should have made up a lie. But what was the point now? I had a feeling they knew more about me than they were letting on anyway. It was probably the only reason I was alive and Indigo wasn't.

"A tornado," I said, mustering a smile.

The hairs on the back of my neck were standing at attention. Inside the pocket of my hoodie, I felt Star quivering. I was pretty sure they didn't know about *her* at least.

"Why you little . . . *liar*," Dorothy spat. "How dare you!"

I opened my mouth to lie—an actual lie this time. To say that no, I hadn't come from Kansas at all.

It was too late. Dorothy's face was burning with aggrieved

rage. "I am the only one. There can only *be* one."

My gut twisted. I understood. We had the same story. It was like we were wearing the same dress to the prom. Only it wasn't a party. Dorothy thought her landing here was fate—that it made her special. Another girl from Kansas meant that it was just a regular occurrence and that she wasn't special at all. Or—worse—that I was here to take her place.

I did my best to scramble, trying not to trip over my words. "Your Highness, I'm just a regular girl from Kansas. I'm *nothing* like you. You're a princess. Look at you. Me, I'm not interested in that. I just want to be myself—I'd never want anything that you have."

I was only trying to placate her, but as I spoke the words I realized they were true. I didn't want anything Dorothy had. I didn't want to be anything like her.

Dorothy hooted in derision. "More lies! If you come from where I come from, all you *do* is want. And if you had even the smallest taste of what I have, you would never stop wanting."

She tapped the tip of one of her shoes as if to illustrate her point. "There can only be one," she repeated through gritted teeth.

Dorothy rose to her feet. Her face was pinched with barely suppressed fury. "Take her away," she said.

The Scarecrow turned to her. "Your Highness," he said in a calm, soothing voice. "Maybe we should let the Tin Woodman review the charges against her first?"

The Tin Woodman pulled out his stupid piece of paper and cleared his throat to read aloud. But Dorothy wasn't having it.

"Take her *away*!" Her scream reverberated up through the room, ringing in my ears. Her face had turned a deep red, and her fists were clenched so tight at her sides that they were vibrating.

My legs buckled inward. I felt like I was watching the whole scene unfold from somewhere far away. From my new, distant vantage, I searched myself, looking for any shred of the strength and anger and stubbornness that had always served me so well. For any secret weapon buried deep within that could help me out of this.

I found nothing. I collapsed to my knees, shaking.

No one else in the room even flinched. "Amy Gumm of Kansas," the Tin Woodman said calmly, "you will be tried for your crimes of treason one week from today. . . ."

For the first time, Ozma acted on her own accord, letting out a high, lilting giggle. Dorothy's eyes were still drilling through me.

"If found guilty," the Tin Woodman said, "you will be sentenced to a Fate Worse Than Death."

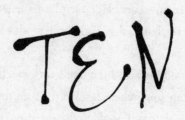

TEN

My prison cell was a perfect cube, all white, without a speck of dirt anywhere. The walls were white limestone, freshly scrubbed, and the tiny bed in the corner was all white, too.

As soon as the Tin Woodman had slammed the cell door behind me after shoving me inside, the door had simply disappeared, like it had never existed. I pressed myself against the cool, smooth surface of the wall where it had just been, searching for a crevice, a seam, any sign at all that there was a way out—that there had ever been a way in. I didn't find anything.

There *was*, however, a window in the room. It was no bigger than a foot wide, and it neatly framed a little swatch of the starry night sky. So Dorothy must have finally decided to let the sun set after all. When I stood on my tiptoes, the glittering green vista of the Emerald City was barely visible, poking up into the blackness.

To get to this dungeon, I'd been escorted down what had felt like hundreds of stairs. It seemed impossible that there could be a window all the way down here, deep in the bowels of the palace. But there it was.

It had to be magic. Was it the stairs that were just an illusion, or the window? And why was there a window in here anyway? It seemed unlikely that my captors would care whether or not I was comfortable.

Well, it was clean. And there was a view. That comprised the entirety of my prison's luxuries. When I sat down on the bed in the corner, I found it hard as stone. That's because there was no mattress to speak of: the bed felt like stone because it *was* stone.

I sat there trying to think of what I was going to do next while at the same time trying to suppress my mounting sense of panic. Meanwhile, Star was investigating, sniffing the walls, clawing at the floor, probably searching for an exit or maybe just something to eat. She wasn't having any luck on either count. When she saw that I was awake, she abandoned her quest and jumped up onto the bed next to me.

I tried to keep my eyes open. I could sleep when I was dead, and if I didn't want that particular sleep to come very soon, I had to find a way out.

But I was too exhausted. I didn't even really know how long I'd been awake for. Before I knew it, I was out.

When I woke up, the sky outside my window was still dark. For how long? I wondered. Dorothy controlled the sun in the sky. According to Indigo, she basically controlled time itself around here. How was I ever going to escape power like that?

"Star," I said, "we are completely and totally screwed." On top of everything else, I was becoming one of those people who talked to their pets.

I'd barely been here a day, and I was already starting to feel insane.

In desperation, knowing it would do me no good, I stood and banged my fist against the wall until it was throbbing with pain. I tried to move the bed to the window, but it was rooted in place. When that didn't work, I jumped up and tried to grip the edge of the window to hoist myself onto the ledge.

I just hung there limply. I had never been an athlete and, unfortunately, I was never going to become one. Even under pressure of death.

I screamed. I screamed until my throat hurt. I didn't get so much as an echo in response. It was like the walls absorbed everything I could throw at them.

My whole body felt like one big bruise, but none of this was doing any good. I was just wasting energy.

I lay down on the bed to think and soon I was asleep again.

When I woke up and saw that the moon was still shining through the window, I finally realized why they had put the window in here in the first place. It was there to make me go crazy. To keep me guessing about how long I had been here, to give me hope that there was some way out.

I turned around with a start at the sound of a key in the door. Wait—what door? But then it was there again: a thin black line began to appear out of nowhere, a black rectangle that drew itself along the blank white wall. Even after all this I still felt a little thrill at seeing magic in action.

But then the door began to swing open and that thrill was instantly gone. I wasn't sure who wanted in, but, whoever it was, I knew it wouldn't be anyone good.

I was on my feet, my fists clenched. If I was going down, I was going down fighting.

The face I saw a moment later as the door disappeared into the wall was so unexpected that it took me a beat to put it into context. I shuffled his features around in my head like a puzzle, trying to place them.

He stepped into the room, and instantly I recognized his shaggy hair and glowing green eyes.

It was the boy who'd never told me his name. The one who'd saved my life back at the pit.

"You!" I exclaimed, my balled fists unballing and my spine relaxing. For the first time in—literally—I didn't know how long, I let myself entertain the thought of hope. He had saved me once. Was he here to save me again?

The boy just put a finger to his lips and waved toward the window. That's when I noticed the crows for the first time. There were several of them, all perched on the window ledge on the other side of the glass, peering in.

One of the birds cocked its head. The thing had ears—human ears, grafted awkwardly to either side of its head. A second passed, and the crow next to the first one cawed loudly, staring at me. It blinked, once, twice, with big human eyelids.

I cried out in frightened surprise, but the boy rapped against the glass a few times and they disappeared into the night.

"You have to watch out for them," he explained. "They're called Overhears. The Scarecrow makes them in his lab. They're spies, but the good part is that they're pretty stupid. It's ironic, really—the one thing he hasn't figured out is how to give them brains. They can see you and hear you, but they're too dumb to understand anything, so they're not so good at reporting any of it back. If you're careful around them, they're mostly harmless. Another one of his failed experiments."

"Who are you?" I asked. Here he was, acting like just waltzing in here was no big deal. And he wasn't making any moves to save me. Maybe I shouldn't trust him.

"Sorry. I guess I never introduced myself. I'm Pete," he said. "You don't have to whisper now that they're gone, though."

Pete? The name sounded too ordinary for him. Anyway, while it was useful to finally know his name, it wasn't really what I'd been asking.

I wanted answers. "No." I said it firmly, placing a stiff period carefully at the end of the word. "*Who are you* meaning why are you here? Meaning, what do you want with me? Meaning, how did you get in here? Meaning, who the *fuck* are you?"

Without meaning to, I was screaming. I hoped the Overhears were long gone by now.

Pete rolled onto his heels, taken aback by my outburst, but he answered my questions calmly.

"I'm Pete," he said again. "I'm here because I know that you can go crazy down here with no one to talk to, and I don't want you to go crazy. So I lifted a key. I work in the palace." Pete glanced nervously over at Star, who glared at him from underneath the bed. She didn't trust him either. "I'm here to keep you company. For as long as I can, at least."

Nothing about this story made any sense. How had he found me at the exact moment I'd landed in Oz? How had he found out I was down here? If I was in a magicked prison cell with no door, how had he just "lifted" a key? He was definitely not telling me everything. Which led me to my next question: Was he really on my side?

"You work in the palace?"

"I'm a gardener."

"So you work for *her* then."

He might as well have been the window, for all the good he did me. Simply another thing to torture me with false hope.

Unless he wasn't here to give me hope at all.

"I'm just a gardener," he said. "I work for the head gardener. The head gardener works for the royal steward. I've never spoken to Dorothy."

He was lying. There was no question in my mind: his eyes were too big and luminous. You couldn't hide anything behind eyes like those.

And yet . . . he had already saved me once. Why would he have done that if he was working for Dorothy?

Pete slumped against the wall. I hadn't moved from my

defensive position in the corner. "Should I go?" he asked. He looked, in that moment, just like a little kid. "I really didn't mean to upset you. I thought it would help."

"If you go," I said, "I'll kill you."

I only said it because I was angry. But it gave me an idea.

Without warning, I lunged for him and grabbed him by the throat before he could react. I shoved my knee into his groin. Pete's mouth widened into a perfect *O* of shock. I didn't think I would be able to take him in a fight, but *he* might not know that. If I scared him enough, maybe he would think I was more dangerous than I really was.

It worked, I think. At least, he didn't resist.

"Give me the key," I said.

"You can take it, if that's what you want," he said. "I'll give it to you. But it won't do you much good. It's not just the lock that's keeping you down here. The moment the cell's unoccupied, all the alarms will sound. They'll know you're gone; they'll catch you before you can make it three feet, and they'll throw you right back in here. That's if you're *lucky*. More likely, they'll skip the trial and just send you straight to the Scarecrow. Trust me— if you think this is bad, that's worse."

I cocked my head. I thought about loosening my grip on his neck. Instead, I tightened it and nudged my knee forward an inch. He grimaced, but didn't say anything.

"If I take the key and leave you here in my place, the cell won't be unoccupied. No alarms, then."

At that, Pete raised his eyebrows in surprise. Maybe he hadn't expected me to be desperate enough to trade my freedom for his. Honestly, I was a little surprised myself.

Still, that was all the reaction I got. "You could," he said calmly. "If that's the way you want to play it. It still wouldn't do you any good. We're deep underground here, and the entrances to the dungeons are always guarded. You might get out of the cell, but you still have to get past the guards."

"It's worth the risk."

"Maybe. Maybe not."

He was right, of course. I felt defeat seeping in through every pore. It was useless. I dropped my hold on him and walked over to my so-called bed where I perched myself on the edge and buried my face in my hands.

"Hey," he said. I felt his hand on my shoulder and looked up to see him standing over me. "If it means anything to you, I've been trying to think of a way to get you out of here. I can't find one. You're too important to Dorothy—it's a miracle I managed to get the key and sneak down here at all. But I'll find a way, okay? I still have a few tricks up my sleeve."

"Why?" I asked, my eyes suddenly pooling with tears. "Why are you trying to help me?"

He flipped his palms to the ceiling as if to say, *Why not?* "Because it's the right thing?"

He sat next to me on the bed, keeping a safe distance between us.

I rolled my eyes. "No one does anything because it's the *right* thing," I said.

"You do."

"I do?"

Maybe that was true, but even if it was, how would he know it? We'd known each other for all of twenty minutes total.

"*You* do," Pete said, this time with emphasis. "Except when you threatened to kill me, that is."

I had to laugh at that.

"But I didn't *actually* kill you, so it doesn't count."

"Seriously," he said. "Everyone in the palace has been whispering about Dorothy's latest prisoner. I knew it had to be you. The girl I rescued from the tin farm. Ever since I saw you, I just had a feeling. I feel responsible for you."

Only then did it occur to me that this was the first time I'd ever had a boy in my bed. The circumstances were less than ideal.

Not that it mattered at a time like this. I was trapped in a cell in a strange kingdom, facing an inevitable sentence of a Fate Worse Than Death. It wasn't the moment to be shopping for a boyfriend.

"How did you know I would be there?" I asked. "When my trailer crashed by the pit. If you work all the way over here in the palace, how did you know I was there? I mean, you got there right in the nick of time. Any later and I'd have fallen in."

"I just had a feeling," he said, shifting in his seat. "I just—I don't know. It was just like someone was calling me there, so I went."

Part of me didn't care that he was obviously still lying. He'd been right—after all the hours locked away in here, all alone, it really did help just to have him sitting next to me. Just to hear another human voice, to be able to ask a question and get an answer back, even if it wasn't the right answer.

Then that faraway, distracted look crossed his face again, the same look I'd seen him get the day I met him, just before he left me. It was the look of someone trying to place a distant tune that only he could hear.

His body seemed to flicker in and out, to grow hazy around the edges, but it was so faint I couldn't be sure it wasn't my imagination. It reminded me of the hologram of Ozma we'd seen on the road.

He stood up abruptly. This time, I thought I knew what was coming. "I'm sorry," he said. "I have to go."

"Why . . . ?" I asked.

"I'm sorry," he said again. "I'll try to help you if I can." Then, before I could protest, before I could even stand to say good-bye, he had pulled a big brass key from the pocket of his loose, white gardener's pants. He walked across the cell in three quick strides and plunged it into a space in the wall where there was no keyhole. The stone rippled around it like he'd just dropped a pebble in a pond.

The door appeared. He pushed it open.

"Pete," I said. My voice cracked unexpectedly as I said it. I just wanted him to look at me. He didn't. He stepped out, the door sealed up, and I was alone again.

ELEVEN

After that, I really lost track of time. I slept, I sat, I slept some more and forced down the disgusting bowls of porridge that would now and then, without warning, materialize on the ever-pristine floor of my prison.

I looked out the enchanted, evil window. Sometimes it was night and sometimes it was day. When the moon was out, I tried to judge the passage of time by its phases, but it was no use. It would be full one moment and a thin thumbnail crescent the next, and then—when I turned away and looked for it again—gone entirely.

I wasted about fifteen minutes trying to play hide-and-seek with Star, but it was pointless. There was no place to hide except under the bed, and anyway, only Star was small enough to fit down there.

With nothing to do except think, my mind kept returning to my mother. I was ashamed of myself for how little I'd thought about her since I'd come to Oz, but now I couldn't stop wondering whether she had made it through the tornado, about whether she was searching for me or whether she was laid up somewhere, drunk or stoned or whatever else.

If there was even a chance she was out there, looking for me or hoping I'd make it home okay, then I couldn't give up. I'd made a promise to myself that I'd do anything to help Ollie and his family, thinking that my mother was beyond my help—but now I realized that, no matter how far away my mother was, no matter how far gone she might be, I would always feel a sense of obligation to her.

Then again, it's not like I was in much of a position to help *anyone* right now. Honestly, I could use a little help myself.

After two or three days—I think, but who knew?—Pete came to me again.

"I don't have long," he said, stepping through the door. His voice was strained with uncharacteristic panic. "Your trial is tomorrow," he said. "The news is all over the palace."

I sat up in bed with a start. I had been down here so long now that I'd nearly forgotten I had a trial coming up at all. The wild look in Pete's eyes reminded me that, as bad as things were, they could still get worse.

"What exactly does a trial entail?" I asked, still holding out some irrational hope that maybe I could be exonerated.

He shook his head and looked down at his hands.

"Just tell me," I said. "Maybe there's some trick to it. Things like that always work in fairy tales."

"Do you honestly think this is a fairy tale?" Pete asked.

"Just tell me what to expect."

He sighed, finally relenting. "Her Royal Highness's kanga-roo court. It's a total joke," he said. "I think the only reason she bothers with trials at all is because she likes wearing the big white wig. Once you go to trial, you're already as good as guilty. I don't think there's ever been a not-guilty verdict as long as the court's been in existence."

In the face of my impending Fate Worse Than Death sen-tence, I found that I was surprisingly calm. Maybe it just didn't seem real.

"So what do I do?" I asked.

Pete looked at his hands. He tousled his hair, and then looked back at me in sheepish apology. "We could make a break for it," he said. "Maybe with two of us, we could fight our way past the guards."

We both knew what a dumb idea it was. "That will just get us *both* killed," I said. "What's the point of that?"

"Yeah," he said. "I know."

"What about magic? I mean, this is Oz, right? Isn't there some spell that would work? It doesn't even have to be a good one."

He shook his head. "I never learned to do magic," he said. "I was never good at it, and no one ever thought it was impor-tant for a gardener to learn, especially once Dorothy made it illegal for anyone except her and her friends to practice it. I wouldn't even be able to cast a simple extinguishing spell without it setting off the magical alarms and going on trial myself."

"What about someone else? Do you know anyone who would give you, like, some kind of mystical trinket or something? I mean, I don't know . . ."

"I thought of that. I talked to every illegal practitioner I could think of and none of them will help. It's too risky. Anyway, I doubt anything like that would work down here. There are anti-magic wards everywhere in the dungeons. You'd have to be really powerful to break through them. Like, Glinda powerful."

"Some magic shoes would really come in handy right about now, huh?" I said.

"Seriously. Maybe . . ." He stopped himself.

"Maybe what?"

"It's nothing. It's just—there might be one more person who . . ."

"Who?" I asked eagerly.

"No," he said. "It would never . . ."

"Who?"

He spoke with finality this time. "No. It won't ever work."

"Please," I said. "Whatever you can do. Please just try."

Pete nodded. "Okay," he said. "I'll ask. But it's a long shot. It's the longest shot."

We were both quiet. I scraped my nails absently along the stone walls next to my bed, trying to make a mark. Any mark. It was like with Indigo's tattoos. We all had our ways of saying *I was here.*

"Listen," Pete said. "Amy."

I jerked my head up. "Yeah?"

He pulled something out of his pocket and stepped over to me.

"It's not much. But maybe you can do something with this." From out of his pocket, he drew a small kitchen knife, and pressed it into my hand.

He was right. It *wasn't* much. But it was something, and he was giving it to me.

"Thank you," I said. I leaned up to his face and kissed him solemnly on the cheek.

"I'm sorry I can't do more."

"I will make it," I said firmly. At this point, I didn't really feel like I had any choice but to keep believing that. Then I remembered one more thing. Something important. "Wait," I said. And I ducked under the bed to retrieve Star.

I'd hated her from the moment my mother brought her home. I'd hated the responsibility of taking care of something that I never asked for, and I'd hated the way my mother seemed to care more about a rodent than she did about me. Or, she had cared about her until she'd *stopped* caring. Star and I were kind of in the same boat that way.

An unexpected well of emotion opened up somewhere behind my ribs. She had been a faithful companion since I'd gotten here. She was the last thing I had left to connect me to where I came from. And she had been a good friend. Even if she couldn't talk.

I cupped her furry body in my palms and gave her one last kiss on the forehead.

"Take her for me," I said. "Keep her safe for me."

I had hated her and now didn't want to let her go. Star was not so sentimental. She crawled from my hands and into Pete's without looking back at me.

"Great," he said. "Just what I've always wanted. A rat."

I smiled. "Just do it."

He lifted her up to his face and let her lick him. "Fine. I'll take her," he said. "But I'm not keeping her forever. Just until you're safe and you can take her back." He dropped her into the breast pocket of his shirt and she squealed happily.

"Go," I said, giving him permission so he wouldn't have to ask.

"I don't . . . ," he said.

"Just go. I'll be okay. But if you know anyone who owes you a miracle . . ."

"I'll see what I can do," Pete said.

He placed his key in the wall. The door opened. I watched him go.

TWELVE

I was ready for them when they came for me the next day. I had paced my cell all night making plans, none of them very good. If I was going down, I was going to do it kicking and screaming. Not to mention biting, clawing, and hair-pulling. And, of course, stabbing. My knife—tiny as it was—never left my hand.

I heard them coming long before they reached me. The Tin Woodman and his metal men made a lot of noise descending all those flights of marble stairs.

As they creaked toward me, I crouched in the corner nearest to where I knew the door would appear and waited. I didn't really know what I was going to do when they got here, but tackling the Tin Woodman as soon as the door opened and then making a break for it would be a start. It wasn't the best idea I'd ever had, but at least it was something.

Thunk, crash, creak, thunk. My heart began to pound. It was do-or-die time.

I was so focused on where the door was about to appear, and what I would do when it did, that I didn't even notice when the room began to fill with hazy purple smoke until it was so thick I couldn't see a thing. When it had cleared away, an ancient-looking woman was standing in front of me.

Her nose was big and crooked and bulbous with a big, hairy wart on the very tip. Purple rags barely covered her sagging, wrinkled flesh. And to top it off, she wore a hat. A black one, so weathered it was almost gray, its point standing at attention.

A witch, I thought.

She looked impossibly old, her face one big wrinkle with eyes that were coal black and seemed to go on forever. When I looked into them I somehow knew in one glance that she was as old as Oz itself.

A strong, cold breeze hit me in the face.

I stepped back. I didn't know whether I was supposed to be frightened or happy. Mostly I was just confused.

"Who are you?" I asked. I could hear the footsteps of the Tin Woodman getting louder. "How did you get in here?"

"I'm Mombi," she said in a scratchy voice. "And how do you *think* I got here?"

"*What* are you, then?" I asked.

She gave me a sly wink. "*Another* question that you already know the answer to. But I'll give you a hint anyway: I'm the Wicked kind. Now are you coming with me or not?"

I was happy she wasn't the Tin Woodman, but, like Pete, I had no idea who this person was. I wasn't going to just run away with her right off the bat.

"Well?" she asked impatiently, tapping her pointy toes against the floor as I stared at her. "They're almost here. I can get you out of here, but you have to make up your mind quick. Will you join me? Yes or no?"

Yes or no. This was the kind of thing you read about in fairy tales. What she meant was that if I wanted her help, I would have to agree to something. She just wasn't going to bother telling me what until it was too late.

Thunk, stomp, thunk, squeak.

"What's the catch?" I asked. "I'm not giving you my first-born, if that's what you want."

"Oh," she said. "That won't be necessary. The second-born will do."

Seeing me blanch, she let out a long, hearty cackle. "You're smart," she said. "I suppose you're right to ask. There's *always* a catch with us wicked witches. But I don't care much for babies— I've already had a few bad experiences with them, if you want the truth. No, you can keep your disgusting spawn. Don't see how you'll manage to get any children at all if you stay here, though. Dorothy'll have you dead before sundown."

We heard the key begin to turn in the lock outside.

Mombi sighed as the door in the wall began to appear. "Girls your age," she said, shaking her head. "Always takes you forever to get out of the house. *Now* we're going to have to fight." She backed up into the corner and squeezed her body so tightly against the wall that it almost looked like she was sinking right into it. "At least I see you have a knife already." She nodded to my hand where I was clutching my weapon so hard that I thought I might be starting to lose circulation. "Let me just give it a tiny little enchantment to make it more useful."

She wiggled her pinkie and thumb in my direction and clicked her tongue a few times. When I held my knife in front of me, I saw that it was pulsing with a purple glow.

If this was going to make it more useful, it was just in time: the door swung open and the Tin Woodman stepped into the room.

"Amy Gumm," he announced, "it is time to face your judgment."

It took him a beat to realize that I wasn't alone. "Guards!" he shouted. "Seize the girl! And the witch!"

He fanned the blades of his hand out in front of him as he lunged for my new ally, his crew rushing into the cell behind him.

Sword-Arm was in front of me, advancing with sword outstretched, backing me into a corner. I stepped out of her way, ducked under her, and thrust my kitchen knife toward her chest just as she pivoted to face me. I missed, but I was surprised at how close I'd come, at how the weight and heft of the knife felt so natural.

Suddenly I knew exactly when to thrust and when to parry, when to go high and when to go low and when to twist away. I felt like I could do some real damage with this thing.

So I sliced and diced and feinted as the Tin Soldiers all scrambled to grab me. A line of bright red blossomed across Sword-Arm's cheek as I connected. I pulled back at the sight of it, but the knife urged me forward again. I gave the head on the bicycle two flat tires in no time, sending him sprawling onto his side on the floor, where he struggled to pull himself upright with his weird, handlebar arms.

When the one with the panel covering his mouth—the one who had killed Indigo—grabbed my arm and twisted it behind my back, I pushed against him with my free arm and wiggled loose. He put out his arms in an almost shrug, offering himself up for another attempt, like he was daring me to fail at checking him again.

Then he charged at me, this time crouching low to deliver some kind of deadly head butt.

I ducked out of the way at the last moment but he spun quickly around and caught me in the back, slamming me to the ground. I lay motionless for a second, the wind knocked out of me. He nudged me with his foot, roughly rolling me over. Grabbing me by the neck, he hauled me to my feet and pulled me close to him, so close that I could tell by his eyes if not his mouth panel that he was smirking.

I was over this. I had been through too much. I had seen too much.

I had been angry before. At Madison. At my mom. But I had never felt anything like this. I could feel myself seize up, every muscle contracting at once, gripped by what Dorothy had done to Indigo, by what she had planned for me. But instead of stuffing it down, or blurting out something stupid, I struck.

I jabbed the blade of Mombi's knife into the *thing's* eye socket.

It was for Indigo. It was for me, too.

Blood spurted everywhere as he slumped against the wall and collapsed. I looked down at the knife, at the Rorschach pattern of blood splattered on the ground. I wanted to believe it was the knife that had done that—not me—but I wasn't so sure.

I felt sick to my stomach, still not quite believing it, but Sword-Arm was on me again, and she was mad. In one swift motion, she knocked my blade from my grip and it went clattering to the ground. I was now defenseless as she shoved me up against the wall.

I punched with my fist, but the hard metal of her arm hurt me more than my punches hurt her and I screamed through clenched teeth. She raised the shiny blade of her deadly arm over her head and I braced myself.

"Mombi!" I yelled.

Without dropping her own attack on the Tin Woodman, Mombi reached her free hand into her robes again and pulled out what looked like a ball of purple yarn. She hurled it in my direction and as it looped through the air it began to unspool, its threads becoming indistinct and unfocused, twisting and curling in a hundred different directions. When the ball hit Sword-Arm, it instantly began to wrap itself around her, covering her in sticky, purple cobwebs. She struggled against it, but her weapon was stuck in midair. Mombi's magic had bought me some time.

"I can hold them for a few seconds, Amy!" Mombi shrieked from the other side of the room. "Now will you join us or not?"

I knew I had no other choice. "Done," I cried.

Mombi reached out a hand. I dove across the room for it and grabbed on tight.

As I touched her, the purple rags began to billow out from around her body. The rags curled around the two of us, enveloping us both in a cocoon as the Tin Woodman and his henchmen faded away along with the room itself.

I was smoke now, too.

"Welcome to the Revolutionary Order of the Wicked, Amy," Mombi hissed as we disappeared.

THIRTEEN

Mombi let go of my hand as we materialized someplace dark. Someplace so dark I couldn't see my hands. But even without being able to see, I could still feel the coldness of the knife in my clenched palm.

The darkness washed over me—a darkness like I'd never experienced before.

"Where . . . ," I started, and then trailed off, feeling a dizzying, spiraling sense of panic. What had I gotten myself into?

My breathing was getting shallower and shallower when a bright spark appeared in the blackness, just inches from my face. When my eyes focused in on it, I saw a tiny, glowing spider crawling through the air. As it moved in a zigzagging spiral, Mombi's body slowly faded into view next to me. I looked down at myself and saw that I was now illuminated, too. The light was confined to our bodies, though. Everything around us remained as dark as ever.

"Where—where are we?" I asked the witch, the words catching in my throat. What had I gotten myself into?

"You'll know in good time, my dear," she said, wiggling her eyebrows. "There's a lot for us to talk about, and I could use a nice, long nap. All that teleportation will take the wind right out of an old girl like me. I'm sure you agree."

It wasn't until she said it that I realized I was exhausted, too. My legs were shaky, every bit of my body was sore, and my arm was throbbing with pain. I felt like I could sleep for a thousand years.

Then I started to remember what had happened and my knees began to buckle in on themselves as the memories washed over me. The escape. The fight. The squishy, sick feeling of my knife burying itself in my foe's eye socket and the thick geyser of blood that had come squirting out.

It couldn't have been me. It felt more like something I had seen on TV than something that had actually happened to me.

I would never have done that. I *couldn't* have. The girl who fought Sword-Arm to a standstill had known what she was doing. I'd never hurt another person in my whole life. Well, not with my fists, at least.

I felt the knife in my hand. It felt good. It felt like it was part of me. Suddenly I understood.

"It was the knife, right?" I asked Mombi. "It's magic. It was telling me what to do."

Mombi swatted the question away. "Pish tosh," she said. "The knife's enchanted, certainly. It will whisper in your ear a little bit—tell you where to move, teach you a few tricks. But it can't make something out of nothing. It can't help you if you don't have it in you somewhere." Her mouth spread into a wide grin, revealing a jammed-together row of rotting brown teeth. "Good thing you *did*," she said.

From the way she said it, I knew she meant it as a compliment, and I felt a twisted sense of pride rising in my chest. I tried to shove it back down. The fact that I had what it took to stab someone's eyes out was nothing to be proud of.

No, I corrected myself. Not *someone*. Some*thing*. And that *thing* had been helping the Tin Woodman. That *thing* had been responsible for killing Indigo. I had nothing to feel guilty about.

Mombi winked at me as if she knew exactly what I had been thinking. She reached out and wrapped her knotted, spindly hands around my closed fist. "Now," she said. "You won't be needing that for a bit."

"No!" I said, more angrily than I meant to, squeezing hard as she tried to pry my fingers open. The knife was mine. I didn't want to give it back. It could keep me safe.

Mombi clucked her tongue but didn't really seem to care. "See? That's the spirit. We'll make a Wicked one out of you yet, now won't we?"

I tried to pull my hand away, but she held it tight.

"Don't worry—you'll have more weapons than you know what to do with soon enough. But in the meantime . . ." Mombi mumbled a few words under her breath and I felt my fingers unlocking against my will. She took the knife and tucked it into her cloak. "Thattagirl," she said. "Don't you worry about a thing. You're here now, and safe. And you're free." Then she chuckled at something. "Well, *sort of*," she said, before letting out an uproarious cackle. Her laughter was still echoing around me as her body began to curl in on itself, like she was turning herself inside out. Then she was gone, and everything was dark again.

Free. But was I? In some ways, it felt like I had traded one prison for another.

We'll make a Wicked one out of you yet.

What had I gotten myself into?

I stood there, waiting for my eyes to adjust, but they didn't. Maybe it wasn't even dark at all: maybe it was just like outer space, where it's only dark because there's nothing to see.

I was alone.

I had been lonely a lot in my life—enough to know that there are different kinds of lonely. There's the lonely I had felt at school, surrounded by people who only paid attention to me long enough to remind me that they didn't like me. There was the lonely I felt when I was with my mother, which was different from the lonely that I felt when I watched her leaving just before the tornado hit, and different from the lonely that I felt when my trailer was being whisked away from everything I'd ever known.

Then there was the bottomless loneliness that I'd felt in Dorothy's sick, white dungeon, the kind of loneliness that had made me feel like I was running through an endless maze.

Standing there in the dark, it was like all those alones had just been tiny, interlocking pieces of a picture so big that you could only see the whole thing from a mile away. Now it was clear: I had nothing except myself. No matter what happened, it would always be that way.

And yet: I took a step forward and was surprised to feel solid ground underneath my feet. I took another. I stumbled on something and caught myself before I hit the ground.

I was just about to move forward again when I heard a voice echoing all around me. It belonged to a woman, and it was kind and gentle and strangely familiar. "I think you're starting to understand," she said. "It will take a while, but you're getting there."

I stopped in my tracks and jerked my head up. "Who's there?" I called out to the emptiness. "What do you want from me?"

Instead of an answer I heard the sound of fingers snapping. Just like that, the world returned to me. It was less like a light being turned on and more a blindness being suddenly lifted.

I was standing in a huge cave, the rocky walls pulsing eerily with a dim purple phosphorescence. High above my head, clusters of stalactites dangled perilously from the rocky ceiling.

In the center of the cavern a massive tree loomed, its trunk as thick around as five people, overgrown with vines and moss and tiny flowers. Hundreds of limbs curled upward until they merged with the rock formations on the ceiling; a tangle of roots covered the ground before disappearing into the walls.

The longer I looked at the tree, the more I couldn't decide where it ended and the cave began.

"Why does there have to be a beginning and an ending?" the voice asked. "If you ask me, it's all middle."

I spun around, trying to figure out where it was coming from, and saw nothing.

"Who are you?"

And from out of the tree, a squat, round old woman in a shapeless white dress and a pointy white hat emerged like she was walking through an open door. Except there was no door. There was no opening in the tree at all.

"People have called me lots of things over the years," the woman said. "It happens when you get old. But *you* can call me Grandma Gert." She brushed a stray flower from her silvery-white cloud of hair.

Her face was old and wrinkled but it was nothing like Mombi's. It was round and kind and so chubby that she had at least three chins. Maybe four. Her eyes twinkled as she smiled at me.

Grandma Gert. I liked the sound of that. There was something about her that I trusted.

It was all so strange. I should have been afraid. Or angry. Or at least startled or confused. I felt none of those things. When Gert reached out for my hand, I let her take it and clasp it between her own, squeezing tenderly, and I realized what I *did* feel. It was a warm sense of peacefulness starting in my chest and spreading through my body.

"Welcome home, dear," she said.

"Home?" The word startled me, and when I repeated it, it caught in the back of my throat. I had no idea where I was, except that it was about as far away from *home* as I could possibly get. And yet . . .

"You're a long way from Kansas, I know," she said. "But there's more than one kind of home. And you're right. You *are* on your own. We all are, and we all have to learn it sooner or later. If you have to be alone, though, wouldn't you rather be alone among friends?"

Alone. I looked up, startled. How had she known what I had been thinking, back there in the darkness?

Grandma Gert's face flushed with embarrassment. "Oh dear," she said quickly. "I'm sorry, Amy. Sometimes I forget how strange it can be at first. I don't do it on purpose—but when someone's thoughts are as loud as yours it can be hard to know the difference."

It took a moment for me to understand what she was saying.

"You can read my mind," I said. Or maybe I just thought it.

The old woman nodded. "Something like that. Please don't be afraid—it's almost always what's right there on the surface. I try not to go too much deeper than that. Not without permission."

I didn't know what to say and then I realized I didn't have to say anything at all. Anything I could say, Grandma Gert already knew.

There was actually something comforting about that.

She was staring deep into my eyes. "Thank you," she said. At first I didn't know what she was thanking me for and then I did. It was for understanding. For not being afraid.

Then she gathered herself up, dropped my hand, and squared her shoulders.

"There will be plenty of time to talk about all of this later. First we need to get you cleaned up." Her eyes drifted down to my scratched, bruised arms and bloody T-shirt. "Mombi certainly does know how to start a fight."

Gert waved her hand, and the tree at the center of the cavern began to transform before my eyes. The roots swirled at my feet, the branches drew themselves down from the ceiling, the trunk began to melt like tar into the ground.

When it was done, she and I were standing next to a deep pool where the tree had stood before. Foamy white water bubbled up from somewhere beneath the ground, and steam wafted off the surface. It smelled clean and fresh.

"Go ahead," Gert said, placing a hand on the small of my back and nudging me forward. "It will heal you."

She didn't have to tell me twice—I stepped right into the spring, not even bothering to take my clothes off. I didn't need to: they began to disintegrate as soon as they touched the water.

I didn't care that they were gone, and I didn't care that I was naked in front of an old woman I'd just met. The minute the warm, clear water touched my bare skin, I felt my muscles melting as bubbles spun around me. I looked down at myself and watched, astonished, as days' worth of dirt slid right off my body. But I was also surprised to see exactly how hurt I really was. Bruises peppered my arms and legs. Thick red tendrils of blood slipped from a gash across my abdomen that I didn't remember getting in the first place.

When I looked up, I saw that Gert was beside me in the water, still fully clothed, her white dress billowing around her. I wasn't sure why the water hadn't affected her clothes the way it had mine. I hadn't even noticed her get in with me.

She looked concerned, too, frowning down at my wounds. "This may hurt, Amy," she said.

"Huh?" I asked, stretching. "No—it feels wonderful."

"Take a deep breath," she said, her tone now serious. With no further apology—before I'd even had a chance to do as she'd told me—she put her hand on my head and shoved me under the water.

The wound on my belly throbbed now with a deep, searing pain. Instinctively, I opened my mouth to scream as I struggled against the old woman's grip. It was no use. Invisible hands grasped me from somewhere deep below the water, holding me in place. Somehow, I knew that all of them belonged to Gert.

I was on fire. I had escaped Dorothy, escaped the Tin Woodman and his metal army, only to find someone I trusted—someone who wanted to help me—and it had all been a trick.

All she meant to do was kill me.

Why? I screamed in my head, knowing she'd be able to hear. *Why would you do this?*

Sometimes only pain can heal, a cold, distant voice answered.

Just when I thought my lungs would burst—just as I felt consciousness beginning to leave me—the hands let go. My body floated up to the surface, where I gasped for air and found my footing on the smooth rocks lining the pool.

I spun around and faced Gert angrily. "Why?" I demanded again, this time out loud. "Why would you . . ."

"Because it was necessary," Gert said shortly, pursing her lips. "I saved your life."

I didn't believe her at first, but my fingers touched smooth skin when I reached for my wound. I looked down. No gaping bloody hole. No invisible sutures. No scar. The wound had healed like it had never happened at all.

The bruises were gone, too. My skin looked dewy and softer than it had ever been, peachy-pink like all the dead skin had been sloughed off, as if every imperfection healed from the outside in.

It didn't matter. She had saved me, okay, fine, but that wasn't the point. The point was that it still felt like a betrayal. Gert had been one thing, and then she had become something else. I didn't understand why. I didn't know if I wanted to.

You had to trust me, Gert said. Her lips didn't move. *But you also have to learn not to trust anyone. Even me.*

She sank slowly into the pool, and then she was gone.

By the edge of the water, I saw that a stack of towels and a gorgeous silk robe had been laid out for me. Had Gert put them there when I wasn't paying attention? Or had they just appeared by magic?

I didn't really care. I wanted to stay in here forever, but I knew that I couldn't. When I felt the water beginning to turn lukewarm, I reluctantly stepped out and dried my newly healed body. I couldn't help thinking that this was all another trick— something to try to lure me into a false sense of security. But my clothes were gone. I couldn't walk around naked. The robe felt soft against my skin.

Gert reappeared as soon as I looped the belt around my waist, as if she sensed I was ready to move on to the next part of whatever fate awaited me. "They're waiting," she announced.

"They?" I asked, not looking at her. "Who's they?"

I crossed my hands over my chest like a five-year-old. Gert's face softened.

"Forgiveness doesn't come easy for you, I see. Sometimes you have to bend so as not to break, dear."

"You manipulated me," I said. "I know it. You used your magic on me to make me think you were my friend."

"Maybe I did and maybe I didn't," Gert said. "But if I did, maybe it was for a reason? And *if* I did, then what's stopping me from doing it again?"

I glanced suspiciously at her, and she shrugged. I guess I would have to take that as an apology.

I didn't know where we were going or who was waiting for us, but I followed Gert obediently as she led me out of the cavern and through a series of caves. I didn't particularly want to, but I knew by now that I didn't really have a choice.

We walked through a room that was entirely empty except for stark silver walls, and as we moved through it, the air changed. It was heavy and humid all of a sudden.

Clouds hovered near the ceiling of the cave, spitting down raindrops on our heads. A thought suddenly occurred to me: if these witches could make weather indoors, if they could control it—could they create a tornado?

Did they bring me here? I wondered.

"If we could do that we would have done it long ago," Gert said curtly. "Your arrival in Oz is no coincidence. Someone— or something—sent for you. But whatever force might have brought you here is beyond even the witches' knowledge."

I just ignored her.

Gert paused when we reached a new tunnel. She reached up and adjusted the collar of my robe before pulling me into another room that was almost entirely taken up by an enormous table made of what looked like glittering black diamonds, surrounded by rough wooden chairs. Mombi stood at the head of the table, smiling at me, well, wickedly. At her sides were two other people I'd never met before. It wasn't a huge leap to guess that they, too, were witches.

"Amy," Mombi greeted me from the other side of the table. "I trust you've recovered from our journey. I was very pleased at the gumption you showed back in the dungeons. And we're all happy to have you with us."

My eyes immediately snapped to her left. Standing there was a boy with smooth olive skin who looked like he was around my age, maybe a little older. His dark hair stood on end as if he had stuck his fingers in a light socket years ago and hadn't bothered to comb it since. He was cute, sure, but there was something arrogant in the way he looked at me with pale gray eyes. Or maybe not arrogant—maybe he looked angry. I straightened and stared right back.

Who was he? The idea of Gert or Mombi having kids just didn't seem right. And he was a little scary, really. Which was saying a lot given the fact that he was sitting next to Mombi.

"She had a nasty slice in her side, Mombi," Gert said, looking her in the eye. "But she didn't much care for the healing process."

Mombi didn't blink. "Tin Soldiers. The cell was protected. I had to improvise."

Gert nodded, but I didn't think she believed her. Was she suggesting that Mombi was just testing me out?

Standing on Mombi's other side was a curvy, statuesque woman wearing a tight purple wrap dress. A hood concealed her face—but when she pulled it away, my heart skipped a beat and then sank.

It was Glinda. Glinda the not-so-good witch. The one who was besties with Dorothy, who had made the Munchkins her slaves and was using them to mine giant holes all over Oz.

She wasn't wearing PermaSmile, but she was smiling at me.

She spoke in a sickeningly sweet voice that scraped at the back of my spine.

"No rest for the Wicked, is there, Amy?"

FOURTEEN

A chill rushed through my body. I should never have come with Mombi, should never have trusted Gert. But what choice did I really have when I was standing in the palace dungeon, about to go on trial for a Fate Worse Than Death, the Tin Soldiers advancing? It's not like I had a ton of options.

"She's one of *you*?" I asked. My voice echoed through the cave.

Was this some kind of trap? Was this Dorothy's idea of a twisted punishment? They'd rescued me, cleaned me up, and now they were just going to turn me over to Dorothy's evil pink BFF?

Like hell.

I took a step back. And another. Then I turned toward the mouth of the cave and began to run. I'd have to navigate the weird maze of caves we'd come through, but it beat being trapped in the room full of witches with crazy superpowers behind me. And if Grandma Gert could read minds, who knew what the others could do? No, I had to get out of here.

Out of nowhere, I slammed into a cold, hard surface and then slid down awkwardly onto the stone ground. But there was nothing there. I'd run into an invisible wall.

Glinda's laugh echoed around me. I guess it probably *was* funny. From her perspective, I mean. I must have looked like a duped Wile E. Coyote falling off a cliff.

I felt my face turn red. I wasn't embarrassed. Or at least, I wasn't *just* embarrassed. I was scared. And I was angry. But I couldn't fight it as an invisible hand clawed into my shoulder, pulling me up to my feet. It set me standing again, turned me around to face my captors, and marched me back toward them.

"Amy," Mombi said warningly. "We made a deal. Remember? You agreed to join us when you took my hand."

"I didn't know what I was agreeing to," I said, twitching against Gert's hold on me.

"Your ignorance makes no difference. The spell was cast. You're bound to the Order now."

"Bound?"

"When I rescued you from your cell, it was under the condition that you would join us. You agreed. The spell was cast and I couldn't undo it if I wanted to. You're one of us now."

I crossed my arms over my chest and glared at Glinda. "I know what you did to the Munchkins," I spat at Glinda. "You may look sweet, but I know who you are."

"Oh!" Glinda exclaimed. She laughed again, high-pitched and lilting. "I'm not who you think I am," she said.

She didn't so much stand as pose, seeming acutely aware that she was the pretty purple flower in a sea of gray and brown and black. "I'm not Glinda. I'm Glamora, her twin sister. She's the Good witch; I'm the Wicked one. Of course, she's also the one who's turned Oz into the hellhole it is now, so it's really all relative."

Then that laugh again.

I eyed the witch suspiciously. A twin? That seemed like a convenient excuse. As I thought back to my first day here in Oz, it was true that she didn't look *exactly* like the woman I'd seen in the field. Mostly, it was a matter of style. Rather than Glinda's bouncing curls, this witch had her strawberry-blonde hair pulled into a severe bun. And though her dress was just as fancy as the one I'd seen Glinda wearing in the field that day, it was simple and elegant, nothing like the frilly nightmare Glinda had worn.

"You say *Wicked* like it's a good thing," I said.

"You're getting the hang of it." Glamora's voice was glittering mischievously. "Down is up, up is down. Good is Wicked, Wicked is Good. The times are changing. This is what Oz has come to."

I looked around at the faces of the Wicked, or formerly Wicked. I wanted some answers. "How did you find me?" I asked slowly. "How did Mombi know I fell from the sky? How did you know I was there in the palace?"

We have eyes within the palace. And the palace has eyes everywhere. The rest I'm afraid I had to obtain from you.

The thought popped into my head. A thought that wasn't mine.

"Amy. Sit. Let us explain," Gert said, this time out loud. I ignored her command and her concerned gaze. I didn't want to look at her. "Sit," she repeated, this time a little louder. I resisted, but found I had no control over my own limbs. It hadn't been a request.

Fighting each step as I went, I walked over and sat down in a cold metal chair.

"Oz has changed," Gert said. "The trees don't talk. The Pond of Truth tells lies, the Wandering Water stays put. The Land of Naught is on fire. People are starting to get old. People are forgetting how it used to be."

"It used to be the three of us would never have imagined we'd be standing in the same room together," Mombi said in her raspy voice. She gestured to herself, Glamora, and Gert. The boy still hadn't said anything. He was just standing with his arms folded across his chest. He didn't really look any happier to be here than I was. "Wicked witches aren't supposed to work together. But that was before Dorothy."

Gert could see that I wasn't buying it. More than see, I guessed, she could read it in my mind. I wondered if she was included in the once-Wicked, too. "We call ourselves Wicked to show that we stand against Dorothy and everything she represents," Gert said. "Wickedness is part of Oz. It's part of the order of things. It's always been the Good versus the Wicked. Magic can't exist without Goodness. Goodness can't exist without Wickedness. And Oz can't exist without magic."

"No matter *what* Dorothy might think," Mombi said. "Glamora. Show her."

Glamora waved her hand across the stone table, and it rippled as its surface transformed into a dark pool of water. Then she waved her hand again, and a picture began to form in the pool, reflecting up from the bottom.

It was a map, and it was divided into four equal triangles, each one its own color. Blue, red, yellow, purple. At the center was an irregular blob of green.

"This is Oz," Glamora said. One by one, she pointed at each of the quadrants. "Munchkin Country, Quadling Country, Winkie Country, Gillikin Country." Blue, red, yellow, purple. As she pointed, their names appeared in dramatic script. "Here on the edge"—she ran her finger along the perimeter of the rect-angle—"is the Deadly Desert. It protects Oz from outsiders. No living thing can cross the Deadly Desert without using powerful magic. Anyone who touches its sands will turn instantly to dust. Or, that's how it used to be."

She jabbed a long purple nail at the blob in the center. "And *this* is the Emerald City. Where Dorothy lives."

Then she passed her hand over the pool again, and the colors disappeared, replaced by shimmering white dots, little pricks of light covering every inch of the map. "The white lights represent Oz's magic," Glamora said. "Its lifeblood. This is what Oz used to look like. And this"—she snapped her fingers—"is what it looks like now."

The light dimmed and faded until most of the map was a dull, washed-out gray, dappled with a few gaping black holes here and there. There were still a few glittering spots spread across

Oz's four quadrants, as well as one spot in the south that was particularly bright, but other than that, the vibrant, shimmering landscape of just a moment ago was gone.

Except for at the very center of the map. The green blob was glowing with more intensity than any other spot, burning so bright that I had to squint to look at it.

I looked up at Glamora and then around the table, where Mombi, Gert, and the boy were all watching me expectantly.

"We need your help," Mombi said.

"The magic is disappearing from Oz," said Gert.

"It doesn't look like it's disappearing," I said, gesturing toward the center of the map. "It's just *moving*."

"Correct," Glamora said with a narrow-eyed smile. "And can you guess *why* it's moving?"

I looked at her blankly, and then it dawned on me. I remembered the pit in Munchkin Country that my trailer had fallen into, and Glinda with her Munchkin machine. I remembered what Indigo had told me about *magic mining*.

"Someone's taking it," I said. Glamora arched a perfectly plucked eyebrow, waiting for me to figure out the rest. "It's Dorothy," I realized. "Dorothy's stealing the magic."

"Now you've got it," Glamora said. "And losing its magic to Dorothy will mean the end of Oz. That's why you're here. We need you to stop her."

I sat up straight. I didn't know the first thing about magic. I didn't know the first thing about *Dorothy*. "Me? I just got here. How am I supposed to stop anyone from doing anything?"

All eyes turned to me at once. The boy fixed me with an especially hard gaze. Finally Mombi spoke.

"Simple. You're going to kill her." She looked right at me and said, "Dorothy must die."

FIFTEEN

I opened my mouth to protest, but all that came out was laughter. Everyone was surprised—no one more so than me. I tried to stifle it, but it had been so long since I'd found something funny, and soon I couldn't control myself. It all came spilling out. The fight, getting suspended, my mother jetting off to her tornado party, the trailer lifting up off the ground and landing me *here*. I thought about who I was back in Kansas, and who I was in Oz. What had I done to make them think I was a potential teen girl assassin? I mean, I got suspended for *not* punching Madison Pendleton. I had maybe been responsible for Indigo's death, but it was only because I'd been trying to save an innocent monkey's *life*. Taking someone down off a stake in the ground was the opposite of taking someone out. This was madness.

Across the table, the witches just sat there staring at me like I was a crazy person while I laughed hysterically. The boy frowned so hard, his eyes turned into slits. Finally, after a few minutes, I managed to calm myself down and wiped my eyes with the back of my hand.

"You want *me* to kill *Dorothy*," I said. It was so ridiculous that I didn't even know where to start.

"That's the idea," Glamora said. The look in her eyes said she didn't think it was very funny at all.

I couldn't believe they were being serious. "Um, I think you've got the wrong person. Before I got here, the last fight I had was with a pregnant girl. And I lost."

"I saw you back in the palace," Mombi said. "In your cell. You managed to hold your own in there. I don't see why you couldn't do the same with Dorothy."

I had to admit, that was true. But I was still sure that the knife Mombi had given me had done half the work. And anyway: "That was different," I said. "That was magic, I'm sure of it. But I couldn't *kill* someone. I wouldn't even know how."

"We'll teach you, of course," Glamora said. "Everyone has to start somewhere."

They were acting like we were talking about learning how to sew. This is not what I signed on for. When I had met Indigo on the road, I was just planning on making my way to the Emerald City and maybe getting one of those cool moving tattoos. This was way heavier than anything I expected.

"Listen," I said. "I have my own problems. I'm sorry about what's happening to Oz—I really am—but I don't see what you think I can do about it. I'm not even *from* here." I wasn't from here. But even as I said it, a little part of me couldn't help but feel that because of Indigo, because of Ollie, because of my time in the cell . . . I was linked to Oz somehow.

Glamora cocked her head. "Dorothy's not from here either," she said. "And look what she's done with the place."

Gert drove her point home. "It's precisely because you are not from here that we think you can do this. You're from the same place as her. You know how her mind works. You understand her."

I wasn't from here. I was from Kansas. Just like Dorothy. I'd come to Oz on a tornado. Dorothy had changed their world once, and now they expected *me* to help them change it back.

"People from the Other Place have always had a special place in ours," Gert said. "The Wizard. Dorothy. Now you. We don't know what power it was that brought you to Oz, but we know that if you're here, it must be because you have a role to play. We want to make sure it's the right role."

I shivered. The story was true. *The Wizard of Oz* had been real. Dorothy Gale had really been swept up by a tornado and brought to the Land of Oz. True, what I was living now didn't seem like the kind of storybook tale I was used to. But it didn't mean they didn't exist.

For the first time, the boy spoke up. His voice was low and gruff.

"Gert, Glamora, and Mombi believe that you are our only hope." He sounded like he wasn't so sure about that. "My job is to train you."

"Are you a witch, too?" I asked. It came out in a more confrontational tone than I'd meant it to, but I didn't care.

The boy looked offended. "I'm a warlock," he said drily. "Or a wizard, if you like that better. It doesn't really matter, does it?"

Gert looked over at him as if remembering her manners. "Amy, this is Nox. He's the newest member of the High Council of the Order of the Wicked. He's the strongest fighter we have."

"Good for him. No offense or anything, it's just, I'm not a killer. I'm not the girl you're looking for here. I think it would be pretty amazing to know what you guys know. But you all have magic; you know what you're doing. I'm sure you can handle her without me."

I probably should have been scared of these people—they called themselves the Order of the Wicked, after all—but talking back to them felt good. Then again, lately I didn't seem to be able to keep myself from talking back to anyone, really.

"You haven't been trained yet," Glamora said. "You don't know who or what you are yet. Oz is different. *You* can be different here. You can be stronger. We'll teach you how to do all of it. To fight. To use magic."

"Amy," Gert said. She placed a reassuring hand on my back. "We're going to teach you to be a hero."

Me. A hero. The idea of having power—of learning magic—rattled around in my head. But reality chased after it: missing Mom, scary Dorothy, a circle of self-proclaimed wicked witches who wanted to make me into an assassin. Besides, even if they could teach me all that stuff, it wouldn't change who I was on the inside. Salvation Amy from Flat Hill, Kansas. Just a trailer-park girl with a bunch of stupid dreams that would never come true.

Weirdly, something my mom had told me once came back to me: *You are not where you are from.* She'd meant it to cheer me up. To make me believe that growing up in Flat Hill didn't have to define me for the rest of my life.

But the witches thought I was special *because* of where I came from.

It's more than that, child. Much more.

Gert was fishing around in my brain once more.

I looked at Nox again. He stared back at me and gave me a shrug like, *See if I care.* He was the only one—except me, of course—who didn't seem thrilled about this whole idea. Even if I agreed with him, I couldn't help taking it a little personally. What did he have against me anyway?

"What happens if I say no?" I asked.

"You *can't* say no," Mombi said. "The pact, remember?"

"I told you," Nox said, not even bothering to look at me. "Just because someone dropped out of the sky doesn't make them the key to saving us."

What was wrong with these people? I felt my blood begin to boil. Nox turned to Mombi and shrugged. And that shrug is what put me over the edge.

"I'm in," I said quietly.

Mombi looked at Gert, who nodded as if to say that my words were true. But they weren't. I had to say yes to joining the Order—I didn't seem to have a choice in that. I was bound by the pact I'd made with Mombi. But I was determined to find a way out of the whole teen assassin part.

And Gert knew it.

A few minutes later, Gert led me to my room. "We let Glamora decorate. Of all of us, she misses the creature comforts of Oz the most."

My cave room wasn't pretty—it was majestic. It was the kind of bedroom I'd always wished for growing up. There was a circular bed that seemed to be sunken into the center of the floor, piled with pillows and silky bedding in rich shades of red. And in the center of the ceiling, instead of a chandelier, there was another upside-down tree. This one was way smaller than the one I'd seen before. And it was in bloom. Black branches held out strange but beautiful poppy-like blossoms, big and white with a blush of pink almost the exact color of my hair. The pale gold walls were covered in wallpaper with those same pink flowers bursting across it. When I looked closer, I realized they were actual flowers. More tiny flowers grew along vines that stretched from the floor to the ceiling, stopping in the middle to swirl into paisley loops. Beneath my feet, a rug made from golden fur rippled.

"What happens now?" I asked. "You lock me in here until I agree to be your killer and actually mean it? Because I know that you know I didn't."

"No, we train you. I know that you aren't ready, child. Just put one foot in front of the other. The rest will come in time."

She sounded so sure. Like she knew something that I didn't.

"And if it doesn't?" What would they do to me if I didn't do what they wanted?

"There is something you don't know about being bound—we can't hurt each other as long as we are in the circle. There is much to fear outside the circle, but you don't have to fear that."

I felt myself exhale and nodded slowly. Whether or not she was telling the truth, her answer would have to be okay for now. I just wished I could read her mind, too.

"No matter what, you'll still be a witch."

"But what kind?" I asked.

"Good question, child," Gert said, slinking off into the dark.

SIXTEEN

I was standing in the middle of an all-white cave. Nox had led me there, then excused himself to change into clothes that he could better torture me in. I waited impatiently.

If I was being honest, the decor of this cave was kind of freaking me out—which was saying something, considering all the others I'd seen.

I stood barefoot on the skin of some giant animal I didn't recognize. Maybe it was some magical Oz beast or something. A track of fire lined the ceiling, illuminating the cave. The white stone walls looked like some kind of stone—opal, I guessed—that shimmered with layers of other colors, depending on the light. White razor-sharp spikes jutted out around me like some kind of medieval climbing wall. Scattered around the room were strange iron machines that looked like either exercise equipment or torture devices.

Training with Nox was going to be fun.

I was already wearing the training uniform. It felt more like lingerie than athletic wear, with a silky tank top and pajama bottoms. The top was clingy and it had some sort of bra thing built in that made my flat chest look a little less flat. Say what you will about these witches, but they valued style.

Giant swings hung on opposite ends of the cave. Of all the places to sit in this cave, they looked innocent enough. I ran my finger along the seat of one and slipped into it. When I shuffled back with my feet, I realized the air was beginning to fill with smoke coming from the floor. I jumped up quickly.

The smoke began to take shape. Familiar figures materialized before me. I backed away, but there was nowhere to go. I was already pressed up against the jagged wall of the cave.

They must have followed me here, traveling through shadows the same way the Tin Woodman had appeared on the road when he found me, Indigo, and Ollie. I wasn't going to stand back and let them take me away for a trial. I looked around wildly for a weapon and spied a rack with some kind of torture devices in the corner. I could only imagine what Nox had planned for us today. I stretched my arm out, but it was too far to reach. I inched toward it.

Dorothy's pink lips pouted at me as she advanced. Her gingham dress, half formed, was just smoke and a hint of cleavage. But her face was there in all of its terrifying glory—and her laugh echoed in my ears even though her plasticky mouth didn't move. The Tin Woodman stood a couple of steps behind her.

"Nox!" I screamed.

Before Dorothy could reach out one of her glinting red nails at me, Nox appeared in the entrance of the cave. Insanely enough, it looked like he was almost smiling.

"Help me!" I cried.

He walked right through the image of Dorothy, and just like that she disappeared. The Tin Woodman disappeared, too, and the ears and hair and tail that I assumed would have made up the Lion vanished with a growl. I was left standing in the white room, staring at Nox.

"*You* sure took your time!" I yelled.

"I just wanted to get your adrenaline going." He smiled a cocky smile, rocking back on his heels. *He had done that?* Even as my anger rose up, I noticed despite myself how good he looked in his training gear. He was more muscular than I would have thought, biceps and quads and muscles I didn't know the names of made up his—possibly magically enhanced—form.

"Why would you do that?" I snapped. "What is wrong with you?"

He just shrugged. It was turning into his signature move. I considered storming out, but my feet stayed rooted to the furry ground.

"*How* did you do that?"

"What I see in my head, I can project out into the space. But it only can last for a few seconds. I just meant to give you a scare, see how good your reflexes are."

"I saw something like that on the road to the Emerald City. Queen Ozma was giving a speech—"

"Not the same thing, really. That was more of a capture."

"A what?"

He leaned in close.

I didn't move. I hadn't exactly spent a lot of time alone with any guys. Tutoring Dustin hardly counted. And he wasn't a witch or wizard or whatever it was I was supposed to call Nox. He was annoyingly—and maybe not so annoyingly—even hotter up close.

"Ouch!" I felt a pinprick of pain on my scalp as Nox leaned back, holding a strand of my pink hair. He pulled something out of his pocket, and folded it together with my hair in his fist.

"Memoria," he whispered.

When he opened his hand, there was an emerald inside.

"This moment is now captured forever. There are emeralds like this embedded in the road. They're meant to deliver messages, scare people, spread Dorothy's decrees. Basically a way for the palace to keep us in line."

He tossed the emerald on the ground. An image rose up from the stone, hazy at first and then snapping in focus. I was rolling my eyes at him. He was leaning in to pull my hair. But it almost looked like he was giving me a kiss.

The image disappeared as quickly as it had appeared.

"So is *that* your superpower? Making people see things that aren't there?"

Nox didn't answer. He disappeared in a blink and reappeared beside me. "I can make them see things that are there as well. Like Mombi said, I'm a fighter. We should get started."

When he moved into his fighting stance I noticed a speck of green paint in his black hair.

"What?" he asked, noticing my staring.

He must be Oz's mysterious graffiti artist. The one tagging the frowny faces I'd seen in Munchkin Country.

"Nothing," I said quickly. "I'm ready." He was working really hard to put up the whole "fighter" front, but I wondered what else was there beneath the surface. What else it meant to be a boy witch.

"Liar," Nox whispered with a mean glint in his eye. "Don't worry. The spring will be able to heal you up when you break something."

"I'd prefer not to get hurt in the first place," I countered.

"Is wit highly valued in your world? You seem to rely on it."

"Is being a total jerk highly valued in your world?" Sarcasm was how I survived back home. I wasn't about to give it up now.

His gray eyes opened a little wider. "Your words will do nothing against her unless you can use them in a spell."

I sighed loudly. If they wanted me to train, I would train. A few self-defense techniques would certainly come in handy around here. For that matter, they'd come in handy if I ever made it back to Dwight D. Eisenhower Senior High and had to face down a leaner, meaner, postpartum Madison Pendleton.

Still. Just because I was willing to learn how to fight, it didn't mean I was going to assassinate anyone. I suspected Nox knew it.

"Why don't you just give me one of those magical knife things and be done with it?"

"I could do that," he mused, pulling a knife from one of his black boots and throwing it from one hand to the other. He tossed it in my direction, but I wasn't fast enough and it fell to the floor with a clatter. I let it lay there, wishing I'd never said anything. "But you might drop it," he finished with a smirk.

"I wasn't ready," I argued.

"Would you rather *have* the knife or *be* the knife? It's that simple. And that hard."

He opened his hand and the knife whizzed into it. I'd seen Mombi do the same thing before. He slid the knife back into his boot, then spread his arms out wide at his sides, daring me to punch him.

I curled my hand into a fist and took a weak, halfhearted swing at him. Nox hopped back and rolled his eyes. "Give me a break," he said. "You have to *try* or it's no fun."

Before I could respond, Nox took his own jab at me, aiming right for my chin. I rocked back on my heels, barely getting out of the way in time, and then, without thinking about it, I hit back. For real now.

This time I connected square in the center of Nox's chest. My fist hit a hard wall of flesh and muscle. My knuckles stung from the impact, but he didn't flinch. It was like he hadn't even felt it.

All he did was laugh. "All right," he said. "Well, that's something, at least. Now do it again. This time, *I'll* try, too."

I looked at the cocky expression on his face. I wanted to wipe it off, just to show I could. So I swung with all my strength and almost fell over from the momentum as he stepped easily out of the way. His smirk hadn't wavered for a moment.

"Keep going."

I kept punching, getting angrier and angrier with every try. Nox dodged each blow as smoothly as if I were moving in slow motion.

It took me until I was sweaty and out of breath to realize that something wasn't quite right. Nox was more than just fast.

"That isn't fair," I said. "You're using magic."

"Of course I am. Lesson one: she'll be using everything she has against you—and I promise it will be a lot more than I'm using right now."

He had a point.

"Fine," I said. "Then why are we even bothering at all?"

When he opened his mouth to reply, I took it as an invitation to hit him right in the solar plexus. His eyebrows shot up as his arrogant smirk transformed into a grin.

"Aha," he said. "Lesson two: your fists aren't your only weapon. Your *weapons* won't be your only weapon either. Dorothy's biggest vulnerability is her—"

I kicked him in the stomach with everything I had, and he went stumbling backward, his mouth wide with surprise. That would show him not to underestimate me.

But instead of retreating, or even slowing down, he came flying right back at me. This time I was ready for him. I ducked.

Over the next hour, Nox didn't let up. He just kept coming at me, using his fists and feet and elbows and knees and everything else he had. The whole time, he never stopped talking—pointing out everything I was doing wrong.

And everything I was doing wrong was *everything*. The way I was standing. The way I was avoiding his gaze. The way I was holding my hands.

But for all I was doing wrong, there *was* one thing I was doing right. I wasn't letting up any more than he was. I was aching and exhausted, but I kept going.

"Stay loose," he said. I didn't know how he had the breath to keep talking when he was moving twice as fast as I was. "Don't waste your energy keeping your muscles tight. Don't focus on where I am. Focus on where I'm *going* to be."

Before the sentence was finished, Nox was gone. I spun around just as he materialized behind me, already ready for him, and caught him right in the jaw. Finally, for the first time, he flinched in pain. But before I could draw my arm away, he'd grabbed me by the wrist and held my closed fist against his face. I tried to pull free, but I couldn't.

He just stared at me, his gaze intense. I couldn't look away any more than I could move my arm. Energy crackled between us, and I felt a strange pull to him. Moth to flame. Magnet to magnet. Stupid girl to impossible, slightly mean witch boy. Wizard. Whatever.

"Close your eyes," he said. "I want you to feel something."

"I already feel something," I said. "*Tired.*"

"Just do it," Nox said.

So I closed my eyes and felt a strange, warm energy pulsing through my body, starting where my fist still touched his face

and traveling up through my arm and shoulder into my chest.
It wasn't hot and it wasn't cold. It was like nothing I'd ever felt
before—including the time when I was little and I put my finger in a lightbulb socket to see what would happen. That had
hurt like there was no tomorrow. Like the surge of electricity
was killing every cell as it flowed through my arm. This was the
opposite. This felt like every inch of me was waking up.

"What is it?" I asked.

"Isn't it obvious?" He let go of my hand and it dropped to my
side, heavy as stone. "It's magic," he said.

Suddenly I felt a breeze. I opened my eyes.

We weren't in the training area anymore. Instead, we were
standing at the edge of a grassy plateau that jutted out from the
mouth of a cave at the top of a mountain.

The sun was bright and perfect and the sky was brilliant blue
with just the slightest tinge of lavender. I looked down over the
edge of the precipice we stood on and caught my breath. We
were don't-look-down high. We were skyscraper-high. Not that
I had ever been in one, but I imagined this is what it felt like. The
drop between us and the treetops was dizzying. Below us was a
vast expanse of wildness.

In the distance, fields and flowers gave way to a lush, dark
forest. Farther on the horizon was a hazy, shimmering mountain
range that blocked the rest of Oz from my view—mountains so
high that their peaks were hidden by a thick veil of quickly moving clouds.

Everything was still and quiet. This was a different quiet

from the creepy, dead quiet of Munchkin Country. This quiet was pristine and charmed and full of life. It felt like Nox and I were the only two people in an undiscovered world.

"How'd we get out here?" I asked. My voice came out in a whisper.

He looked at me like I was the dumbest person alive. "You have to stop asking those kinds of questions," he said. "You know exactly how we got out here."

Of course I knew. It was the same as the answer he'd given me before.

"Magic," I said under my breath, without even really meaning to.

"Yup," he said. "I zapped us up here. I can't work the same kinds of teleportation spells that Mombi can, so we didn't go far. The Order's headquarters is all inside these caves." He gestured at the cave opening behind us.

I breathed deep, enjoying the first fresh air I'd tasted since I'd been taken to the Emerald Palace who knows how long ago. I felt it buzzing in my lungs and my whole body tingled. It was the same feeling I'd felt back in the caves when I'd touched Nox's face and closed my eyes.

"I think I feel it," I said finally. "The magic."

"You can't *not*. Not up here," he said. "This is Mount Gillikin. It's one of the most magical spots left in all of Oz. Dorothy hasn't quite gotten to stealing it yet—it's too much trouble. See those mountains a ways off? They move. Every night, they rebuild themselves; every day they're different than they were the day before. Can't build roads through them. Can't even draw a map. You never know what you're going to get. Some days they might be covered in snow, other days they could be so hot you'll get sunstroke. Or anything in between. People go up those mountains and they never come back. Sure, you can get past them—you can fly, or teleport, or whatever—but it's not easy. They're part of what keeps Gillikin Country more protected than the rest of Oz. Still, it's only a matter of time."

"It's incredible."

"All of Oz used to be like this. There was so much magic floating around that you almost couldn't help picking it up here and there. Now most of it's just in a few scattered spots like this, places Dorothy can't be bothered with."

"Maybe she'll never bother," I said. "Why does she need more than she already has?"

Nox snorted. "You don't know Dorothy. The more she gets, the more she wants. That's the way it is with you people," he said.

"*You* people? What people?"

"People from your world. Like Dorothy. The Wizard. Like you, probably. Magic's dangerous for outlanders. You're not built for it."

"But you're going to teach me anyway. That's what Mombi said."

"They think the risk is worth it," Nox said. "Not everyone agrees."

"You don't think I can handle it. "

"Maybe you can and maybe you can't. I don't really know

you. What I think doesn't matter. The question is what *you* think." He shrugged.

I shook my head. I needed more.

"It's your choice," he said. "It's not magic that makes you who you are. It's the choices that you make. Look at Dorothy."

"What about Dorothy?"

"That's exactly what makes Dorothy evil."

SEVENTEEN

After my training session with Nox, it was a relief to see Gert. I didn't know what she had in store for me, but I had a feeling it wouldn't involve having to hit anyone. Despite the whole almost-drowning-me-on-purpose incident and her being up in my brain all the time, she had *not* told the others that I had no intention of killing Dorothy. I was still confused about what it meant to be a witch—a *Wicked* witch, for that matter—but somehow she seemed less *Wicked* than the rest. Maybe it was stupid Stockholm syndrome, that thing people get when they start liking their captors. But I didn't feel like I was a captive when I was with Gert.

Gert's room was like an old-fashioned apothecary, with a wall of glass jars filled with a million different liquids, big canisters heaping with I don't know what, and plants and herbs I didn't recognize. The light was dim, but warm and cozy, too. I couldn't figure out where it was coming from—although there were candles crowding almost every surface, none of them were lit. Her walls were covered with some kind of white gold, which further intensified the glow.

In the corner leaned a broom made out of wood so dark it was almost black, with long, thorny bristles. I reached out to touch it but drew my hand back when Gert spoke sharply.

"You're not ready for that yet, dear," she warned. I looked at her, but she smiled like it was no big deal and began to bustle around the cave.

"Amy," Gert said. "I know this is all new. I know you're scared." She walked over to a shelf and absentmindedly plucked a jar down before glancing at it, shaking her head to herself, and placing it back in its spot. "But we need you," she said. "And I have faith in you. And now, for our first lesson. I like to think of this project as my little *Get Witch Quick* scheme." She giggled at her own joke.

She sat back down on a stool on one side of a big wooden table in the middle of the room and indicated that I should follow suit. Every inch of its surface was covered with candles, and as she looked down at them, they began to light, one by one.

Gert's face glowed in the light that she'd made. She smiled, a secret, satisfied little smile, and then clapped her hands and they all went out. "Your turn now," she said.

"How?" I asked. I was confused. She hadn't taught me anything yet. Wasn't I supposed to say a spell or wave a wand or brew up something with eye of newt? From what Nox said and from what I'd seen so far, magic only *looked* easy. It took concentration and practice and time.

Gert waved her hand in the air, and as she did, sparks trailed behind it, like tiny, crackling fireflies. "Think of magic like electricity in your world," she said. "In Oz, it's all around you. It flows through the ground and the sky and the water. It keeps Oz alive. In most places, there's not nearly as much as there used to be, but it's still there."

"Okay . . . ," I said. It sort of made sense, but not really.

"To use it," she went on, "you just need to know how to find it. You need to gather it up and tell it what to do. It's just unstable energy. Magic always wants to be something different from what it already is. It wants to change. That's what makes it magic. And that's what makes lighting a candle the simplest bit of magic you can do. You just take the energy, and you tell it what to be. In this case: heat."

It always wants to be something different from what it already is. Now *that* made sense to me. It reminded me of myself.

I frowned at the candles. I stretched out my fingers and moved them through the still, slightly damp air around me, trying to get back to that place Nox had taken me to—that tingly, warm feeling.

Nothing.

"You have to want it," Gert said. "Do you want it?"

"Of course I want it," I said. I did, didn't I? I passed my stiff palm over the candles.

Again, nothing happened. The wicks remained completely flame free.

"Do you really, child?"

"Why wouldn't I?"

"Forget about what you are supposed to do. Just do what comes naturally to you."

I slumped over. "I hate to break it to you," I said, "but *none* of this comes naturally to me."

"Amy," she said. "It will. Soon. What you did in that cell with Mombi, part of that was the knife, yes. But an even bigger part of it was coming from *you*. You have the talent. Once you learn how to harness it properly, you'll be unstoppable."

I couldn't help but remember the fact that I had hurt someone, or something. He deserved it, but still. It felt so easy in the moment. Maybe too easy. I remembered what Nox had told me, about how dangerous magic was, about how it corrupted people from my world. How they wanted more and more. It was magic that had made Dorothy who she was now. What would it do to me? What if, in training to fight Dorothy, I became just like her?

"You're not Dorothy, dear," Gert said. I felt myself shiver involuntarily. She must have overheard my thoughts. "Don't worry. I'll make sure you never become her." I wondered if Gert was making this promise just to stop me from worrying, or if it was a promise she could keep. "Which leads us to a very important question." She paused, and looked me up and down appraisingly. "Who are you?" she finally asked.

I pulled back, surprised at the question. "What?"

"If you're not Dorothy, then who are you?"

I didn't know how to respond. "Um," I said. "I'm Amy?"

"I bet there are a million Amys where you are from, dear.

Amy is what you are *called*." Gert laughed liltingly. "One thing you have to understand," she said, "is that all magic users have our own specialties. We each have our own affinities for certain kinds of magic. It has to do with your personality. Once you understand what kinds of magic you're best suited for, it will be easier. But before you can do that, you need to know who you are. The essence of what makes you *you*. So. Who are you?"

I thought about it. Before I'd gotten to Oz, I would have been able to answer the question more easily, I think. But I also think I might have answered it wrong. Now, I didn't know where to begin.

Was I the Amy Gumm I'd always been, who took care of my mother even though I sometimes hated every vomit-y, thankless moment of it, who got by in school not even breaching the surface of all that potential that Dr. Strachan said I had? Was I Salvation Amy, the girl who always took the bait when Madison Pendleton pushed me too far? The girl who couldn't keep her mouth shut literally when her life depended on it? The girl whose future looked as bleak as the Kansas sky she stared at every night through her tiny circular trailer window?

Or was I someone more extreme, someone I never imagined—a killer. A warrior. A girl who could stab someone in the face and know that she was doing the right thing? A girl who had strength she never even knew about?

"Who am I supposed to be?" I asked.

"It's not a matter of who you're supposed to be. The truth is, I already know exactly who you are. But my telling you—that won't do you any good at all. You have to be the one to figure it out. Here, try again. Light the candles."

I focused in on myself. I imagined the candles flickering and then lighting up.

But still, nothing happened.

Gert's face didn't betray any expression. I searched it for disappointment, but I couldn't find any at all. She just clapped her hands together and smiled. "I think that's enough for today," she said. "You'll meet with Glamora next. Now *that* should be interesting."

I shrugged and stood up. As I got to the doorway, though, I turned back around to face Gert one more time.

"What about you?" The question that had been bouncing around in my mind came tumbling out just like that. "Are you really a Wicked witch?" I asked. "You said you were, but . . . you don't seem Wicked to me."

Gert's smile faded. "That's a complicated question," she replied shortly, averting her eyes.

"I think I can handle complicated at this point," I said.

She just sighed. "They used to call me the Good Witch of the North," she said. "But that was a long time ago."

"What happened to you?" What makes a Good witch turn Wicked? And if she couldn't stop herself from Wickedness, how could she stop me from following Dorothy's path?

"I knew Dorothy when she was young, when she first came here. When all she talked about was home. But I saw something else in her even then—she wasn't honest with herself about what

she wanted. She said she wanted home but she also wanted rec-
ognition. She wanted the world to sit up and recognize what
she'd done. She couldn't get that in her world so she came back to
ours. But here she was living in the shadow of Ozma. So she neu-
tralized Ozma and took the reins herself. But even that wasn't
enough for her. She wanted more."

"I want things, too."

"You want things to be right. There may be a boy you want
to kiss, or you may want your mother to get better. But you don't
have what she has—more *wanting* than would fill that Kansas of
yours, I'd imagine."

"What if you're wrong?" I asked quietly.

"I'm not wrong." Gert's voice was firm, unwavering. "Now
go. You need to get all the rest you can before meeting with
Glamora tomorrow."

Was Gert *still* Good? I wondered, and if not, why? Her mouth
formed a thin firm line that said she would not be answering
anything else, at least not today. I found myself turning and
leaving the room—and not of my own volition. Gert's invisible
hand gave me a push.

Back in my own quarters, I was more tired than I should have
been. Somehow, I was even more exhausted than I'd been after
that morning's training session with Nox. By the time I'd finished
wolfing down the bowl of tasteless green gruel that had materialized in my room, I was so exhausted that instead of bothering to
take my clothes off, I collapsed into the bed still dressed.

My bed was barely a bed at all—it was just a bunch of pillows and sheets piled into a sunken pit in the middle of my room. But I'd already discovered it was more comfortable than any mattress I'd ever slept on. Sinking into it felt like sinking into a dream.

Despite how tired I was and despite how good it felt to finally get to lie down, I heard Gert's thoughts echoing in my head as I tried to settle into sleep. *Who are you?* I should have had an answer to that. *Everyone* should have an answer to that. But I didn't.

My first lesson with Glamora was something completely different.

When I stepped into her room the next morning, she looked up from behind a jewel-encrusted vanity that was unlike anything else in the caves.

Actually, Glamora's entire quarters were like nothing else in the caves. It was pretty easy to forget we were underground at all.

There were rugs hanging from the walls of the cave in rich purples and reds, and carpeting the floor. Her bed was heaped with white fur, and there was a whole wall covered with mirrored closets so stuffed with dresses that the doors were all standing half open. One just contained jewelry, necklaces and rings and earrings spilling out onto the floor.

She stood from her vanity and moved to a tufted couch with a mirrored table before it. She stared at it and a tea set appeared. She beckoned me to sit.

"What are we doing?"

"We're having tea."

As I sat down, a tiered tray of pastries poofed into existence right next to the tea set. The tray was laden with inside-out sandwiches and square doughnuts and little scones with what looked like gold-leaf chips.

My mouth watered. After practically starving in Dorothy's dungeons the idea of eating something that didn't taste like sulfur weakened my curiosity. Why not just sit and eat with the crazy purple witch? But was she trying to get to know me? Was this some kind of supernatural test I wasn't even aware of yet? Would we read the tea leaves when we finished the tea?

I was so hungry that I reached out for a tiny cookie that looked like a little pane of stained glass. Glamora slapped my hand away.

"Wait till the hostess pours before you touch anything," she ordered. "You'll need to be careful of even the smallest of gestures when you begin your mission. Everything you do will be watched. You'll need to get close to Dorothy, and Dorothy is smarter than she looks. Anything could give you away." She finally gestured for me to eat and I took a bite of one of the gorgeous petits fours. The flavors changed magically in my mouth, from layer cake to chocolate sorbet to some kind of banana pudding.

This all came as news to me. No one had told me the plan yet. "So I'm going to be going, like, undercover or something?" I asked, my mouth still half full of pastry. Glamora looked at me disapprovingly and didn't answer my question.

"Don't talk with your mouth full. Now, pour me a cup of tea."

We spent the next few hours reviewing manners—certainly something I had zero experience with back home. How to walk, how to speak. How to serve. She taught me how to curtsy and even how to *look* at Dorothy.

While the lesson with Gert had been full of conversation, almost like hanging out with a friend, Glamora was all business, barely even pausing on one topic before she'd moved on to the next. By the time it was over, my head was swimming with what felt like useless information.

And there was going to be a lot more where that came from. As I was leaving, she handed me a stack of books—architecture, art, etiquette, and a couple of novels.

"Everyone in Oz under the age of two hundred has read these. We'll discuss them all next time." She sat back down at her vanity and turned away from me, toward the mirror. Her hairbrush picked itself up and began brushing her hair.

What was I going to do, challenge Dorothy to trivia? Bore her to death?

"*All* of these?" I asked incredulously. It would take me at least a month to read *half* of what she'd given me.

"You'll manage," Glamora said. "And one more thing. I don't think you like me very much. And I *know* you don't trust me. That's a good thing. You shouldn't trust me. But you shouldn't trust anyone else here either. Every smile, every kind word—every cookie—it's all done with one goal. And that's a dead princess."

"I know that," I said defiantly. "What's your point?"

"My point is that in Dorothy's world, words like *Good* and *Wicked* are meaningless," Glamora replied. As she ran her brush through her hair, it began to deepen in color, from fiery red to a deep, rich auburn. She smiled sweetly as she spoke, like she was trying to do me a favor.

I knew what she was doing. She was trying to shake my faith in Gert. But why?

EIGHTEEN

"What is wrong with that woman?" I asked Nox as he escorted me to dinner on the night of my first lesson with Glamora. He took the books she'd given me and they dematerialized into thin air—I presumed back to my room where I could study them later.

He looked at me wryly. "You got yourself beat up and you're learning how to do magic—but you're mad about reading a couple of books?" He laughed. "Glamora should be the easiest part of your day." But the corner of his mouth was turned up just barely in a way that suggested he knew exactly how difficult Glinda's twin could be.

"There's just something about her," I said. "Something that creeps me out."

"She's Glinda's twin," he replied. "What do you expect? Imagine having your other half turn on you, and knowing that one day you'll have to face her in battle."

I stopped in the hallway. Nox turned to look at me, his face aglow from the tracks of fire that lit our way from above. There was the barest hint of impatience beneath his cool surface. I picked at it like a scab.

"Gert asked me who I was, but the truth is I don't know who any of *you* are. Not really. And I don't even know one detail of this big plan that supposedly hinges on me."

"You don't have to know every turn of the road in order to walk down it."

"It would help to know the destination."

"You do—we're taking down Dorothy."

"You know what I mean. Can't you drop the good soldier crap for a second and just be a person?"

He paused for a second, as if seriously considering the question. Finally, he said, "Only Mombi and Gert know the whole plan. The rest of us only know pieces. That way if someone gets caught, all isn't lost."

"But what if—?" The sound of Glamora clinking a glass prevented me from asking more questions.

"Some stories aren't mine to tell," Nox said curtly. Then, as if feeling bad, he added, "Welcome to your first official dinner with the Revolutionary Order of the Wicked." And with that, he led me into the dining room.

The dining room was formal like Glamora. But spooky, too. The table was a round piece of slate suspended in air in the center of the cave. The walls were a warm chocolate brown with real live honeysuckle flowers growing all over. The table was set with black china. Another upside-down tree was suspended over the table.

Mombi, Gert, and Glamora were already seated.

Nox nodded toward a chair and then took the one next to it. I sat down nervously.

I hadn't had a sit-down dinner with my mom since I was twelve. Our trailer only had a foldout table that Mom had covered with tabloids and unpaid bills.

Gert mumbled a few words under her breath, and our glasses filled with red liquid. I guessed if we were old enough to fight, we were old enough to drink wine.

The plate in front of me was again piled with green goo. At least I had a reason to appreciate Glamora now. Her tea parties might be the only appetizing food I'd be getting from here on out.

"Well . . . how did our girl do?" Mombi asked, looking at me.

"She had absolutely no manners," said Glamora crisply, all too eager to answer first. "Whatever they were teaching her on that tin farm, they should be ashamed."

They weren't teaching me anything. If I followed Mom's example I wouldn't even know how to use a fork. When she actually bothered to eat, Mom's food of choice was Bugles right out of the bag. Or if I pushed hard enough, cereal right out of the box.

"But she has fine bone structure. Don't you think, Nox?" Glamora continued, winking at Nox.

I swallowed a gulp of the wine, which tasted vaguely like

flowers. Did Glamora actually just give me a compliment? And what was with the winking?

"Amy has great potential," Gert jumped in.

Potential was a word that had hovered over my head for the last five or six years at school. Wasted potential. Had it followed me here?

Mombi pressed the subject. "Did she accomplish anything without your aid?"

"No, but she will," Gert said.

Mombi sighed.

"We don't have much time."

"It's just that for a girl who says so much, she does not yet know herself."

Ouch. It sounded different when Gert said it just to me instead of saying it in front of everyone else. Plus, they were talking about me as if I weren't sitting right in front of them.

Nox cleared his throat. *Here we go,* I thought. Now he has a chance to really lay into my failures.

"You can't judge her now. She's doing the best that she can under the circumstances."

The wineglass slipped in my hand. I caught it, but not before a few drops spilled on the table. Nox glanced at me and raised an eyebrow. Was he seriously defending me?

Glamora erased the spill with a wave of her hand.

I looked up at Nox. It didn't make any sense. Mombi studied him appraisingly, as if she was just as surprised as me.

"It takes most charges years to learn what we want her to do in a month," he explained. "She isn't even from here. What did you expect? No one can do that." Suddenly I realized why he was being so nice. He genuinely sounded like he couldn't wrap his head around the idea of me ever being a real witch.

"*You* did," Mombi countered.

"I was a kid. It's easier."

"Dorothy did," Glamora added.

"I can speak for myself!" I blurted. "And honestly, what do I really have to know how to do in order to be bait?" I had put it all together in my head. I was now a fugitive from the palace—and one who Dorothy had a very *personal* interest in. They wanted to use me to distract her. That had to be it.

"I'm right. I'm bait, aren't I?"

Gert opened her mouth to answer—probably to say something comforting—but she stopped herself. She actually looked surprised, which was a real feat for someone who could read minds. But then I realized she wasn't looking at me. I swiveled in my chair to follow her gaze and gasped. Standing behind me were two girls, dripping in blood.

They weren't like any girls I had seen before. The tall one had red hair and a deep purple scar in the center of her forehead, about the size of a silver dollar and as smooth as exposed bone. The other girl had blonde hair and piercing green eyes and a small, heart-shaped mouth. But honestly it was hard to focus on that, because, while half of her face was flesh, like mine, the other half was made out of metal, the two sides bolted together with big, thick screws. Her neck was the same—divided down the center—and her left arm was metal too. I couldn't see her legs under her pants, but I wondered if her whole body was the same way.

The two girls were leaning against one another. Or rather, the tin girl was leaning into the taller one. I couldn't see the wounds underneath all the blood, but she looked more hurt.

Mombi was at the girls' side in a blink. "Where? What?"

"Quadling Country. The Lion," mumbled the tall girl with the round scar.

Mombi disappeared in a plume of smoke. Instead of helping the bloody girls, it was clear she'd gone to check out the *where* and the *what*.

Nox twitched beside me at the word *Lion*. He leapt to his feet, Gert quick to follow.

Nox picked the tin girl up in his arms. A smile flickered through the woozy pain on her face.

"Melindra, it's going to be okay. I've got you."

For the first time since I met him, Nox looked like he cared.

Gert's hand glowed as she touched the girl's arm. "Let's get her to the spring."

Before I knew it, the girls and Nox and Gert were gone. When I turned back to the table, Glamora leaned back in her chair and took another bite of the goo.

Being abandoned with no explanation didn't bother me. What bothered me, suddenly, surprisingly, was how much more Nox cared about helping this other girl.

* * *

"Sit," Glamora commanded at our next lesson, pointing to her vanity as we entered her cave. I was distracted, still irked by what had happened over dinner the night before. Those girls had shown up covered in blood and I was here to learn how to curtsy? I slouched away from her, knowing how much it would bother her. I didn't sit. I touched her things instead. The vanity was covered with little glass figurines that looked like maybe they were once part of a really ornate chess set. I rolled a glass queen in my palms and heard a deep exhale from Glamora like she was trying to keep calm. I rolled my eyes, too. It was a small act of protest, but it registered like an earthquake for Glamora.

"Sit," she ordered again without raising her voice, but she snatched the figurine from my hand and placed it back on the vanity. The other figures moved back into place, too, on their own. I wondered if Glamora's real gift wasn't etiquette but some kind of witchy OCD.

I obeyed this time, sitting on the chair but immediately twisting away from the mirror to face her. She took her hair out of its intricate bun and it fell in pretty waves well past her shoulders, framing the deep *V* of her purple dress and impressive cleavage. With her hair down she looked even more like her evil sister.

"I may not have Gert's or Mombi's gifts but I do have many things to teach you, my dear," Glamora said.

I reached for the queen figurine again. It moved away from me.

Glamora sighed. "Showing is sometimes better than telling."

I looked up at her as she placed her perfectly manicured hands over her face and then pulled them away like she was playing peekaboo with a toddler. I gasped. Her right cheek had a lunar-shaped hole in it—I could see her tongue. I could see her perfect white teeth.

"What happened to you?" I asked, horrified.

"Family can hurt us better than anyone."

"Why would Glinda . . . What happened?"

"Glinda wanted to make sure that no one mistook me for her anymore. Looking exactly like your enemy can potentially be an advantage when we are on the brink of war, and she didn't want me to have that advantage."

Glamora didn't seem embarrassed or ashamed of it—but letting me see her scar was clearly a big deal, especially for someone so beautiful. And Glamora was still beautiful, even with her face carved up. Beautiful was in the way that she moved and spoke. Beautiful was an action as well as a description.

"Why don't you use the spring?" I asked carefully.

Glamora ran her fingers over the scar almost lovingly. "When she faces me, I want her to face what she's done."

I shook my head. "I've seen her. I've seen what she's become. You don't really think she'll see this and beg for forgiveness, do you?"

I wondered if she was hoping that there was some part of her that still did. That was hoping Glinda would see the scar and be sorry. I knew a little about hoping for that—and I knew a lot about being disappointed.

Glamora laughed, a big bell of a laugh that went up so high that I felt like I needed to cover my ears.

"There is no more room for forgiveness. Not for me. I want the scar to be the last thing she sees before I end her."

Glamora's eyes studied mine, waiting for some kind of reaction.

"She didn't kill you," I said slowly. "She was clearly close enough to do that. But she didn't kill you."

"When you're a witch *and* a twin, you're connected. I used to be able to see what she was doing, I could feel when she was in pain. But since she did this, I don't feel her anymore. I don't see her anymore. There's a chance that if the knife went all the way through me, then it would go all the way through her as well. Killing me could very well end her own life."

"But isn't that true for you, too? If you go after her, you could kill yourself."

"That's the difference between us. I wouldn't hesitate if the outcome was ridding the world of her evil."

I stared at Glamora as she touched her cheek and the scar disappeared, and she looked perfect and whole once again.

When I first saw Glamora just a few days ago, I thought she was the scariest thing in the world because I had thought she was Glinda. But now that I'd seen the *real* Glamora, I wondered if maybe she was scarier than Glinda after all.

"Now let's get started, shall we?" She put her hand on my shoulder and gently turned me around to face the mirror. There were only two mirrors back home in the trailer. The broken one in our tiny bathroom and the one over my ten-million-year-old dresser that was warped and had a kind of fun-house quality that made my face appear even narrower than usual. I spent as little time as possible looking into either one of them.

This mirror was different. Or maybe I was.

I caught my breath. There was something tough in my eyes. Tougher than before if that was even possible. The pink was washing out of my hair, giving way to dirty blonde.

Cheap hair dye.

"Very pretty," Glamora said, looking at me without an ounce of irony or fake sincerity.

I tried to get out of the chair, but she put her hands on my shoulders and pushed me down.

"Very pretty," she repeated with the same certainty as Gert when she'd asked me who I really was. Like she wanted to make sure I believed her. Like she somehow knew that no one had actually called me that in my entire sixteen years.

Since I got here, Glamora had been judging my every move based on some crazy standard of etiquette. So the kind words threw me.

"What's underneath is everything, Amy. But that doesn't mean you can't enhance it. Beauty has its own kind of magic. And the appearance of something can have power, too."

She tossed her own hair, and it changed from deep auburn to pale lavender. Then back again.

She touched my hair.

"What will it be?"

"You don't like the pink?"

"When I first saw you, Amy Gumm, your hair was the thing that gave me hope for you. For all of us."

"Seriously?"

Glamora scrunched up her perfect nose as if hair color were something too sacred to make light of.

"When Dorothy landed here in that precious gingham number I knew she was trouble."

"You knew Dorothy when she first arrived?"

"Back then I was where my sister was. That is, until she found her place at Dorothy's side. No one else sensed it, I don't think—but I did. Something about that much sweetness didn't feel right. But you, you didn't have an ounce of sweetness and that hair was just the exclamation point."

"Thank you?" I said. "I think."

"It is a compliment. I'd take a million Mombis over one Dorothy. I don't know about your tin farm, but here, sugar can be a poison." She fluffed out my hair with her hands, as if shaking off the Dorothy cloud that passed over her face.

"I want to keep it. I like the pink," I said, more brightly than I usually said anything.

Glamora's fingers passed through my hair, adjusting the color—first blue, then green, then back to pink—a better pink—with depth of color and shine that my hair had never had even when it was its natural color, the dirtiest of blondes. Now it was just north of cotton-candy pink. I remembered rinsing out my hair in the sink of the trailer just a few days and a tornado ago. I had thought that changing my hair would change something about my gray little life. And now? Now I had the perfect shade of pink and more change than I knew what to do with.

She blinked and my cheeks were rosier. Again and my lips were a deep red gloss. And again and a delicate pattern of green and gray shadow made half-moons over my eyes. And again and my lashes seemed to grow a quarter of an inch. One more time and glitter showered from above me.

Glitter made me think of Madison. Sparkling like a damn disco ball in the hallway back at school—

But then I saw that Glamora's glitter was nothing like Madison's. It knew exactly where to go—highlighting just above my cheekbones, my eyelids. Dusting my clavicle and shoulder blades. Complementing what she did with the makeup. Not like blush but like something more natural. Or rather, supernatural.

In the mirror, I saw Nox appear in the mouth of the cave. I hadn't seen him since yesterday, when he'd disappeared with the injured girl.

"Is she . . . ?" I asked, turning to face him.

Nox's mouth opened but nothing came out as he stared at me. Glamora giggled.

Nox found his voice.

"She's doing fine," he said with a cough. "The wounds were deep, but she's strong."

Glamora's eyes lit up on Nox. "What wonderful timing you have. Doesn't she look beautiful?" She winked, but I couldn't tell if it was at Nox or at me.

Soon after Nox's arrival Glamora had declared we were done for the day so Nox walked me back to my room—but that could have been because my room was on the way to his room.

I wondered what Nox's room looked like. He probably slept on the floor or some austere stone slab like the one back in my cell in the Emerald City.

Nox didn't comment on my makeover.

"What happened to them?" I asked Nox as we walked. "What was that scar in the middle of her forehead from? Why did the other one—why is she . . . did the Lion do that to her?" I thought of the girl's bloody, half-tin face and shuddered.

Nox shook his head. "Melindra's been half tin for a long time. She is one of the few people to escape from the Scarecrow's labs."

"The Scarecrow did that to her?" I'd seen him in the throne room. But he had looked pretty harmless compared to the Tin Woodman.

He nodded and continued. "Annabel's a Horner. *Was* a Horner—from Quadling Country. Their horns contained powerful magic. Dorothy offered large rewards for them. There aren't any Horners anymore."

I tried to picture a unicorn horn in the center of Annabel's pretty forehead. Magical or not, having something growing out of my forehead was not something that would have gone over well where I came from. But when I imagined someone trying to chop it off, I shuddered. Ollie's wings, Melindra's arm and face, Annabel's horn—the body part count was rising every time I learned anything new about this place.

"They're just kids," I said slowly. "They should be going to school. They should be doing normal kid stuff like having fun and torturing girls like me."

Nox shook his head like the idea of kids being kids had never even been a possibility for any of them. He sighed and looked at me like I didn't understand anything. "When Dorothy rolls through a town, she takes the adults—the people who can work. Some of them go to work for Glinda in the magic mines, or for Dorothy in the palace. Some of them get brought to the Scarecrow to be his toys."

"His toys?"

"He got it in his big brain to 'help' Dorothy. Finding ways to extract magic. Helping the Tin Woodman build a better army. But in his spare time he experiments."

While I digested this he went back to Dorothy. "Sometimes she'll take some of the kids, too, but most of them get left behind."

"So you guys scoop them up and put them to work for you instead."

It sounded like an accusation, like I was judging them. And maybe I was.

Nox nodded.

"Is that really any better?" I asked.

He just shrugged. "It was for me," he said. "I was one of them. It was Mombi who found me. My parents were dead. I was almost dead myself. It was Mombi who taught me magic—taught me everything I know now. She taught me to be a person again. If it wasn't for her . . . ," he trailed off.

I tried to imagine Nox as a little boy, but I couldn't. I couldn't imagine him being carefree or vulnerable or innocent. I tried to imagine Mombi rescuing a little boy, taking him in, and being a mother to him. That was even harder to imagine.

"And as repayment she made you fight?"

"Dorothy took everything from me. Dorothy took everything from those kids back there. I *choose* to fight," he said fiercely.

Sometimes it felt like we were in the middle of some argument that I had already lost. He was just so sure of everything. But what if he was sure about something that was more wrong than right? I didn't know what to say to that so I didn't say anything until we got to the opening of my cave. I dragged my fingers through my freshly colored hair and mumbled a good night.

"I liked it before."

"What?" I asked, turning back to him.

"That face."

"My face?" He liked my face before? Was this a setup for some kind of insult?

"Don't get me wrong, Glamora's magic is effective. But it's almost a shame to see it change. I haven't seen one with so much written there—every thought right there on the surface. It's a rare thing in a place like this." For the first time I didn't think that he was trying to hurt me. Maybe he spoke only one language. The truth, and nothing but. It had stung like hell, but it made what he was saying now sound all the more real. In a place like this, that little bit of truth might be a compass in an upside-down world.

"But I suppose Glamora's thinking ahead. If you're going to

fight Dorothy, you need to build a wall instead of a window."

"Is that what you did?"

He shrugged noncommittally.

"I don't think mine was ever a window." His chin jutted up the tiniest bit further into the air, like he was rising above something.

I wanted to know what. But he was already walking away.

NINETEEN

The next day I woke to see that Glamora's makeover had stuck. Pink cheeks, perfect hair. But the change in my appearance didn't help me with my lessons.

In the morning I saw Nox for training, which resulted in more bruises for me to wash off in the spring. With Gert, I still wasn't able to produce any magic. Finally, almost out of sympathy for me, she cast a listening spell with the snap of her fingers and we listened to Glamora singing in her room. Later, I found some small success with Glamora. I poured tea without spilling a drop.

After dinner I found a trunk in my room filled with dresses. A note in Glamora's purple cursive said *Wear one.*

Was it a reward? Was it possible that in all my classes, I was doing best at the etiquette? If Mom could see me now . . .

I sifted through the gowns and pulled out a pretty pale gray one that somehow complemented my hair. It was strapless silk and floor-length. Although I wasn't much of a fan of dresses, this one seemed to know exactly where to hug and exactly where to fall. I didn't know if magic could be woven into fabric or not, but it was perfect.

A few seconds later, a bat wearing a purple ribbon flew in, landing on my bed.

It wore a note around its neck, written in the same purple script: *Follow me*.

I followed the bat deeper into the labyrinth of the mountains into a cave I hadn't been in before. It was totally Glamora, grand, like old movie Grand-with-a-capital-G. A real crystal chandelier hung from the ceiling, and a bank of what I could only guess were windows along one wall overlooked a stunningly realistic panorama of the Emerald City. But the real spectacle was beneath my feet. The floor was made of glass, and underneath it was rushing water. It must be the water that fed the spring. The effect was like standing on top of a river. It made me dizzy—for a second I almost lost my balance.

"It's not nearly the same as my ballroom back home, but it will have to do. . . ." I spun around at the sound of Glamora's voice to find her in the corner, watching me.

Just then, Nox appeared in the doorway of the cave.

"You didn't wear the suit?" Glamora accused sweetly.

Nox made a face and shook his head, as if whatever she'd left for him was too awful for him to even consider.

Glamora waved her arms and music filled the air. It was somewhere between jazz and pop with a soulful pretty voice that wrapped and unwrapped itself around the beat. It was a love song. If I didn't know better I would think that Glamora was trying to play at matchmaking. . . .

"Very well, but a gentleman never keeps a lady waiting," Glamora insisted.

I stifled a laugh, not sure which was funnier: the idea of me being a lady or him being a gentleman.

But the laugh didn't escape because Nox was striding toward me, rearrranging his face and his swagger to make it seem like this was his idea entirely.

He gave a little bow. His pointy hair didn't even move when he bent over. I curtsied, determined not to give in too easily to what must be another one of Glamora's etiquette lessons.

Nox took my hand and pulled me closer, putting a sure hand on the small of my back, steadying me. We began to dance. I breathed him in against my will. He smelled like the healing spring back in the caves, fresh and alive and full of magic.

Glamora called orders at us after every rotation we made around the room.

"Posture!"

"I don't know how they dance where you're from, but here in Oz no one leads."

"You are equal partners in the dance. In the circle. In life."

I couldn't help but laugh at that one.

"Are you ever serious?" Nox finally demanded, but even he was starting to break under Glamora's ridiculous instruction.

"Are you ever *not*?"

The dance wasn't quite a waltz—something that I'd never

done but had seen in enough old movies on TV. It was more of an elaborate pentagram that crisscrossed the room over and over.

Another couple appeared beside us—a pretty woman with caramel skin and green hair, and a handsome man beside her in a top hat. I opened my mouth to ask who they were.

"Illusions," whispered Nox as a Munchkin appeared behind him.

"Look at your partner!" Glamora barked.

In seconds the ballroom had filled with fake couples, swirling around us.

It made sense that Nox could do this. He was the most coordinated, most physical being I'd ever met. But still, with every step we took in unison, I grew more aware of him. Even if he was annoying, and arrogant, and too serious all the time, I had to admit it: he was hot.

I didn't look up. I didn't want him to see anything other than indifference in my eyes.

Prom was coming up in a couple of months back at school. There were already posters in the halls with a really cheesy silhouette of a couple lit from behind by the moon. The theme was "A Night to Remember." I was never going to go to prom anyway. And it's not like anyone would be dancing even remotely like we were now. But I suddenly realized that this might be as close as I would come to "A Night to Remember." Dancing with a witch boy who didn't want me here.

As we danced, I dared to steal glances at his face. In this moment, Nox didn't look like he didn't want me here. Maybe it was years of Glamora instruction, and he was simply good at being a gentleman. Maybe it was the tapping of her foot to the music against the floor that was almost hypnotic. But he didn't look completely tortured.

"Remember," Glamora said, her voice floating across the dance floor. "This isn't a battle. Unless it is—in which case you should still keep your eyes on one another, to make sure that no one makes a move that isn't wanted." Glamora laughed, like it was an inside joke with herself.

Nox's face shifted suddenly, like he was remembering something.

"You think that you're too good for us," Nox said, the brightness of his voice not matching up with his words.

"Excuse me?" No one ever thought I was too good for anything. I grew up in a freaking trailer.

"Gert says you're holding back. You're afraid to be like us."

"That's not true. I'm afraid to be like Dorothy. Not the rest of you."

"You're already like us, you know. You wished for this. You wished to be as far away from your mom as you could get and your wish came true."

"How do you know that? And anyway, that doesn't make me Wicked. Or formerly Wicked either," I argued. I tried to drop his hand but he wouldn't let me go.

"You're afraid to do anything but wish for things to happen to you. You wish you could go show up on your dad's doorstep, meet his new wife and new kid—you wish you could say all the things you want to say to him. You wish you could have left your mom on your own. You've wanted to run away for almost as long as you can remember. But it took a tornado to do it. You couldn't even make that happen on your own."

He gripped my hands even tighter and pushed me forward in the dance like I was a puppet.

Why was he saying all this? More importantly, how did he know?

Gert. Nox wasn't in my head reading my thoughts. Gert was. She'd fed him my secrets, my entire life it seemed.

I had never done anything, he was right. I did go through my life just reacting to other people. When I was young I had escape plans—big, grand, dumb ones. I was going to start fresh somewhere where no one knew me and no one would call me Salvation Amy. But that part didn't sting as much as the Dad thing did. I did think about going to visit him, all the time. I'd have some excuse like I was selling candy for school. And I would see the life he left us for. The pretty wife who was no prettier than Mom before she started with the pills. The little girl or boy, technically *my sister or brother*, who she was pregnant with when they moved away to Jersey. I was going to show up and meet them and warn that little girl or boy that one day Dad would get tired of him or her, too.

Glamora tapped her foot on the glass floor to the beat of the music. "You're losing the beat, Amy."

Nox leaned in and dropped his voice to whisper words that I hadn't heard since I stepped into Oz.

"Am I right, Salvation Amy?"

The room spun. I wasn't sure if I was dizzy from him or from my anger. I dropped his hand.

He reached for me—but his hand missed me completely and grabbed the air next to me.

I was standing in a new spot. Across the room from where I started.

"What the hell? How did I . . . ?"

Had I—? Was it possible—? Had I moved myself across the room?

Don't you see? You did it. I heard Gert's voice. She appeared in the center of the room. She'd been here all along. I felt hot. More specifically, my hands felt hot from casting the spell.

She had done this on purpose, made Glamora and Nox bring me to this room and beat at me until I couldn't take it anymore. Like dipping me under the spring, she did what she thought she needed to do. But this time she'd gone too far.

The room spun again. My hands got hotter—light seemed to shoot from them. Not the gentle glow I'd seen from Gert. A searing red glow. Like darts of fire.

The fire darts seemed to be seeking Nox. But Nox lit up with a weird blue light of his own and the darts seemed to deflect off him. More darts came off my hands even though I wasn't actually directing them. They shot straight up into the air and showered down like firecrackers.

I was angry. Too angry. No-turning-back angry.

I wanted to run away from him, from Gert, from all of them, but I couldn't move. Nox made a beeline toward me and grabbed my glowing hands with his own. In a blink we were standing outside the caves on the same spot he'd taken me the first day of training—the peak of the mountain, this time looking out into a deep black sky dotted with strange constellations where the familiar ones should have been.

These stars were different from any stars back home. For one thing, they were brighter. For another thing, where the constellations I was used to never seemed to match the images they were supposed to resemble, these formed themselves into clear pictures the longer you gazed at them. There was a horseshoe and a bear and a tiger and a dragon, all as clear as pictures in a book.

"Gert thought *home* was stopping you from doing magic. We had to push. We had to know." He pointed into the distance. "Look. That one's always been my favorite." As he pointed, a group of bright-white pinpricks rearranged themselves into the image of a bicycle. As I looked at it, a memory came back to me: my mother teaching me to ride a bike when I was five, before we'd moved to Dusty Acres.

It was the first time I'd ever tried it without the training wheels, and Mom had promised to hold on so I didn't fall. But at some point, as I'd raced down the hill, the wind in my hair, I'd let out a whoop of triumph. I was doing it. It was only at that moment that I'd realized Mom had let go. I was on my own.

That was when I went crashing to the curb. When I crawled back to my feet, my knee scraped and bloody, my bike in a tangled heap on the ground, I'd looked up the hill to see my mom standing at the top, clapping for me.

I had been pushing back thoughts of Mom on a regular basis now. All Gert's talk of forgiveness had planted a seed that I did not want to let grow. I'd told myself that all I'd been thinking about was where my fist was going next. About trying to light a candle just by thinking about it and remembering all the stuff in all the books Glamora had given me.

But it wasn't true. She was still there no matter how much I didn't want her to be. And now, standing on the top of the mountain with Nox, all I could think about was my mother.

I was an idiot. For a few minutes I had been thinking about prom and dancing with Nox and how he maybe didn't hate it— and he was just following witchy orders.

And somehow that almost made me more angry.

"It matters how you do this," I said through clenched teeth, staring him down. "What you do to get there. You can't just *kill* someone. The ends do not make it okay."

His eyes shifted away from mine and then back again. I saw something pass over his face. Guilt. Regret. No, it was maybe something else—like curiosity or realization—like he was happening upon completely new information.

Like it had never occurred to him that I would be hurt or mad or anything like that. Like being able to do magic trumped everything.

"We're the only ones *willing* to take her down. The only ones capable. It's us or nothing. We're doing one bad thing for the good of Oz."

"Do you ever not speak the witch party line—do you ever

make a decision that is all your own?"

His eyes flicked away from mine.

"Do you always ask so many questions?"

"Do you ever ask *any*? You know absolutely everything there is to know about me and I don't know anything about any of you. Not really."

The cockiness from the dance floor was gone. He slipped out of it so easily it was a surprise.

"Do you really want to know who I am?" he asked.

I should have said no and backed away from him. But even though I was mad at him, I still wanted to crack him open and see what was inside. I nodded.

"I'm not Nox."

"What?"

"Nox is just the name Mombi gave me. I don't remember my real name. I remember my parents. Their faces. The way they smelled and sounded. I remember the day that they were taken from me. But my name washed away with them. And there's no one alive who remembers it."

"Nox . . ."

"It was in the beginning. When Glinda and Dorothy were just starting to mine everything and everywhere. Glinda hadn't figured it out yet. She wasn't using the Munchkins. She was just using her own magic to mine magic. She blasted a hole in the center of the town and boom. She hit the water table. Everything flooded. We climbed up to the roof. There was this old weather vane up there that was so rusty it didn't even move when the wind blew. I remember my mother told me to hold on to it no matter what. And I did. But my mom didn't. Or couldn't. I wanted to let go, too, but I held on like she told me to. When the water went down, no one in the village was left except me."

I inhaled sharply.

"Did Mombi find you then?"

"Later, much later I think. I went from town to town. I stole when I had to eat. I slept where I could. Sometimes people were good to me. And sometimes they were horrible. Mombi saved me during one of those horrible times. I stumbled upon the wrong town. The Lion was there. But so was Mombi."

He glanced up at me, then looked away sharply. He didn't want my pity.

"What I said back there when we were dancing—I'm sorry I had to do that. I needed to get a reaction from you. You've been fighting all along. You raised yourself. I had an army and three witches."

Something hit me all at once. "What Gert said about magic— how can you use it if you don't know who you are?"

"I know exactly who I am."

"But you said . . ."

"I am a fighter. I am a member of the Revolutionary Order of the Wicked."

It occurred to me—maybe Mombi hadn't rescued him out of the kindess of her heart. Maybe she had done it to make a perfect soldier. If all Nox had was a faded memory of some woman who may have been his mom, all Nox had ever really had was the Order. And all his magic came from there—from the person they made him. He was as pure as the magic that ran through the spring. He was all magic. Hardly a boy at all. He was the knife that he told me he could train me to be.

I wasn't sure if I pitied him or envied him. Would I trade away the few good memories of my mom to get rid of all the bad ones? I thought the answer was yes, but who would I be without those memories? Who was Amy Gumm without her past?

I was running away from home. Nox was marching toward home. Home was battle for him.

And maybe it was for me, too.

Nox grabbed my hands suddenly. "Magic is just energy that wants to be something different," he reminded me. "So take what you're feeling right now and turn it into something different. Turn it into magic."

I looked at Nox. I wished this moment had been the starting place for today's lesson. Not what he did on the dance floor. But I pushed that aside and I tried to do what I'd seen him do. Tried to do what I saw Glamora and Mombi and Gert do. Be both in my skin and a part of the magic around it. I felt the energy coursing through my body like warm water. I thought of my mother. I thought of the question Gert had posed: *Who are you?*

I focused on my sadness, the sadness I'd felt for my whole life, and I willed it to be something different. To change.

I thought of my mom again in the kitchen of our trailer, telling me what a disappointment I was. The image blotted itself out, becoming a fiery red light.

And then it happened. It was snowing. White, glistening flakes were falling all around me, around me and Nox. He looked at me with an expression that was somewhere between pride and awe.

"See?" he said quietly.

I stretched my arms out and spun around, laughing. The snow was accumulating.

"No one does this right away, not even me," Nox said quietly. "You have power."

I reached out my hand and let some flakes fall into it. It didn't melt. It wasn't snow, I realized. It was ash.

I looked up at Nox in surprise.

"Your fire burned up the sky," he explained.

For a second, I was disappointed. Snow would have been so pure and beautiful. But ash made so much more sense with who I was.

"We should get back. Gert's going to want to talk to you," he said suddenly.

We walked back inside. I didn't take his hand this time. I'd rather fall down in the dark.

TWENTY

When I got to Gert's cave, she was standing in front of the scrying pool again.

"Don't be too mad at Nox. He did what I asked of him."

I could feel my anger bubbling up again, but I stayed in one place and my fingers didn't feel like they were on fire. Yet.

"I'm not even sure if Nox actually knows how messed up this is. But you do. Why did you do this? Why did you tell Nox all that stuff about me? He has no right to know!" I was somehow certain that Gert's moral compass pointed north, but she was ignoring it for the cause.

"Because we're running out of time," she said simply, gazing calmly into my eyes. Every line in her round face was fixed in its sincerity and certainty.

"So that justifies everything? You get to just root around in my head and mess with me because it's convenient for you?"

Gert shook her head. "I'm sorry, Amy. It's funny—we

actually need your sense of good around here. Things have gotten murky after so many years fighting her. We need someone to remind us that not everything is complicated."

She was apologetic for the hurt she'd caused me, but not the action. Did that mean that she would do it all over again if she had the chance? If it meant I would agree to take down Dorothy?

"I couldn't think of any other way. Magic can be triggered by our strongest emotions," Gert said, turning away from me. "It worked, didn't it?"

Gert focused on her scrying pond. It was smaller than the one in the war room. Although I was still bristling with frustration over her witchy doublespeak, I moved closer to see what she was doing. Ripples began moving inward toward Gert's finger as she mumbled words under her breath.

A face began to appear in the water. I narrowed my eyes. A familiar face.

"Mom," I spat.

There she was. Looking completely the opposite of the angry, pill-popping mess who had stormed away from our trailer. Before the tornado. Before Oz. It all felt like so long ago.

She had a small Band-Aid on her forehead, her hair was pulled back in a ponytail, and she was wearing jeans and a pullover sweater I'd never seen before. She looked nice. She looked clean. But she looked sad, too.

"Is it a trick?" I demanded without looking up. Maybe there was a part of me that couldn't believe she had changed so much. Maybe there was a part of me that didn't want to believe she had changed so much without me there to help her.

"It's not a trick, Amy."

"I thought there was no way to see the Other Place."

She waved a hand dismissively. "There are more things that can be done than people think. I can't let the witches in on *all* of my secrets, now can I?"

I reached out to my mother, feeling hopeful and scared at the same time. The water rippled through my fingers but I couldn't touch her.

The unfamiliar room she was standing in was small and gray and the furniture was that foam and wood kind that I'd seen in doctors' offices. Where was she? Was she in a shelter? One of those places they put people who have been displaced by disaster? She was looking under the cushions of the couch, then she moved on to a tiny kitchen area and began rifling through the cabinets.

My gut twisted. I knew what she was doing. She was looking for her stash.

"I don't need to see anymore," I said. I'd seen this horror show before. But I couldn't pull my eyes away. Her face lit up like she'd found what she was looking for. She pulled it out and held it at arm's length.

It was a sweater. My red one. It was a little too tight and had a tiny hole in the sleeve, but it was my favorite because it was the only thing I owned that was actually designer. It was dirty, covered in what looked like the red clay roads for which Dusty Acres was named. It had probably been tossed from the trailer during the cyclone. She hugged it to her chest.

She wasn't using. She was just missing me.

I balled my fists in anger. I had spent years trying to clean her up. And the thing that finally made it happen was getting rid of me.

"You can access magic from the good places as well as the bad, you know," Gert said softly.

I laughed. "Maybe you haven't looked around in my head enough. There *are* no good places."

"You *can* decide what kind of magic you practice. Just like you can decide who you are. In the end, it's really the same thing. But you don't have to be angry."

"What if I want to be angry?" I snapped. "Don't I have a right to be angry?"

Gert just shrugged evenly, but I kept going.

"Look at what I did back there when I was angry. I set the sky on fire and made it snow ash. Being angry *works*. It works a lot better than anything else I've tried."

"But imagine if you didn't have to start there. Imagine if you got to start somewhere good."

"Yeah, well," I said. "I can imagine a lot of things. That doesn't mean they're possible."

"Anything is possible, dear. Look around you."

I laughed bitterly. "Oz—where all your worst nightmares can come true."

"Look at us," Gert said, ignoring me. "We witches spent our lives fighting each other. Now we live under the same roof. Working together for something greater. It just goes to show . . ."

I tried to imagine becoming besties with Madison Pendleton after years of her torturing me. I shook my head.

But Gert wasn't talking about Madison Pendleton, not really. She was talking about my mother. I felt like if I forgave her, I was just asking her to hurt me again.

"Why are you pushing this?" I asked. "My mom's a million miles away. It doesn't matter."

"She's the voice in your head."

"And you want yours to be in there instead?"

"I want *yours* to be, Amy."

I refused to look at her, refused to be taken in by those warm, grandmotherly eyes. I knew what was behind them.

I kept staring at the water but when Gert didn't respond, I looked up to see her fading into white smoke.

Well, clearly she was done with this conversation. I looked back down. The image of my mom was fading away. As it did, the water began to bubble.

Steam began to rise from the roiling, angry water. The pool was boiling, and I knew it wasn't part of Gert's spell. I was the one doing it.

Forgiveness can get you places, I guess. But sometimes you need to light a fire.

I sank into my bed that night without bothering to change out of my gown. I'd seen Mom. I'd done magic. It bugged me that even now, my mom was tied to everything I did. Was she seriously still screwing with me from a gazillion miles away?

I couldn't blink away the image of her in the scrying pond, all cleaned up and holding on to my sweater. It made me sad. It made me miss her. But it didn't magically erase the years of other, grimmer images.

Sleep felt as far away as home.

The next morning, I was almost glad to remember that I had a session with Nox. I needed to punch something. That I would get to punch *Nox* was an added bonus.

On my way to the training room, Gert's and Glamora's voices wafted out at me as I passed Glamora's chambers. Something about their tone—hushed, yet sharp and full of warning, like they were talking about something secret—made me stop just outside to listen in.

"Don't encourage it, Glamora."

"Whatever do you mean?"

"You know *exactly* what I mean. That girl has more cracks in her than the road of yellow brick. Nox will break her in two."

"Or she'll break him. Don't pretend you were never young. She has no real connection to any of us. But she and Nox— there's something there."

"We are bound. She is warming to me—"

"That's not enough. You know that I have my own suspicions about exactly who it was that brought Amy to Oz. There are few people with enough power to summon someone from the Other Place, and if my hunch is correct, we both know that a simple binding won't be enough to hold the girl to us. But I can think of a stronger glue. . . ."

"She's starved for it, certainly. But I don't know if our boy is capable of love. He wasn't built for it. *We* didn't build him for it."

"It's funny, Gert," Glamora said. "All that mind reading, and you still can't see inside the heart. Our boy is starved for it, too. He just doesn't know it yet."

I backed away, shaking my head, and rushed down the hall. I did *not* feel that way about Nox. Maybe he wasn't the total jerk I'd thought he was at first, but that didn't mean anything. It definitely didn't mean he felt anything for me.

TWENTY-ONE

My pulse was still speeding when I got to the training cave. Seeing him was already going to be different after last night—dancing together, hearing his story for the first time, and feeling the magic that had finally surged through me.

When I walked into the cave, he wasn't alone. A glint of tin caught the light and blinded me for a second. It was the girls who had interrupted our dinner the other night, covered in blood. They looked fine now—better than fine. Annabel, the tall one with the unicorn scar, was stretching, while Melindra, the half-tin girl, leaned against the wall with her arms crossed, staring at me.

Something about the way Melindra flicked open her metal lashes reminded me of Madison back home. Like she already hated me and we hadn't even met yet.

"Melindra and Annabel will be joining us today," Nox explained to me without looking up. "Melindra, Annabel," Nox said. "This is Amy."

"We *know* who she is," Melindra said. "The girl who fell out of the sky in a tin can to save us all." There was something sarcastic in her voice, but there was something else, too—like she couldn't decide whether she was supposed to be suspicious of me or if she was hoping everything they said about me was true.

"Nox told me that you escaped the Scarecrow's labs," I blurted. I'd been spending too much time with Glamora. One of her helpful hints about meeting new people was to tell them something you know about them. But for some reason I don't think she meant bringing up that horrific time the person was tortured by a mad scientist Scarecrow.

But Melindra suppressed a smile, and I could see that it wasn't such a mistake at all. She was proud—proud of who she was and of what she had been through.

"They wanted to make me join the Tin Man's secret police," Melindra said. "I wasn't going to let that happen. So I got out of there and came here. No one's ever done that before."

I was impressed. I'd needed Mombi's help to escape, but this girl had done it on her own. I wanted to ask her how but now didn't seem like the best time.

"We need to see if Melindra and Annabel are ready to go back out there," Nox said.

"We're ready," Annabel volunteered, without looking to Melindra to back her up. I couldn't believe it—they'd been torn apart by the Lion, but there was still no question of not going back.

"Okay, then show us what you've got. Amy can spar with

the winner," Nox said. He still hadn't looked at me, and now he turned around to busy himself with the equipment.

"Don't even," Annabel warned, watching my gaze follow Nox.

"Don't what?" I asked.

The girls both giggled. It was weird to see the flesh-and-blood side of Melindra's face contort in laughter while the metal side stayed stiff and emotionless.

"What?" I asked again.

"We've seen that look before," Annabel said. "Trust me, it's not worth it. Nox only cares about the cause. There's no room inside him for anything else. Not that plenty of people haven't tried." She shot Melindra a knowing glance.

"I'm not . . . ," I started, but I could feel myself blushing. "I don't . . ."

I stopped myself.

Nox returned, handing a knife to Annabel, who thanked him with a flirty smirk. Nox ignored it. Or maybe he just didn't notice it in the first place. Melindra shook her head at the knife and instead offered up a clenched fist. As she lifted it to her chest, a thin, glittering blade folded out from the top of her wrist as easily as a bird would stretch its wings. She looked out at me from behind it with a smirk.

Great, I thought. Melindra was a human Swiss Army knife, like Sword-Arm back in the palace. At least this one was on my side. She *was* on my side, right?

I leaned against the wall and watched the girls spar. I felt myself shrinking, in danger of disappearing again. I didn't want to have to fight either of them. They'd both been at this way longer than I had. Plus, they seemed to hate me.

Why though? And what was Annabel trying to say about Nox? Was he playing me? Had every moment between us been planned to make me a better fighter?

I heard Annabel scream and I looked up just in time to see Melindra's blade slashing across her chest, a bright-red streak of blood blossoming on her shirt. And then, just like that, she disappeared in defeat. Off to the spring, I guess.

Melindra didn't drop her fighting stance. Nox looked over at me.

"Your turn, Amy. Keep your elbows up. You've been dropping them. And Mel, you're a half step behind where you usually are. Focus."

A few seconds later, it was me standing opposite Melindra, a knife from Nox in my hand. Although I had trained plenty of times with him before now, I was nervous to be facing someone new.

I didn't have time to be nervous: the fight had begun.

Melindra was so light and fast on her tin feet that sometimes her metal and flesh seemed to blur together as she danced around me, landing jabs in my sides and chest.

It was clear that she was using magic, too. I tried to summon the power I'd found the night before with Nox. I was pretty sure that I wasn't allowed to set my opponent on fire, but other than misdirection, that was basically the only magic I knew how to do. Not that it was working now—I felt my hands go hot a few times, but no flame appeared.

I dodged a blow from Melindra and something made contact with my shin—her metal meeting my bone. I made a desperate, errant swing and a miss at her flesh side before her other leg sideswiped mine, taking me down to the ground in an ungraceful heap.

"What do you think, Nox?" Melindra put a hand on her hip triumphantly. "Still too slow? Am I ready now?"

She reached out her hand to help me up. I ignored it and leapt to my feet.

We went at it again. This time, Melindra moved even faster than before, slashing and diving and feinting around me as I stumbled forward like my feet were made of cement, struggling just to keep my balance and avoid her blade as it whipped through the air in every direction.

"Look at you," she said, not pausing in her attack. She swung her leg toward me in a powerful kick and I barely managed to get out of the way in time. "All this training and you're fighting like it's your first day. Am I making you nervous? Or is it someone else?"

I lunged for her, urging the fire to my hands, but it didn't come. Melindra disappeared just as I was about to grab her, and I whirled and ducked just in time to avoid getting a haircut—or worse—as her sword grazed the top of my head.

"Oh, did I make you mad?" she asked.

She jumped up and seemed to hang in midair for a split second as she pulled her knees to her chest before whipping them out like a jackknife and shifting her momentum, flying straight for me.

Her feet collided hard against my breastbone, and before I knew what was happening I was on my back on the stone floor again, the wind knocked out of me. I watched with dazed double vision as she turned a graceful backflip and landed like it was nothing. Melindra whipped out her arm and pushed the tip of her blade into my throat, looking down on me with contempt.

"Poor little Amy," she said. "All of Oz is depending on you and you can't even take out a sorry half girl like me."

She was pressing hard enough to hurt without actually breaking the skin. But the message was clear. *I could kill you if I wanted to, but for now I'll be nice.*

"Shut up," I wheezed through clenched teeth, still struggling to breathe.

"Not the best way to impress boys," she said, shifting her eyes sneakily toward Nox. "Especially a boy who cares more about the cause than anything else."

"Shut up!" I spat again, feeling my face go red with anger.

"They all think you're so special. I don't know why. You can't even do a simple spell. Go ahead. Try." She pressed her blade harder. My face burned; my fingers tingled with heat.

Nox finally stepped in.

"Melindra," he said, grabbing her by the arm. "That's enough. Let her go. She's doing her best." From the disappointed way he was looking back and forth from her to me, I felt like I had let him down twice. First by letting her beat me, and then by not fighting back once she had me pinned.

Melindra rolled her eyes and snorted contemptuously, but she pulled her weapon away. "Don't give her false hope, Nox," she said. "You know as well as I do that you're too good for her."

She looked back at me. "Not so talented after all, are you? Just another outlander who thinks she's special. We get used to that around here, you know."

I'd had enough. Enough of being picked on. Enough of other people telling me what to do. Enough of feeling powerless.

"Shut up!" I screamed, my words reverberating through the stone chamber.

The burning feeling that had been building in my body rushed through me at once, and I lit up: I was on fire. The flames came shooting out of my chest in huge, curling tongues that all rolled together into one giant ball of fire that exploded out of me, rocketing straight for Melindra.

She stepped aside casually and the fireball shot right past her, hitting the wall of the cave with a pathetic fizzle. Nox's mouth dropped open in surprise, but Melindra was unfazed. "That's really the best you can do?" she asked with a sneer. I pushed past both of them without a word.

When I showed up in Gert's cave she looked at me. "You burned your pretty hair," she said, sounding completely unsurprised.

"Teach me," I said. "I'm ready. I want to learn."

"Get some rest," she said. "Meet me in the training room tomorrow. You'll learn."

* * *

When I walked into the training room the next morning, it was empty except for a single stalk of corn growing in the center of the room.

"You ready for this?" Nox asked, appearing at my side without warning.

I glared at him. "What are *you* doing here?"

"Gert asked me to help," he said without looking at me, and, as if she'd been summoned by her own name, Gert materialized out of nowhere. She drew her hand up in front of her and whispered something, and tiny green shoots began to spring up through the stone floor, quickly unfurling themselves into stalks taller than I was. Taller than Nox. Soon there were hundreds of them, and the cave seemed to magically expand to make room for an entire cornfield that had grown all around me.

I looked up to find that the ceiling had been replaced by a cold and artificial blue sky. When I glanced back at Nox, he was already disappearing into the green.

"Find him," Gert commanded.

I lurched ahead, ready to chase after him.

Gert's invisible hand stopped me. "Not like that. Pay attention. I like to say a few words when I cast a spell. It helps me focus. And it will also help you as you're learning." She wove her hands together and whispered an incantation: "What I seek, I shall find, what I see, will be mine."

A white orb formed between her hands and rose like a flare, pausing in midair. Waiting for someone to follow after it.

I took a step forward.

Gert gave me a look of consternation. "No," she said. "Make your own."

"What if I set the whole place on fire by accident?"

She shook her head. She was frustrated with me, I could tell, but in her frustration—in her squinted, lined eyes and pursed lips—I could see something else, too. Something I didn't see very often. She wasn't just doing this because she wanted me to be able to help the Order. She wanted to teach me because she was worried about me.

"I'm here," she said. "I'll be helping you. But you *can* do it on your own. You're almost there already. Just imagine what you want to happen. And then concentrate on that, and only on that. The magic is everywhere. It's waiting for you to take it and make it your own."

I closed my eyes, and my brain went right back to yesterday, when Melindra had me pinned to the ground.

"No, no, no," Gert said, clucking her tongue. "Not that. Pick a moment not so filled with emotion this time. Try not to let the anger fuel you anymore. It's too unreliable. Too uncontrollable. Pick an innocent moment where you aren't setting the world on fire."

I remembered my first training session with Nox, him leaning into me, his hand on my shoulder.

"Yes, there you go."

I imagined reaching out for him with my mind, searching for him.

Something was happening. I could feel the tingle of energy rippling through me, seeping out through my pores. I pushed at it, shaping it, trying to make it into what I wanted.

In my mind's eye, Nox turned from me and began to walk away. He grew smaller and smaller, and then he looked over his shoulder and beckoned for me.

I opened my eyes.

An orange ball of fiery energy, no bigger than a fist, was spinning in the air in front of me. I had done it.

Nox, I thought. *Where are you?*

At that, the flare jittered and shot ahead, into the corn. I followed it as it twisted and turned through rows and rows of stalks, not dropping my singular focus on finding him. It only took a few minutes before I found him sitting on the ground, looking bored.

His eyes lit up in pleased surprise when he saw me.

"You didn't think I could do it, did you?" I asked. He just shrugged like, *Hey, can you blame me?*

"Now I have to find you," he said, standing. "Go ahead. Just *try* and hide from me. But I'm warning you—I could find you anywhere."

Over the course of the next week, I learned how to use misdirection to hide from Nox in the cornfield. I learned how to direct my fiery darts at a target instead of setting structures (not to mention myself) on fire. I learned how to concentrate on what I wanted—which meant *figuring out* what I wanted. It wasn't easy, but Gert and Nox were patient.

Every afternoon, I would spar in the training room with Melindra or Annabel or Nox. I was still so much slower than the rest of them but I could tell I was getting better.

After a few weeks, I was stretching in the training room, about to go up against Melindra, when Mombi materialized in the corner of the room. I hadn't seen her or Glamora in days.

"What is she doing here?" I whispered to Nox.

"Ignore her," he said under his breath. But it was hard to ignore someone like Mombi. It felt like some kind of test. Was she here to check up on my progress? To see if I was ready yet? I still hadn't beaten Melindra, which didn't bode well.

Now that I'd fought her a million times, along with Annabel and Nox, I'd realized that Melindra was by far the best of us all. Most of my sparring sessions with her just boiled down to staying out of her way, which I'd gotten good at doing.

But she'd also seemed to develop a grudging respect for me. Now, when we fought, she was all business, not bothering to insult me or snipe at me. She always beat me. Then again, she almost always beat Nox and Annabel, too. When she had me where she wanted me, she'd just shrug, toss her hair, and raise her arm and its built-in blade up in victory.

Today, as Melindra and I began, I could feel Mombi's critical eyes tracking me as I moved and dodged Melindra's weapon. I managed to hold my own, ducking every time she swiped at me with her arm. I was proud that I hadn't let her get within striking distance. This fight was lasting longer than most of our previous ones had, and I could tell we were both getting tired. Maybe today would be the day I'd finally beat her. Maybe all I'd needed was an audience.

Melindra forced me back toward the corner, near where Mombi and Nox stood. "She's still reacting," I heard the old witch mutter. "Not acting."

Her words hit me in the gut almost as hard as Melindra did.

"Oof," I cried as Melindra surprised me—feinting with her blade and then kicking me right in the stomach. Now she reared back, ready to strike again, this time with the sharp metal blade of her tin arm.

I did the only thing I could think to do. I disappeared.

I found myself outside of the cave where Nox had taken me the night I made it snow ashes. I took a second to catch my breath again. Mombi's words had affected me more than I'd expected them to. I'd thought I'd made so much progress, learned so much in the past few weeks. But in an instant, she made me feel like all those lessons hadn't even happened.

It made me angry that Mombi had shown up for just one fighting session and was passing judgment on me—she didn't care how I was doing, how much I'd changed. All she cared about was whether or not I was ready to fight.

You are stronger than you think. Stronger than Mombi thinks, I told myself. *You can take Melindra. Gert believes in you. So does Nox.*

I repeated these lines a few times like a mantra until I began to believe them. I thought about Gert's training, focusing on something other than anger to feel the magic begin to thrum in my fingers.

I concentrated on the room again and materialized just as Melindra was righting herself after having fallen through the air where I should have been standing. Without hesitating, I flipped through the air, and pinned Melindra to the ground.

Melindra's eyes widened with surprise. "Ow," she said. "Not fair!"

"There's no such thing as fair out *there*," I said. I'd learned as much from Nox.

I jumped to my feet.

"Need some help getting up?" I asked, extending a hand to Melindra. When I stole a glance at Nox, I saw him watching intently. It could have been my imagination but it looked like he was actually on the verge of a smile.

I didn't dare look at Mombi.

Melindra took my hand in her metal one, crushing my bones just a little too hard. She leaned in.

"Let me guess," she hissed. "He told you you were special. He took you to a place he never takes anyone else. Sound familiar?"

Something twisted in my gut, but I managed to keep a smile on my face. It was the halls of high school all over again.

Salvation Amy's jealous. She wishes this were her *baby.*

I squeezed even harder and narrowed my eyes. "Never underestimate a girl from Kansas," I said.

Before Melindra could say anything back, Mombi had stepped

in front of me. She was looking at me like she was seeing me for the first time.

"You handled yourself well against our best," Mombi declared. "Training is over. The Lion is on the move, heading toward the village of Pumperdink, just south of here. We leave at first light."

TWENTY-TWO

"You were good back there," Nox said. "Really good." He had caught me in the corridor below the training area as I was heading to my room. It was dim and narrow down there, with a hazy, purple light that glowed from somewhere within the rocky walls.

"Thanks," I said. "Melindra had it coming. She's too used to winning. She let her guard down."

"Yeah," he said. "But you beat her fair and square. You've gotten so much better. It's not just the magic. It's the rest of it. I don't even think you know you're doing it. The way you move; the way you think on your feet. You've gotten so good so fast. You're a natural, you know."

"I wonder what happened," I said.

He gave me a funny look. "What do you mean?"

"I mean, I was never like this before. Back home. Where does it come from?"

"Amy," he said. "It comes from *you*."

I couldn't help thinking back on what Melindra had said after

I'd beaten her. She had just been trying to provoke me, but that didn't mean it wasn't true. In some ways, I wondered if she was the only one that I could trust around here. At least she was for real with me.

Everyone in this place had an ulterior motive. It wasn't even all that ulterior. Everything anyone did, everything they said to me, was all designed to push me in one way or another, was all meant to force me into becoming the person they thought I was. To become the weapon they needed. Nox was no exception. It would be stupid to think he was.

And yet, every now and then, it was like he was trying to tell me something that had nothing to do with Dorothy, or with the cause.

"What do you think you would be like?" I asked. "You know, if it weren't for Dorothy. If you'd had the life you were supposed to?"

He looked at me in surprise, like it was something he had never even considered. "I . . ." He paused. "I don't know. That's the funny thing, isn't it? As much as I hate her—as much as I wish Oz was how it was supposed to be, that we could all just be happy—I would be a totally different person, then. I can't even imagine who I would be. Maybe someone better, I don't know. Maybe someone worse. I like who I am." He rolled his eyes and laughed ruefully to himself. "Maybe I owe her."

"Let's not get carried away here," I said. But I knew what he meant. It was like me and my mom. Yeah, she'd been pretty crappy at the whole parenting game, but what if she hadn't been? Who was to say I wouldn't have turned out like Madison Pendleton?

"My whole life has been about fighting her, you know?" Nox was saying now. "Who will I be when she's gone?"

"Do you think it will ever really happen?"

He tilted his head, pushing his fingers through his wild mane of hair, looking both vulnerable and certain of something. "I know it will," he said. "I wasn't sure at first, but now I know."

"How?"

"I don't know who brought you here or how they did it. But I know there was a reason for it. You're here to help us. And I know you can do it."

Suddenly I was aware of how close we were standing—so close I could smell his familiar sandalwood scent. I felt a pull toward him. One I didn't just attribute to magic.

"And then what? Then who will we be?"

He leaned in toward me the tiniest bit.

"Then everything changes," he said quietly. "Then I'm different. You'll be different, too. You're different already. I knew it from the beginning, but . . ."

I leaned toward him now, too, and, as if I were channeling Gert, anticipated something I really wanted. Wondered if I actually could make it happen. Without any magic at all.

Suddenly his face changed and he looked away. "You have to promise to be careful tomorrow," he said. "I didn't want to bring you, but Mombi wouldn't listen. The Lion's no joke. You have to promise me you won't do anything stupid. I—we need you too much. You're too valuable."

For a second, I'd thought he'd been saying something different. But now his jaw was set, and I remembered again.

"I know the deal," I said. "I know why I'm important to you." I was testing him now. I wanted him to correct me.

He stared at me for what felt like the longest time. But he didn't say anything else.

I turned around.

"Dorothy must die. I get it. But in the meantime, what are you living for?" I asked.

He didn't answer. "I have to go," he said. I was already walking away. "There's planning to do. You should try and get some sleep."

TWENTY-THREE

A screeching sound woke me in the middle of the night. When I opened my eyes, still groggy, I saw it. A bat.

It was zigzagging around my room, wings flapping, howling with a voice that was ten times bigger than its body.

I knew what it meant. It was a signal. It wanted me to follow it.

When I got to the war room a few minutes later, everyone else was already there, dressed for battle and clustered around Glamora's scrying pool. Melindra and Annabel had grim looks on their faces. In other words, some things were the same as ever.

"What is it?" I asked.

"The Lion's moving faster than we thought," Gert said. "It's time to go."

Glamora pointed to the pool, where the shadowy image of an enormous lion breaking through the door of a small thatched house appeared. It was too dark to really make him out, but he didn't look so cowardly to me. He looked mean—and hungry.

Behind him, I could see other silhouettes. The bumpy outlines of some kind of reptile, and a furry blur that looked like it might be some kind of enormous rodent.

"The Lion spent so long afraid of every creature in the forest. Now he commands them," Nox whispered.

"What are those things?"

"You name it. If it has claws and teeth and it drools, it probably answers to the Lion." I felt myself shiver as my imagination filled in the blanks.

"What are they doing?" I asked quietly, fighting back the irrational fear that he could hear me.

"What they do best," Glamora replied. "Going door-to-door. Some of the villagers he'll capture to bring back to Dorothy; the rest of them he'll kill. For fun. After he eats, of course." She trailed her fingers through the water, and the image disappeared in a swirl of red. "It's too late for this village—it's already lost. But he'll be on to the next one soon, and if we act fast we can stop him before he gets there."

"Not to mention get to *us*," Nox said.

"Exactly," Mombi interjected. "He's less than a hundred miles from us. If he gets any closer, we run the risk that his senses will be able to see past the magical barriers that keep us hidden here." She looked at me. "I hope what I saw yesterday wasn't a fluke, Amy. This isn't a test anymore."

"Mombi," Nox said, cutting in. "Please. Think about it. Amy should stay behind. We can't risk her on something like this. It's too dangerous."

Mombi dismissed him with a wave of her gnarled hand. "We've already been through this, Nox. I wouldn't expect you, of all people, to let your feelings get in the way of what must be done. We need all the strength we can muster tonight."

"If we can't count on Amy now, when all the rest of us will be there, she won't be much good alone against Dorothy anyway," Melindra added, shooting a sidelong glance in my direction.

I was annoyed. They were talking about me like I wasn't even there. And why was Nox trying to prevent me from going? Didn't he think I'd improved? "I'm going," I said coolly, all heads turning in my direction. "Melindra's right. And I'm a member of the Order now. I'm not just going to hide out here while everyone else fights."

Nox's forehead creased in frustration, but he let it drop. It was settled.

Mombi, Gert, and Glamora left the war room to make the final preparations. I was about to leave when Nox pulled me aside. "Here," he said, pushing something hard into my hand.

I turned the object over in my palm. It was a knife, but it wasn't *only* a knife. I could tell it was special just by the way it felt. It was heavy, heavier than it looked, and it was almost vibrating with something that I now recognized immediately as magic.

I didn't want to like it. I didn't want to like anything that Nox gave me. But I couldn't help it: the knife was too beautiful. It was nothing like the kitchen knife that Pete had given me. It had a glinting silver blade with mysterious symbols engraved into it. The hilt was smooth and white, and was intricately carved into the figure of a bird with wings outstretched, ready to take flight.

"I carved it by hand from a Kalidah's bones," he said, looking down to avoid meeting my eyes. "The blade's made from the

claw. Gert spelled it and Mombi sealed it. It's designed to channel your magic for you—to store it and make it easier to access.
Not so different from Dorothy's magic shoes, really. Except,
hopefully, you know, not totally evil."

I rubbed my fingers over Nox's handiwork. It must have taken
hours. I knew that he'd done it for the cause, so that I could be a
better fighter. But it was still a gift and it was still beautiful.

"It will protect you," he said. "And there's another spell
attached to it, too—push the wings down."

The wings didn't look like they would move, but when I
pressed gingerly on them, they ceded easily to my touch and
folded up neatly against the side of the bird's body. As they did,
the knife sparkled in my hand and then evaporated into smoke
that drifted off into the air.

"Where'd it go?" I asked.

"It's still with you," Nox said. "Just not anywhere someone
else can find it. Now picture it in your hand again."

I looked down at my empty, open palm and imagined I was
clutching the weapon. Its image entered my mind, and as it did,
I was holding it again.

"Thank you," I said quietly. I wrapped my fingers gently
around the hilt. I couldn't remember the last time anyone had given
me anything, and this was something that Nox had made just for
me. Something magic. I felt my spirit lift inside myself. The corners of my mouth threatened to turn upward, but I didn't want him
to see how happy the present had made me. "What kind of bird is
this?" I asked. It didn't look like any bird I'd seen before.

"It's a Magril—a bird that's native to Gillikin Country. It spends half its life as a beetle, and when it's an adult, it goes to sleep for a year and wakes up as this majestic creature."

"Kind of like a butterfly."

"Kind of like you," he said. I didn't have an answer to that.

I didn't need one. At that moment, Mombi appeared before us. She looked down at the knife and up at me, and then Nox.

"It's time to go," she said.

We all gathered a few minutes later in the training room—me, Nox, Gert, and Mombi—and held hands. Glamora would be staying behind, along with Melindra and Annabel.

Melindra complained about being left behind—she wasn't the type to want to miss out on any action—but she seemed placated when Mombi reminded her that it was important that our most skilled fighter guard the headquarters in case it was a trap. Melindra didn't look happy about it, but she knew better than to argue with Mombi.

I felt myself envying her. Now that it was time to go, I suddenly wondered if I should have been so eager to fight.

But it was too late to think about that. In the training area, we all stood in a circle, all of us chanting at once as we worked together to cast the spell that would take us to the village.

Glamora took a step back, still chanting, and stepped out of the circle, followed by Annabel and Melindra. We all joined hands.

Nox looked over at me. "Hold on," he warned me with a sly, nervous grin.

He squeezed tight.

I felt an invisible force start to lift me, then it yanked me upward like a bullet, and we shot straight up.

I screamed and closed my eyes, knowing I was about to be smushed like a bug against the roof of the cave.

Instead, I felt wind on my face. I opened my eyes and found that my body was horizontal, my arms strained to their limits as I held on to Nox. Everyone else still had their eyes closed, their mouths forming the same chant over and over and over, and we were all fanned out like skydivers in formation, the mountain below us, hurtling out of sight.

We were flying.

It was the most incredible feeling I'd ever had. The sensation of free-falling made me giddy and light-headed, like I was a balloon and my insides were helium. I laughed, almost forgetting that I, Salvation Amy, was on my way to battle the Not-So-Cowardly Lion and his army of monsters. How could my stomach tie itself into knots about what was coming when I was busy tumbling into the sky?

"It never gets old," Nox said, opening his eyes. "In case you were wondering."

His normally spiky hair was flattened against his head by the wind, but for some reason his voice came out normal, like we were still standing right next to each other in the training room.

"You could have warned me," I said. "I thought we were going to teleport."

"It takes too much energy to teleport this many people," he said. "By the time we got there, we'd all be ready to pass out from exhaustion. This is more efficient. Plus, it's fun."

"Won't they see us coming?"

"Nope," Nox said. "We're traveling in the Space Between Space. They can't see us if we're not really here. It's how we passed through the mountain."

"Oh," I said, pretending I knew what he was talking about.

"I'll explain later," he said.

"Should we still be chanting?" I asked nervously, seeing that both Mombi and Gert still had their eyes squeezed tight.

"Nah," he said. "The takeoff is the hard part. Now that we're on our way, it only takes Gert to keep us in the air."

"What's Mombi doing then?" I asked.

Nox wiggled his eyebrows and lowered his voice to a conspiratorial stage whisper. "Mombi's afraid of heights," he said. "She's not casting a spell. She's saying her prayers."

"Who exactly do wicked witches pray to?"

Nox laughed. "Who knows? She's just trying to stay distracted so she doesn't piss herself before we land."

Our ascent had slowed down by now and we floated easily through the air, a mist of lavender clouds hovering just inches above our heads. In the distance, the sun was rising over the Deadly Desert. Instead of looking down, I looked at Nox as he took in the landscape.

Seeing him like this, away from the caves, away from the cause, I could almost see the boy he could have been. The boy he *would* have been if Dorothy had never come back. He looked happy. He looked beautiful.

Then he turned dark again. "Almost here," he said. I followed his gaze and saw thick, black smoke rising up from a forested area at the foot of a mountain range, curling into the sky.

"Get ready," Gert said, not opening her eyes. "We're coming in for a landing."

The knot in my stomach tied itself right back up as our velocity reversed itself and we hurtled for the ground, picking up speed.

But her warning was unnecessary. We landed like feathers in a field on the outskirts of what must have been Pumperdink. It was on fire, its small, dome-shaped houses consumed with flames as panicked townspeople raced in every direction.

The smell filled my nostrils and stayed there, churning. It was disgusting—a horrible combination of smoke and blood and burning flesh and other things, I'm sure, that I didn't even want to know about.

As I looked around, unsure what to do next, I saw something moving above me. Monkeys—they were weaving through the burning sky. The almost humanlike way in which they swooped and dove into the chaos made me shiver.

"Mombi and I will take down the beasts left in this village and save as many of the children as we can," Gert said, turning back to me and Nox. "Amy, you go with Nox to find the Lion. Send a summoning spell when you've got him in your sights. Don't try to defeat him yourselves—he's too powerful for either of you to take on without us."

Nox nodded and Mombi and Gert disappeared.

He balled his hand into a fist, and when he opened it he was holding a glowing ball of blue flame, which he blew on gently. It spun from his hand and hovered a few inches in the air. Nox blew on it again—it circled lazily around us, then darted back and forth for a few seconds before zinging off in the opposite direction of the village, leaving a trail of blue energy in its wake.

Nox jerked his head wordlessly toward the forest on the other side of the field. I pulled the knife he had given me out of the air, like he'd taught me to do, and his eyes met mine. The rest of his face was stony and emotionless, but his eyes were flashing with something else that I couldn't place. Pride, maybe? They seemed to be saying, *See? This is it. This is what I told you about.*

I nodded, hoping he knew that I understood. And we went racing off, chasing the light.

It got darker as we went farther into the trees, until finally the only illumination was the dim light from the tracing charm that was leading us. But my training served me well now, and my feet nimbly avoided every obstacle as if I'd run down this path a thousand times.

After a few minutes, we heard a roar in the distance. Nox put a finger to his lips and slowed down until we reached the edge of a clearing.

"Stay back," Nox whispered. "They won't notice us yet if we're careful."

The clearing was crowded with animals, some I recognized and others I didn't. There were foxes and crocodiles and wolves and tigers and bears. A few were walking around on their hind legs, while others were pacing on all fours. It was a nightmare zoo—a menagerie of wild mutated animals of every size and shape. These were the Lion's beasts.

Did the Lion command every animal in Oz, or did they have a say in the matter? I wondered, thinking of Star. If anyone was stubborn enough to show a little backbone, it was my pet rat. With any luck, Pete was keeping her nice and safe, but if she ever had the bad luck to meet this guy I hoped she would give him a good, hard bite.

The beasts had surrounded a group of Gillikin people, who were lined up neatly in the middle of the clearing like they were waiting for something.

Or maybe like something was waiting for *them*: at the front of the line, I saw the Lion himself for the first time in the flesh. He had been a vague, hazy shadow in Glamora's scrying pool, but now, in person, I realized exactly how terrifying he really was.

Really, he was barely recognizable as a lion at all. He looked like a monster, like some warped nightmare version of the king of the jungle. He was huge and golden, with bulging, grotesque muscles and a filthy, snarled mane. His lips were curled back, baring a mouth crowded with sharp, long, crooked fangs.

"Is that what he's always looked like?" I asked under my breath. Nox just shook his head and signaled for me to keep watching.

There were about ten townspeople in line. At the front of it, a trembling man with a top hat and a purple beard stumbled forward to where the Lion stood. He clasped his hands in front of him, and I could tell that he was pleading with his captor, but they spoke too quietly for me to hear what he was saying. I snapped my fingers, casting a listening spell. As I did it, I felt energy flowing out of my knife and into my body. The knife made magic so much easier.

"We've given you everything that you asked for," the man was saying. "We have nothing left. Please, just leave us alone. We're Dorothy's loyal subjects. We'll help you in any way we can."

"There's still plenty you can give me, Mr. Mayor," the Lion said. He widened his jaw lazily, almost like he was yawning. Thick ropes of drool rolled down his chin as he leaned forward on his haunches. The mayor levitated a few inches off the ground to meet him.

I couldn't tear my eyes away. At first it looked like the Lion and the man were kissing. But they weren't—their mouths were inches apart, not quite touching. The man looked like he was struggling, but then his mouth fell open, too, as his face contorted in pain and something that looked like red smoke came spewing violently out of him. I couldn't tell whether it was vomit, or blood, or something worse. Whatever it was, the Lion lapped it up hungrily.

"What's he doing?" I asked in horror, gripping Nox's arm.

"The Lion eats the fear of others," Nox explained in a whisper. "It's how he survives. How he gets stronger."

As if proving Nox's point, the Lion's muscles rippled and bulged. He was changing. He was growing.

The man was changing, too—his beard went from purple to gray in a matter of seconds. His rounded cheeks turned gaunt as the Lion finished and dropped him to the ground. The mayor gasped for air, suddenly old and frail, but smiling, too. I realized I understood why. He wasn't scared anymore.

"Hopefully you won't ever have to face him," Nox said. "But if you do, try not to be afraid."

Not exactly possible, I thought, looking at the smiling old mayor.

"What will happen to the mayor now? Will they let them go?" Nox just shook his head sadly.

As we watched, a hyena and a giant rabbit, who was probably as tall as I was, grabbed another victim from the line and led him forward to their leader. The rabbit seemed to be the Lion's second in command. He was on his hind legs just like the Lion. He had sharp buckteeth and giant, watery, bloodshot eyes. The hyena, also walking on two legs, was every bit as creepy. He looked nervous, jumping at every sound in the woods around him while he assisted the rabbit. And there were a lot of sounds to react to with a zoo of animals behind them.

"We have to stop them," I whispered to Nox.

He shook his head. "Not alone. I'll call Mombi. There's no way to do it without blowing our cover though, so be ready." I took a deep breath and prepared myself as he conjured another ball of light from his hand and sent the flare spinning out into the darkness. This was it.

The orb went whizzing into the trees, and as it did, a wolf lurking on the edge of the crowd pricked up his ears, jerked his head up, and let out a howl, his quick eyes darting from the ball of light straight over to its source.

That source being me and Nox.

The Lion looked up from his second victim, trying to find the cause of the commotion. With a wave of his arm, he released his beasts like a violent tide that came right toward us. I had seen a few members of the Tin Woodman's guard. They were eerily organized and obedient. But the Lion's army was different— they were wild and disorganized, each one of them operating on its own.

The wolf sped ahead of the pack in a gallop. Nox stepped forward and, in one swift motion, pulled out the sword he'd had strapped to his back, meeting the wolf with a gut-opening slice.

And then we were surrounded. Nox ducked and feinted and swung, flames trailing behind him, but every enemy he sent flailing to the ground was replaced by another.

I couldn't help Nox, and Nox couldn't help me. A group of winged monkeys had descended from unseen perches in the trees and were now spinning around me like furry little gymnasts, clawing and snapping with pointy little fangs. They were quicker than I was; even when I used my magic to dodge out of their way they seemed to know my movements before I knew them myself.

Don't be afraid, I reminded myself. I lunged, pulling my knife through the air, trying to be fearless.

One was bigger than the rest, and more vicious-looking, too. He flew right for me, claws outstretched.

I raised my knife, ready to fight, but then I hesitated, remembering what Indigo and Ollie had told me: that the winged monkeys were under Dorothy's control. No matter how horrible they seemed now, they weren't attacking me because they wanted to. They were doing it because they had to.

My split second of sympathy cost me. The monkey wrapped his hands around my neck and his legs around my waist. He was stronger than he looked, and I struggled to disentangle myself as he squeezed my throat tighter and tighter, chattering maniacally, his rancid sour-milk breath hot against my cheeks. I gasped for air, feeling myself grow dizzy.

Nox got to the monkey just in time, wrenching him from me just as I was about to pass out. He snapped the monkey's neck before tossing him to the ground.

"Why did you do that?" I cried. "If you clip their wings they won't be enchanted. They won't serve Dorothy."

Nox looked at me like I was insane. "Amy," he said. "In case you hadn't noticed, this is a war. Now's not the time to start worrying about the plight of the poor monkeys."

I looked at the dead monkey on the ground, its wings now folded over him like a pathetic blanket. There wasn't time to dwell on it, though. The rest of the monkeys had closed in on us. We were surrounded. But I pulled out my knife, hoping I could defend myself with as little collateral damage as possible.

I wielded my blade almost instinctively as the next monkey sprung at me, striking him in the chest. He screamed, collapsing. I couldn't tell if he was dead. I hoped not, but there was no way to find out: another one was on me already.

This one got close enough to swipe at my stomach before I

managed to take him down. He slid to the ground in a heap of fur and feathers. They kept on coming, but Nox and I were a good team: we made quick work of them. Some writhed in pain, others seemed to give up immediately, almost like death was a relief.

As the bodies piled up around us, I realized Nox was right. It was them or us.

I looked up to find another wave of beasts descending on us—this time a group of giant crocodiles lumbering toward us with swords and spears. I remembered the bumpy shadows in the scrying pond, lurking behind the Lion. They were even worse in the light: slimy green skin. Triple rows of teeth exposed and ready. They were slower than the monkeys, but more massive. I didn't know how my knife could penetrate their thick reptilian skin.

"You ready?" Nox asked. He whirled around into a crouch, his back pressed against mine, and we prepared to fend the attackers off.

"I'm ready," I said, ignoring all the blood and the pain in my left arm from where the monkey who'd tried to strangle me had bitten down with his sharp little teeth.

Then everything stopped.

The hyena dropped to the ground, and a split second later the rabbit did the same. What the hell? Were they dead? I looked around.

They were frozen. Every beast, every creature of the forest—all frozen, as if someone had pushed a giant pause button. But how?

I looked immediately to the Lion. Had he done this?

But he seemed as surprised as Nox and I were, dropping the girl whose fear he'd been feasting on into a heap on the ground and looking up. During the fight, he'd been happy to let his henchmen take care of business while he enjoyed his dinner, but now he was interested.

This isn't good, I thought, nervously shifting my grip on my blade. Whatever spell had just frozen all our other enemies didn't seem to have any effect on the Lion himself.

And I still had no idea who had cast it.

The Lion rose up on his legs in a fury, and roared into the sky.

Then I understood. I could feel her coming, could feel the warmth of her energy suffusing my body. It was Gert.

TWENTY-FOUR

I looked up to see Gert descending from the sky. She landed in the middle of the clearing amidst the strange, museum-like menagerie of the Lion's still-frozen henchmen. Without a word she raised her hand and a solitary lightning bolt appeared from above, coursing silently through her body.

I gasped. What was happening? I stared at her squat, round body as it began to glow with energy; her face burning with a fury that was almost inhuman. For the first time, I thought I understood why she called herself *Wicked* now.

At that moment, the citizens of Pumperdink, who had been just as frozen as the Lion's beastly army, seemed to be released from her spell. They began shouting and scurrying around, scattering in every direction, running for their lives. I looked at Nox.

"She's using everything she has to hold the beasts," he said. "But it will take all of her concentration. The Lion's too strong for her. We need to protect her until Mombi gets here. She'll know how to finish him."

He sprung forward. "Let's see how you deal with someone who's not afraid of you," he snarled. He thrust his hands up and a torrent of sizzling blue energy came shooting out. Growling in anger, the Lion leapt through the air and landed with a crash at Nox's feet.

But Nox had disappeared. He materialized behind the Lion just in time to take a swing at him.

If it had been baseball, Nox would have hit a home run. If the Lion had been a normal Lion, Nox would have sliced his head clean off from behind. But this wasn't a game, and this Lion made the lions I'd seen in the zoo look like kittens. Nox connected with a *thwack*, but all it did was make the Lion mad: he spun around and lunged again, and Nox barely managed to get out of the way in time.

I still hadn't moved. I couldn't help it. Maybe Nox wasn't afraid, but I was.

But when the Lion grazed Nox's cheek with his claw and I saw blood, my body forgot all about fear and sprung into action. I held my knife close, drawing out as much magical power as I could from it. I zapped myself to Nox's side. At last I was finally getting used to fighting like this.

The Lion jumped back, momentarily surprised. He hadn't been expecting me, but it only took him a second to get his bearings and charge, unhinging his jaw and leaping for me.

I didn't let myself flinch. Instead, I took advantage of the moment and thrust my knife forward into his gaping jaw, hoping that at least *there* he was vulnerable.

I was right. I was lucky.

My blade sank to the hilt and when I pulled it out, hot, sticky blood gushed out of the Lion's mouth. He recoiled and let out something that almost sounded like a whimper of pain.

At first I thought I'd actually done it—finished him, with that one blow to the spot where he was vulnerable. It would have worked in a video game. But the Lion wasn't going to be beaten that easily.

With blood still pouring down his face, he pivoted and, in a flash, wrapped both of his massive paws around Nox's neck. "The runaway," he said, in a tone that was velvety and smooth, almost a purr. He was looking at Nox, but it was clear he was talking to me.

He cocked his head and sniffed, his nostrils flaring as if he could still smell the Other Place on me.

"Everyone in the kingdom is on the lookout for you, little one. I thought I was just out for a snack tonight. I never expected to find *you*. Dorothy will be so pleased when I bring you back to her. Let's make a trade. You give up and come with me and I'll let your friend go."

Nox's eyes met mine, fierce and sure. *Do not make a deal*, they seemed to be saying.

"I'm not going anywhere with you," I said, trying to sound more certain than I was. "He doesn't mean anything to me."

The Lion shook out his mane and gave me a wicked smile. "Very well," he said. He opened his enormous jaws and, as I watched in horror, blue smoke began streaming out of Nox's eye sockets and nostrils. Blue, the color of his magic. Nox began to shake.

"Stop!" I screamed. I raised my knife and prepared to throw it, aiming it at the Lion's head—but I hesitated. What if I hit Nox instead? What if it didn't work? I had been training, but I still wasn't ready for something like this.

As I stood there, paralyzed by self-doubt, Gert whooshed by me in a streak of white light. As she came to a stop, the beastly guard she'd been holding motionless with her spell began to stir to life all around us. They were still looking dazed and sluggish, but it would only be a matter of time before they recovered their bearings. In other words, we were screwed.

Gert clapped her fists together and as she pulled them apart, Nox went flying from the Lion's grip and landed in the grass a few feet away.

"Take me instead," Gert hissed at the Lion. "I'm an old woman, but I have more for you to feast on than the two of them combined."

"No!" I cried, but she ignored me. The Lion looked her up and down, considering the offer. He must have known that I was more valuable than either Gert or Nox. But he was hungry and hurt. He probably figured he could take her first and still have me when he was done with her.

The Lion nodded. Gert stepped forward.

"Stop!" I shouted again, leaping forward to pull her away. I couldn't let this happen. But Gert had other ideas. She flicked her wrist at me and I went falling backward to the spot on the ground where Nox was already lying. When I tried to stand, I found that all of my muscles were frozen.

Gert just shot me a sly smile.

It was only then that I knew what she was playing at: Gert was fearless. There would be nothing for the Lion to suck from her. I hoped she had something better to give him in its place.

The Lion had no idea, though. He pawed at the ground and smiled greedily as he unhinged his mangled, blood-soaked jaw. Gert didn't so much as pause. She looked up at her old enemy with a glint of cheerfulness in her gaze and she pursed her lips into a kiss.

A flash of light blinded me for a second as the Lion began to stiffen and writhe. He tried to pull away, but it was too late.

The stream of energy coursing between his mouth and Gert's was white, not blue like before. And it was coming from the Lion, not from her. Her body was shaking like a leaf as she absorbed it.

Every muscle in the Lion began to shrink, like a balloon deflating. His eyes widened in something that looked like surprise.

No. Not surprise. Cowardice. Instead of giving him her fear, she was draining him.

Now. Gert's telepathic voice echoed weakly in my head like a whisper down an empty corridor. I realized that I could wiggle my fingers again. I could move.

Nox realized it, too. He jumped to his feet and lifted his sword one more time. At that same moment, Gert collapsed in a heap. She'd done what she needed to do.

Nox sliced at the Lion's belly and blood gushed from the

wound. The Lion tried to roar, but all that came out was a high-pitched squeal.

I was on my feet then, too. I dove forward, ready to finish him off once and for all. But I was too late. Even in his weakened state the Lion was somehow already bounding away, retreating back across the clearing and into the forest, his army of beasts following their leader.

Her plan had worked. She had beaten him. I stood up, ready to cheer.

But Nox was standing, too, and he didn't look nearly as happy. "We almost had him. Where the hell was Mombi?"

I had been wondering that, too, but when I saw that Gert was still on the ground, everything else went out of my head. She wasn't moving. She was lying in front of us like an overstuffed rag doll, her arms and legs splayed out at the wrong angles.

"Gert . . ." I knelt by the witch's side. Nox was already crouched over her, trying to pull her up and into his chest.

"Hold on," Nox was whispering. "Mombi's on her way. We'll get you to the spring."

Gert's lips trembled. She was trying to smile. For me. For Nox. But her soft, fleshy body was spreading out into formlessness, almost like she was melting before my eyes as she sprawled, convulsing, on the ground. What she had taken from the Lion must have been too much to absorb, even for her.

The green grass beneath her turned from green to brown to black charred dirt. It was as if someone had taken a torch to it.

Nox placed his palms on Gert's chest and bit his lip in

concentration. Blue sparks glittered at his fingertips but immediately petered out.

"Come on," I muttered, willing his magic to work. He did it again, and again nothing.

Suddenly Gert's arm shot up and she grabbed my wrist, clenching tight. Her lips began to move—she was mumbling something under her breath. At first it sounded like she was speaking a different language, but when her lips stopped moving, I was able to understand her words in my mind.

It was an incantation. *"North, South, East, West, wind, fire, sun, earth, protect her and keep her. Protect her and keep her."*

Now I was crying. "Gert," I managed to say. "Please. I need you."

Nox was ignoring us, still trying desperately to use his magic to bring her back from the brink.

"Come close, dear," Gert gasped. Her face was once again the warm, kind face I'd first seen when I'd woken up in the caves, frightened and alone. I saw the witch—Good or Wicked, it didn't matter anymore—who had comforted me and fed me, who had helped me find my magic. I leaned in over her.

She tilted her head up and kissed me on my brow. I felt warmth wash over me. It started where her lips met my forehead and bloomed all over, until my skin was somehow coated in Gert's kiss.

"Gert, no . . . ," I gasped. What had she done? She needed every bit of strength to hold on. Whatever she had given me, I didn't want it. I didn't want a good-bye.

"This will keep you safe," Gert said.

"You have to do something," I croaked at Nox, tears streaming down my cheeks. He had finally given up and sat back, and had silently watched Gert bestow her kiss upon me. "Please. Save her. Use your magic. You have to."

Nox shook his head sadly. "There's nothing I can do," he said, looking away.

Gert looked up at me. "It has to be you, child. You have to do it," she said weakly.

"Do what?" I asked, somehow believing that as long as I held on to her gaze then she would hold on to me.

"You have to kill Dorothy, Amy."

TWENTY-FIVE

I woke up the next morning feeling spent and disoriented, my mind a jumble of hazy images that appeared one by one in my head like pages in a horrible picture book.

The burning village. The eerie scene in the forest. Nox's determined face as he fought back an onslaught of beasts.

I felt like I was being plunged naked into a frigid pool as the rest of it came back to me. The Lion's gaping, bloody maw; Gert's tender kiss and the strange way I'd felt the life slip out of her as I'd held her in my arms. Her body dead on the ground.

In the enchanted softness of my bed, I tried to tell myself that it hadn't really happened—that it had all been a dream. It was only when I felt a tingling on my forehead, in the exact spot where Gert had kissed me, that I knew it had all been real.

At that stinging realization, I jolted instantly out of bed and took a shaky step forward, followed by another and another then another until I was in the center of the room, where I stopped in a state of paralyzed panic. I had no idea what to do with myself.

I couldn't go back to bed. I couldn't leave. So I just stood there, trying to will the memories out of my head. I didn't want to think either. But thinking was the only thing I *could* do.

I don't know how long I stayed like that. It could have been a minute and it could have been an hour, but I was still standing in that same position when a ghostly, luminous butterfly came floating through the wall and hovered in front of me. I accepted its entrance without surprise or curiosity. It was like I had been expecting it.

"Find me," the butterfly said, speaking somehow in Glamora's voice, and I nodded and began to get dressed.

I made my way through the Order's tunnels with a numb and heavy feeling. With every step I took, I felt the weight of what had happened yesterday bearing down on me.

The door to Glamora's room was ajar, and I pushed it open without thinking about it, only to freeze abruptly when I saw the witch's reflection in the ornate, gilt-framed mirror of her vanity.

She was crying.

Not just crying. Her entire body was shaking with grief as she hunched over the table in a contortion of pain. She looked so small and powerless—so unlike herself—that half of me wanted to turn and leave her while the other half wanted to rush over and comfort her. I did neither. Instead, I just watched, unable to move, unable to say anything, knowing that she would never want me to see her like this.

Her fiery hair, always so perfectly coiffed, was frizzy and disheveled; a single strap of her elegant silk nightgown drooped across her shoulder. Her face was tired and worn, etched now in a map of sags and wrinkles and that scar on her cheek that she usually kept hidden. She looked like she had aged twenty years in one day. It was hard to believe it was her at all.

But even in this bedraggled and unfamiliar state, Glamora was still Glamora. The liquid pooling in the corners of her eyes was glittering and crystalline, and each tear that rolled down her cheeks and tumbled from her chin made a small plinking noise as it landed on the vanity. Looking closely, I saw that the surface was strewn with a messy scattering of them—tiny, teardrop jewels that just kept on coming.

Glamora was crying diamonds.

Suddenly she seemed to sense me watching her and she looked up. I felt embarrassed to be caught, and embarrassed for her, but I didn't look away. In that moment, I owed her the dignity of an unwavering gaze. It was the least I could do.

"Amy," she said, sitting up straight and tugging the strap of her gown up to a more decorous position. "Come in."

As Glamora spoke, her hair rearranged itself into a sleek chignon. The lines on her face melted away, leaving her as youthful and refreshed-looking as I'd ever seen her. Every trace of vulnerability was gone now. Now she was cool and unreadable.

The jewels on the table caught the light, and I couldn't help but glance over at them. There was something about seeing them lying there in their scattered little pile that chilled me. What kind of person is so hard on the inside that she cries *diamonds*?

Glamora noticed me staring. Somehow she knew what I

was thinking, and she shook her head ruefully. "Magic loves change," she said with a sigh. "Do enough of it and it will warp you in strange ways. It's the first law of enchantment. Use it to change the outside and after a while the inside changes, too. So I traded my tears for beauty. Well, it could be worse, couldn't it?"

"Yes," I said quietly. "It could." But I wasn't so sure.

"If you think I'm bad, you should see what comes out when my *sister* cries," she said. I couldn't tell if she was joking. But then she clapped her hands, signaling that it was time to change the subject and get down to business.

"Now then," she said. "We suffered a great loss yesterday. An *unimaginable* loss. As you know."

I waited for her to go on. "What you may *not* know," she continued, "is that Gert was by far the most accomplished magic user in the resistance. More powerful than me or Mombi; more powerful than any of the witches in the Order's other cells. Perhaps the only person in Oz whose power could rival my sister's. They didn't make her the Good Witch of the North for nothing, you know." She rolled her eyes and sighed, momentarily recalling some old rivalry before moving along.

"Without Gert, we no longer have the power to reliably hide ourselves from Glinda and Dorothy. They will be looking, and it's now only a matter of time before they find us. As a result, we have decided to move our plans forward earlier than expected." She folded her hands primly in her lap.

"Good," I said.

Glamora gave me a careful once-over. "Do you understand what that means?"

I was pretty sure I did, but I took a second before I answered, just to let it sink in. "Yes," I finally said, sitting up straight and squaring my jaw in resolution. "It means it's time for me to do what I came here to do." As I said the words out loud, the numbness inside me seemed to let up. Not a lot, but enough that I actually felt something other than a dull and aching emptiness.

Mostly anger. Cold and burning anger at the same time.

"Are you sure you know what you're agreeing to?" Glamora asked.

I didn't know why she cared.

"I understand," I said, tossing my hair defiantly. "It's time for me to kill Dorothy."

Glamora nodded, satisfied. "I wish more than anything that I could do it myself," she said. "But it has to be you. There's no other way."

At first I thought she meant it to be something like an apology, but then I noticed the way her shoulders had tensed up in a barely concealed combination of rage and regret, and I realized that she was actually envious of me. That, to her, it was a privilege.

Well, maybe it was.

With that, the witch stood and ran her hand along her nightgown. It rippled like water and resolved itself into a more presentable outfit for the day: a tailored tweed suit in a somber mauve shade, cut primly to the knee.

"No matter what the occasion, we must present the proper

face to the world," she said, sounding like she was speaking more to herself than to me. "Now, come. We have to have a talk with Mombi. You'll be leaving for the palace today."

Mombi had showed up a second too late; a second after I'd laid Gert's lifeless body onto the ground. At just the second when it didn't do us any good.

She'd come swooping in through the trees in a swirl of purple light, fists clenched and eyes blazing, ready to fight, but when she saw me and Nox, she stopped in midflight and hung in the air. A look of sick understanding passed across her face. She landed with a thump before kneeling and placing a hand to the side of Gert's face.

"There was a child . . ." She stopped to collect herself. I had never imagined that Mombi could seem so *human*. "I couldn't leave her. I thought Gert would be able to handle it on her own. I thought . . ."

She betrayed no emotion after that. Instead, she bowed her head and began a solemn chant.

I somehow knew instinctively that this wasn't a spell to bring Gert back to life. There are some things that no amount of magic can accomplish, and this was one of them. This was a ritual to lay Gert to rest.

Mombi's muttered words were unintelligible and ancient-sounding, with a wandering melody buried somewhere deep below their surface. The chant sounded like one of those weird songs you sometimes hear flipping through dials on an old radio only to pause on a station that barely comes in, the tune so far away that it's hard to tell if it's even a tune at all or if it's just static.

The old witch passed her hands up and down along Gert's body as she sang, and as she did, Gert began to melt into a pulsing, flickering puddle of mystical electricity that slowly seeped its way into the earth.

Whatever magic Gert still had left in her, she had given it back to Oz now.

Then Gert was gone without a trace, like she had never been there at all.

But she *had* been there. She had sacrificed herself to save us. No, forget that. She had done so much more. Even if I had never quite been able to figure out—never really been able to tell where the Good ended and the Wicked began for her—I had known, by the end, that she had believed in me. Not just as the one who would be able to defeat Dorothy, but as Amy Gumm.

None of us spoke as we joined hands and shot up through the trees and into the air. There was nothing to say. This time I didn't bother looking at the ground as we soared over Oz. I had seen enough for one day.

Mombi had disappeared as soon as we were back in the caves.

Nox took me by the hand and walked me back to my room. He pressed a gentle hand to my shoulder. I opened the door and stepped inside, not looking back.

That was yesterday. Now it was today.

Glamora and I found Mombi in the war room, seated at the table across from a girl I'd never seen before. She looked terrified. Her shoulders heaved silently as she cradled her face in her palms.

Glamora and I each took a seat.

"This is Astrid," Mombi said. The girl rocked back and forth, not looking up. "Until last night, Astrid was a servant in the palace. Today, she has been given the opportunity to join our cause. Astrid, meet Amy."

"Hi," I said, not quite understanding where this was going.

"If all goes well, Astrid will be returned unharmed to the palace when our mission is complete." Mombi cast a meaningful, ominous look in Astrid's direction. "If she chooses to make a nuisance of herself, things will not be so pleasant for her."

If all goes well. Then I got it. Astrid hadn't decided to join the Order. She hadn't been rescued from a burning village. She had been kidnapped. That was why she looked so scared.

A chill shot down my spine as I remembered that things were never easy around here. Good and evil were always changing places with each other.

For the first time, Astrid looked up at me. Her eyes were big and pleading, pooled with tears. Her chin trembled as she looked desperately at me, like she was hoping I'd be the one to save her. But I was out of pity. She would have to choose her own fate, just like the rest of us.

I looked back to Mombi. "Tell me what I need to do," I said.

A satisfied smile crept across her withered face.

"Well, you need to *become* her, naturally."

I leaned back in my seat, knowing that with witches, it only tangled things up when you asked too many questions. It was easier to just wait for them to explain themselves.

Mombi proved true to form. "Today you will assume Astrid's identity and take on her job as a servant in Dorothy's court. You will infiltrate the palace and ingratiate yourself with the princess. You will learn her habits and her hatreds. You will learn when she goes to bed and when she wakes up in the morning, her fears and her weaknesses and her secret prides and sorrows. In the guise of little miss Astrid here, you will learn everything there is to learn, and you will relay it back to us. Then, when the time is right, you will strike."

At this, Astrid let out an anguished, choked squeal.

"She looks nothing like me," I said. "How am I going to impersonate her?"

Mombi sprung to her feet, reached into her cloak, and pulled out a dagger. In one sudden motion, before the poor girl even knew what was happening, Mombi had grabbed a fistful of her hair and yanked.

Astrid's head jerked backward. She yelped again, and when she saw Mombi raise her knife into the air, the yelp became a scream.

The blade flashed through the air. I held my breath.

But instead of slicing the maid's throat open like I'd anticipated, Mombi simply lopped off a large hank of her white-blonde hair.

"Now," Mombi said. "Go ahead and say your name four times."

Astrid sat there, frozen. "Say it!" Mombi screamed, so loudly that even Glamora jumped in her chair.

"A-Astrid," the girl stammered uncertainly.

"No stuttering!" Mombi said sternly.

Astrid gulped. "Astrid, Astrid . . . Astrid," she finally managed to spit out.

Mombi smiled. "Good girl," she said, and she began to crush the hair up into a tight ball before gesturing to me to come forward.

"Here," she said, thrusting it out. Reluctantly, I took it from her.

"What do I do with it?" I asked, holding it up.

"Eat it," she said.

"*Eat* it?"

"Eat it."

I looked over at Glamora, who nodded calmly.

Seriously? Avenging Gert meant eating some other girl's disgusting hair?

Trying not to grimace, I shoved every bit of it into my mouth. To my surprise, it crunched when I bit down, and then, after a few more chews, it melted onto my tongue like cotton candy. Well, not *just* like cotton candy. It still tasted like hair. But at least it went down easy.

Then nothing happened.

I gave Mombi a quizzical look. "It didn't . . . ," I said.

"It will take effect slowly," she replied. "Now come on. Let's give these two some private time while we wait for the spell to work. Glamora's quite a skilled interrogator, you know."

She laughed when she registered my look of surprise. "Everyone always assumes I'm the one who does the dirty work around here," she said. "Little do they know, I'm the *nice* one. Looks aren't everything, you know." She beckoned impatiently from the doorway.

I had to force myself not to look over my shoulder as I left.

"What's she going to do to her?" I asked Mombi nervously when we were outside.

Mombi waved a hand. "Oh," she said. "Nothing much. You know how it goes. The maid always has the most valuable information. And the maid *always* cracks under pressure."

Nox was waiting for us in the training room. He still seemed shaken from yesterday, but I could tell he was trying to cover it up.

"Your job is simple for now," he said. The scrying pool rippled, and a map appeared. This time, it wasn't a map of Oz. I studied it for a minute and realized it was of the palace. "Astrid is a servant, but she's at the bottom of the food chain—she doesn't spend much time with Dorothy. Change that. Get close to the princess. Listen to her. Find out her habits, her routines. Find out when she's vulnerable and what she's vulnerable *to*. You'll only have one chance to hit her. And we want you walking out of there alive."

"How long do I have before I kill her?" I asked.

"Don't worry about that for now," Mombi cut in. "A spider weaves her web slowly and carefully. A witch—well, a witch is like a spider. At least, this witch is."

"So you *don't* want me to kill her?"

"Don't you worry. You'll get your chance to be Wicked. But I'll let Nox explain all that."

Nox waited a beat and then began rattling off instructions.

"For now, you're there to watch and learn. You're there to blend in. Remember: you are Astrid, not Amy. And you are *not* to make any move against Dorothy without a direct order from us."

"And how am I going to *get* that order?" I asked, annoyed at how impersonal he was being.

"We already have an operative in the palace who will be watching you. When the time is right, that person will bring you instructions. While you're in the palace, try to avoid using magic. There are security measures everywhere, and magic is off-limits for maids. They're a little lax on that rule—if it weren't for travel spells and glistening charms, nothing would ever get as clean as Dorothy likes it, so they tend to turn a blind eye, so as long as you keep it to the small stuff it shouldn't be a problem."

"What about my knife?" I asked, knowing that I'd feel safer if I could have it at the ready.

"Summoning it shouldn't be a problem," he replied. "That's not really a spell anyway, since the knife is always with you. You're just activating it. Just don't summon any demon guides or cast any reincarnation spells, okay?"

We both smirked at the irony of it. Just a few weeks ago I was struggling to use enchantment to blow out a candle and now we were talking half-seriously about me performing serious A-grade magic.

"Well, you never know," Nox said, shrugging. "Anyway, if you do need to use magic that you think will set off the alarms—and I don't recommend it—it will be pinned to your location. So get the hell out of there before anyone can find you."

"I'll do my best," I said.

"The Emerald Palace," he said, turning his attention back to the scrying pool and pointing to a small square buried in a complicated grid of interconnected shapes. "These are your private quarters. You're three floors down from Dorothy and . . ."

Suddenly I wasn't paying attention. My stomach began to lurch. Something was happening to me.

I had almost forgotten the spell Mombi had cast. The enchantment was beginning to take hold.

The map of the palace in the scrying pool had disappeared and my reflection replaced it.

At least—I *thought* it was me. It was hard to be sure. My face was no longer my own. I was turning into Astrid.

My eyes shone back at me, no longer their familiar brown color but now the bright blue of a swimming pool.

Then my pink hair was a radiant, corn-silk blonde.

I stared at my reflection, trying to make sense of it.

I hadn't noticed back in the war room, but it turned out that Astrid was pretty. She was definitely prettier than me. Her nose was a bit bigger, yes, but in a way that made her face more interesting. She had a small, heart-shaped mouth and a perfectly symmetrical oval face with high cheekbones and a chin that was neither too prominent or too simpering.

I was still trying to get used to my new face when I realized the rest of me was changing, too. It wasn't the most pleasant experience: my skin felt like it was being ripped apart as it stretched to make room for my new bones. It turned out Astrid was tall.

When I instinctively put a hand to my cheek—just to make sure that it was still there, I guess—I noticed that my fingers were now long and slender. It looked like I'd had a manicure recently, too.

"Call me old-fashioned," Mombi said, admiring her own handiwork, "but I liked the pink hair better."

I barely heard her. I turned to Nox, suddenly feeling scared, suddenly unsure if I was really ready for any of this.

His face looked ashen for a minute, but then he swallowed hard and smiled. "Don't worry," he said. "You're still Amy."

When I looked back into the pool, I couldn't say that I agreed. There was no trace of the old me. I was no longer Amy Gumm.

A short time later I was wearing the maid's green uniform I'd seen on Astrid earlier.

After I had put it on Glamora surveyed me, twirled a fiery tendril of hair around her finger in thought, and finally nodded in approval. I couldn't help feeling proud of myself. "Remember what I've taught you," she said. "Astrid may be among the lowliest of the servants, but she knows what forks to use; she knows the steps to the dances. Being a maid is only one step removed from being a princess. Don't do anything to remind them you're neither."

She grabbed my shoulder with one hand and placed the other

on my spine, jerking me upright. "Watch your posture. Dorothy can't *abide* a sloucher, and neither can I. Walk around like that and you'll be fired in a week. Or worse."

I looked into the scrying pool mirror one last time. Like Mombi, I missed my pink hair. And while I knew I wasn't Amy Gumm anymore, I didn't feel like Astrid either.

I was still looking at myself when Mombi spoke up. "Enough of this. It's time for you to go."

She reached into her robe, pulled out something that looked like a pebble, and dropped it into the pool. I leaned over to watch as it rippled in concentric circles and then began to glow. When I looked up, Mombi was already gone.

"She's always been awful at good-byes," Glamora said sadly. "But I'll say one: Good-bye, darling. You'll be fabulous." She opened her arms and pulled me into a deep hug. It was nice of her, but I think we both knew she wasn't Gert.

After a moment, she let me out of her embrace. "I'll let the two of you say your farewells in private," she said, blowing me a final kiss before leaving.

It was just me and Nox now. I'd never seen him so quiet. He was staring at the scrying pool, which was showing the map of the palace again.

"I have a list of Dorothy's likes and dislikes and schedule. Memorize it and then destroy it." He held the list out toward me. When my hand grazed his, he grabbed on tight.

He closed the gap between us without taking a step and his mouth closed over mine before I could speak. He was kissing me. I closed my eyes and let go of everything except him for a few seconds. I had never kissed a boy before so I had nothing to compare it to. But I was sure that whatever it was like, kissing Nox had to be different.

Because *Nox* was different. Power and magic flowed between us like when he'd first showed me what magic was. But it wasn't magic at all this time. It was something completely human. Things we couldn't or wouldn't say with millions of words were all there, all at once. Everything we shared and everything we were was contained in this single perfect moment.

When we broke, he was breathing hard and I wasn't breathing at all. The candles in the cave suddenly blew out. Was it us? Or had Mombi sent a gust telling us to hurry up?

He composed himself, letting his arms drop to his sides. But he was still standing within kissing distance.

"That will never happen again," he began.

My stomach dropped. *Was it that awful?* I wondered.

"But it would be too bad if it didn't happen once," he finished. "I just wish I'd gotten to do it when you still looked like yourself."

I wasn't hurt. I didn't have time to be hurt. And he was right. He didn't want us distracted by each other. It was too dangerous. Until Dorothy was dead, I couldn't care about the way I looked, or about what Nox thought about me, or about what Glamora had done to Astrid.

I didn't know what was Good or Wicked anymore. All I knew was what was *right*.

"What do I do?" I asked.

"Isn't it obvious?" Nox pointed at the pool, which was still glowing in concentric circles, pulsing outward from where Mombi had dropped the pebble. He smiled a smile that looked like a secret. "You jump."

I couldn't wait any longer. If I didn't do it now, I'd never have the guts. So I took a deep breath and a running start and dove headfirst into the shallow water.

TWENTY-SIX

A moment later, I emerged out of a full-length mirror in a sloppy somersault. As I righted myself I realized I was in a dim, musty room that was so small I could almost touch both walls by stretching my arms out. I wasn't even wet.

I stood up and looked in the mirror. Astrid stared back at me. I touched the cool glass—solid now, no way back—and reminded myself that this was me standing there. This was me in Dorothy's dumb servant attire: frilly white shirt, pleated green skirt, apron, and red patent-leather Mary Janes that seemed like a mocking approximation of Dorothy's sky-high pumps. Cute.

I smoothed down my skirt and adjusted the apron, looking around while fighting back a wave of nausea at being in one of the palace's tiny rooms. I needed to get used to it quick. After all, this was my new home.

The servants' quarters weren't much better than my cell had been. There was a little white bed with threadbare sheets printed with Ozma's faded crest and a dresser with peeling paint that had seen better, grander days. A small silver bell sat on top of the dresser. That was pretty much it.

It made my room back in Dusty Acres seem lavish. And *that* room hadn't even had walls.

I yanked open the top drawer of the dresser, not expecting to find much. I was right. There were three uniforms identical to the one that I was already wearing, and a couple of plain cotton dresses—one in a plain green satin and another in white. Glamora had told me that every maid had two dresses aside from her uniform—one for escorting Dorothy to parties and one for her monthly day off.

So this was it.

It didn't take long to search the rest of my sad accommodations. I got excited for a second when I reached underneath the mattress and pulled out a battered old book. Maybe it was a diary. Some extra insight into servant life would come in handy. Hell, maybe Astrid had documented the one day a month Dorothy sunbathed in the warm glow of the Emerald City's Rusty Knife Recycling Pile. That'd make my task easier.

Either I wasn't that lucky or Astrid wasn't that interesting, or both. It was just a dog-eared copy of a trashy-but-famous Oz romance called *The Quadling and the Nome*, one of the more boring books Glamora had forced me to read during our cram sessions.

I tossed it aside in frustration and sank down onto the bed. I was all alone for the first time in weeks, and I had absolutely no idea what I was supposed to do next.

Out of boredom, I opened my palm and was about to light a small magic flame when I remembered Nox's warning not to use magic. I snapped my hand shut and leaned back. So much for my plan to pass the time by staring at fire. I sighed.

"Boredom," I said aloud, "thy name is assassin-ing."

It was only then that I realized I was overlooking the one friend I *did* have in the palace. Well, make that *two* friends. Friend Number One: Star the Rat. Who was, in theory, still being kept safe by Friend Number Two: Pete.

Pete. I'd almost forgotten him. Was he here? Did he know I'd managed to escape? I wondered. Or how I'd managed to do it?

Even if I found him, there was no way of telling him I was okay. I was Astrid now, and even though I had a good feeling about Pete, my witch-trained side knew I couldn't take any unnecessary risks. I was supposed to follow the plan. *Watch and wait*.

I sat. I watched. I waited.

I almost jumped out of my maid's costume when the bell on the dresser rose a few inches into the air and began to ring.

I knew it meant that someone in the palace needed service. I knew about the bell because Astrid knew about the bell. The spell Mombi had cast didn't give me access to her memories—not exactly—but it did give me a vague sense of her instincts. What Astrid would do in this situation came through as a foreign tickle in the back of my mind.

I walked over to the bell and cautiously picked it up. It rang louder.

I held it at arm's length toward the door. It got louder still. When I placed it back on the table, the tinkling chime faded.

It was like a game of hot and cold. The bell was telling me which way to go.

So me and the bell walked out the door, down one hall and then another and another and another. At each corner, I listened carefully, judging which way to go. The bell was getting louder and louder as I roamed through the palace. How big *was* this place?

When I reached a carved oak doorway, the ringing stopped. I'd really been hoping the bell would lead me to one of the normal doors, but of course it put me in front of this monstrosity at the end of the hall. The door was carved into a landscape scene that twisted and moved as I stared at it, almost like crude animation. In it, dozens of blackbirds repeatedly dropped dead over an endless field of corn.

I knocked, and then jumped back as a blackbird exploded into a puff of feathers beneath my knuckles.

An impatient, somewhat familiar voice told me to enter. My heart sank when I saw the Scarecrow sitting on the edge of his bed in the center of the room, waiting for me. Or rather, waiting for Astrid.

"Yes, Your Royal Scarecrow?" I chirped in my sweetest voice, even though I was shaking on the inside. I was face-to-face—and alone—with the monster who'd experimented on Melindra. I felt my hand tingling and I was comforted with the knowledge that my knife was there if I needed to summon it.

The Scarecrow's room looked less like a bedroom and more like an enormous, filthy study. Every surface was cluttered with loose papers and dirty plates and bits of straw. The whole place smelled stale and moldy, like the bootleg firewood our neighbor used to wheelbarrow around Dusty Acres. Lying on the floor near my feet I noticed a bound leather book open to a drawing of a monkey's internal anatomy, with little notes in shaky hand-writing penciled in the margins.

I shivered and forced myself to look away, letting my eyes travel upward, where walls of bookshelves stretched beyond the reach of the candlelight.

"Well? What took you so long?" the Scarecrow snapped. My eyes snapped, too, back down to where he sat, his creepy button eyes looking right through me. "Why didn't you just zap yourself to me?"

"Zapping is forbidden in the palace," I said, the words out before I could even think about them.

I let out an internal sigh of relief when the Scarecrow seemed exasperated but not suspicious. "You should know by now that those silly rules don't apply when *I* ring," he grumbled. He gave me a meaningful look.

Oh no, I thought. *Please please please don't tell me he's Astrid's secret boyfriend.*

But he just scowled as he gestured toward a square metal tray that was sitting on a table next to his bed. "I'm feeling duller by the second here."

Doing my best not to disturb his mess, I carefully stepped over piles of junk and picked up the tray.

It took everything I had to stay calm when I saw what was actually on it: knives and scalpels and curved needles and pliers and an assortment of other things I didn't even want to think about. Some of them were still bloody.

These were probably the same tools this monster used to dissect and experiment on innocent Ozians. On people like Melindra.

And what did he want *me* to do with them? I was still trying to figure it out as he casually leaned his stuffed body against his bed's ornate headboard and started removing a series of straight pins from his scalp, dropping each one carefully into a metal wastebasket near his feet.

I noticed that they had blood on them, too. I cleared my throat and nodded toward the horror show of instruments on the tray.

"What would you like me to do with these tonight, Your Eminence?" I kept my voice detached, like a good, subjugated servant girl, even as my skin crawled at the scene before me. I hadn't been prepared to face the Scarecrow within minutes of my arrival. I hadn't been prepared for the Scarecrow at *all*.

He looked me up and down with his dead and shiny button eyes. "I want you to do the same thing I always want. What's gotten into you?" Without waiting for me to answer, he plucked a scalpel up from the tray I held and began carefully using it to break apart the stitches that held his canvas skull together. "I got started without you. The syringe is already filled."

I noticed it then: a syringe with a needle at least four inches long was sitting right there next to the rest of the bloody utensils. I picked it up, wishing I'd learned a spell to keep my hand steady.

When I turned around the Scarecrow was lifting the flap off his head, revealing his brain.

I'd seen a monkey brain once in biology class. This was kind of like that, only pinker and goopier. The whole thing was suspended in red, gelatinous mush that I'd mistaken for blood.

I picked up the syringe. I gave it a little squirt like I'd seen nurses do on hospital shows. Where was I supposed to stick it? My borrowed Astrid instincts were quiet. Maybe the magic only went so deep, or maybe she'd done such a good job blocking out these traumatizing scenes that they didn't transfer over, or maybe my own instinct to run away screaming was overriding my Astrid sense.

Either way, I stood there holding the needle like a dummy.

When I waited a moment too long, his gloved hand shot up and grabbed my wrist with a steel grip. His hold was tight, yet I could feel his straw insides crunching as he squeezed. I almost flinched away, but that wouldn't be an Astrid move. I kept my eyes downcast and frightened.

"Get it right, girl. Or I'll be the one sticking needles into *you* next."

"Yes, sir," I said meekly, adding a shudder that wasn't entirely feigned.

When he let go, I went for it, jamming the needle into the pinkest part of his brain mass. Part of me hoped there might be an air bubble in the needle or something, and my next job as servant girl would be mopping bits of Scarecrow off the walls. I pushed the plunger, releasing the fluid. The Scarecrow let out a long moan of relief. His head lolled over to his shoulder and a little felt tongue I didn't even know he had dangled limply from his mouth. I willed myself not to throw up.

"Ahhhh," he moaned again.

I pulled the needle out and put it back on the tray, slowly backing away.

"Do you know how many brains I had to drain for this stuff?"

The thing is, he wasn't looking at me. It sounded more like he was talking to himself; he barely seemed to remember I was there at all.

"It's exhausting," he continued, "but it's the price they must pay to have the finest brain in all of Oz."

"Yes, sir," I mumbled.

"I'll sew myself back up. It's good to let it breathe for a bit." He waved me away, a bit of straw escaping from his cuff. "Take the trash on your way out, girl."

I grabbed the wastebasket, almost tripped over myself curtsying, and got the hell out of there.

As long as I didn't think too much about it, and if I followed my feet and let the spell do the work, I knew my way around the palace. After only one wrong turn, I finally found my way to the kitchen, which seemed as good a place as any to dispose of the Scarecrow's garbage. It was empty now for the brief window between cleaning up after dinner and getting ready for breakfast. The place was even more huge than I had expected, which was fitting considering the size of the palace.

Not to mention the size of Dorothy's appetites.

One wall was lined with a row of old-timey stoves while a

row of sinks dominated the other. At the end of the kitchen was a fireplace, a small fire dancing behind the grate. I tossed the whole wastebasket in. It burned down to dust in an instant.

When I turned around, I was no longer alone. Ozma was standing in the doorway. She wore a nightgown so sheer I could see her pale, almost translucent skin through it. Her big green eyes were unblinking, glowing brightly in the kitchen's candlelight.

I was pretty sure she hadn't noticed me.

I held my breath and stepped aside into a shadow. But as I moved, the princess let out a lilting giggle and I saw that her eyes were trained right on me. I'd been discovered.

"Pardon me, Your Majesty," I said, curtsying deeply and praying I hadn't done anything technically against the rules.

Again, she giggled. It had a manic, almost crazed quality to it.

"Is there anything I can do for you?" I asked quietly and carefully. "May I assist you to your quarters?"

She smiled and clapped her delicate hands together. "Quarters! Halves!" she exclaimed in delight, and then her face immediately drooped into a frown. "And have-nots."

So this was the One True Princess of Oz. It was obvious to anyone that she was broken somehow. I wondered if this was what she did every night—if she just wandered around the palace reaching for whatever shiny objects caught the attention of her spooky green eyes and spouting weirdo puns. I turned to go. I didn't want to be around if she started banging on pots and pans or something.

But as I tiptoed around her into the empty hallway, she called after me.

"Dorothy knows," she singsonged. I stopped and turned back, wondering what she meant. What if there was a little bit of Ozma still in there?

"What does she know?" I asked, forgetting myself.

She began to sing. "Backward rivers, Dorothy knows, Lion's den, Scarecrow's nose."

Oh. It was just more nonsense.

What happened to you? I wondered. But I knew it wasn't worth it to ask.

Ozma's hand reached out for mine as I tried to skirt past her. Her grip was surprisingly strong for someone so frail and thin that I could practically see through her.

I tried to shake her loose, to no avail. "Ozma. Your Majesty. You have to let me go or I'll get into trouble."

She gave me an angelic smile and patted my hair with her free hand. It was like my mom mid-bender.

"What does the owl say?" she asked me.

I inspected her face to see if there was even a hint of under-standing, if there was anyone at all at home. It didn't look like it.

I'd taken too long to respond, so this time her question was louder, echoing through the kitchen. "What does the owl say?"

"Please be quiet, Your Majesty," I hissed, but when it looked like she was about to ask me again, I gave in. "Who! The owl says who."

"Are you?" she demanded, cocking her head to the side.

"Astrid," I replied, trying to stay calm, her clammy hand still on my wrist. "I'm Astrid."

"Mm mm mmm," she replied, pointing at my chest. "Naughty liar."

I yanked away from her, more violently than I'd intended. Ozma teetered like an antique vase and then started to fall over. I had time to picture the princess of Oz cracking her head on the cobbled kitchen floor; that'd make for a pretty atrocious first night of espionage. I leapt forward to steady her.

Before I could even apologize for almost knocking her over, Ozma latched on to me. She put her lips right up against my ear.

"I'll never tell," she whispered.

And then, out of nowhere, she grabbed my chin and turned my head, kissing me softly on the cheek. Her lips were soft and smooth.

What the hell?

I pulled back gently and looked at her. Her eyes were wide open, too. She was still studying me. This time, though, she let me go. Without another word, Ozma resumed her wandering, leaving me in the kitchen to wonder if my cover was already blown.

TWENTY-SEVEN

"Today is a beautiful day to be in Oz!"

The lilting, sweet voice wafted across the crowded table in the servants' mess hall where I was eating breakfast with the rest of the maids.

I was starting to sweat, and not just because this was the first time my Astrid identity needed to stand up to mass scrutiny; it was humid in the mess hall, the room seeming to trap all the heat from the kitchen. There were about twenty girls huddled shoulder to shoulder around the long, rough-hewn table—no boys. The butlers and footmen I'd seen hustling around must take their meals at a different time.

Jellia Jamb sat at the head of the table—the one who'd spoken with such unironic chipperness about what a beautiful day it was to be a servant. Jellia was in charge of the downstairs staff. She had a sickly sweet smile on her face and she looked like she was a few seconds away from bursting into song. She poised her fork above her plate and held it there. Everyone else followed suit.

Jellia was pretty, with rosy pink skin and golden-blonde hair. As the head maid, her uniform was a deeper, richer emerald green than the rest of our pale, washed-out shades that were somewhere between sea foam and olive.

Somewhere in the back of my mind, I'd hoped I'd get the chance of a glimpse of Pete when the staff gathered, but no luck. If I was going to see him, it wasn't going to be at mealtimes.

We were dining on a spread left over from Dorothy's dinner last night, which meant we were eating dinner and dessert for breakfast. Braised ribs. Truffle-infused mashed potatoes. Chocolate cake. The fact that my mouth was watering felt like some small betrayal of the Order. Even the maids' food in the palace was a million times better than what the Order cooked up in the caves. Still, I would have given anything to have Gert make me some green goo again, something other than the table scraps of a flouncy despot. And, back at the caves, I could eat without feeling that everyone was staring at me, picking up on whatever giveaway Ozma had noticed the night before. Green goo was a lot less stressful and a lot more ethically delicious.

"Praise Dorothy," Jellia said, and nineteen forks descended in unison. Mine was just a second behind.

Glamora was right. The girls had perfect manners, and in that moment, I was thankful that she'd trained me so vigilantly. But there was something else, something a little eerie. They were more than perfect—they were synchronized. Every girl's fork met her lips at the exact same moment and touched down on their plates again, like clockwork.

"Dorothy has been very generous. She was pleased with last night's service. She didn't actually say so, but I could tell. She didn't have a single complaint. Well, except about the bread, but that wasn't our doing, and I'm sure Her Highness knows that. Aren't we lucky to work for someone as kind and understanding as Princess Dorothy?"

This girl was cheerful. Too cheerful. Dorothy wasn't even *here* and this was at least the eleventh compliment she'd heaped on the princess before we'd even started eating.

And I'd hate to see what happened to the poor person who screwed up Dorothy's bread—whoever that was.

"Astrid, are you all right?" Jellia asked as I took a braised rib from the serving dish at the center of the table.

I looked up, startled. "I'm fine."

"You never eat that," the girl next to me, whose name I'd learned was Hannah, said suspiciously.

"Maybe she's trying to put on some weight," offered another maid named Sindra. Her eyelashes were extra-long and she'd tied her hair into tight pigtails, almost like an homage to Dorothy.

I swallowed hard. Was Astrid a vegetarian? Had my stomach just given me away?

I shrugged as lightly as possible. "I guess I'm just extra-hungry this morning," I said, trying to match the other girls' perky tone and keep pace with their synchronized eating. "If it's good enough for Dorothy herself, it's certainly good enough for me!"

That seemed to satisfy them. Jellia nodded as if my logic was too unimpeachable to argue with, and I went back to trying to chew daintily, hoping I wouldn't make any other mistakes.

I kept my antennae up for intel, but the only subject of conversation was *Dorothy*. Which should have been a good thing, considering that she was the one I was really here to learn about. Unfortunately, no one was sharing any useful information. It was all about how beautiful Dorothy was, or how kind she was, or how lucky we were to be working for the greatest person in all of Oz.

It was weird. They were like a creepy, overeager maid sorority.

By the end of breakfast, I found my fork moving in time with the other maids. I found myself nodding when they nodded, chewing when they chewed, blinking when they blinked. Part of me was proud for how easily I'd blended in, a necessity if I was going to complete my mission. But another part of me wondered if maybe the whole automaton routine wasn't coming a little too easily.

Was it magic? I wondered. A spell to make us as orderly as possible? Did Dorothy have some kind of charm working to keep us from eating like slobs or tapping our forks? Or was the clockwork perkiness machine just the maids' way of dealing with the constant fear of living under Dorothy?

Breakfast didn't last long. Jellia merrily reminded us how much work we'd been blessed with and hustled us off to our tasks. Every room in the palace was cleaned every day, regardless of whether or not anyone was using it.

"I wish we could use magic for this," I said leadingly to Hannah, glancing at her over our big bucket of soapy water. We were hunched on our hands and knees, scrubbing oil stains from the floor of the Tin Woodman's suite.

My floor scrubbing was pretty half assed, since I was too busy checking out the Tin Woodman's living space to really bother with my job. Except that his room was almost as boring as mine. The room was completely devoid of personal effects whatsoever, other than spare parts. The only thing that interested me was a strange contraption that was bolted to the wall, made up of two long metal brackets that held an ancient-looking mattress suspended about a foot off the floor in a perfectly vertical position. Just under it, a pair of boot-shaped scuff marks had become so etched into the wood that I was sure *no* amount of scrubbing would remove them.

At first, I couldn't figure out what it was. Then it dawned on me. This was the Tin Woodman's bed. He slept standing up.

The whole place gave me the creeps. On the other hand, at least we weren't cleaning the Scarecrow's room—that would have been terrifying—not to mention it would take all week.

Hannah shot me a sidelong look and lowered her voice. "You know using magic would be wasteful, Astrid. Dorothy needs it, every drop. Besides, doing the work the old-fashioned way is comforting to Dorothy. It reminds her of how she used to clean the farm back in the Other Place."

"You don't need to lecture me about comforting Dorothy," I replied quickly. "It's my whole reason for being here."

Hannah smiled at me and I smiled back, hoping to match her cheerily vacant quality.

"I'm so glad our slaving away makes Dorothy feel better," I muttered, pretty sure Hannah wasn't the type to detect sarcasm.

"It really does!" Hannah exclaimed. "It reminds her how far she's come."

The soap we were using had a lemony, peachy smell. I wondered if this was the soap that her auntie Em used to use back in Kansas, before the tornado whisked her away. What could have happened to turn that sweet, innocent farm girl into this magic-hoarding fascist?

I wasn't going to get any useful assassination tips out of a frightened airhead like Hannah, so I decided to poke around and see if there was any way I could get her to give up some information about Pete. Even posing as Astrid, I figured tracking down the only other anti-Dorothy person I knew of might be helpful, and surely servants cozying up wouldn't raise any red flags. Not that I wanted to cozy up with Pete.

"Have you seen that boy around with the crazy green eyes?" I asked casually. "I wonder when he takes his break."

Hannah looked up at me, surprised.

"Who? You mean one of the guards?"

"No, I think he's a gardener."

"Oh, don't be silly, Astrid," she said.

I blinked. "What do you mean?"

"You know any fraternization is strictly forbidden."

"Oh," I said, trying to figure out a way to cover my mistake. Before I could, Hannah leaned in close enough to whisper.

"I let Bryce—you know, the baker I was telling you

about?—sneak into my room the other night," she whispered. "But don't tell anyone. I don't want to get punished for Smuttiness again."

"I promise I won't," I whispered back.

"I'll keep an eye out for your boy, too," Hannah said. "But I haven't seen anyone with eyes like that."

I leaned in close to the floor, trying to scrub away a particularly stubborn piece of dirt. Who *was* Pete?

After we finished the Tin Woodman's suite, we were allowed a fifteen-minute break in the servants' mess hall. For a snack, Jellia brought out an array of stale muffin bottoms. Apparently, Dorothy ate only the tops.

While the other girls ate with a chorus of "oohs" and "aahs"— I guess muffin butts were a treat around here—I took a moment to study the postings on the mess hall walls. There were a ton of brightly colored signs about proper cleaning techniques and uniform maintenance, but also a color-coded schedule of palace personnel. I tried to memorize it, particularly the times when the guards changed shift. Knowing when there could be gaps in Dorothy's protection would definitely come in handy. The big wild cards were the Scarecrow and the Tin Woodman. They weren't in the habit of posting their schedules anywhere, even though I knew they were always somewhere in the palace. The Lion, too, was rumored to be around.

The idea of seeing the Lion again, after what he'd done to Gert, made me sick.

But it wasn't my job to be sick. It was my job to get past them, and I'd have my hands full enough with that as it was. One thing at a time. First, get a read on Dorothy's comings and goings, then—

"Are you not eating, dear?"

It was Jellia. She'd sidled up next to me without my noticing.

"I will," I replied quickly, waving at the fluorescent step-by-step guide to mopping. "Just feeling like I could use a refresher. I want to stay sharp for Dorothy."

Jellia nodded approvingly and handed me a muffin butt wrapped in a napkin.

"Good girl," she said. "Just remember to keep your strength up. It's important."

Jellia wasn't kidding around. By the end of that first day I was so exhausted, I collapsed immediately onto my tiny bed. What'd felt stiff and lumpy the night before now seemed to my aching body like the most comfortable spot in all of Oz. The calluses on Astrid's hands hadn't prepared me for how intense a full day of nonstop cleaning could be.

I made it through. One full day posing as a maid, and no one seemed suspicious. Well, except for Ozma, but I hadn't seen her around at all that day. And Dorothy's guards didn't come knocking down my door, which meant Ozma had kept her mouth shut. That was a relief.

Better yet, I didn't see any more of the Scarecrow's brains after that terrifying first night. Rumor was he'd locked himself up in his laboratory—wherever that was no one seemed to know—hard at work on some project. In the meantime, we maids were instructed to leave his daily hay bale delivery outside his bedroom door. Secret science experiments were obviously ominous and something I should look into, but I was mostly just relieved the Scarecrow didn't have time for his creepy dalliances with Astrid. Through the night, the bell next to my bed remained mercifully silent.

Today I'd mastered the routine and gotten used to my new body. Tomorrow, I'd work on getting closer.

The next day was more of the same. Cleaning my way through the palace alongside Hannah and the other maids, I started to put together an idea of Dorothy's day. I didn't get to see her or actually wait on her—it was more her absence that painted a picture. The bitch cast a long shadow.

First, I observed the hustle and bustle in the kitchen, the cooks preparing Dorothy's breakfast. We're talking a thorough inspection of bacon here, because Dorothy apparently doesn't like it too crispy. That bacon then went upstairs on a tray, presumably to undergo a thorough inspection by Jellia before being allowed to be delivered bedside by a shaky maid.

The first room on our cleaning circuit, as outlined in Jellia's thorough flow chart, was Dorothy's solarium. It was her preferred location for midday tea with the ladies. I was partnered with Sindra, which meant I did most of the cleaning while Sindra gazed longingly at all of Dorothy's gaudy decorations. After the solarium, our next stop was the nearby bathroom, where Sindra and I came upon a well-to-do woman in an elegant sundress, staring into the mirror like she was trying to psych herself up before skydiving. This was one of Dorothy's ladies. She pretended not to notice us.

"That's Lady Aurellium," Sindra gossiped on our way out. "Her husband used to be the Master of Coin."

"I didn't even recognize her," I said, then took a chance. "Horrible what happened to Lord Aurellium."

Sindra snorted. "Well, he shouldn't have told Dorothy what she couldn't spend the palace reserves on."

I didn't press her further, but it sure sounded to me like something dark had befallen Lord Aurellium. And now here was his wife, a playdate for Dorothy. So she spent her days entertaining the important people of Oz she hadn't yet executed or driven into hiding.

Around teatime, we almost crossed Dorothy's path. It was impossible not to hear her coming. Her red high heels clicked unnaturally loudly through the halls, as if amplified by magic. Not to mention she brought with her the heavy footfalls of her bodyguards and the tittering of her entourage, a group of gaudily dressed Dorothy-appointed beauty experts and jesters, all of them constantly jabbering about how wonderful she was. I wanted to get a look at my target, but Hannah yanked me away.

Dorothy was never alone, I realized. It was unclear whether that was a tactical decision—or maybe even she couldn't stand to be alone with herself.

After teatime, Dorothy either took a nap or met with her council of advisers, or possibly both. Either way, we weren't allowed on the upper floors during that time, lest we disturb Her Greatness.

There was no way the maids didn't see how screwed up everything was. But they went cheerfully along. Or, at least, they pretended to. Never for a moment did they doubt Dorothy's magnificence and kindness and perfection.

It was like they were brainwashed. Either that or scared out of their minds.

Later that day, a whistling Jellia and I were sweeping dirt from the narrow hallway that ran between the palace and the Royal Gardens when the unmistakable clanking of metal parts came echoing in our direction. The unspoken rule among the maids was to stay out of sight of Dorothy and her advisers—particularly the metallic Grand Inquisitor and his Tin Soldiers—except that wasn't an option now. There weren't any doors or exits in our little hall; either we ran back toward the palace in the direction of the incoming metal man, or we ducked into the Royal Gardens where servants were strictly forbidden.

Jellia's giddy facade melted under a fresh burst of panic. She froze, clutching her broom and staring down the hall. I grabbed her and pulled her over to the side of the hallway, our backs tight against the wall. She was shaking.

"It's okay," I told her. "We haven't done anything wrong."

"But—but what if she didn't like the song I was whistling?" Jellia stammered.

Before I could answer, the Tin Woodman rounded the corner. The last time I'd seen him had been in battle and for a moment I tensed up, half expecting him to come at me. But he didn't so much as glance in our direction. He didn't recognize me—couldn't recognize me. I tasted blood and realized I'd been biting the inside of my cheek.

"Please, please don't, it was just an accident!"

The Tin Woodman was dragging a young man along by the elbow. He wore the emerald-plated armor of the palace guards. He thrashed against the Tin Woodman's unforgiving grip to no avail. From around the young guard's neck hung a cardboard sign that said Crime: Wandering Eye.

"I didn't mean to look at her!" the guard pleaded.

"Silence," came the Tin Woodman's icy reply.

As they went by, I made the mistake of meeting the young guard's eyes. I should've kept my gaze downcast and subservient like Jellia. Desperate, the guard tried to lunge in my direction.

"Please!" he screamed. "Help me! This isn't right!"

I could've done something. Cast a fireball spell. Summoned my knife and saved that guard. I wanted to save him because I couldn't stand to see that fear in his eyes. But then the Order's whole plan would've been blown. Disgusted with both myself and the situation, I looked away.

The Tin Woodman shoved the guard onward, out into the Royal Gardens. He didn't bother closing the door all the way. After a moment, I crept over to peek outside.

"Astrid!" Jellia hissed. "What are you doing?"

I shushed her and watched as the Tin Woodman led the guard to a sunny bed of overgrown sunflowers. They stopped there, the guard still pointlessly struggling. I wondered what Wandering Eye meant. Had he checked out Dorothy? What was the punishment for that?

The sunflowers shuddered, then parted, and there stood the Lion, stretching in his sun-drenched napping spot. I couldn't believe it. Here I'd been dumbly sweeping away while Dorothy's beast slept right outside the door. The Lion looked totally recovered from his battle with Gert. His thick muscles rippled under his coat of golden fur as he drew himself up, looming over the guard.

The Tin Woodman exchanged words with the yawning Lion but I couldn't hear them. I had to stop myself from casting a listening spell, again remembering Nox's warning about using magic. Whatever they said, it made the guard collapse to his knees.

A moment later, the Lion crooked one claw delicately against the guard's face, the motion so smooth I almost missed it. Something that looked an awful lot like a Ping-Pong ball sailed in an arc away from the guard's face and into the waiting, open maw of the Lion.

It was his eye, I realized. The Lion had flicked out the guard's eye and swallowed it. I backed slowly away from the door.

"What did they do to him?" Jellia whispered, her curiosity proving to me that the maids weren't entirely oblivious and brainwashed.

"You don't want to know," I replied. "We should get out of here."

So this was what I was up against. A psychotic midwesterner with a reservoir of magic who was never alone, surrounded by loyal killers that would disfigure one of their own without a second thought. Meanwhile, I'd received no further instructions from Nox or the Order, and hadn't seen any sign of Pete, my one sort of friend in the palace.

Sure. This whole assassination thing would be a piece of cake.

TWENTY-EIGHT

On the third day, there was a flutter of activity among the staff. Someone important had arrived in the palace.

"The Wizard!" Hannah whispered in excitement as she headed off to clean the north wing while I gathered my materials to handle the south.

"The Wizard?" I asked, hoping for more details. But Hannah was already scurrying away.

Neither Glamora's lessons or Gert's had ever touched on the Wizard. Honestly, I'd forgotten all about him. Hadn't he gone back to the Other Place in his balloon? What was he doing in Oz? As usual, I was two steps behind.

But the Wizard was definitely here. I decided to detour past Dorothy's solarium, knowing that if she kept to her regular schedule she'd be in there. It wasn't on Astrid's normal cleaning route for the day, but that was a risk I'd have to take. I needed to find out more.

The hallway was totally clear, and I made sure to keep my

footfalls light. The door to the solarium was ajar, probably because Dorothy figured no one would have the guts to eavesdrop. I pressed myself against the wall outside the open door, peeking into the room. Inside, Dorothy was stretched out on a green velvet divan with ornate, gold legs. Next to where she reclined, a tower of little finger foods and pastries overflowed with snacks. Dorothy wasn't even bothering to lift a finger: the cookies were floating right from the tray and into her mouth.

I did a double take when I saw who was sitting across from her on a brocade couch: Glamora.

No. Of course not. It was Glinda. She was wearing a slinky pink slip dress, her red hair piled in a perfectly coiffed updo, and she was sipping primly from a pink teacup.

"I don't trust him," Dorothy complained. "Why does he have to come here at all? I let him do what he wants; I let him get away with using magic. Can't he just stop pestering me?"

"The Wizard may be an irritating ally," Glinda replied. "But he would make a dangerous enemy. Let's keep him happy." It was freaky how much they looked and sounded like each other. Hearing Glamora's voice coming from Glinda's mouth made me miss her sister a little. Even if I'd never liked her that much in the first place.

"I don't see why I can't just kill him," Dorothy complained. "It would make everything so much easier. I hate him, and I hate his dumb little hats."

"The Wizard is from your world," Glinda reminded her. "That makes things more complicated. His magic is unpredictable.

Trying to kill him could easily backfire. As long as we keep him on our side, he's harmless. He might even be able to help us. You know as well as I do that we share . . . similar goals."

"Hmph," Dorothy said. "I just want him out of my life."

"Patience, Dorothy," Glinda warned. "Why don't we take a look and see what he's up to? I agree that it's better to keep a careful eye on him."

Dorothy let out a loud sigh of frustration. She clapped her hands together and I snuck a peek to see what they were doing. Their attention was directed at a painting of a pleasant woodland scene that hung on the wall, over the fireplace. I took the opportunity of their distraction to watch more closely.

"Magic picture!" she barked. "Show us the Wizard."

At Dorothy's command, the picture began to rearrange itself, like the paint was still wet and an invisible brush was creating a different scene. Suddenly the trees became a face I recognized: the Tin Woodman. Then another face formed. This was one I'd never seen before. But I had a good guess as to who it was. It was an older man with a narrow face, mischievous eyes, and overgrown, almost hornlike eyebrows. He had a small, jaunty top hat sitting on the baldest part of his almost entirely bald head.

The Wizard was having lunch with the Tin Woodman. Even their voices carried crystal clear through the magic of the painting. It was like watching one of those high-def TVs my mom always talked about putting on layaway. It made me nervous, knowing Dorothy had access to this kind of power. I wondered what the limits of her spying were.

I also wondered if I might be able to use this magic painting myself instead of relying on old-fashioned sneaking around.

"Why don't you just tell her how you feel?" the Wizard asked casually, leaning back in his chair and buttering his scone.

The Tin Woodman looked up from oiling his joints with a scandalized expression. "I couldn't possibly. I—"

In the solarium, Dorothy turned to Glinda and I yanked my head back behind the door frame. "He's trying to turn him against me," she hissed. "Listen to him."

Glinda shook her head. "That's not what it sounds like to me. It seems to me that they're discussing a matter closer to our mutual friend's stuffed heart."

"No!" Dorothy groaned. "Not *this* again."

I tentatively leaned in to see Glinda shrug, put a red-clawed finger to her red-painted lips, and point at the painting, where the Wizard was patting the Tin Woodman's shoulder sympathetically. He tried to swat it away with one of his knife-tipped hands, but the Wizard jerked back just in time to avoid getting sliced.

"It's useless," the Tin Woodman said. "Everything I do, I do for *her*. And still, she will never love me the way I love her."

I almost gave myself away by laughing out loud, but swallowed it just in time. The Tin Woodman was hopelessly in love with Dorothy!

Really, it wasn't funny. It was sick. Well, okay, maybe it was a little funny.

Then I remembered what I knew about the Tin Woodman.

He'd lost a love and accidentally chopped off his limbs with an enchanted ax. But what if the ax hadn't been enchanted at all? What if the Tin Woodman was just a guy who was known for taking things too far in the name of love?

"Why not start small?" the Wizard was advising. "Ask her for one dance at the next ball. That couldn't hurt, could it? And maybe it will lead to something else."

The Tin Woodman's forehead crumpled like aluminum foil, then smoothed itself out again as he considered the idea.

"Perhaps."

"Ugh! It would *literally* hurt! He has knives for fingers," Dorothy complained. She clapped her hands again and the painting changed to a motionless, pastel image of a sunny seascape. "Enough! Encouraging the Tin Woodman's pathetic crush is treason. I could have the Wizard's head for that."

Glinda waved off the suggestion. "Oh, hush," she said. "You can't blame him for that. We've *all* found ourselves having those conversations with your metal admirer. He *never* changes the subject; it's impossible *not* to encourage him. Anyway, we shouldn't be rash. Remember when you disposed of the Wogglebug and then, a few months later, you wanted another?"

"I remember," Dorothy grumbled begrudgingly.

"There were no more Wogglebugs. And there is only *one* Wizard."

Dorothy conceded with a nod and a pout, but I wasn't so sure. It looked like she might still prefer a world with no Wizard at all.

Glinda stood up. "Well, my dear . . ."

Glinda looked ready to leave, so that was my cue. I slipped away from the door and padded quietly down the hall. I wasn't so bad at this spy stuff and I didn't even have a magic painting. Now, I just needed to figure out what to do with everything I'd just learned.

In the banquet hall, scrubbing endlessly at the shiny marble floors, I had plenty of time to consider my next move.

I had so many questions. Why wasn't the Wizard back in the real world where he belonged? Why didn't Dorothy trust him? And what made him and *his* magic so dangerous that they couldn't risk dealing with him?

But I wasn't just thinking about what they'd talked about. I was also thinking about that picture, wondering exactly how far it could see. Nox had warned me about using magic, but I wouldn't be casting anything, since the painting was already enchanted. It was probably safe, right?

I rushed through the rest of my cleaning. It wouldn't be up to Jellia's standards, but I didn't care. I needed to do something. I'd been gathering information for three days and still didn't have a concrete plan to get closer to Dorothy. I could keep playing maid and, in the meantime, let Dorothy go on murdering her enemies and disfiguring her allies, all the while wasting my days cleaning until I slipped up and got beheaded for the crime of Soap Scum. Or, I could take a risk, speed things up, and use her magic painting.

Yeah. Worth it.

I tiptoed back to the solarium. This time, it was empty.

I looked both ways down the corridor to make sure no one was coming, and crept into the room, approaching the picture. It had changed again. Now it was a painting of a quaint little cottage, like something you'd see in a dentist's office.

I wasn't sure it would work. The picture was probably just a normal painting without Dorothy's magic to make it do its thing. Even so, I looked around nervously one more time, and then faced it.

"Magic picture," I whispered, trying to mimic Dorothy's sharp command, only quietly. "Show me—"

"Ahem."

I'd been caught. Without thinking, without even turning around, and definitely without considering Nox's warning about magic, I cast an invisibility spell. My cover was blown. Escape was now the only thing on my mind.

I disappeared only for a second. Before I could even move my invisible feet, a feeling like getting splashed by a bucket of cold water came over me. Just like that, I was visible again, my spell canceled. I stood smack in the middle of Dorothy's solarium, exposed.

The Wizard stood before me.

TWENTY-NINE

The Wizard took a step toward me and tipped his hat, revealing a bald, shiny head with a horseshoe of curly gray hair. He smiled at me with a mischievous twinkle in his eye and gave a little bow.

I'd expected to come face-to-face with one of Dorothy's underlings or maybe even Her Awfulness in the flesh. With some effort, I calmed the fight-or-flight reflex, especially since flight had already failed. The Wizard wasn't one of Dorothy's allies, but that didn't make him one of my friends.

"Oh, excuse me, sir," I managed to get out, trying to play it cool. "I was just dusting."

The Wizard looked pointedly at my empty hands.

"Yes, well," he replied thoughtfully, "spick-and-span as this whole place appears, I suppose one would need an invisible maid for the invisible dust."

I let out a nervous laugh that was only half feigned.

"I don't know what you mean, sir," I said, and tried to walk around him. The Wizard took a step backward, getting in my way. He smiled at me again and tipped his chin, almost like we'd just accomplished some kind of fancy dance step. It took some menace out of the moment. Even so, I took a second to size the old man up.

The Wizard looked like a handsome, aging movie star. His clothes were perfectly tailored, his suit a stiff brocade like it was cut from a tapestry. Soft silk ruffles peeked out from his collar and cuff links with little silver *W*s punctuated his wrists. He touched the brim of his hat as I appraised him. Compared to the rest of his outfit, the black hat with its black band looked simple and worn, almost like it came from another time.

"It must have been a trick of the light," the Wizard said impishly, waving at the solarium's dozens of twinkling windows. "A sleight of body, perhaps."

I knew he was screwing with me but I stared at him with the inoffensive blandness I'd picked up from the rest of the maids.

"If that's all, sir, I have more chores to be done," I said with an excess of politeness.

The Wizard fixed me with a mysterious, catlike smirk. "Ah. That's what we like around the palace. Initiative. Gumption. *Spunk.* It seems to me that I used to know someone else like that, too."

My mind immediately went to the most obvious person: he was talking about Dorothy.

"Of course, I'm speaking about myself," he said. He gave me a sly wink, like he knew it wasn't what I'd been expecting him to say. "What's your name, child?"

"Astrid," I said quickly. Maybe too quickly. This guy was crafty, I didn't want to give anything else away.

Of course, I knew what everyone knew about the Wizard—that he'd come to Oz in a balloon, that he'd set himself up as its ruler in Ozma's absence, and that he wasn't a real wizard at all, just a guy with a lot of fancy tricks. And, of course, there was the fact that he had supposedly *left* Oz just around the same time Dorothy had, to go back to his own world. *My* world.

Clearly, some parts of the story weren't quite accurate—for starters, he was still here in Oz. But for some reason, in all my lessons with the Order, Glamora and Gert and the rest had never brought up the Wizard at all. Had he ever really left in the first place? Did they know he was here? I wondered how it all connected.

The Wizard had turned away from me and was examining the painting. He leaned in close, like he was super-interested in the brushwork, and then stepped back and ran his finger along the edge of the gilded gold frame.

"I see you missed a spot, Astrid," he said, holding up his index finger, which was perfectly clean. "You'll have to be careful about that next time. You're lucky it was me who noticed. Others around here get quite upset when things are where they don't belong."

"It won't happen again, sir," I said. I inched toward the door, but part of me wanted to stay. It seemed like the Wizard was trying to warn me, which meant maybe I could trust him. Or at least get some valuable information out of him, making this whole excursion to the solarium not a total screwup.

"How long have you been working in the palace, Astrid?" he asked, seeing me linger.

I hesitated. "Several years now," I said finally, figuring it was a vague enough answer that it was probably safe.

"And what do you think of your job? Of the princess?"

"It's wonderful, sir," I said. "I'm so lucky to be able to work for someone as wise and beautiful and generous as Dorothy."

"Ah yes," the Wizard replied, as if we were discussing the weather. "Dorothy certainly has ways of keeping her servants smiling. After all, the minute you start grumbling, you'll be sent off for an official Attitude Adjustment from the Scarecrow."

"I—" I wasn't sure how to respond. The Wizard seemed like he was tempting me to be critical of Dorothy. I wanted to trust him. But he'd already caught me doing magic and I didn't want to give him more ammunition if he wasn't on my side. He almost seemed to be hinting to me that he was—but just because Glinda and Dorothy hated him didn't mean he was a good guy.

"The Scarecrow is so brilliant," I finally said. "Without him, we wouldn't have so many of the advances in magical technology that make Oz the place it is now."

The Wizard smiled sadly and fiddled with his boutonniere. "Of course," he said. "Where would Oz be if not for the Scarecrow's great experiments? Ravens with human ears; men with bicycle wheels instead of legs—it's a glorious world we live in now, isn't it? It almost reminds me of the one I came from." At that he looked back up at me. It was almost like he was trying to gauge my reaction.

I didn't let myself react. "Yes, sir," was all I said.

"I hear," the Wizard mused, "that the Scarecrow is working on his greatest experiment yet."

I perked up. This was exactly the type of information that would be valuable to the Order. I had to be careful not to seem too interested, though.

"In his lab, sir?" I asked casually.

"Oh yes," the Wizard replied. "Day and night in his secret laboratory. Not sleeping. Probably working his fingers to the . . . well, I'm not sure if the Scarecrow actually has bones. But you get the point."

I nodded enthusiastically and tried not to choke on my own fake sincerity. "He sacrifices so much."

The Wizard's face lit up.

"Those who have sacrificed always have the most to lose," he said, watching me closely. "Ever hear that expression, Astrid?"

I shook my head. "No, sir."

"Ah. You will, my dear. You will."

What the hell did that mean?

Before I could ask, the Wizard tipped his hat and strolled out.

My heart was pounding on my way back to my room. What was the Wizard trying to tell me? Did he have some clue as to who I was or what I was here to do? It was like trying to put a five-thousand-piece jigsaw puzzle together without the picture on the box.

Ozma. The Wizard. The palace was full of cryptic oddities that I couldn't quite get a handle on. Who could I trust?

It was almost like the universe wanted to provide me with an answer when I opened my door to find Pete sitting on my bed.

THIRTY

I jumped back and gasped. I had been starting to wonder whether Pete even existed at all, and now he was sitting on my bed without a care in the world—like he belonged there.

I had to remind myself that it wasn't my bed. It was *Astrid*'s bed. Which meant he was here to see her, not me. But why?

All I wanted to do was run over to Pete and hug him—to tell him *It's me, Amy, and I'm okay.* I wanted to tell him about Mombi and the Order, and about Gert, and how she had died. About why I was here and what I was going to do. I couldn't tell him any of those things, though.

I closed the door behind me just in case anyone passed by in the hallway, and then tried to get my head together.

"What are you doing here?" I asked, in the most noncommittal voice I could manage. I didn't want to seem *too* surprised to see him. I still didn't know why he was in Astrid's room. What if they were friends?

A thought struck me. What if they were a *thing*? That would be awkward.

Pete stood up from the bed. His face spread into a wide grin and he stepped over to me and wrapped his wiry arms around me in a huge hug. I didn't let myself give in to it, but I didn't fight it either.

"You made it," he said, sounding choked up. "You're here."

My entire body stiffened. I pulled myself out of his grip and pushed him away.

"Of course I'm here. It's my room."

"I came as soon as I could. Sometimes it's hard for me to get away."

I didn't know what Pete was playing at. Yes, he had been kind to me. He had been my friend. But he'd been cagey, too, and I still didn't know who—or what—he was. I still didn't know if I could trust him, given what I now knew from the Order.

As much as I wanted to, I knew that I couldn't. Nothing was safe around here.

"I don't know what you're talking about," I said carefully. "And I'm not supposed to have anyone in my room. You should leave."

Pete put a soft hand on my shoulder. "It's okay, Amy," he said. "You don't have to pretend—I know it's you. Your secret's safe with me. At least, it's as safe as Star is."

He reached into his pocket and pulled out my pet rat. When her little white face peered up at me and she gave a squeak, I couldn't hold back anymore and tears welled up in my eyes.

All the uncertainty and fear and strangeness of the last few weeks came flooding through my body at the familiar sight of her. I reached out my hands and Star crawled into them.

"How did you know?" I asked, looking up at Pete. "How did you find me?"

"You can change your face, Amy, but I'd know you anywhere," he said. It wasn't any kind of answer. I wiped a tear from my cheek and studied Pete. His expression was as impassive and mysterious as his words.

I clasped Star to my chest.

"Is there something wrong with my disguise?" I asked. It was something I'd been worried about since my run-in with Ozma, and if Pete could see through it, what was to stop someone like Dorothy or Glinda from realizing I wasn't who I said I was?

"That's not it," Pete said. "Whoever cast the spell knew what they were doing. It will fool them all. Everyone except me."

I suddenly remembered what they'd told me before I left the Order—that I'd have a handler in the palace, another one of the Order's agents who would be keeping an eye on me. Someone to watch my back and, eventually, give me instructions.

I wondered if that someone could be Pete. It would make a lot of sense—he could have been the one who had led Mombi to me in the first place, when I was back in the dungeon.

But I knew that I wasn't supposed to have any contact with my handler at all. Not unless it was totally necessary. I wasn't even supposed to know who it *was*. If it was Pete, I was pretty sure he wouldn't be risking the plan by sneaking into my room.

"I asked some of the other maids about you," I said.

"They'd never heard of a gardener with green eyes."

"Yeah, they don't really know me around here," Pete replied. He sat back down on the edge of my bed.

I stayed standing. "You told me before that you worked here."

"I do. It's complicated."

Complicated. The word thudded between us. It was my least favorite word. Dad had used it just before he left me and Mom and never came back. I felt myself getting angry again.

"How am I supposed to trust you when you won't tell me the first thing about you?" I asked, my voice rising. I'd used up all my subtlety in my conversation with the Wizard. I was done with all this coy crap. "'It's *complicated*, Amy. I *can't* tell you, Amy.' It's a bunch of bullshit! You need to start explaining."

As I raged, I felt my palm open. Magic tingled my fingertips like they were itching, and I knew it was my knife. It wanted to come to me. Whether or not *I* trusted Pete, my knife didn't. It was trying to tell me something—that he was dangerous. For now, though, I willed it to stay out of sight. I'd already slipped with my magic once today, it couldn't happen again.

Pete sighed and looked up at me with apologetic eyes. "Look," he said. "I don't work in the palace, exactly. Not inside, at least. I'm not really even supposed to be in here. I work on the grounds—in the greenhouse."

The greenhouse. I'd seen it from the window when I'd been cleaning.

I sat down next to him on the bed. It made sense—sort of. At the very least, it explained why he always smelled vaguely of flowers.

It didn't explain *everything*, though. I knew in my gut that there was more to his story.

But wasn't there always more to everyone's story around here? To survive in Dorothy's Oz, a person had to have their secrets. I would let Pete keep his.

For now.

"How did you get back here?" he asked me. "*Why* are you back here, after what almost happened? Who disguised you? Who are you working for?"

He took my hand in his and clasped it tight, but I looked away. If Pete could have his secrets, I could have mine, too.

"Long story," I said.

Pete frowned, but I didn't care. I was just giving him a taste of his own medicine.

"I have time," he said.

"Good. That means you have time to tell me about the Wizard," I replied, reminding myself to stay focused on my mission.

Pete bit his lip. "Okay," he said, disappointment in his voice. "If that's what you want to talk about."

"Spill it," I commanded.

"There's not a lot to tell," he said, averting his eyes. "I don't know a lot about the Wizard. No one does."

I pulled my hand away and placed it in my lap. Star was racing around the room, sniffing everything. "Tell me what you *do* know, then. Why is he here? What happened? What's his deal?"

Pete paused like he was trying to decide how much was safe to say, and then nodded. "There are different theories. The Wizard

left in his balloon just before Dorothy used magic to go home.
You know that part of the story."

I nodded.

"For a while he was gone. And then he wasn't. That's where
it gets a little hazy."

"Someone brought him back?"

"Maybe. Or maybe the balloon never took him home at all.
No one really knows. What we do know is that somewhere along
the way, he spent some time with the witches. That's how he
became a *real* wizard instead of a fake one."

I jerked my face toward him in surprise. "What witches?"

"The ones who are left—the ones Dorothy didn't kill. Not
counting Glinda, obviously, though her twin sister is one of
them. Their leader's a witch named Mombi. Anyway, between
the time the Wizard left and the time he showed up back at the
palace, she and the Wizard became allies. They aren't anymore,
though. He came back to the palace pretty soon after Dorothy
returned. Apparently he and Mombi had a falling out."

Now *this* was getting interesting. Still, I kept my face expres-
sionless. I didn't want him to know that I knew Mombi or any of
the other witches.

"I talked to the Wizard today," I said. "He was weird. He caught
me doing . . . something, but I don't think he cared. I think he
might know who I am."

Pete's eyebrows raised. "It's possible," he said. "The Wizard
always seems to know more than everyone else. It has something
to do with the kind of magic he uses. It's different from the usual

Oz magic. He's a real wizard now. The question is what *kind* of wizard he is."

Exactly. The usual question: Good or Wicked?

"Dorothy doesn't trust him," Pete continued. "But she thinks she can use him. I don't even know if the Wizard himself knows whose side he's on."

"What if he's figured me out?" I asked. "What if he tells Dorothy what he saw?"

Pete twisted his mouth in thought. "I don't think he'd do that," he said. "But I'd stay away from him if I were you."

I nodded, but I wasn't so sure. What if the Wizard was supposed to be my contact here in the palace? His arrival pretty much synchronized with mine, and if everyone believed he'd had a falling out with Mombi that could make for good cover. There was still so much I didn't know.

"What about Ozma?" I asked. "I saw her, too. I think it was the real Ozma, not one of her holograms."

Pete's face twitched, just barely, but enough for me to notice. "She's around. I've never met her. She's not herself—Dorothy did something to her. Listen, just ignore her. That's what everyone else does."

"She kissed me," I said.

"That sounds like Ozma," he said. "She's in her own little world. It's kind of sad."

Suddenly his eyes glazed over. His hands trembled at his sides. He tried to shove them in his pockets.

"Pete?" He began to flicker.

"I have to go."

Before I could stop him, Pete slipped out the door and into the hallway. He didn't even say good-bye.

At my feet, Star tittered and scratched. I picked her up and snuggled her against my chest, sighing.

"Well," I said to my loyal pet rat, "at least I have one ally here I can trust."

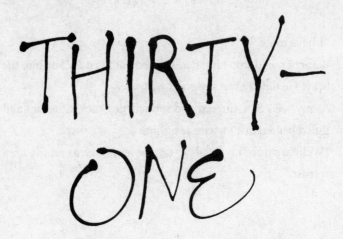

THIRTY-ONE

"How about you carry a poison capsule in your little jaws and drop it into her mint julep? Think you could pull that off?"

Star stared at me, then scratched my chest with her tiny claws and went back to sleep. I guess she wasn't into my idea.

It was early the next morning. I hadn't slept well and had spent most of the night tossing and turning, much to Star's chittering annoyance, and now I was up before the magic bell at my bedside had even summoned me to my chores.

I sighed and plucked Star from my body, placing her back on the bed. As I pulled on a clean uniform, I couldn't help rolling my eyes at the prospect of another day of redundant chores. The mysteries around the palace—Ozma, the Wizard, Pete—were piling up, but I still wasn't any closer to figuring out a way to kill Dorothy. How many days of boring housework would I have to put up with before the Order made contact? If I wasn't careful, way more careful than I'd been yesterday in the solarium, it wouldn't matter. I'd be back in the dungeon.

Turning to face the mirror, I checked myself for presentability and then searched my still-strange face, looking for a sign of what Pete had seen in it—the thing that had tipped him off that I wasn't who I appeared to be. I found nothing.

I almost jumped out of my shoes at a knock on the door.

Now *this* was new—before, if someone had needed me, they summoned me with the magic bell. No one had ever knocked on the door before.

"Just a moment!" I called out nervously, grabbing Star and shoving her under my bed. "Stay," I whispered urgently. She seemed to get the picture.

When I saw Jellia waving cheerily at me from the other side of the threshold, I stifled my surprise. Maybe she did a weekly inspection of the maids' quarters. If so, I hoped Star would have the rat-smarts to stay out of sight.

"Astrid!" she chirped. "How pretty you look! And aren't you just the luckiest girl in the world today?"

I fixed a robotic grin across my face. "Every day is lucky when you work for Dorothy," I replied.

Jellia chuckled. If she sensed my complete lack of sincerity, she didn't let on about it. "Now that's the attitude we like around here," she said. "But today's luckier than most, dear—you have a very special assignment. You're going to help me prepare Dorothy for her activities. How does it feel to be the new second handmaid?"

I stepped back in genuine surprise. "Me? Dorothy's new lady-in-waiting?"

"Yes, *you*, you silly goose," Jellia said. "Don't act so surprised! You've been here longer than almost anyone, and you've proven yourself just as loyal and lovely as any of us. Now come—we don't want to keep Her Highness waiting."

"But what about Hannah?" I asked, following Jellia down the hall at a businesslike clip. As of yesterday at lunch, Hannah had been the second handmaid. She hadn't been in her seat at dinner, but I'd just assumed Dorothy had needed her for something. What had happened to her?

Jellia looked over at me and shook her head sadly. "Hannah is in the infirmary," she said. "She won't be returning to service in the palace."

That didn't sound good. I put a hand to my chest, trying to mask my curiosity with sisterly concern. "What happened to her? Will she be okay?"

"Unfortunately, the Lion took a liking to her. *Too* much of a liking." She sighed. "It wasn't the poor thing's fault—the Lion has always had appetite issues. There was nothing Hannah could have done."

"Did he . . . eat her?" Images of Gert melting on the floor of the forest clearing back in Gillikin flew into my head. She had died trying to protect me. To protect all of us. Meanwhile, the Lion was still alive, maiming guards and running around attacking innocent servant girls for no reason.

"Well—not *all* of her," Jellia said. Her smile had never wavered. "She'll be fine in no time, and after she recovers enough, the Scarecrow will repair her body. She'll be better than ever. She's actually quite pleased. It's an honor to enter the service of the Tin Soldiers."

Pleased. Sure. I was burning with anger. Being mauled by a lion and becoming one of the Scarecrow's gruesome science projects was supposed to be an *honor* now? As the heat rose in my chest, I felt my invisible knife again, pulsing along with my heartbeat somewhere inside my body. It wanted to come out. It wanted to do some damage. I willed it away.

"Is the Lion still here? In the palace?"

"No," Jellia replied as we turned a corner and headed up the grand staircase toward Dorothy's quarters. "Glinda decided it would be best for him to return to the forest for the time being. We don't want another incident, and he hasn't been himself since—" Suddenly she stopped herself.

"Since what?" I'd wondered if he'd been affected by what Gert had done to him in the woods but I couldn't see anything specific the day I saw him in the garden.

She looked away. "Never mind that. Aren't you excited about your new assignment?"

I *was* excited, but not for the reasons Jellia thought I should be. I was scared, too. Getting close to Dorothy was part of my mission, but this was all happening so quickly.

I knew from listening to the other girls at mealtime that being one of Dorothy's ladies-in-waiting was a coveted position, reserved only for the most cheerful and pliable of the servants.

"Why me?" I asked.

"You've impressed the princess over the years. And you've

impressed *me*." Jellia lowered her voice and leaned in close. "You work well under pressure, dear. You'll need that."

I thought about our encounter with the Tin Woodman in the tight confines of the garden annex. I assumed Jellia had blocked that incident out, stored it down in her special utility closet of denial. Apparently, it made more of an impression than I thought.

"That, and . . ." Jellia glanced over at me, sidelong, "the Wizard also put in a good word for you."

I stopped in my tracks. "The Wizard?"

"Oh yes. He came to me just last night and told me how pleased he was with your dusting. True, the Wizard is always full of compliments, but not usually when it comes to housekeeping. You must have made quite the impression. I thought it was only fair that you get your chance."

"I was just doing my job," I said, still not sure what to make of all this. Was the Wizard trying to help me? Was he working for the Order, helping me make my way into Dorothy's inner sanctum?

Jellia turned to me and looked me up and down, mistaking my confusion for reluctance. "If you aren't up for this, Astrid, I'm sure any of the other girls would jump at the chance."

"No, of course I am. It's just—poor Hannah."

"This isn't the time for mourning. We go on," she scolded. "We only have one job, and that's to please Dorothy."

Yeah, Jellia kinda needed a slap. But all these maids were so brainwashed, I couldn't fault her for being callous.

We arrived at the door to Dorothy's private chambers. It was green and heavy and gaudy as hell, carved from solid emerald and etched with an ornate floral pattern, the grooves lined with gold and jewels.

Jellia gave me a last once-over before we entered.

"Here," she said, digging into the pocket of her apron and pulling out a little gold pot. "We're not really supposed to use it, but just a little bit won't hurt." She unscrewed the lid and held it out to me.

I cautiously dipped my finger inside and came back with a glob of shimmering, greasy stuff that reminded me of lip gloss. Indigo's face popped into my head and I closed my eyes for a second, remembering what she'd told me about it. I smeared it across my lips, feeling a tingle as the PermaSmile took effect. It wasn't exactly comfortable—it felt like the corners of my mouth were being held apart by clothespins—but I guessed that was better than accidentally letting Dorothy see me frown.

I returned the canister to Jellia and she took a little for herself, refreshing her smile before placing the goop back in her apron. When her hand came back out, she handed me a silver hairbrush.

"Remember—it's a thousand strokes. Not a thousand and one and not nine hundred ninety-nine. Don't lose count. Dorothy will know. She always does—we've lost more than one girl that way. If there's one thing to say about Hannah, it's that she certainly *could* count."

Jellia knocked on the door and, after getting no response, pushed it open. As she entered, she looked over her shoulder and whispered back at me with one more bit of advice. "Whatever you do," she said, "don't touch the shoes."

Dorothy's room was wall-to-wall pink. Pepto-Bismol pink, cotton-candy pink, sunset pink, and every nauseating shade in between. A canopied bed was encircled with pink silken drapes; the floor was wall-to-wall pink shag carpet; and the ceiling overhead was covered in what looked like pink rhinestones that would probably make you go blind if you stared at them too long.

If Madison Pendleton ever made it to Oz, I thought, she could probably get a job as Dorothy's personal interior decorator.

In the center of the room, a few feet from the bed, some kind of green powder had been sprinkled onto the carpet in a wide circle. Inside it, a little black terrier was racing around in excitement, chasing his own tail.

I knew exactly who *that* was. Toto. When he spotted us, he bared his tiny teeth at me and growled.

Jellia stepped carefully around him. I did the same, and as I did, Toto lunged at me but hit an invisible barrier. Undaunted, he got back up on his little feet and tried again. I jumped, despite myself.

"Don't mind him," Jellia said, waving her hand. "He's having another time-out. He's a sweet little thing, but he sometimes has problems controlling himself."

It was no surprise that Dorothy's little dog was as vicious as she was. As for Dorothy herself, though, she was nowhere to be found.

Jellia pulled the fluffy bedspread a hair tighter as she passed by. "Yoo-hoo!" she singsonged. "Your Majesty!"

There was no response.

"She's probably in her favorite place," Jellia said, pulling open a door.

Calling it a *closet* was an understatement. It was as big as one of the caves back in the Order. There were dresses, mini and maxi, corseted and flowy, and ball gowns and short-shorts and skinny pants. The clothes were endless in their variety, but they all had one thing in common: they all bore a familiar, blue-checked print.

When I reached out and ran my fingers against the fabric of a checkered jumpsuit, it dislodged itself from the others and floated out ahead of us as if it were being worn by an invisible model. I touched a hat next, and it joined the dress on its strut down the runway.

Jellia gave me a sharp glance and touched both items, launching them right back to their original spots. I grimaced in silent apology.

We continued through the closet with no Dorothy in sight. Besides Her Royal Awfulness, there was something else that was conspicuously absent amidst the rows and rows of clothes: there wasn't a single pair of shoes.

We finally found Dorothy in the back, stretched out on a chaise covered in pink paisley swirls. She was wearing a long, silk robe—still in that blue gingham pattern—and the toes of her red heels poked out from underneath it.

Even in her pajamas, she never took them off. Did she *sleep* in them?

"You're late," Dorothy said icily, looking up from a fashion magazine called *Her Majesty*. Her own face PermaSmiled at me from the cover.

"I'm sorry, ma'am," Jellia said, casting her eyes to the floor. "There was a disturbance with one of the other maids. Astrid here will be taking Hannah's place."

Dorothy glowered at me. "Can she count?"

"She's a wonderful counter," Jellia said. I nodded in agreement, but Dorothy had already stopped caring. She threw her head back and stretched, clapping her hands together.

"Where are we on the guest list for the ball?" she demanded.

"Everyone who's anyone will be there," Jellia asserted. "Jinjur, Polychrome. I even heard from Scraps, the Patchwork Girl."

Dorothy frowned, like she wasn't all that impressed with her guest list. Well, maybe if she weren't always exiling and executing people, they would want to come to her parties.

"Whatever," Dorothy snapped, and pointed to the tray of nail polish that was sitting on a small vanity in the corner. "Anna. Nail polish."

It took me a second—and a look from Jellia—to figure out that *Anna* meant me. I nodded shyly and brought the tray over, wondering where I was supposed to put it. Jellia just tapped it quickly and it floated right out of my hands, hanging steady in the air.

"What would you like today?" Jellia asked, surveying the rainbow of polishes. I was happy to see that at least when it came to her manicures Dorothy had a sense of variety. There must have been at least a hundred different colors.

Dorothy sat up and swung her feet to the ground. As she did, her shoes made a ruby-red comet's tail through the air. I had to stifle a gasp. It was like they were glowing from the inside, like they wanted me to notice them.

Jellia and Dorothy were prattling on, deciding on the best nail art for the day—*stripes or swirls or sparkles?* They sounded like they were talking from the end of a long tunnel. I couldn't take my eyes off the shoes. I was transfixed.

So beautiful. So shiny. So perfect.

Whoa, get a grip, Amy.

I'd taken pride in wearing the same ratty pair of knockoff Converse since freshman year. They were broken in, comfortable, and something the Madison Pendletons of the world wouldn't wear in a million years. I'd never given a crap about shoes before, especially not the bedazzled variety. So why now? Something wasn't right.

Even as I reasoned with myself, the glow from the shoes intensified. I realized they were shining just for me, that Dorothy and Jellia couldn't see them, not like I could. They were calling to me.

A numbness spread over the skeptical part of my mind.

I wondered what it would be like to have people wait on me the way we were waiting on Dorothy. What it would be like to have a closet full of dresses. What it would be like to have power.

Power that came from those shoes.

I want them, I thought. *I need them.*

I should just take them.

I was vaguely aware of my body moving, my hands clenching

and unclenching. Slowly, I reached toward Dorothy's feet.

"Astrid," Jellia warned, yanking my elbow back.

I ignored her. I wanted those shoes.

"*Astrid!*" she said again, this time angrily. She snapped her fingers right in my face, tearing my eyes away from Dorothy's feet. I blinked. Looking up at Jellia, I felt like myself again, and I knew that the shoes had been doing something to me.

Jellia just glared, as if to say *Didn't I warn you?*

Dorothy was busy holding up a bottle of polish to the light, thinking about her impending manicure. When I glanced in her direction, I saw her eyes narrow and her mouth twitch up in the tiniest sneer. Had she noticed? Did she know what her shoes were doing?

"Astrid," Jellia ordered firmly, "the princess needs her hair brushed."

"One thousand strokes exactly!" Dorothy snapped, still not looking up at me.

I took a deep breath and moved behind her. I grabbed the brush from my pocket and pulled it slowly through Dorothy's thick auburn locks. Her hair smelled like lemons and sunshine. I expected there to be a rotten note underneath, but there wasn't. It was all sweetness and light. *This is what evil smells like*, I realized.

One, two, three, four . . . I counted silently, being careful not to yank too hard when I hit a rare tangle. It was actually sort of relaxing—I felt much better now that I had something to focus on other than the shoes.

"Let's do the hearts," Dorothy finally decided. "Use the pink glitter. Blue for the base." She extended her hands to Jellia and I realized that there was something gnarled about them. The rest of Dorothy was perfect, but her hands looked like an old woman's.

Jellia pulled up a stool and picked out the first color. Dorothy began to hum a low waltz under her breath while Jellia got to work.

Jellia was an artist. Her fingers moved delicately and quickly over Dorothy's nails, tracing the outlines of tiny hearts without even the tiniest mistake. Still, you could tell it wasn't easy. Jellia's brow crinkled in concentration and it quickly began to shine with sweat as she worked.

"Tell me the gossip," Dorothy demanded. "No one ever tells me anything. There must be something interesting going on in this palace of mine. I know you know. The servants always do."

"Let me think," Jellia said. As she spoke, she glanced up at me, probably to check on my progress. I was at two hundred. I met her eyes, flashed her a reassuring smile, and then nearly nicked the back of Dorothy's ear with the brush.

Dorothy didn't even notice, she just went on humming her stupid waltz. But Jellia did, flinching on my behalf at the close call. That's how it happened.

Jellia's hand slipped. A drop of nail polish fell from the brush. I watched it go, as if in slow motion.

The sparkly pink polish landed in a blob on the pink carpet.

Dorothy shrieked.

The thing is, the polish almost matched the color of the

carpet. Even if it wouldn't come out, it was just a tiny little drop. No one would notice. But Dorothy would know.

"You idiot!" she screamed.

Jellia didn't move. Her lips twitched at the corners of her frozen smile. "Princess Dorothy—Your Highness—I am so *very* sorry. It . . ."

She dropped to her knees in panic, dabbing frantically at the carpet with a handkerchief to blot out her mistake. But Dorothy put her hand out to halt the maid.

"Don't. You'll just smear it and make it worse."

Jellia looked up, eyes impossibly wide above her frozen smile. But Dorothy was over it. Sort of. She shook her head.

"Should I send for soap and water?" Jellia asked. "I'm certain I can have it out in a moment."

"Soap and water," Dorothy repeated, snorting. She muttered something under her breath and a sizzle of energy sparked from her fingertips. The minuscule stain instantly disappeared. "The atrocious mess is not the point, Jellia. The point is that you were careless. Very careless. I'm used to better from you."

"I'm sorry," Jellia repeated, still trembling, sitting back down on her stool. "So *very* sorry. I can't imagine what came over me."

I swallowed. In a way, Jellia was covering for me. I'd distracted her.

Dorothy's voice suddenly filled with syrupy kindness. "Oh, Jellia, dear. You can't cry over a little spilled nail polish. I'll think of *some* way for you to make it up to me."

I resumed my brushing. *Two hundred and one.* I hadn't forgotten my place. Jellia picked up the bottle of polish. I expected her to be relieved, but she was still quivering.

"I'll just need to think of the appropriate punishment," Dorothy said.

"Yes, Your Highness."

"I wonder what it should be. . . ."

Jellia's hand was shaking so much that she had to put the bottle down again.

"Did I tell you to stop?" Dorothy asked. Jellia's eyes widened and she picked the bottle back up to continue. Her mouth was still stretched ear to ear but the rest of her face was crumpled in terror.

This was what Dorothy did to people. I had known Dorothy was cruel, but the joy she took in her cruelty filled me with disgust.

I thought of Madison Pendleton and all her minions, the people who had taken the same delight in tormenting me back in school. I thought of Gert, and of Indigo, and of Ollie hanging from the little post by the side of the road. I thought of all the new orphans in the village of Pumperdink.

Then another thought came to me. It seemed so clear. I hadn't heard from the Order since I'd gotten here. Maybe they'd forgotten about me. Regardless, I was within clear cutting distance. What if this was my best chance? If I was going to kill someone, I needed to be in control, and not rely on someone else to tell me when the time was right. Nox had made that mistake in the woods—he'd waited for Gert and Mombi before attacking the Lion, and look where that had gotten us. It had gotten Gert killed.

I could do it now. Dorothy was distracted, completely absorbed with punishing Jellia. She would never see it coming. She wouldn't even have time to scream.

My heart was racing, but I took a deep breath. I didn't pause in my brushing. *Three hundred and seven.*

I shifted positions ever so slightly and dropped my free hand out of Jellia's line of sight, just behind Dorothy's back. My knife materialized in my hand, its warmth spreading up through my arm.

I wrapped my fingers tightly around it. No one had noticed. I was inches away from her neck. Without even consciously casting a spell, I heard Dorothy's blood pulsing through her veins.

I had the bitch right where I wanted her.

I pulled my elbow back and raised the knife so that it was just a centimeter from Dorothy's spine. Would it be quicker to slit her throat or stab her in the back?

I hesitated. A moment ago, I'd been possessed by a pair of pretty shoes. Was that happening again? Were they controlling me right now? No. I *wanted* to kill Dorothy. I could undo everything she'd done, return the beauty and magic to Oz, create a happily ever after. It was all just one blade stroke and one seriously ruined carpet away.

Was I ready, though? Was I ready to be Amy the Assassin? God knows Dorothy deserved it, but—

Dorothy let out a high-pitched, ear-shattering scream that rustled the rows of dresses. She jumped up from her chaise, knocking it over. The brush snagged on her hair and flew out of my hand. I froze, unsure whether to hide the knife or lunge forward and stab her.

"Guards!" she bellowed.

Shit, shit, shit, I thought in panic. I made a split-second decision—maid or assassin—and willed the knife to disappear. I was pretty sure Jellia hadn't seen it. But had Dorothy? Had she sensed the magic? I decided playing dumb was the best option.

The Tin Woodman appeared in a burst of smoke, his ax poised to attack. "Your Majesty!" he said. "What's wrong?"

My eyes darted around, looking frantically for a way out, just in case Dorothy pointed a finger in my direction.

Instead, Dorothy had righted the chaise and climbed atop it, shaking, but also managing to delicately smooth out her robe. Jellia stared up at her in confusion and I followed her lead.

Dorothy could barely get out the words. "A—A," she stuttered. "There was a—" She pointed to the corner, and every muscle in my body relaxed when I saw that it wasn't me she had been reacting to. She had no idea I'd been about one second away from killing her.

"Catch it," she wheezed, pointing to the corner just in time for us to see a tiny brown ball of fur streaking under the skirt of one of her floor-length gowns. "Kill it!" Dorothy screamed, jumping ridiculously from foot to foot.

A mouse. It was just a mouse.

The Tin Woodman looked at Dorothy with concern. "Of course, my princess," he said, with something approaching actual tenderness in his voice. He stepped forward and began to carefully pull the clothes aside. "I can't imagine how upsetting this must be for you."

"No," Dorothy said. She reached out blindly, found the top of my head, and used it for balance as she lowered herself back onto the chaise. Her fear seemed to have suddenly twisted into something else. "Not you."

"Princess?" the Tin Woodman asked, confused.

Dorothy thrust a long, half-manicured nail at Jellia. "You. You catch it."

The maid's face was stoic. "Yes, ma'am," she said quietly. Jellia dropped to her hands and knees and began to crawl across the floor, disappearing behind the dresses. We all watched her.

"Did I tell you to stop, Amanda?" Dorothy snapped. "My hair's not going to brush itself, now is it?"

I picked up the brush. *Three hundred and twenty-eight.* I didn't even know *what* I was feeling anymore as I went back to work. *Three hundred and twenty-nine.*

The garments rustled and every now and then we caught a glimpse of Jellia as she searched, but ninety strokes of the brush later she still hadn't emerged. Dorothy, the Tin Woodman, and I all watched intently.

"It would be an honor if you let me catch the foul creature," the Tin Woodman suggested finally. "With my speed and training, it would take me no time at all."

"No, you'll get oil on my dresses," Dorothy said irritably. "I guess I have to do *everything* around here."

Even with a concerted effort not to look directly at them,

I noticed that Dorothy's shoes were glittering brighter than before. She twirled a finger in the air and a pink bubble materialized at the tip of her nail.

"Come on out, Jellia," she ordered, "now that you've disappointed me on every possible level."

After a few tense seconds Jellia emerged on her hands and knees and crawled back toward us, her face ashen but still PermaSmiling eerily, her hair messy and matted with sweat.

"Stay," Dorothy commanded. Jellia froze on her hands and knees.

Dorothy gave a little flick and the pink bubble went spinning. It twisted and darted in the air the same way Nox's tracing charm had, back in the forest outside Pumperdink the night that Gert died. After a few seconds, it zipped into the pink folds of the closet and, not thirty seconds later, returned, now rolling along the ground. Inside the glowing bubble-gum orb, a tiny mouse barely bigger than my thumb squirmed and scratched.

Four hundred and ninety-nine. I kept on brushing. The ball spun across the carpet right up to where Jellia still knelt.

The maid looked up at Dorothy in fearful anticipation.

"Pick it up," Dorothy said.

Without rising to her feet, Jellia complied, and as she did, the bubble faded away, leaving just the mouse in her hand.

"Now kill it," Dorothy said.

Jellia paused, looking down at the mouse's little face. "But Dorothy. Your Majesty—"

"Do it."

"How?"

Even the Tin Woodman seemed a little confused as he looked on. He cocked his head curiously and swung his ax over his shoulder, waiting to hear what the princess had in mind.

Dorothy giggled girlishly. "Oh, Jellia," she said. "I *knew* you were stupid but I didn't know you were *that* stupid. I mean, all you have to do is squeeze."

"But . . . ," Jellia said.

"Jellia, it's you or the mouse," Dorothy said, the sweet, girly tone gone from her voice and replaced by an icy coldness.

I wanted to look away, but I couldn't. Dorothy's favorite maid took a deep breath, closed her eyes, and made a fist around the little animal. She clenched it tight and, as she did, I heard a single squeal. Her eyebrows scrunched together in distress.

"Make sure he's dead," Dorothy instructed.

Jellia clenched tighter. A trickle of blood spilled out from between her fingers, but she placed her other hand underneath in time to catch it before it hit the carpet.

"Good girl," Dorothy cooed. "See? Was that so bad?"

Jellia opened her fist, where the mouse lay inert, now just a little ball of fur and blood. "Where should I . . . what should I do with it?" she asked in a strangled voice.

"You have pockets in that frock of yours, don't you?" Dorothy asked. "I want you to hold on to it. To remind you of what happens when you disappoint me the way you did today. As well as to make sure I never see one of those disgusting creatures in my palace again."

Without a word, Jellia took the mouse's little corpse and placed it in the front of her apron. Dorothy applauded in delight.

"Wonderful. All is well. Now go wash those hands. I can't have any mouse guts on my nails, now can I?"

Jellia stood and left the room, and Dorothy let out a little giggle.

"She's lucky I didn't make her eat it," she said, and looked directly at me for the first time. "Isn't that right, Alison?"

I nodded mutely, literally biting my tongue. The Tin Woodman chuckled adoringly.

Five hundred sixty, I counted off in my head, trying to keep my temper in check. I should've stabbed her.

THIRTY-TWO

The next morning, I held Star extra close before depositing her safely in one of my bureau drawers. My mother's rat wasn't happy about being confined, but now that I knew how Dorothy reacted to rodents, I wasn't taking any chances. I couldn't let her run around free.

A night's fitful sleep hadn't helped me shake the events of yesterday. Could I have actually done it—could I really have sliced Dorothy's throat? I had been ready—or so I thought. Why did I hesitate? Was I that weak?

I told myself that I didn't want to ruin the Order's plans—they'd told me to wait—but I knew that wasn't entirely it. I'd chickened out.

I slammed out of my room, frustrated with myself, and headed off to meet Jellia. We had an appointment to go through my new duties as Dorothy's second handmaid.

When I found her in the empty banquet hall, Jellia was more distracted than I'd ever seen her. Unruly strands stuck up on her normally perfectly coiffed hair; her smile flickered every now and then into something *almost* like a frown.

Also, she smelled. Like, *really* smelled. She was still carrying around the poor little mouse's body in her apron and apparently it was starting to decompose in there, giving her a foul, rotten stench that turned my stomach.

Worse yet, the first thing she told me was that there had been a change of plans. I'd already been demoted.

Her tone was impossible to read when she said it. "After yesterday's debacle, Astrid, the princess has decided that you are not the best girl for the job."

My heart sank. That was the last time I would brush Dorothy's hair, the last time I would find myself in her royal chambers with a clear shot. Had I wasted my best opportunity to kill her? Had she realized that's what I'd been about to do, after all? I was back to square one. No path to Dorothy, no contact from the Order, and no sign of Pete.

Would I be stuck here forever, abandoned by the Order, and fully transformed into Astrid? Gradually, I'd stop being afraid of being found out and transition into the other maids' perpetual state of Dorothy-induced anxiety. Amy would be gone and I'd just be another blank-slate maid, stuck in a place somehow more monotonous and horrific than Kansas.

I returned to my mind-numbing chores. Scrubbing floors, sweeping, hand washing an endless supply of gingham skirts that I could swear hadn't even been worn. And then, as if my day wasn't already gloomy enough, the sun went down a little after midday.

"It's the party," one of the other maids told me during our break. "Her Highness needs all the beauty rest she can get before the big day. We should just be thankful she turned the Great Clock at all."

So now sunlight was dictated by the condition of Dorothy's skin. Perfect.

The day—or night, I suppose—wore on. As I went about my work, I found my anger growing. Yesterday, it'd been Dorothy and her psycho actions that had set off my temper. Today, it was the people who'd convinced me this was a good idea in the first place—Glamora, Gert, especially Nox—and left me stranded in this horrible place where the sun didn't even shine anymore. Weren't they worried about me? How much of this did they expect me to endure?

As I aggressively dusted the lamps in Dorothy's reading room, Jellia and her stench swung by.

"It's time for the Scarecrow's hay delivery," she said, keeping her distance, probably self-conscious about her own odor. "Run that up, would you?"

I grunted a yes. I hadn't seen the Scarecrow since that first night. He'd been locked away in his laboratory, working on this hush-hush experiment, his finest work according to the Wizard. The maids had been taking turns lugging his daily bales up to his room and leaving them outside his door. The bales were starting to pile up. I imagined the Scarecrow—shriveled and wrinkled from not stuffing himself—and shuddered.

The bale was heavy, but after all my training with Nox it felt good to do something a little more physical than dusting. By the time I'd ascended halfway to the Scarecrow's chambers, my palms were raw from the bale's wire handle and a sheen of sweat had spread down my back. When I finally reached the top, I dropped the bale with a thud, preparing to push it the rest of the way down the hall. That's when I noticed something that didn't quite fit.

Outside the door to the Scarecrow's room, an exceptionally short, dark-haired maid seemed to be fiddling with the doorknob. I didn't recognize her. Was she new? Hadn't she been warned not to enter the Scarecrow's space without permission?

I left the bale and rushed down the hall. If the Scarecrow came back, this Munchkin girl would be his next experiment. I'd seen enough maids tortured this week, thank you very much.

"Hey," I hissed. "What're you doing?"

Startled, the maid turned her head in my direction. I skidded to a stop just a few feet away. That wasn't a maid at all.

It was a monkey clumsily disguised in a maid's uniform. And it wasn't a *she* any more than she was a maid.

She was Ollie. His face was no longer gaunt and blistered and the hair had grown in over his scarred wrists. He had put on a little weight. He was wearing a dress.

"On a special mission from the Scarecrow," Ollie growled at me. "Go find something else to clean."

I could tell he was lying. A half smile played on Ollie's face—mischievous and sad all at once—like I was just another puppet maid to be brushed off and pitied. He went back to his tinkering and a second later the door popped open with a click. Ollie waddled inside, not seeming to care that I'd caught him picking the lock.

"Ollie, wait—!"

Before the door could slam shut, I slipped in after him.

As soon as the door closed, a cyclone of fur sprung at me, Ollie's feet slamming into my chest and knocking me backward onto the filthy, junk-strewn floor of the Scarecrow's room. Before I could recover myself, he was crouched on top of me, pinning my arms down.

"Don't scream," he hissed, his angry face inches from mine. "I don't want to hurt you, but I will if I have to."

"What are you doing?" I whispered back. "It's me."

I realized how stupid I was being. I had been so excited to see him alive that I'd forgotten what I looked like. Ollie had no way of recognizing me in my borrowed face. It'd been so long, he might not have even remembered me as I used to look.

"Just keep your mouth shut," he said. "I'm here for some information and then I'll be on my way. If you know what's good for you, you'll pretend this never happened."

I couldn't suppress a smile. Even after all this, it was still hard to get used to a talking monkey, and it was even harder to take him seriously when he was wearing a dress. I could have screamed with joy. Who cared that his claws were digging into my arms so hard that they were going to leave bruises? Ollie was alive! Not only that, he was up to something. Anyone breaking into the Scarecrow's chambers was a friend of mine.

I could have flipped him over and freed myself without much effort. Even with his monkey strength and reflexes, I was certain he wasn't half the fighter I'd become. It made me proud to think about, but I didn't struggle. I didn't want to escalate the situation and risk a real fight where either one of us could get hurt. I nodded like the milquetoast maid I was supposed to be.

Ollie's grip slackened for a moment, but then his monkey brow wrinkled as if realizing something. His brown eyes narrowed into slits and his grip intensified.

"You said my name," he said with a menacing growl. "How do you know me?"

"I—" My mind raced. Did I dare break my cover? The last time I'd seen Ollie, he was bailing on me and Indigo. I didn't blame him for running, but it didn't exactly recommend him as trustworthy.

Before I could come up with a suitable lie, Ollie leaned down and sniffed my neck. When he lifted his face up, he looked totally confused.

"You smell like—" I realized he was trying to place my scent.

I thought of Star; she had recognized me immediately. I hadn't questioned why at the time—I'd figured it was just some animal owner sixth sense, but something else was even more likely. My Astrid disguise didn't change my Amy scent.

"The girl from the road?" Ollie asked, a baffled look on his face. "The one who saved me?"

Screw it. I nodded. "Amy," I reminded him.

"You look different," he said, still not totally sold, still not releasing my arms.

"It's a disguise," I replied. "And it's a hell of a lot better than yours, by the way."

Ollie replied with a toothy grin that would've put even the most habitual PermaSmile users to shame.

"Amy the Outlander! But how . . . ?"

Ollie sprung off me and I rose to my feet. Before I was even all the way up, the monkey's strong, furry arms were wrapped tight around my waist—so tight I could barely breathe.

"I'm sorry I ran off on you," he panted. "It wasn't my best moment."

"It's okay, Ollie." I patted him on the head and he slowly released me, stepping back and looking me up and down. "Where have you been?" I asked. "How did you get away?"

"I made it to the Dark Jungle," he said. "There's a group of Wingless Ones there, and they've started a small resistance among the animals."

"Like the Order," I said, musing out loud.

He shook his furry head. "No," he said sharply. "*Not* like the Order."

"What's wrong with the Order?" I asked in surprise.

"They can't be trusted. What's the difference between a wicked witch and an evil princess? Are you working with them?"

"There're a lot of differences," I said defensively. He looked at me suspiciously. "They trained me. They taught me magic. I can fight now. I'm going to change things. We could join forces and—"

"Never," he cut me off firmly. "We recognize what the Order is doing. But we have been enslaved too many times. We have known witches and wizards, and we will not be bound to anyone."

Bound. I was bound, too—Mombi had used that very word to describe it. But that wasn't why I was here. I was no one's slave, and I was acting of my own free will.

Wasn't I?

I let the question go for now.

"Why are you here?" I asked. "Are you looking for your parents?"

"My parents would turn me over to Dorothy the second they saw me."

"Then why?" I waved at our surroundings, thinking of their sadistic owner. "You know you're nuts breaking in here, right?"

"I don't have a choice," Ollie replied. "It's my sister. Maude. She's here somewhere. The Scarecrow has her."

"Is your sister . . . ?"

He answered my question before it was out of my mouth. "She's a traitor, too—one of the ones who kept their wings. But she's still my sister. I can't let him have her. I can't let him . . ." His eyes glistened as his voice trailed off.

I knelt down to Ollie's level and grabbed his hands in mine. I squeezed them tight. "What does he want from her?" I asked urgently.

"I don't know," Ollie replied. "The Wingless Ones have our spies in the palace, but all they were able to tell us is that she was taken. That the Scarecrow has plans for her."

"What kind of plans?" I asked, thinking of the big experiment the Scarecrow was hard at work on.

Ollie looked down at his little red patent-leather slippers. They matched mine, right down to the square, gold buckles.

"Maude was always special," he said slowly. "A genius. The smartest monkey our kind had ever seen. Maybe smarter than the Scarecrow himself. It's possible . . ."

"He wants her brains," I said.

Ollie nodded, shaking loose from my hands and clenching his fists. "She tried to convince me to stay—to keep my wings and become Dorothy's slave. She thought that compromising was our best chance for survival. For the first time in our lives, I was right and she was wrong. Those who have sacrificed always have the most to lose," he said.

Frustrated, Ollie pounded his fists against the floor, stirring up loose pieces of straw. I wanted to comfort him, to tell him everything was going to be okay. But how could I? For all I knew, Maude could already be dead, her liquefied brains jammed into one of the Scarecrow's needles.

Then something else occurred to me. *Those who have sacrificed always have the most to lose.*

"Ollie," I began carefully. "What does that mean? That thing you just said."

He looked at me blankly. "That is the motto of the Wingless Ones," he said. "To remind us how much we have sacrificed for others, and how much we have lost because of it. It reminds us that compromise is death—that we must remain free."

I let the words roll over in my head. Where had I heard them before?

Then I knew: the Wizard had used that exact phrase. It hadn't made any sense at the time—I'd had no idea what he was talking about. He had hinted that something terrible was going on in the lab. He had used the motto of the Wingless Ones. He had been trying to tell me something. But why? Whatever his reason, it definitely wasn't a coincidence.

Ollie paced across the Scarecrow's floor, gazing into the distance. "The last time I saw Maude, Dorothy had just handed down my punishment. She allowed the Winged Ones to confront me before I was taken to the field, to be strung up. Maude spit in my face and told me that she hoped my punishment would improve my thinking."

He winced as he told the story. I knew the feeling. Every unkind thing my mom had ever said to me was etched in my memory, too.

"Ollie—"

"My point is, it doesn't matter. It doesn't matter that she abandoned me. She's my sister. I won't abandon *her*. I need to find her. I don't care what the risk is."

I nodded. "All right," I said matter-of-factly, "I'll help."

It was a split-second decision, not something I really thought through. But I'd hesitated yesterday, with Dorothy right under my knife, and that'd just bought me another day of feeling useless. If I could strike a blow against Dorothy and her regime, no matter how small, I was going to do it. That was my new policy. Screw waiting around.

But Ollie shook his head. "No, it's not your fight. I have to do it myself."

"It may not be my fight," I replied. "But I know the palace better than you do, and I'm not a monkey wearing a dress. You'll get killed if you keep traipsing around like that."

"I wasn't *traipsing*."

"It was a miracle I spotted you instead of someone else." I shook my head, thinking about the Wizard, the serendipity of it all. "I have a better chance of finding Maude than you ever would."

An affronted look passed over his features, but then Ollie paused to consider it. "What would the Order say about this?" he asked. "What do they care about my little sister?"

He was right. I knew exactly what Nox would have said: that one winged monkey—no matter whose sister she was—wasn't worth risking my cover. That my mission was about something bigger and that nothing could get in the way of it.

Well, maybe all that was true. But they weren't here. They didn't understand what it was like to stand by and watch Dorothy's casual cruelty, to feel like a powerless coward hidden under a borrowed face. I was tired of waiting. I was my own person. Bound to the Order or not, I was still going to make my own decisions. And I felt deep down in my gut that this was the right one.

"The Wizard told me the Scarecrow is at work on something big. Something that could make everything the Order is fighting for irrelevant. They'll probably thank me for finding out what it is," I told Ollie, even though I knew it probably wasn't true. "If Maude's a part of it, I promise, I'll get her out."

Ollie scratched the top of his head. "I don't know. How will you even find her?"

"I haven't quite worked that out yet," I replied.

"No way," Ollie said, shaking his head. "You don't even have a plan and you want me to just leave? Abandon my sister? No way."

"You don't have a plan either," I reminded him. "And besides, I have this."

With a flourish, my dagger appeared in my hand. I stuck it under Ollie's chin and he held up his hands, eyes widening.

"Easy, Amy," he said, glancing down at the blade. "What's your, um, point?"

"My point is, you'll die," I replied. "You won't last another hour here unarmed and in that ridiculous outfit. I've got weapons, I'm trained, and I sort of blend in. I've got a way better chance of finding her than you."

"All right," Ollie grunted, gently placing his hand on top of mine and pushing my dagger away from his neck. "I get it."

I realized suddenly how long we'd been talking. Jellia would have noticed me missing by now.

"You should get out of here." I walked to the window and flung it open. "I promise I won't let you down."

I looked back at him. Ollie nodded slowly, admitting to himself that I was his best option. As he walked toward me, he pointed a furry finger toward my chest.

"I'll give you until midnight tomorrow," he growled. "The Wingless Ones have a secret entrance in the Royal Gardens. If you're not there, with my sister, I'm going back to Plan A——"

"Cross-dressing?"

Ollie grimaced. "You joke, but this is serious."

"I know," I replied, trying to sound confident. "I won't fail."

"Thank you," he said quietly when he was at my side. "You're the first kind human I've met since Dorothy took over."

Ollie stood on the toes of his servant's slippers and gave me a soft, tender peck on the cheek. Then he flung himself out the window, easily grabbing on to the branch of a nearby tree and scampering into the leafy cover, disappearing into the darkness of Dorothy's artificial night.

No more waiting. I had made a promise to myself that I would help Ollie. Now I had a chance to make good on it.

THIRTY-THREE

The first step of my plan was to get out of the rest of my chores.

I found Jellia in the banquet hall, scrubbing the floors on her hands and knees. Normally, sunlight spilled in through the hall's massive windows, but with night having already fallen, Jellia was forced to do her scrubbing by candlelight. Somehow, that made it even more depressing.

Before I approached, I took a few big whiffs of her dead-mouse stench—enough to make myself look queasy. Then, I staggered toward her, dragging my feet.

"Astrid," she snapped, looking up. "Where have you been?"

I draped a hand across my forehead. "I'm feeling ill," I told her. "My stomach . . ."

"This is no way to work yourself back up to second handmaid," Jellia lectured.

"I'm sorry," I pleaded, clutching my stomach. "But it's better for me to get my rest than to puke all over Dorothy's freshly cleaned carpets this close to the ball, isn't it?"

She tilted her head, knowing I had a point. She forced a smile and I saw that there was a small fleck of red lipstick on her teeth. It made me feel even sorrier for her than I already did.

"Fine," Jellia said. "But we need you tomorrow. Bright and early. No excuses."

I left the banquet hall practically doubled over, straightening up only when I was sure no one was watching. I didn't go back to my room like a loyal maid on the mend.

Instead, I headed for Dorothy's solarium.

I'd memorized the maids' schedule and knew the solarium had already been cleaned today. And, in cases of vanity-induced solar eclipses, you could always count on the room dedicated to sunlight being totally empty.

Nonetheless, I approached cautiously. I'd picked up a feather duster on my way here. This time, if I got busted—by the Wizard or anyone else—at least I'd have a plausible excuse. Just some extracurricular dusting around the magical artifacts.

The solarium was eerie in the early evening moonlight. The rainbow of lounges all appeared drained of color, like a furniture vampire had passed through. The dozens of floral arrangements that Dorothy demanded be changed weekly all drooped, their expected sunlight having never appeared.

Just as I'd hoped. It was empty.

I tiptoed across the room to Dorothy's magic picture. Currently, it depicted a sprawling poppy field under a starlit sky. It was beautiful, actually, the only thing in the solarium that didn't look washed out.

"Magic picture," I whispered. "Show me Maude."

Wherever Ollie's sister was being held, it was somewhere dark. I couldn't really even see her, only matted, sweat-slick fur that rippled with labored breathing. I could make out a set of leather straps holding her down on some kind of table. It looked pretty grim.

Well, I consoled myself, at least Maude was alive.

Then, I heard the Scarecrow. I jumped at the sound of his voice and whipped around, almost drawing my knife before realizing it was coming from the painting.

"These damn calculations," he muttered. "Why won't they just add up?"

A raven squawked in response.

"I know," the Scarecrow hissed at the bird. "They *will* all laugh at me. Call me stupid. Call me . . ."

He trailed off. I heard a rustling sound, the scratching of straw shifting around, and then the Scarecrow's wrinkled, felt-gloved hand gently caressing Maude's cheek. She didn't even have the strength to move away, although I could hear her breath catch with revulsion.

"Maude, my dear," he said musingly. "Do you ever get the feeling you're being watched?"

Did he feel me using the magic painting on him? It would make sense for the Scarecrow's laboratory to be warded somehow against magical invasions, especially since it was so hyper-secret.

I glanced over my shoulder, but the hallway outside was still quiet.

I thought for a moment. I wasn't sure if the Scarecrow had some kind of magical alarm system on his lab or if he was just paranoid—either way, I didn't want to risk it. And anyway, looking *inside* didn't help me find the lab's location.

"Magic picture," I whispered. "Show me the *outside* of the Scarecrow's lab."

The painting went gray for a second as if it was thinking, then one building on the palace grounds filled the entire frame.

The greenhouse. *Pete*'s greenhouse. Was the Scarecrow's lab somewhere in there?

As if in answer, one of the grotesque crows with the huge, human ears landed on the edge of the greenhouse's roof as I watched. Then I saw another one and then another, all of them flying from someplace behind the greenhouse.

"Magic picture," I whispered, morbidly curious. "Show me the way in."

With a lurching motion, the painting's image pushed through the front wall of the greenhouse, zooming past the rows of flowers and through a latched hidden door. There, partially hidden away behind a small grove of trees, was the biggest birdcage I'd ever seen. The gilded bars stretched up at least three stories high, and I could make out a flurry of black feathers rustling inside.

An aviary.

The ravens were circling and diving in and out of the cage. There were hundreds, maybe thousands of them, cawing and cackling, crowding every available perch, their human eyes bulging, their ears twitching. My stomach turned. It was disgusting.

The cawing was too loud. Someone in the palace would hear.

"Enough," I hissed at the painting.

The movement and sound immediately stopped, replaced by the painting of the poppy field at night.

I had learned enough. I still didn't know exactly where the door to the lab was hidden, but I had a good idea, and I'd pressed my luck in the solarium long enough. I turned and headed back to my room.

When I opened the door to my bedroom, part of me couldn't help hoping that Pete was waiting for me again, but I was alone. I could've used some information about the greenhouse. And, more importantly, I needed a friend right now. Someone to tell me I wasn't crazy for what I was considering—breaking into the total horror movie that was the Scarecrow's lab.

I pulled Star from her hiding place and cradled her in my lap, softly stroking her soft white spine. There was one more obstacle left to consider. If I was going to rescue Maude, I needed to get the Scarecrow out of there first. My plan to do that? Not entirely sane.

"Hey, Star," I said. "Know anything about arson?"

Of course, Star didn't reply. I found myself laughing in spite of the danger. The Wicked Witch of the West, she had some good ideas.

How about a little fire, Scarecrow?

THIRTY-
FOUR

I breathed a sigh of relief the next morning when the sun came
up like normal. Dorothy must've gotten enough beauty sleep.
The Great Clock was turning again.

I went through my daily chores as usual, boredom and nervousness mingling dangerously in the pit of my stomach. Ollie was
going to meet me in the Royal Gardens at midnight, which meant I
had to rescue Maude as close to that time as possible. I could manage hiding my pet rat in my room, but what was I going to do with
a winged monkey? No, I had to time this out perfectly.

I found Jellia at the end of my shift. Two days of that dead-
mouse smell had caused some major cracks to form in her jovial
exterior. Her eyes were red-rimmed, her smock wrinkled and
flecked with smudges, and her hair was in total disarray. Worst
of all, her lips were taut and stress sores had formed at the corners of her mouth, probably from too much PermaSmile.

The other maids had been keeping their distance and Jellia,
not the least bit oblivious to the effects of her pungent aroma,

had assigned herself chores that kept her isolated. As she finished cleaning out the kitchen's grease traps, I went right up to her like nothing was wrong.

"Hey, Jellia," I said, smiling gratefully. "I just wanted to say thank you for giving me the day off yesterday. I feel much better."

A fragile smile spread across Jellia's face. For a moment, she seemed to regain some of her pep. "Of course, Astrid. Think nothing of it."

Without hesitating, acting like the smell didn't even bother me, I went in for a hug. I squeezed Jellia tightly and, after a moment's hesitation, she hugged back. And then she clung to me for a few seconds longer than normal hug-length, letting out a little whimpering noise.

"It'll be okay," I whispered to her.

When I pulled back, Jellia wiped the corners of her eyes. "Thank you. I needed that."

I sincerely thought Jellia needed some cheering up and I wanted to make her feel better. So I felt a little pang of guilt as I walked away holding the master key ring I'd fished from the non-smelly pocket of her smock. She was the only maid entrusted with access to every room in the palace, which meant I had no choice but to pickpocket her. I hoped she didn't realize the keys were missing until the morning, when I planned to find some way of giving them back to her—losing them would just be one more thing for Jellia to freak out about. Still, it had to be done. Hopefully, the worst-case scenario was Jellia spending a sleepless night worrying about her keys instead of a sleepless night gagging on mouse smell.

I made it back to my room and waited for nightfall. Lucky for me, Dorothy was still on her twelve hours of beauty sleep kick, so the moon rose promptly and the palace went quiet. It was actually kind of nice for the servants; without Dorothy raging around, they could relax.

I held Star close before I departed.

"If I don't come back," I told her, "find a way to give everyone the plague."

I crept upstairs to the Scarecrow's room without seeing another soul. The hay bales were still stacked next to his door, awaiting their hideous fate of being stuffed inside the burlap folds of a maniac.

I needed to make this look like an accident.

I approached the wall sconce closest to the bales, the one right next to the Scarecrow's door. Inside, the ornate oil lamp glowed brightly. I produced my knife and slid it against the base of the lamp, just hard enough to create a small crack. Oil began to leak out, dribbling slowly down the wall, onto the floor, and then seeping into the nearest bale.

Now I just needed to create a spark.

Before I realized what was happening, my dagger began glowing white-hot. Was I doing that? Or was the dagger helping me along?

Regardless, the blade sizzled up against the oil spillage, igniting it. Blue flame spread from the wall to the bales, which immediately started to crack and smolder. Soon, they'd all go up.

Using Jellia's keys, I slipped into the Scarecrow's room,

shutting out the growing cloud of smoke behind me. I kicked some of the trash from his floor—more straw, loose papers, discarded scrolls—toward the door, knowing that they'd catch when the fire spread.

If a fire in his room didn't draw the Scarecrow out of his laboratory, I didn't know what would.

Next, I climbed out the same window Ollie had left by yesterday, clambering onto the tree. I wasn't nearly as graceful as he'd been—the branches scratched my face and the backs of my hands, creaking under my weight, but I managed to climb down, carefully and quietly.

Above, I could hear shouts from the Scarecrow's floor. Smoke was now spilling out from the window I'd climbed out of. From my position halfway down the tree, I had a pretty clear view of the palace grounds. A few stories up, the fire crackled, louder and louder. I watched and waited, slowly beginning to dread that he wouldn't come. That I'd become an arsonist for nothing, endangered my cover, and let Ollie down.

But then I saw a lanky shadow step away from the recesses of the greenhouse. It was him! The Scarecrow crossed the palace lawn on long strides, his head tilted up to see the furnace glow emanating from his room. He'd taken the bait.

When he was out of sight, I dropped the rest of the way out of the tree, landing softly at its base. In the distance, the dome of the greenhouse was glowing with the huge reflection of the full moon. It wasn't far now.

The palace grounds were just as beautiful at night as they

were during the day. But, lit as they were by delicate lanterns and glittering tea candles, they didn't offer a lot of cover. I sprinted across the lawn, hoping everyone would be too distracted by the fire to spot me.

In his haste, the Scarecrow had left the greenhouse unlocked. I rushed through the door, the fragrant smell of flowers immediately wiping away the charred scent of the palace. I paused for a moment, catching my breath and listening. All I could hear was muffled shouting from the palace—no guards chasing after me, no Tin Soldiers clanking in this direction. Just a caw or two escaped from the dark recesses of the greenhouse. I'd made it. So far so good.

The greenhouse was filled with rows and rows of flowers like nothing I'd ever seen before. There were huge roses with blossoms bigger than soccer balls and bright-red poppies that opened and closed their petals every few seconds as if they were breathing, expelling pale pink pollen into the air as they did. There were tulips whose colors changed every few seconds, cycling through all the colors of the rainbow, and towering sunflowers that sparkled in the near darkness, their petals seeming to give off their own sunlight.

The rows of plants went on and on and on. This, I realized, was what Oz should be like everywhere. Dorothy wasn't just satisfied with stealing the magic from Oz—she was also stealing what the magic created. Someday, I hoped that I'd have a chance to see some of these plants growing in the wild, out of Dorothy's reach.

But not tonight.

I hurried toward the back, the sound of the crows getting louder and louder, until I was only steps from the aviary. It was now or never. I ignored my fear, unlatched the door, and stepped into the cage.

Inside, they were everywhere. On perches high above and on the ground, pecking at seeds that were sprinkling down from a wrought-iron feeder hanging from the ceiling like a chandelier. Standing careful guard.

Despite their vigil, they ignored me.

I kept my breath shallow and steady, hoping that Pete was right, and that neither their hearing or vision was very good, trying not to think about their razor-sharp claws and even sharper curved beaks.

I'd only had a narrow glimpse of the Scarecrow's laboratory, but I got the feeling it was underground. There weren't any staircases that I could see in the aviary. Most of the floor was covered in seed, feathers, and bird crap.

Except the birdbath. That, oddly enough, was mostly clean. Stranger still, the ravens didn't perch there.

I approached, tiptoeing past the birds that scavenged for seed at my feet. I ran my fingers along the edge of the birdbath, examining it for a button or a latch or anything else that might give me a clue about what to do next.

Nothing.

The stagnant puddle of water in the bath's basin was murky and black and stinky with mildew. It was impossible to see what was down there . . . which made it a perfect hiding place. I had an idea. I held my knife out and willed it to fill with heat like it had back in the palace. The weapon felt eager to please, turning orange, the color of an almost-extinguished ember. I concentrated harder and turned up the juice until it was shining so brightly that it hurt to look at it.

I plunged it into the fountain, the water steaming as it came into contact with the blade. I could see through the cloudy pool to the bottom where my knife illuminated something dark and round.

A button.

I jammed the butt of my knife against the button, and it gave easily.

The birdbath disappeared right out from under me, and I almost tipped over and fell flat on my face. I managed to keep my balance, though, and looked down to see that where the bird-bath had stood just a few seconds earlier, a small round door like a manhole had appeared in the ground. I leaned down and tenta-tively lifted it—inside, a stairway spiraled into darkness.

From somewhere high above my head, I heard a loud *Ka-caw!*

Then, an excited rustling. I'd gotten their attention.

Another crow cried out, and then another and another until they all seemed to be screaming at me.

A rumbling sound began to build as my peripheral vision clouded with a fluttering blackness. The rumble got louder and louder, and then I realized what it was: it was the sound of hun-dreds of birds flapping their wings all at once. They were all flying right for me.

With no time to worry about what was down there, I stepped through the door and plunged down the twisting stairway. I felt like I was running for my life, trusting my feet to find their purchase against the treacherous stone stairs. They didn't let me down. Nox had trained me well.

The door slammed shut behind me and everything suddenly went completely black. Able to see exactly nothing, I stopped and looked up and waited for my eyes to adjust.

They didn't. I decided to light my knife up again, finding it even easier the second time than the first, and held it aloft. Or tried to. I hit rock a few inches above my head. I climbed back up the staircase and examined the back of the door, but it didn't have any handles or buttons. I had no idea how to open it back up. *Well*, I thought, *at least it will keep the crows out*. Plus, I might be trapped. With no other direction to go but down, and only my knife to light the way, I descended.

When the steps finally ended, I looked around, the glow of my knife lighting up an entire room. The Scarecrow's House of Horrors was almost as I had imagined it to be. Except worse.

There were two long metal tables set up with horrific instruments like the ones I'd seen in his room, and a metal chair with restraints on the arms and the legs. I was pretty sure that's what Maude had been strapped into yesterday. So where was she now?

Next to the chair was a square, squat machine, with a bunch of circular dials and gauges on it. It was attached to a long leather tube. I didn't want to know what that was.

Against the wall was a huge shelf lined with big glass

jars—the kind that Gert kept her dried herbs and potion ingre-
dients in. But these jars weren't filled with mandrake root and
nightshade dust.

Many of them held what looked like brains floating around in
some kind of glowing green liquid. I stepped closer. They were
pulsing. They were still alive, I realized in horror. It wasn't just
brains—there were other body parts, too, ears and hands and
tiny little white wings. From baby monkeys? I shuddered.

I turned my attention to a wooden drafting table, which was
papered with sketches and anatomical diagrams. There were
monkeys, Kalidahs, a chicken, and a few other animals I didn't
even recognize.

I tore my eyes away and began looking for signs of actual life.
"Hello?" I called out. "Is anyone here? Maude?"

I wasn't really expecting an answer, but then I heard a noise,
a barely audible moan coming from behind a metal door I hadn't
noticed in the back of the room, on the other side of the boxy
machine. The moan came again, louder this time, and I knew
that as afraid as I was, there was someone, or something, on the
other side who had it a lot worse than me.

I held my breath before opening the door, picturing all the
terrible things I might find.

The next room was smaller and filled entirely with rusty
metal gurneys. They were caked in dried blood, but at least there
were no bodies on them.

Then I saw her. In the back of the room, a tiny monkey in a
frilly pink dress was cowering in a metal cage that was barely

big enough to contain her. Feathers from her twisted, mangled wings poked through the bars.

"Maude?" I asked gently. "Is that you?"

She looked up at me with scared, big brown eyes. They looked like Ollie's only minus the mischief. But the rest of her was not at all like Ollie. Her head was freshly shaved and her arms were wrapped with cloth bandages.

I crouched down next to her. "I'm here to get you out," I said in the gentlest voice possible.

"Who . . . ?" she croaked wearily.

"I'm Amy. Ollie sent me."

"Ollie?" Her eyes filled with momentary hope before clouding over again. "No," she said. "He would never . . . why would he help me when I was so terrible to him?"

"Why *wouldn't* he?" I asked.

"He was right about everything. I should have listened." Her eyes rolled back into her head.

"Maude," I said, snapping my fingers in her face. "Can you move? We need to get out of here."

She nodded, but otherwise she didn't budge. She was out of it; I'm pretty sure she thought I was a dream.

I started looking around for the keys to her cage, then realized I didn't need them. The Scarecrow would know Maude had escaped, so screw it. I bashed the lock with my dagger until it broke open.

The banging seemed to wake Maude up a bit and her eyes focused on me. I leaned in and helped her out of her prison and onto the ground, but when I tried to lift her into my arms to carry her, she brushed my hands away.

"I can walk," Maude said. As an afterthought, she reached over her shoulder and felt for her wings, like she had forgotten whether or not she still had them. As she brushed her fingers through the matted feathers, I couldn't tell if she was relieved or disappointed.

She didn't say anything—she just reached up and grabbed my hand and hobbled along beside me, past the gurneys and through the door into the main lab.

I could hear the crows outside, their mad *ka-caws* echoing down the passageway. We weren't going to be able to leave that way.

"Is there another way out of here?" I asked.

Maude either didn't hear my question or chose to ignore it. Her eyes had filled with rage. She was staring at the Scarecrow's machine.

"Did he use that on you?" I asked, my voice somber.

Slowly, she nodded.

Hell with it. Why stop wrecking stuff now? I walked to the machine and shoved it over. It crashed loudly to the ground, its gears spilling out and spiraling across the floor like loose change. I looked back at Maude.

"He'll only fix it," she said.

"I know," I replied. "But I'd love to see the look on his stupid straw face when he finds it."

Her cracked lips twitched, not quite smiling, but I thought I saw a spark of happiness in her tired eyes.

"What did he do to you? I asked. "What is the Scarecrow building down here?"

"I don't . . . I don't remember."

She put a hand up to her shaved head, her eyes squeezed shut in pain. I couldn't tell if it was physical or mental. Did it hurt to think? Or did it hurt to remember what had been done to her?

"He drained me . . ." Maude knuckled the back of her head. "He's trying to make himself smarter." I thought of Ozma and wondered if maybe the Scarecrow had drained her brain, too.

"But why?" I asked, looking around at all the equipment. The wall of specimens. It had to be something more than the Scarecrow having brain envy; nothing went on in this palace that didn't somehow benefit Dorothy.

"He's trying to . . . he's going to . . ." She drifted off, going hazy.

And then, suddenly, the birds went silent.

"What has gotten into you? Be quiet, you dreadful beasts!" I heard the Scarecrow shouting at the ravens. He was back. The fire must've been put out. We were out of time.

"Oh no . . ." Maude moaned, her knees went weak, and I felt her almost collapse next to me.

I grabbed her by the shoulders. "Tell me there's another way out of here."

She shook her head, her eyes drifting toward the staircase. "Only through there."

Trapped. My only option was magic.

"Take my hand," I told Maude, trying to sound confident. "I'm getting us out of here."

I had never gotten that comfortable with the travel spell that Mombi had taught me, but at this point, I had to risk it. It was dangerous—Gert and Nox had told me time and time again that I should never travel without clearly visualizing my destination, otherwise I was liable to end up teleporting myself into the middle of a brick wall.

I closed my eyes and tried to picture the Royal Gardens. I'd never actually been out there, only glimpsed them that day when I saw the Lion pop the eye out from that guard. What did I remember?

The sunflowers. A sprawling bed of overgrown sunflowers where the Lion had been napping. I pictured the flowers, but it wouldn't do to travel into them, not unless I wanted petals and stems sticking out of me. I imagined the space directly above the flowers; the cool night air, the moonlight, the Royal Gardens. I focused on the details that would be *below* me, imagining the empty space where we'd travel.

It would be the most powerful spell I'd ever cast. And the most important.

My dagger throbbed in my hand. It wanted to stay and fight. Not a sound strategy, but that's the kind of instinctual advice you get from a magic object that's primary purpose is stabbing.

Distantly, I heard the Scarecrow shuffling down the steps. He was close, but I was already imagining myself far away. . . .

"Hold on to me," I whispered. Even my own voice sounded as

if it came from down a tunnel, the magic building up within me.

I felt Maude squeeze my hand and then I let go—not of her, but of this place. I heard a wooshing in my ears, felt the magic pulling me apart, and then we were gone.

THIRTY-FIVE

Maude and I materialized right above the sunflowers, just like I pictured, and tumbled in a heap through the petals and leaves, stems cracking beneath us. The ground was soft, the landing not too rough. We'd made it. We were alive.

I'd completed a travel spell. The most complicated magic I'd ever done. And it worked. I felt laughter bubbling up within me.

"You okay?" I asked Maude, my throat suddenly dry, like I'd been dehydrated.

"Yes," she croaked back, and we began crawling our way out of the flowers.

I was exhausted. The spell had worked, yeah, but all my appendages had that pins-and-needles feeling, and I had the vague sense that I'd left part of myself behind, like the magic had taken a price.

Also, considering how powerful the spell was, I worried that Dorothy might have felt it or detected it somehow. There was nothing I could do about that now.

Ollie was waiting for us. All I could see of him were his eyes. They were unblinking and glowing yellow, shining down at me.

"You fell out of the sky," he said to me, baffled.

I waved at him weakly. "No big deal."

As I struggled back to my feet, Ollie locked eyes with Maude. I don't know if I'd been expecting them to hug or what—the last time they'd seen each other she'd spit on him, so maybe that was pushing it—but they didn't. It was awkward, neither one of them sure what to say, until Maude finally broke the silence.

"You came back for me," she said softly. "After everything—"

Ollie cut her off with an embrace. He held her tight and Maude squeezed back, although I noticed her fingers brushing over the stubs where his wings used to be. I let them have a moment, looking toward the palace. The Royal Gardens were on the other end of the grounds, away from the greenhouse and the Scarecrow's burned bedroom. The windows on this side were dark, empty. There weren't any patrols around, but I didn't want to take any chances.

"Sorry, guys," I interrupted. "But you need to get moving."

Both monkeys turned to me. Maude bit down on her lip, looking suddenly nervous about something.

"There's just one more thing," Ollie said, glancing surreptitiously at my dagger.

My shoulders slumped. I was already exhausted from the night's events, I didn't know how much more I could do.

"What is it?"

"You need to cut off my wings," Maude replied.

I stared at her. "Uh, what?"

"The wings are tied to Dorothy's magic," Ollie explained somberly.

"As long as I still have them, she has power over me," Maude finished. I noticed her flexing her wings as she spoke, as if trying to commit the feeling to memory. "I won't be able to leave the palace grounds with them."

Ollie had already unclipped a pouch from his belt, opening it up to reveal sutures and some clean rags. I glared at him.

"You knew we'd have to do this."

Ollie nodded. "Yes. Sorry I didn't tell you, but . . . you volunteered."

I flipped the dagger around in my hand, gently clutching the still-warm blade, and held it out to him.

"You do it," I said.

Ollie looked from me to the blade, then at Maude. I could see him trying to steel himself, to find the courage to accept my challenge. After a moment, he looked away.

"I . . . I can't," he said quietly. "She's . . ."

She was his sister. Of course he couldn't mutilate her. That job fell to me.

Maude grabbed my hand.

"Please," she said quietly. My stomach clenched. "You've already opened my cage. Now set me *really* free."

Cutting them away was the easy part; my knife was sharp and hot. The worst part, the part I worried would stick with me, was the sound they made. And how the wings began to flutter on their own.

Blood poured down my hands, so dark it was almost black. The heat of my blade cauterized the wound some. Ollie huddled beside me, staunching the blood and suturing where needed.

"I am so sorry. I am so sorry," I kept repeating. I don't think she heard me. I didn't know a spell to numb the pain or I would've used it. Maude bore it without a scream or even a whimper, knowing that we needed to keep quiet.

Softly, almost under her breath, she hummed a strange, sad song. It sounded like a children's song.

"Our parents used to sing that to us," Ollie whispered. "A nursery rhyme about learning to fly. I don't even remember the words."

Maude wasn't crying, so I held my tears back, too. The least I could do was be as brave as she was.

When the first wing fell to the ground, Maude lost consciousness. I checked her breath, just to make sure she was still alive, but I didn't try to rouse her.

Ollie cleaned and bandaged the first stump while I moved on to the other. This one took longer, my arms heavy and weak.

When it was done, Ollie lifted her into his arms, cradling her like a baby. She stirred, looked at me blearily.

"Thank you," she murmured.

I nodded and opened my mouth to say something. Instead, I found myself collapsing onto my knees. Ollie leaned close, his face now level with mine.

"Come with us," he said urgently, and jerked his chin in the direction of the stone wall that separated the Royal Gardens from the Emerald City. "I can bring you to the Dark Jungle and the other Wingless Ones."

I trusted the monkeys. But even though I still hadn't heard from the Order, I knew I had to see this thing through. I shook my head. "No," I replied, gritting my teeth and trying to pull it together. "My mission is here."

In the darkness, I couldn't tell whether the look on Ollie's face was admiration or pity.

"In that case, Amy of Kansas," he said. "You need to stand up."

I struggled to my feet, every muscle sore and aching. I felt like I might crumble back to the ground at any second. When I was finally up, Ollie shifted Maude into one arm and held out his other hand to me.

I reached out to grip it, thinking that he was just saying good-bye. But he pressed something metal into my palm. When I looked down, I saw that it was a tiny silver arrow, no bigger than the needle on an ordinary compass.

"It will lead you to the Wingless Ones," Ollie said. "Keep it safe. Keep it with you. Use it to find us when you need us most."

I blinked at him, shocked. He had made no secret of how the Wingless Ones wanted nothing to do with the Wicked. He knew I was loyal to them, and he was trusting me with this anyway.

"We work for no one," Ollie said, as if he sensed my surprise. "But you have proven yourself. You are our friend, and we will help you however we can."

"Thank you," was all I managed to say.

The words were barely out of my mouth and he was already on the move, carrying Maude toward the shadows of the wall. Once there, he didn't climb over. Instead, he lifted up a flap of grass and disappeared beneath it. A tunnel, I realized. The Wingless Ones had dug a tunnel.

The silver arrow twitched in my fist in the direction of the wall. I now knew there was a way out, but I couldn't yet take it.

I was lucky to make it back to my room, so weak I was practically crawling the whole way, without drawing any attention. At one point, I had to duck behind a curtain to avoid being spotted by a pair of palace guards. They were chatting about the freak accident in the Scarecrow's room. Good. I hoped that meant nobody suspected foul play.

Well, at least until the Scarecrow discovered Maude missing and flipped out.

All I wanted to do was collapse into bed and sleep for a million years, but I couldn't until I got myself cleaned up. As I washed the blood from my hands in the little basin by the cupboard, the sounds of bones cracking and feathers flapping echoed in my head. When I closed my eyes, all I saw were Maude's twisted, injured wings falling into the grass.

I shuddered. Doing Good had been uglier than I'd expected it to be. And the price . . . the price now was feeling like I needed to always be looking over my shoulder. Maybe I'd taken too many risks.

And now, to get rid of the evidence, I needed to take one more. I felt dizzy, like I was spinning out of control, but I shoved it down, doing what needed to be done.

I pulled off my blood-crusted dress and placed it carefully on my bed. Waving my finger at it, I lit it with a magical flame. It burned quickly and noiselessly, its fabric blackening and smoking, hissing and popping. At least no one in the palace would find the smell of smoke out of place.

Though the fire danced across my sheets and mattress, the spell did its job. They remained unharmed by the flames.

I stood there, practically naked, just watching, my arms crossed across my chest until the evidence was finally disposed of. There wasn't even a trace of ash left behind. It was as if it had never happened—the room wasn't even hot.

But I could still see the fire burning on my retinas when I closed my eyes. Much smaller than the one I'd set outside the Scarecrow's chambers. But with more magic. I felt weakened; an emptiness in my core like a hunger.

If Dorothy had detected my use of magic, I'd be in trouble. I needed some support. I needed someone to tell me what I'd done hadn't been a total waste—what was one free monkey in the scheme of things? A minor victory at what cost?

Where was the Order? Why had they left me all on my own?

I turned to the mirror that I'd come somersaulting out of almost a week ago.

"Nox," I said. My voice came out angrier than I meant it to. "Nox. I don't know if you can see me. I don't know if you're listening. But I need you."

There was no answer.

THIRTY-SIX

The hunt was already on when I woke up. From the tiny window in my room, I watched the monkeys circling the grounds. There were dozens of them in the air, swooping and diving. I couldn't help realize that even though winged monkeys are controlled by magic, today they were tethered to long metal chains that fastened in thick collars at their necks and were being held from the ground by the Tin Soldiers, who just stood there looking up at their prisoners like they were flying kites at the beach. I guess with one runaway monkey, they didn't want to take any chances that their magical power over the monkeys might be slipping.

They were searching for her.

I dressed slowly, feeling achy all over, and took an extra second to look at myself in the mirror. I half hoped that maybe Nox would appear there, but he didn't. I kissed Star on the nose and tucked her away safely in her drawer. I think she was getting used to it, or at least had stopped trying to scratch her way out of it.

As I exited my room, I tried to inject a little extra pep in my step to make up for the worn-out feeling in my bones. Maybe I could borrow some of Jellia's PermaSmile.

That reminded me. I had to get her keys back to her. I'd find a way to do it at breakfast. My stomach growled; apparently, starting a fire, overusing magic, and chopping the wings off a monkey made a girl extremely hungry.

Except, there was no breakfast: instead, the maid staff was lined up from one end of the hall to the other, no food in sight.

"What's going on?" I asked Sindra, the maid next to me, as I joined the line.

"Surprise uniform inspection," she replied. Sindra blinked her extra-long eyelashes and shrugged. She didn't seem to have any clue that anything was up. Part of me envied her ignorance.

Jellia marched up and down the line, making sure everyone was in order for the inspection. Her scent was vastly improved; Dorothy must have finally let her take the mouse out of her pocket. She looked sharper than she had in days, but not quite chipper. Jellia knew something was up and it made her nervous.

When she passed me, I saw the tiniest look of alarm flit across her eyes. Her mouth, probably slathered with PermaSmile, didn't move. My pulse raced as I tried to say calm. Had I missed something? Did I have one of Maude's feathers stuck in my hair?

Jellia stepped toward me. She licked her thumb, and brusquely rubbed a spot behind my ear. A spot I couldn't have seen in my mirror.

"Astrid," she spoke quietly, without venom. "You've been slipping in your appearance lately. You're really going to have to learn to be tidier."

When she got close, I took the opportunity to slip Jellia's keys back in her pocket. Her eyebrow arched at me—maybe she felt the tug against her smock—but she didn't say anything more, just studied my face for a moment longer to make sure I was clean. I breathed a sigh of relief as she turned her back on me and continued her march down the line.

The clomping shuffle of metal against marble approached and then I knew for sure that this was no ordinary uniform inspection. Jellia stepped back and faced us. I felt the other girls tensing up at my side as they began to realize it wouldn't be Jellia conducting the inspection.

Jellia cleared her throat. "Ladies, the Tin Woodman and his men are going to ask you some questions. Be honest and concise. As long as you tell the truth, no harm will come to you."

I'd known this might happen, but I hadn't expected it so quickly. I thought I'd have some time to prepare my story. I steeled myself, willing my heart to slow, willing my face to stay smiling and placid as the Tin Woodman came lurching into the room, all business. Jellia curtsied as he approached. The Tin Woodman didn't acknowledge the gesture.

The Tin Woodman made quick work of the line, showing each of us a small picture of Maude and asking each of us about her whereabouts last night.

"Well, I don't know if I recognize the funny little creature!"

Sindra said, her turn right before mine. "It's a monkey! They all look the same to me."

I wanted to reach over and slap her. Of course, I didn't. I didn't even turn my head.

A moment later, the Tin Woodman shoved the picture in my face, and I realized that I didn't have to lie about whether I recognized her. The drawing of Maude was nothing like the Maude I'd rescued the night before. Her fur was neatly combed, and her wings were folded behind her back. She had a pink bow in her hair and was wearing a little pair of green glasses. The little half smile on her face was knowing and shy at the same time.

I looked up at the Tin Woodman. I studied the seams that held his metal face together.

"I've never seen her," I lied confidently, then tried to copy some of Sindra's stupidity. "I don't have any contact with the monkeys. They have lice."

I remembered what I'd seen of the Tin Woodman in the magic picture in Dorothy's parlor, mooning over the princess. I knew his weakness. It should've been like picturing him in his metal underwear, thinking about him writing bad love poetry to Dorothy in motor oil. At that moment, it didn't make me feel much better. He lingered in front of me, taking longer than he had with the other girls.

"The last time this monkey was seen, she no longer had her fur," the Tin Woodman said. "Or her wings. Use your imagination."

I didn't have to imagine. The image would never leave me.

"No fur or wings?" I asked, trying to conceal a wince at the horrible memory. "Shouldn't she be dead?"

The Tin Woodman's eyes flickered. "She will be."

He stepped away from me then, holding up the picture for everyone to take a second look.

"This monkey escaped from the Scarecrow's lab late last night," he said. "She was gravely injured. She could not have escaped without help from someone inside the palace."

No one said anything. Abruptly, the Tin Woodman changed gears, his voice coldly demanding.

"Who is responsible for delivering hay to the Scarecrow's chambers? Step forward."

Everyone in the line hesitated, but one by one, four of us stepped forward, including me and Sindra. The Tin Woodman stared right at me, though. He stepped close again.

"You smell like smoke," he said dispassionately.

Could he even smell with that metal face? Was this a ploy?

I blinked up at him innocently. "My room was close to the fire, sir," I replied.

"Tell me your name, little maid."

"Astrid," I said, feeling less secure in my disguise spell than I had in days.

"Where are you from?"

"Gillikin Country," I said.

Before he could ask any more questions, Jellia cleared her throat loudly behind him. "Your Greatness," she said, addressing the Tin Woodman. "We have duties to attend to and we're already off to a late start. Dorothy will be very disappointed if we don't . . ."

The Tin Woodman gave me a last look. A long one. "Maids,

so good at getting every single detail right," he mused. He stepped away from me, addressing the rest of the line. "If any of you have information on our escaped monkey, you know where to find me. And don't put the hay near the lanterns, you little fools."

Metal hands clasped behind his back, the Tin Woodman strode from the room.

"Off to your duties, girls," Jellia singsonged when he was gone. "Don't dillydally. There's more work to be done than ever."

I was turning to follow Sindra when I felt a hand on my shoulder. It was Jellia.

"Come with me," she said. "I have a special task that you can help me with."

That was unusual. My chest tightened, paranoia fluttering through me. Did Jellia know? Had she figured out that I swiped her keys? That I used them to help Maude escape? I studied her face, but it was as placid and cheerful as ever.

I didn't have any choice except to go with her. As she led me out of the dining hall, I felt my knife whispering for me to call it. But I didn't, not yet. I wasn't entirely sure what Jellia was up to, but I didn't totally distrust her. I would only have one chance to run. I had to make sure I took the right one.

"Of course this has to happen just so close to the ball," Jellia chattered airily as we walked. "The Tin Woodman and his men are ripping apart every room. Turning over every cushion. They don't care that we'll have to clean it all up before Dorothy's guests arrive. And Her Highness will not be pleased if even the slightest thing is out of place. Not to mention that mess in the Scarecrow's room."

It was the closest she'd ever come to complaining about anything. I followed along and listened, wondering what she was getting at.

"You know," she continued. "I've worked in the palace for a long time. I was here before the Wizard, even. I was here during the Scarecrow's rule. I was here when Ozma was still herself. I was here when Dorothy returned."

"That is a long time," I said, trying to sound noncommittal, but I was curious just the same, and not only about why she could appear to be a young girl after so many years working in the palace. I wondered why she was telling me all this—she had never opened up around me before. Maybe that hug yesterday really had made a difference. Maybe she just wanted to talk?

"Oz has been through many changes," she went on. "Oh, people talk about the *real* Oz, but I don't even know what they mean by that. Oz has rarely stayed the same for long. That's the magic, of course. Always changing."

We were climbing the stairs now. Jellia's smile was different from her usual phony mannequin-grin. It was sad and faraway.

"I have some fairy blood, too, you know," she said. By now I wasn't even sure if she was talking to me or talking to herself. "Not anywhere near as much as Ozma, of course. Not enough to make much of a difference. But enough to know that things could have been different."

Finally, we were at my room. I looked over at Jellia questioningly. Why had she brought me here?

"I want you to be sure that your room is tidy," she explained.

There was no hint in her voice that anything was out of the ordinary. "They'll be searching all of them, of course, and I know that you can be sloppy from time to time. I wouldn't want them to find it out of order. It would reflect badly on me."

She stared at me meaningfully. This was a warning. I don't know how much Jellia knew, but she'd brought me here, taken me away from my chores so that I could make sure everything was in order. So that I wouldn't get busted.

"Jellia, I—"

She held up her hand. "I'll expect you in the kitchen for dishes shortly."

Without another word, she walked away. But when I opened the door and stepped inside, I realized I was too late. Everything was out of place. The sheets had been stripped. The mattress had been cut down the center, feathers spilling everywhere.

When I saw the open drawers, overturned on the floor, I felt like I was going to throw up.

Star was gone.

THIRTY-SEVEN

Outside the window, the sky turned from blue to purple to black. Even though it was barely after breakfast, Dorothy had turned the clock.

I couldn't bring myself to care. Star was gone. My room had been ransacked. I was sure they knew about me—about who I really was. The Tin Woodman already seemed suspicious of me. They'd put it all together.

I had to get out of here.

I turned to face the mirror, which was basically the only thing in the room that had been left undisturbed. Could it be the way out, too?

I ran my fingers over the smooth, reflective surface, hoping some kind of answer would reveal itself. "Nox," I said, knowing in my heart that it was useless. "Please help me. Tell me what to do. I need you."

I thought I saw my image ripple, just barely, like when you drop a penny in a pool, and a quick surge of hope rushed through me. But the mirror remained unchanged. Any movement I'd seen had just been my imagination.

I looked at my face, the face that wasn't really my own, and tried to remember what I really looked like. For some reason, it made me wonder what my mother was doing. I wondered how much time had passed since I'd left—I knew that time didn't work the same here as it did back home. Was she an old woman now? Had she found a new life without me? Or maybe a hundred years had passed back in Kansas and she was now long dead. I shivered.

Suddenly I found myself longing for my real face. I thought about taking out the knife and cutting myself to reverse the spell, just to get a glimpse of the girl I had been. If I was going to be captured, or have to fight my way out, I decided I would do it as Amy.

The blade came to me eagerly. It glinted in the mirror.

I was just about to slice my palm open when I heard something behind me. First a rustle, then a squeak. I spun around to see Star emerging from a crevice between the floorboards and the wall, a tiny little space I had never noticed before.

"Star!" I cried. "Where the hell were you? Where did you come from?" I was so overjoyed to see her that I didn't even care that I was talking to a rat that had no way of answering any of my questions. She must have escaped somehow. That's one good thing you can say about rodents: they know how to make a quick getaway. I just hoped she'd done it *before* they'd searched my dresser. Somehow I didn't think Dorothy would take kindly to a maid harboring a rat in her room.

I knelt down to pick her up, but she darted away from me.

"Star?" I stood back up and watched her closely. Something was up—she was frantically running around in a circle like she was trying to get my attention.

"What are you trying to tell me?" I asked.

As if she understood what I was asking, she scurried over to the door and began scratching at it.

She wanted me to follow.

"Are you serious? Now?"

It was a bad idea. Worse than bad. Colossally bad. The Tin Woodman was tearing the rooms apart one by one, the whole palace was in chaos over the missing monkey, and I wasn't sure whether or not I was a suspect. Plus, Jellia had already covered for me once this morning, and I still wasn't sure exactly what *that* was all about. The safest course of action, for now, was to keep my head down and be ready to run.

Or ready to fight.

"Star . . . ," I said.

She squeaked. She'd never behaved like this before. It was a far cry from her lethargic Dusty Acres days, usually spent napping in her exercise ball. Maybe there was some natural phenomena in Oz that made animals smarter. I mean, the monkeys talk after all.

I sighed. They *do* say rats are extremely intelligent. If she wanted me to follow, I would follow.

As soon as I opened the door, Star raced out without hesitation.

I chased after her. I guess if anyone caught me, I could tell them I was trying to strangle the rat on Dorothy's behalf.

I was nervous, still unsure what exactly was going on. But Star wasn't. Star moved quickly and hugged the side of the hall as if she knew that she was supposed to be inconspicuous—as if she knew exactly where she was going, exactly what she was doing.

After a couple of turns, past rooms where other maids were too busy diligently cleaning to notice us, Star came to an unexpected stop, right in front of a life-size statue of Dorothy. I'd probably dusted this a few times—there were others like it scattered all over the palace. In this one, Dorothy peered hopefully toward the horizon (the wall), while clutching a picnic basket, Toto's scruffy head poking out of it. This version of Dorothy reminded me of the sweet, innocent one I was familiar with, the way most people back home thought of her: sweet and smiling, her hair pulled into two plaits. Too bad she was fictional. I looked at the statue. I looked down at Star. She was twitching in expectation.

"Okay," I said, keeping my voice low. "Now what?"

Star rolled over onto her back, then back to her feet, and looked up at me.

I didn't understand rat sign language, but I knew she was trying to show me something. I looked at the statue again. I thought about all those movies where a statue conceals a hidden door and almost laughed, looking down at Star.

"Is this when I, like, lean on the statue and fall through a trapdoor?" I poked stone Dorothy in the eye for emphasis, and nothing happened.

In response, Star started running around in a circle, chasing her tail.

"Star, I don't have time for this," I said. "Things are already screwed up and why am I talking to you, you're a rat."

Star stopped chasing her tail and looked at me, lifting one of her front legs off the ground. It was like she wanted to shake hands.

Rolling over. Chasing her tail. Shaking hands. These were dog tricks.

I looked back at the statue. Toto's front paw was sticking out of the basket. I looked dubiously back at Star, who squeaked. Feeling a little dumb for humoring my pet rat, I shook Toto's paw.

It moved under my hand like a lever. Something inside the statue clicked, and then an almost imperceptible ripple went through the marble, like the shimmer of heat coming off a sidewalk in the summer.

Star squeaked and raced up to the statue's base, running right through it, almost like the statue was a hologram. Tentatively, I reached out and touched what seconds ago had been cold, solid marble. Although it looked no different to the naked eye, now my hand passed right through it.

I glanced down the hallway in either direction. The coast was still clear.

Well, I'd followed Star this far.

I took a deep breath, fighting back the instinct that said I was about to smash my face against a rock, and walked through Dorothy's statue.

I found myself on a stone staircase lit by glowing, shimmering orbs of energy that lined the cracked, ancient walls. I glanced over my shoulder and for a moment I could see the back of the Dorothy statue, but then it faded into solid rock. In front of me was a staircase that led nowhere but down. Great.

I heard Star chittering up ahead, so I pressed on. The ceiling above the staircase was so low and cramped that I had to duck my head to walk down it. *Probably built for Munchkins,* I thought.

I caught up with Star at the bottom. The ceiling opened up down here, the same orbs from the staircase illuminating an ancient chamber with a dirt floor. Dust tickled my nostrils. It didn't seem like anyone had been down here for a long time. I wondered if this was like one of the tunnels Ollie and Maude had disappeared into last night.

"What did you get me into?" I muttered to Star.

We followed the tunnel, the only sounds my soft footfalls and Star's clicking nails. I glanced over my shoulder once and watched as my footprints quickly filled back in, like some invisible force was making sure to erase all trace of my passing. I started walking a lot faster after that. I had the constant sense that something might start chasing me at any moment.

After only a few minutes, the tunnel came to an abrupt dead end. I looked back again and couldn't see the staircase we'd come from, even though it didn't seem like we'd gone that far. Instead, the tunnel stretched on forever behind me. Something told me there was no going back.

A ladder was built into the wall in front of me. It was wooden and rickety and led up through a narrow hole in the ceiling. I tested it, rattling it hesitantly to be sure it would support my weight.

It shook, but it didn't give way. So I put Star in my pocket and began to climb, not knowing where it would lead me. It was a tight squeeze; like the staircase, this tunnel was basically Munchkin-size. I'd never been claustrophobic before, but I was still supremely relieved to see a square of light overhead.

At the top of the ladder, I reached up and lifted a square door. I opened it slowly, peeking out, not sure where I'd be popping up. From above, dirt shook loose into my face.

It was a flap carved into the grass, just like the one Ollie had used the night before. Except this one appeared to lead into a bunch of shrubs. Well, at least no one would be able to see me emerging from the earth.

I crawled and clawed my way up and out, through leaves and thorns and branches. When I was finally able to stand, I looked around, pulled a bunch of leaves from my hair, dusted myself off, and found that I was in the palace's sculpture garden, a place I'd seen in the distance, out the window, but had never been in before. It wasn't that far from the greenhouse, and I was a little nervous to be in the proximity of the Scarecrow's lab again so soon, but no one was around. The search for Maude must have gone to the other side of the palace—to the Royal Gardens—where they'd probably discovered her mutilated wings by now.

The sculpture garden had always looked green and peaceful from a distance. Up close, it was nothing like that at all. Giant topiaries trimmed into the figures of Oz luminaries—the Lion, the Tin Woodman and the Scarecrow and Glinda, as well as others that I didn't recognize—all towered over my head, all of them dark and shadowy in the moonlight as they stared creepily down at me.

Life-size stone statues were mixed in among them. They were made from a flaky, brittle shale; all of them with eyes that seemed strangely lifelike, as if they were watching me sneak through their ranks. I pushed down the sudden desire to draw my dagger.

The statues were carefully arranged along a spiraling stone path through the hedges. They appeared to represent every race and creature in Oz—humans, Munchkins, Quadlings—and also stranger humanoids like an armless brute with a hammer-shaped head, and a gang of sprite-size people with horns sticking out of their foreheads.

As I moved quickly down the path, Star wriggled in my pocket. I reached down for her, but she squirmed free of my hand and jumped onto the stone path. She darted on ahead: this wild-goose chase wasn't over. This time, I didn't question it. Clearly, she had a destination in mind.

So I followed her as she scurried along, trying not to look at the gruesome faces of the statues staring at me until we reached the entrance to the hedge maze.

There I stopped short. This was one place I *didn't* want to go. While the sculpture garden had always looked like a peaceful retreat from the vantage point of the palace windows, the hedge maze, on the other hand—even from a distance—had *always* given me the creeps.

I don't know why. Maybe it was just the way it exuded magic; the way it seemed to change and rearrange itself every time you looked away from it. Even in the dark, the leaves of the hedges were Technicolor-green, so saturated that the color almost bled into the atmosphere.

It seemed like the kind of place you could get lost in. The kind of place you could enter and never leave.

Unfortunately, Star didn't seem to share my fear—she was already several yards ahead of me, and if I didn't hurry, she would be out of sight before I knew it.

"Slow down!" I hissed after her, but she didn't listen. I took a deep breath and followed her into the maze.

As soon as I stepped inside, the leafy walls on either side of me began to rustle, suddenly sprouting little pink buds. The climbing ivy grew and twisted.

My heart pounding, I looked back. The opening I'd just run through was no longer there. It had sealed up behind me with new growth.

"Damn," I swore under my breath. I'd almost expected those frozen statues to come to life, but I hadn't expected the *maze* to.

Keeping Star in my sights suddenly seemed more important than ever—it was no longer just a matter of not losing her. It was a matter of *me* not getting lost. Rats were supposed to be naturally good at mazes, right? Star seemed to have some sense of where she was going, but I knew that, on my own, I would be stuck in here for good.

There was no point in looking back, so I didn't bother.

Relying on a rat to guide me through a magic maze pretty much summed up my last twenty-four hours. I felt out of control, isolated, and uncertain where I was headed. I plunged forward regardless. Sometimes the path was narrow and claustrophobic, the hedges so high I couldn't even see their tops. Then I'd turn a corner into a sweeping cobblestone boulevard where the topiary walls were short enough that it seemed like I might be able to dive over them with a running start.

We turned a corner and found ourselves in a long, leafy corridor—grown over with ivy—where there didn't appear to be any more turnoffs. The hedges stretched out in a rigid line, nowhere to go except straight ahead. Unfortunately, the path looked like it went on forever, extending so far into the distance that I couldn't see an end. The maze felt massive, like an entire world unto itself.

The endlessness terrified me. Even Star slowed down and sniffed at the air, looking around like she was trying to get her bearings.

"Come on, Star," I urged quietly. "Don't fail me now."

The hedge wall on my left was covered in a blooming honeysuckle-like vine that dripped with a sweet-smelling nectar. Without really realizing what I was doing, I reached toward one of the blossoms to sample the nectar—it smelled so sweet and alluring. A purple ladybug landed on the blossom just in front of my fingers and the flower snapped close with a crunch and a squish. I jumped back. The flowers had teeth.

I started forward, wanting to put some distance between me and the flowers. Star ambled along at my side, no longer leading the way.

"What did you get me into, Star?"

Just as I said it, her head popped up into the air and she doubled back on the path we'd been following. She began to examine one of the hedges we'd passed. It looked like any of the rest of them to me, but Star, having now made up her mind, circled around and ran straight toward it. As she did, the branches slid aside, forming an opening as wide as a doorway. I gasped—more from joy than surprise—a way out! Star ran through—and I ran right behind her.

We kept running, no longer obeying the paths laid out by the maze. The walls continued to slide aside for us as we charged on, closing at our backs as soon as we slipped through.

And then, finally, we reached the center of the maze. It was so unexpected that I almost tripped over my feet while skidding to a stop. It was a large, circular area, paved with jagged flagstones. Wildflowers bloomed everywhere, the moonlight beaming down brightly on their open faces.

Dead center in the middle of the plaza was a stone fountain that looked older than time itself. Its water spiraled up into the sky in a corkscrew and didn't seem to come back down again.

Sitting on the edge of the fountain was Pete.

As usual, he had found me when I least expected it. Like the Order, Pete was just another of my supposed allies that couldn't be relied upon.

"You," was all I could manage, still catching my breath.

"Hey," he said casually. Clearly, he'd been expecting *me*. He sat there like there was nothing strange at all about meeting up in the early morning darkness for some fun times in the nefarious hedge maze.

Actually, with the way the bright-yellow half-moon shone on his dark hair, the colors around us supercharged, Pete looked almost beautiful. He looked better than normal—like an artist's rendering of his ideal self. He looked perfectly at ease here, like he belonged.

"You brought me here," I said suspiciously. "You had Star come get me."

"Yes," he said. He stood up from his perch on the fountain but didn't come any closer.

"How?"

"Star may not be able to talk, but it's not so hard to communicate with her if you know the trick," he replied.

More half answers. This was way beyond its expiration date.

"What about the maze? Did you do all that? Do you control it?"

He laughed. "No one controls the maze. Especially not me. It's a living thing—like you or me or Star. If you're kind to it, it remembers. If it's your friend, it will help you." He smiled and gestured at everything around us. "These hedges and I go way back," he said. "So I asked it for help."

What was he saying? That he had trained this place?

I took a step closer.

Who are you? I wanted to ask. *What do you want from me?*

I wanted to ask those things. But I had asked them before. I knew he wouldn't give me a straight answer. And if he somehow did now, I wasn't sure I would like it.

"If you wanted to talk to me, why didn't you just come to my room—like before? Why go through all this?" I asked instead.

"Things are about to get messy around here, Amy," he said. "It's not safe for me in the palace."

I wanted to laugh. "And it's safe in *here*? I hate to tell you this, but the flowers have teeth."

Pete laughed. "Okay, true," he said. "If you make it here to the center, though, you're in the safest place in the whole Emerald City. Maybe in all of Oz. Dorothy's afraid to come in here. Even *Glinda*'s afraid. They should be—it's more powerful than they are. More powerful than Mombi, for that matter."

He raised an eyebrow mischievously.

"You know Mombi," I said. Of *course* he did. I should have known.

"I do," he said. "Mombi and I go way back, too."

"So *you're* my handler. The one who's been keeping an eye on me for the Order. Are you the one who told her to rescue me in the first place?"

Pete shook his head emphatically. "I don't work with the Order. Just because I know Mombi doesn't mean I like her."

"How do you know her, then? Wait, never mind. I don't know

why I thought you'd answer that, since you haven't answered any of my other questions."

Pete's expression darkened. "She may say she's working for the good of Oz, but Mombi doesn't do anything for the good of anyone except herself. Take it from me."

I rolled my eyes and walked over to the edge of the fountain.

"Pete," I said. "Why should I take *anything* from you?"

"I guess you shouldn't," he said. I couldn't decide whether he sounded apologetic about it.

"So what do you want from me? Why did you bring me here?"

"I wanted you to know how to find the center," he said. "I wanted you to understand this place. To introduce you, I guess. It might be useful to you someday."

"Introduce me."

"Yeah."

"You wanted to introduce me to *a bunch of magical hedges*." I was pissed at how evasive Pete was being, but the logical part of me knew this was a valuable place to know about. With things getting hot in the palace, the Tin Woodman sniffing around, the magic I'd used last night—I might need a place with carnivorous flowers to hide in.

Pete just shrugged. He tried to take my hand in his, but I pulled it away.

"And I wanted to say good-bye," he said. "I have to leave the palace. I couldn't before. But Dorothy's weak right now. She's being hit from too many angles. I don't even think she realizes it. I have to leave while I can."

I felt it like a punch in the gut. Mysterious and flighty as he was, at least Pete usually *tried* to be helpful. But now—just like the Order—he was leaving me behind. And I still didn't have any answers. Was it a coincidence that he had just been walking by when my trailer fell out of the sky, that he kept showing up and disappearing?

I backed away from him. Pete was more than he seemed. That much was clear.

"Who *are* you?" I asked.

"I had started to think that there was no hope for Oz," he said, again not answering the question. "Things were just so bad. The day I met you I was walking around looking at all the damage. Thinking there was no way things could ever get better. That we shouldn't even bother trying. And then you dropped out of the sky. You reminded me that there was still Good here. Even if it was just the promise of Good."

Good. There was that word again. Back home, I had always thought of myself as a good person. Maybe a good person with a little bit of a temper, but still *good*. Here, in Oz, it had gotten more complicated—words like *Good* and *Wicked* had lost their meaning. What mattered was right and wrong.

At least, that's what I'd thought. But Pete thought I was *Good*, and the way he said it made me wonder if it still mattered after all.

"It was selfish of me to get so close to you," he went on. "But it wasn't *just* selfishness. I wanted to make you feel like you weren't alone, so that you could be the force for good Oz needs."

His words made me feel unsteady. "I don't know what that means," I said. "I hardly know anything about you. You're not a gardener at all, are you?"

"I wish I could tell you everything, Amy. I wish I could take you with me. But I can't. We all have our secrets to keep." He looked at me pointedly, and I remembered that I was still wearing Astrid's face. "And you're bound to Mombi now. I can't break that. Even if I wanted to."

He knew that, too. What else did he know about me?

I turned away from him and trailed my fingers through the water in the fountain. I half expected to feel something when I touched it—that it would be magical, charged somehow. But it was just water.

Then Pete stood up.

"Wait—" I said. I stood too. "Please." I had so much more I wanted to ask him. Even if he wasn't going to give me the answers.

But he was running his fingers through his hair, looking away. He had more he wanted to say, too, I could tell.

"Don't trust anyone. Don't even trust me. Trust yourself," he said. "You'll know what to do. Be safe, Amy."

Before I could reply, he took a running leap and dove head-first into the fountain. The water was only about a foot deep, but it swallowed him easily. I ran over and leaned into the pool, but all I saw was clear water shimmering over the mosaic-tiled bottom. It was empty. He was gone. I sighed in frustration.

"Looks like it's just you and me," I said to Star.

I thought about following—about jumping right into the pool after him. But somehow I knew that whatever door Pete had just passed through was closed.

With all the magic in Oz, with all the magic the witches had taught me, there was one trick I still hadn't mastered: how to make people stay.

THIRTY-EIGHT

The hedge maze basically showed me the way out, opening up its walls for me. As I passed, the bitey flowers made sweet little kissy noises at me. That didn't really cheer me up.

I returned Star to my room, hiding her back in the drawer and using some of the padding from my ripped-up mattress to make her a bed. I figured the Tin Soldiers wouldn't bother tossing my room twice. After that, I rejoined the other maids, scrubbing and dusting through the rest of the afternoon. No one seemed to have missed me, although I didn't see Jellia anywhere.

Around dinnertime, the sun came back up. Dorothy must've been awake.

The maid staff was only half done with our meals when all of our bells started ringing at once. Something was wrong, and as they led us to the throne room, it wasn't hard to guess what.

It wasn't just the maids. The halls were crowded with people all heading in the same direction: guards, gardeners, deliverymen, cooks, everyone. I even saw the Wizard's hat sailing through the procession.

"They know who it is," someone behind me whispered. "They've discovered the traitor who helped the monkey escape."

Even though I'd barely had time to touch my dinner, I felt sick to my stomach. If they knew who it was, then they knew it was *me*. I knew how Dorothy liked to work: that she was looking forward to calling me out from the crowd in front of everyone, making me beg and humiliate myself while she tortured me with my own fear.

I thought about running. I could teleport myself to the hedge maze and hide in there. I could make it out before the Tin Soldiers had the chance to grab me.

Or I could summon my knife and fight.

I knew one thing for sure: I wasn't going back to one of those tiny dungeon cells. And I damn sure wasn't going to the Scarecrow's lab for any Attitude Adjustment.

Before I could decide anything for sure, Sindra sidled up next to me.

"I just can't wait for things to get back to normal," she said. "You know, I found a metal screw in my bed. The Tin Soldiers must have searched the room. And what if *I'm* the traitor? I mean, I *did* bring up some of those hay bales."

I shook my head. "You didn't do anything wrong," I replied, and picked up my pace to get ahead of her.

As we entered the throne room, my eyes came to rest on the Wizard. He observed the crowd with an inscrutable smirk that didn't quite reach his eyes. He stood in the middle of the crowd, but separate, too, as if he were surrounded by an invisible bubble. Really, it was that people were a little afraid of him. They didn't want to stand too close. I was just surprised that he was down here with all us common servants.

The staff milled about, chatting, some of the maids taking the opportunity to flirt with the guards, but it all came to a halt when the Scarecrow and the Tin Woodman entered. The crowd hushed as the two took their places next to the two empty thrones.

Audible gasps and a smattering of clapping rippled through the crowd when Dorothy sashayed into the room. It was the first time I'd seen her since the incident in her chambers a few days ago, and I noticed with disgust that all the beauty sleep seemed to be working—her skin looked perfect, like a doll's, not a blemish to be seen. The spike heels of her magic shoes—which I pointedly avoided looking at—sparked against the marble with her every step. Dorothy's hair bounced at her shoulders, even more shiny and perfect today than ever. She wore a leather dress of that familiar blue-and-white pattern that hugged her farm-girl curves before fishtailing out at the bottom.

Dorothy sat on her throne, daintily crossed her legs, and regarded us all with an expression equal parts imperious and murderous. At her side, the second throne—usually reserved for Ozma—remained empty. I guessed that the *actual* princess wasn't important enough to get invited to this sort of thing.

The Tin Woodman banged the butt of his ax on the floor.

"Attention!" he shouted, as if everyone in the crowd wasn't already staring at the throne.

Slowly, a thousand-watt grin spread across Dorothy's face, as insincere as a piranha's. She cleared her throat and her voice began to echo through the room.

"My aunt Em used to say there wasn't any such thing as being too generous," she said. "My dear aunt Em was never a princess, of course, but I still try to live by her words. I like to think I treat you all not just as subjects but as friends."

She paused, and the crowd responded with clapping and cheering, not all of it entirely forced. I had to say, this wasn't the Dorothy I'd expected. She might have been a total bitch in private, but she sure knew how to work a room.

"And how am I repaid for my generosity?" Dorothy went on, a hand daintily spread across her cleavage, her tone suddenly wounded. "With betrayal. A betrayal of me, a betrayal of Oz, a betrayal of all of *you*."

Angry muttering began to spread through the room. They were actually *buying* this crap.

I could practically feel her eyes boring right through the crowd and into my skull. I knew that, at any second, she would be dispatching the Tin Soldiers to push through the audience and drag me up to the throne to be punished in front of everyone. My fists clenched. I was scared, yes, but also felt my anger starting to rise. I must be prepared to draw my dagger and make sure Oz's benevolent ruler died first.

"We will have our justice!" Dorothy shouted. "The truth always reveals itself."

Cheering again. They couldn't make up their minds—were they angry or happy? Were they really clapping for the downfall of a traitor? Or because it wasn't them being punished today?

"Bravest Lion," Dorothy said through clenched teeth, "bring me the traitor."

The Lion loped out from the door behind the throne. A murmur went through the crowd. The Lion's ferocious figure was always intimidating but the nervousness sweeping the room was also partly owed to the prisoner he dragged behind him.

Jellia Jamb, the head maid and Dorothy's most trusted lady-in-waiting, her hands bound behind her back.

I lurched forward in surprise, bumping shoulders with one of the guards. He glared at me, but I hardly noticed. I couldn't tear my eyes away from Jellia. This wasn't right. Not at all.

The Lion held her with one paw digging into her arm through the puffy sleeves of her uniform. Her hair was disheveled, her face ashen and quivering. The PermaSmile had been wiped from her face. Her uniform was all torn up.

My mind raced. Was this a trap? Was Jellia going to inform against me? Or was she going to take the fall?

Her keys. Oh no. I'd stolen her keys, they'd figured it out, and now she was to blame.

My fault. This was my fault.

"Come forward," Dorothy demanded, curling a finger at Jellia.

The Lion released her and Jellia stepped forward, righting herself quickly when she stumbled for a moment.

Dorothy looked her up and down, clucking her tongue. Then she stood up and straightened the crooked flaps of Jellia's collar.

"There," Dorothy said, almost intimately, almost like she

was just speaking to Jellia. If I didn't know better, I'd think there was something tender about it.

I held my breath. What was she going to do to her? And, more importantly, what was I going to do about it? I couldn't just stand here while someone else got blamed for my crimes against Dorothy.

"Jellia," Dorothy said, sitting back onto her throne and crossing her legs casually. "You stand accused of freeing the monkey, Maude, from the Scarecrow's private medical facility where she was being kept for her own good. How do you plead?"

Jellia's chin trembled as she opened her mouth to speak. "Guilty, Your Highness," she said.

The room gasped, no one louder than me. Jellia hadn't done it—so why was she confessing to the crime?

"Additionally," Dorothy continued, "we discovered several pieces of evidence in your room suggesting that you have been in regular contact with a ragtag band of magic-using malcontents and usurpers operating out of Gillikin Country."

The Order. She meant the Order.

Jellia was my handler. How could I not have seen it? Getting me close to Dorothy. Letting me check my room this morning. Hell, she'd probably allowed me to pickpocket her keys. Tears welled up in my eyes—tears of belated gratitude, frustration, futility. I fought them back.

Jellia didn't reply to Dorothy's accusation.

The Lion twitched and pawed impatiently at the ground. He growled, baring his teeth, and Jellia flinched away from him. Dorothy stroked his back, calming him.

"Well?" she asked Jellia. "What do you say to that?"

Jellia looked around the room. I tried to catch her eyes, but it was almost as if she refused to look at me. She raised her chin high.

"That accusation is true," she said, her eyes blazing. "I am a member of the Revolutionary Order of the Wi—"

Dorothy lunged forward and slapped her before Jellia could finish. To my ears at least, the slap echoed like a thunderclap. The room, which had started to buzz during Jellia's second confession, went completely quiet.

To even Dorothy's surprise, Jellia didn't look at all cowed. Instead, she raised her head even higher, looking out on the crowd once again. It was like she was shaking off the meek, PermaSmiling, and servile creature we'd all known. Her spine stiffened and her shoulders rose up, like her false persona was an actual weight she'd been carrying. Gone was the woman who'd chastised me for not starching my pleats, the woman who'd carried around a dead mouse for days on Dorothy's orders. Suddenly she looked like a warrior.

I should've known. Should've thanked her for wiping what must've been blood off me. For protecting me.

Dorothy recoiled from Jellia, as if scalded by the brazen impertinence. She gathered herself and shouted, struggling to be heard over the increasingly buzzing crowd.

"Treason! Sass! Unsanctioned magic!" Dorothy shrieked out the charges. "I sentence you to—!"

The ropes binding Jellia's hands burned away with a puff of

smoke. The crowd gasped as Jellia cut off the princess, her voice rising louder.

"People of Oz!" she yelled. "Dorothy's tyranny has lasted long enough! It is time for us to rise up! It is time for us to reclaim the magic that is rightfully ours! My fellow Ozians—in times like these, the Wicked will rise!"

No one knew what to do—the idea of a royal decree being interrupted was so preposterous that even Dorothy had frozen, her face bright red. I heard some boos from the crowd, but a larger part was silent, some leaning intently forward, whispering among themselves. Others edged toward the exits, not wanting to be involved in whatever came next.

I looked over to where the Wizard had been standing and saw that he was gone. But where?

Dorothy stomped her ruby-wrapped feet, more like a spoiled child than a regal princess. "Stop it! I trusted you!"

Jellia turned toward her and, as she did, Dorothy pointed an angry finger at her. It began to glow.

My knife suddenly appeared in my hand, almost without me realizing it, but no one else noticed—everyone's attention was firmly on Jellia and Dorothy.

A crackling bolt of electricity shot from Dorothy's finger, straight toward her former maid. Jellia raised a palm as if to say *Stop*, and it bounced right off her, curling back in Dorothy's direction. Dorothy gasped, but the Tin Woodman flung himself in front of her just in time to absorb the spell, sparks hopping across his metal body.

"Kill her!" Dorothy screamed.

Jellia's outstretched hand began to glow. But before whatever spell she was casting could fully coalesce, the Lion bounded forward and sunk his teeth into Jellia's shoulder. She screamed as the Lion tore into her, shaking her back and forth until her arm came completely off with a sick tearing sound. Those closest to the thrones, including Dorothy, were sprayed with Jellia's blood.

Now people were screaming, running toward the exits. Others remained, too scared to even flee without official dismissal from Dorothy. I stood, frozen, in the midst of the chaos.

The Lion flung his head back—for a moment Jellia's hand was visible between his teeth, then it disappeared down his throat.

"Stay and watch!" the Lion bellowed at the crowd. "See what happens when you raise a hand against the princess!"

Released from the Lion's maw, Jellia crumpled to the floor. Her face was deathly pale, but her eyes finally met mine, her wide eyes serene and unwavering. I felt my knife charging with magical energy. I wasn't sure if it was me doing it or the weapon itself—I didn't care. I couldn't let her suffer for what I'd done.

I took a step forward, but someone grabbed me by the shoulder.

"No," a voice whispered in my ear. I sucked in my breath. "She knew the risks. She knows what she's doing. She was willing to sacrifice herself for you. Don't make it for nothing."

I didn't turn around. I didn't need to. I knew that voice. It was Nox.

The Lion loomed over Jellia, one mammoth paw poised to open her throat. The Scarecrow stepped forward suddenly, putting himself between the Lion and Jellia, his stitched mouth crooked into a smooth smile.

"I want her alive," he said. "I can devise a more appropriate punishment than this barbarism."

The Lion roared, not lowering his claws. He glanced over at Dorothy.

She stood looking down at Jellia, her cold expression in stark contrast to the atomic glow emanating from her red shoes. The crowd went quiet again, collectively inching backward, as if preparing for her wrath. At her feet, the Tin Woodman had managed to pull himself onto his knees, still smarting from Jellia's spell. He grasped the hem of Dorothy's dress and tried to thumb away a spattering of Jellia's blood. Dorothy slapped his hand away.

"Scarecrow, take her away," Dorothy said quietly.

As the Lion and the Scarecrow yanked Jellia to her feet, Dorothy swung her gaze over the crowd. Her cheek was mottled with pinpricks of Jellia's blood.

"Let this be a lesson to all of you," she said quietly, although her voice carried through the throne room. "This is where revolution will get you. In Dorothy's Oz, there is no room for the Wicked."

THIRTY-NINE

"Nox?" I whispered urgently, caught up in the rush of the crowd leaving the throne room. I wasn't sure where he was, or even who he was. I was certain he'd be wearing someone else's face, like me. I didn't want to lose him, not now.

A guy in front of me in a pointed hat with little bells on the brim—part of a juggling troupe, I think—looked over his shoulder at me. He had blond hair and pale skin and a face I didn't recognize.

"Not now," he said. His voice was all Nox. Luckily, everyone was chattering so loudly that they couldn't hear us. "Go to your room," he ordered. "I'll be there as soon as I can."

Then he pushed his way into the sea of people and was gone.

He must've known everything. That I'd jeopardized my mission in order to free Maude, and that Jellia was forced to sacrifice herself because of me. That's what he meant when he whispered to me, I was sure of it. I was responsible for Jellia's horrible fate, but how could I *not* have tried freeing Maude? It was the right thing to do. At least, it seemed so at the time. Now, it seemed like I'd merely traded Maude for Jellia. The Scarecrow's laboratory wouldn't be empty for long. I felt sick to my stomach.

Back in my room I sat on my bed, too full of nervous energy and confusion to even move. I picked Star up and held her, trying to calm myself down. It didn't work. I watched the door, waiting for it to open.

Instead, after what felt like an hour but was probably more like fifteen minutes, Nox's image appeared in the mirror, and he stepped right into my room.

He was still in disguise, still had the yellow hair and round face that looked nothing like his own. But it was him.

"Sorry," he said. "I hate to intrude."

I wanted to wrap my arms around him. I wanted to kiss him. I wanted to tell him everything. About how hard the last week had been, about how lonely and confused I'd been without him.

"Amy," he said, practically before he'd even fully materialized. "You've put us in a terrible position."

He looked at me, and then his disguise faded away, and the Nox I knew—dark and angular and strong—stood before me. His eyes blazed with anger.

"Jellia is going to die because of your pointless risk. She's been a loyal agent for the Order almost since the beginning, and now we've lost her. Because of you."

"I didn't . . ." I began to defend myself, but I didn't know how to finish the sentence. I turned my face away from his. "I had to," I said. "I couldn't let the Scarecrow do that to that poor monkey. And the Wizard told me . . ."

"The *Wizard*?" Nox asked incredulously. "Why would you listen to anything the Wizard told you?"

"He was trying to give me a message," I said. "Trying to tell me that Maude was important. That the Scarecrow was using her to create something. That we had to stop him."

Nox stared at me as if I was the stupidest person alive. "The Wizard is a manipulator, Amy," he replied. "It's what he does. It's how he survives. You can't believe a word he says."

"I can't believe a word *any* of you say," I snapped, my temper flaring. "Maybe if you'd actually told me Jellia was my handler, if I'd *known*—"

"You didn't need to know," he answered. "It wasn't part of the plan—"

"What freaking *plan*?" I practically shouted. Days of frustration, of living in the dark, were beginning to boil in my blood. "You didn't tell me what I was supposed to do. You didn't give me anything to go on."

Nox shook his head. "When will you learn? Some things are bigger than you, Amy."

I didn't want to hear any of that mission-before-all-else crap. So I shoved him. Nox stumbled back, surprised.

"You just left me here," I yelled, jabbing his chest with my finger. "I didn't know if I'd ever hear from any of you again."

Nox caught at my wrists, stopping me before I could shove him again. "Do you think I *liked* leaving you here? Not being able to talk to you or see you, not knowing whether you were okay or not? I did it because I had to, not because I wanted to."

"I'm just a chess piece for you people to move around," I hissed, tearing away from his grip.

For a moment, I thought I saw a look of genuine hurt cross Nox's face. But then he drew himself up, his voice going cold.

"And now you've ruined everything," he said quietly. "We had a plan, and Jellia was part of it. Now she's gone, and every second I'm here puts everything we've worked for at risk."

"You want to make me feel worse?" I asked. "Is that it?"

"I thought I could trust you," Nox said. "I thought you understood what we were trying to accomplish."

At that, I had to look away. I was furious at him for putting me in this position, but it'd been my decision to free Maude, and ultimately that meant what happened to Jellia was on me.

"I'm sorry," I said. "I didn't mean for Jellia to get hurt."

"Being sorry doesn't change anything," Nox said with a sigh. "All it does is waste your energy. And you'll need every bit of strength for what's coming."

I looked up at him. "Are you going to tell me what that is this time? Or are you going to surprise me again?"

"The ball," he said, ignoring my commentary. "That's when we strike."

Of course. The gala that Dorothy had been planning for months was tomorrow night. If only everything could have held off for one more day, we wouldn't be in this situation. *Jellia* wouldn't be in this situation.

"I'd tell you the rest of the plan, but at this point there barely *is* a plan," he went on. "Without Jellia, we're going to have to change some things around. Jellia was supposed to assign you as Dorothy's official cocktail waitress—"

"Cocktail waitress? Seriously?"

"Dorothy has been known to . . ." Nox hesitated. "Imbibe. Quite a bit."

"She's a lush," I said, almost laughing, thinking about my drunken mother sprawled on the couch and how often I'd been her private waitress. "I would have been perfect at that."

"We can't control the new head maid—whoever it is—so we don't know if you'll be in proximity, if you'll even be working the ball."

"I'll find a way," I told him. "Am I going to be on my own again?"

"No," Nox said. "I'll be there, too, but you might not recognize me. And the rest of the Order and its allies will be close by. While Dorothy and Glinda are distracted by the party, they're going to be working to set up magical wards around the palace, to temporarily disable the use of magic. Dorothy won't be able to use her shoes; Glinda won't be able to use her spells."

"What about me?" I asked. "That means I won't be able to use magic either."

"You'll be able to use your knife," Nox said. "But it won't be magic. It will just be a regular knife."

"So I wait for the magic to go away . . . and then?"

Nox looked at me like he was surprised I was even asking. "Then you kill her," he said.

I thought about it for a moment. "This is your big plan? Stab her at a party?"

"Yes," Nox replied.

"And you couldn't have told me that from the start?"

"We needed to be sure about you," Nox replied. "Jellia was supposed to confirm your readiness, but . . ."

I thought of Jellia, bleeding, one arm missing at Dorothy's feet.

"Oh, I'm ready."

"Disabling all this magic isn't easy," he continued. "The palace is well protected. Just getting an agent *in* here is harder than you'd think. To place the wards, we'll need witches strategically placed all over the grounds. They'll only have one chance to act, and they might not be able to hold it for long. Without Jellia, it's going to be much harder. You'll have to act fast. But I'll be here, and wherever you are, I'll be right behind you."

I studied Nox, his face stoic, but his words warm. I couldn't figure him out. Was he using me or did he actually care about me? Hell, I couldn't even figure myself out. Did I want to kiss him or punch him in the face?

"Great," I replied, hoping to be as inscrutable as Nox.

He looked at me seriously. The anger in his face was gone now, replaced by concern.

"I won't let anything happen to you, Amy," he said. "Everything we've done is for this moment. For you. Don't let us down."

And then he stepped through my mirror, disappearing on me

once again. I didn't have a chance to ask him how I could let them down if everything they'd done was for me. It didn't matter. The end result was the same. I was getting out of this strange body and out of this horrible palace. One way or another.

And first, I was going to kill Dorothy.

FORTY

Dorothy quickly named Sindra the new head maid.

Although Sindra tried to be humble about it for the sake of Jellia's memory, she couldn't hide her excitement. She took to the role easily, sliding into her newfound authority as if it had been custom-made to fit her.

She made us draw straws to decide who would clean Jellia's blood from the throne room.

"I'll do it," I volunteered, before the process could even get under way. The other maids looked grateful, even Sindra.

It was my fault her blood was spilled. The least I could do was clean it up.

I'd been concerned with keeping my head down after Jellia's arrest, but it turned out that I had nothing to worry about. In the twenty-four hours before Dorothy's gala, we were all being worked so hard that there was no time for me to do anything suspicious.

Anyway, with the mystery of the missing monkey supposedly solved, no one around the palace seemed to be very suspicious anyway. Dorothy was too egotistical to realize that Jellia had just been the tip of the iceberg. I didn't let myself think about what could be happening to her down in the Scarecrow's laboratory. She only had to hold out for a little while. Once Dorothy was dead, the first thing I planned to do was free Jellia.

So the rest of the maids and I scrubbed and cleaned and dusted every possible surface. We reviewed checklists of each guest who would be attending and their strange and dumb requests. The Governor of Gillikin Country could only have purple sheets; the Shaggy Man wanted a pantry stocked with nothing but baked beans and a closet filled with the finest dirty rags. I didn't bother asking who the Shaggy Man was.

That night, I fell asleep as soon as my head hit the pillow. I'd spent the day working so hard that I hadn't even had a chance to let my mind linger on what was coming.

In my dream, I scoured the cobblestones of the throne room, cleaning up Jellia's blood. It was exactly how I'd spent my afternoon, except when I was finished I didn't move on to preparing the guest bedrooms for the mayor of Gillikin's entourage like I had in real life. Instead, I moved on to the hallways and the ballroom, the kitchen and the solarium, every room of the palace smeared with blood and in desperate need of cleaning. The sounds of my scrubbing echoed through the empty palace. Whatever happened here, I got the feeling it was my doing. I wasn't sure if Dorothy's palace being an abandoned, bloody mess was a good thing or a bad thing.

I woke up with a strange feeling in my stomach. It was the first-day-of-school feeling, but it was the day before summer vacation feeling, too—I was nervous about what I had to do, but excited to know that it was all almost over.

Tonight. Tonight was do-or-die. Literally.

Could I do it? I wondered. Could I really kill another person—even someone like Dorothy?

I put my uniform on slowly, catching a glimpse of Astrid's face in the mirror for what might be the last time. When I was dressed, I pulled my magic knife from the air and turned it over in my hand, admiring it. The shining, intricately engraved blade; the hilt that Nox had carved just for me.

I stared at that knife, feeling the blade pulsing with magic in my hand, and I realized that not only could I do it, but I *wanted* to do it. Seeing what Dorothy had done to Jellia, the callous disregard for her life, and her look across the crowd like *this could be any of you*. Dorothy was a monster.

I couldn't help thinking about what Nox had said when he had given me the weapon, about why he had chosen the Magril on the handle especially for me. He'd told me it reminded him of me because of the way it transformed itself from something ordinary into something special—into something magical and fierce.

I had already changed, I knew. I was nothing like the girl in the trailer park, nothing like the girl who had arrived here in Oz. But was the transformation complete? I had a feeling that it wasn't. When I killed Dorothy tonight, I would be someone different afterward. But who?

I didn't know. I couldn't picture it. Maybe I didn't want to.

That day, as I went about my chores under the careful eye of Sindra, I watched in curiosity as the palace began to fill up with strange visitors. I saw Cayke the Cookie Cook—flanked by bodyguards—her diamond-studded dishpan laden with an assortment of baked goods, a gift for Dorothy. Polychrome, the Daughter of the Rainbow, floated down the hallway and then passed through a wall as if she were a ghost, leaving a misty, multicolored trail behind her. There was a giant frog in a three-piece suit and a top hat; a small, round hairy guy who looked kind of like a really angry troll.

At first I thought *that* was the baked-bean-loving Shaggy Man, until Sindra muttered something under her breath. "Wow," she said. "The Nome King is getting *fat*."

I wondered how many of these people actually *liked* Dorothy, and how many of them were here because they didn't have any choice? Which ones were Order operatives? When everything went down tonight, would the giant frog guy have my back? Would I have to avoid getting clocked by a diamond-studded baking sheet? I wished Nox had given me some idea who our allies might be.

Were all of Dorothy's guests as evil as she was, as corrupted as the Scarecrow and the Lion and the Tin Woodman? Or were they all just here to keep her happy, knowing that ignoring an official invite from Her Royal Highness was basically asking for a palace-mandated Attitude Adjustment?

It didn't matter, I decided. I already knew my enemy. That was enough.

In the late afternoon, Sindra gathered a handful of us in the maids' mess hall.

"All right, everyone," she beamed, clapping her hands excitedly. "I've selected you lucky ones to be the waitstaff at the gala this evening. That means you get the rest of the day off to rest, wash up, and get it together! It's the biggest night of your careers so don't screw it up."

It was the *last* night of my maid career, thank goodness. As the other maids tittered excitedly on their way back to our chambers, I broke off, ducking down a hallway before I even realized where I was going.

The solarium. I needed to do one thing before all this happened. Just in case it was the end.

I passed a half dozen Munchkins in bright-colored formal wear on the way, along with a pair of palace guards, but I kept my eyes straight ahead like I was seriously intent on getting some cleaning done, and no one stopped me.

The solarium was clear, so I shut the door behind me and approached the magic painting.

"Magic picture," I said, quiet but firm, "show me my mom."

It took the painting a moment, like it was having trouble tracking my mom down—what else is new?—but after a stressful few seconds where I worried she might be dead, the painting started to rearrange itself. The seascape gradually shifted to a giant room, possibly an auditorium or maybe a gym. Fluorescent lighting, folding chairs, and a crowd of people, none of whom I recognized.

This didn't look like any of my mom's usual haunts, and at first I wondered if the picture had somehow gotten confused and tuned into the wrong signal. Until the image panned to a table with a coffee urn and bags and bags of Bugles. That was when I knew my mom couldn't be too far away.

There she was, elbow deep into a bag, but somehow managing to look classed up— at least compared to the last time I saw her. Her hair was smoothed into a sleek ponytail, her makeup tastefully applied. She was smiling as she spoke to a woman holding a Styrofoam cup.

"I just wish Amy could be here to see this." In her palm, she held out a coin with the number six on it. Styrofoam Cup gave her a hug and a pat on her back.

"Six months sober," she said. "I just wish it hadn't taken losing everything I care about to get it."

No matter how tough you think you are, there are certain things that just get to you, and they're usually the little things. The ones you don't expect.

I wiped a tear from the corner of my eye. It was only one, but still. I couldn't believe that Mom had changed so much.

It hurt my feelings a little, that she had done it all without my help, but it made me proud, too. Proud of her. Suddenly I missed her very badly.

Yet at the same time I didn't want to go home. I wasn't finished here. Just like my mom had changed, so had I. That place where she was—Kansas—didn't feel like home anymore.

Mom had found purpose without me. And I had surprised myself by finding a purpose here.

I remembered what my mom had said about Madison Pendleton, about how bullies always got what was coming to them.

Tonight, I planned to prove her right.

FORTY-ONE

Sindra was inappropriately excited considering just yesterday her predecessor's arm had gotten hacked off.

"Isn't Dorothy generous?" she asked as we all lined up in the back of the ballroom, waiting for the party to begin. "These new uniforms are just lovely. And so comfortable, too!"

I smiled and nodded. It was true that the smooth green satin of the dress we'd been instructed to wear for the party felt good against my skin, but I thought *comfortable* was a little extreme. For one thing, it was too short, and I kept having to stop to yank down the skirt to be sure my underwear wasn't showing.

Since I'd last seen it this morning, the ballroom had been lavishly tricked out and transformed to the point where it was unrecognizable. A hundred ruby-red disco balls glittered against the dark, domed ceiling, but unlike the disco balls I knew from back home, these weren't suspended by anything. They floated on their own, pulsing in time to the music and dipping and hovering and twirling like shiny beating hearts.

Meanwhile, the wooden parquet I'd spent so many hours hunched over and scrubbing was magically gone, replaced by a transparent dance floor that looked down onto a brilliant, starry night sky, every constellation brighter and closer than they'd ever looked from the ground.

Instead of the usual cloth coverings, the tables were veiled in pink, hazy mist that looked like it had been torn straight from the clouds during sunset. Sprouting from the middle of each table was a centerpiece that I recognized: the giant, ever-changing flower from the greenhouse—the one with the blossom that transformed right before your eyes from a rose to a dahlia to an orchid to a lily and on and on in a kaleidoscopic rush that was enough to almost make you dizzy.

"It's gorgeous, isn't it?" Sindra whispered reverently. "Glinda did the decorating. She always does such a good job."

It's a little *tacky,* I wanted to say, but the truth was, I couldn't help thinking it was beautiful, too. Knowing what was coming—that blood would almost certainly be spilled across the stars—made me feel a little sad.

"Yes," I told Sindra. "It's amazing."

I could feel the magic coursing all around me and wondered how much of Dorothy's power was dedicated to running this place. It must've been part of the Order's plan; with all the magic happening here, hopefully no one would notice the witches performing their wards outside the palace. Not until it was too late.

The doors swung open and as the guests began to stream in, the trays we held magically filled themselves with hors d'oeuvres and drinks. The cocktails were garnished with what looked like real emeralds and rubies that floated upon the surface.

My heart fluttered. It had begun—no turning back now. The only way I was going to get through the night was by convincing myself that nothing was out of the ordinary—that killing Dorothy was just another thing to check off my list of duties for the day. No big deal.

"Okay, gals," Sindra announced, facing the rest of us. "You've seen what happens to screwups, right? Let's, um, do the opposite. Let's make this ball one they'll be talking about for years to come!"

Oh, that won't be a problem, I thought to myself.

The maids dispersed, each of us making our way around the room and presenting the partygoers with their choice of food and drink. I served a group of Flutterbudgets who took forever to decide what to drink, each of them reassuring the next that they were making the right decision, then throwing their selections back like they needed to loosen up more than anything. Next was the stern-looking royal family of Winkie Country, all dressed in sparkling pressed-tin suits that would've made the Tin Woodman envious. They barely looked at me when I passed.

As soon as our trays were empty, they filled themselves up again. No one talked to us or paid much attention to us at all. All we had to do was look pretty and not trip.

The whole place thumped with music and all the guests were laughing and chattering. They gathered around Scraps, the Patchwork Girl, and began to cheer as she pranced and pirouetted in an acrobatic routine that was somewhere between break-dancing, voguing, and gymnastics.

When she cartwheeled into a perfect split, a roar went up from the crowd. Scraps stood and bowed for her audience, and then the music shifted to something slower and moodier. All of the disco balls that had been whirling around began drifting toward the highest point in the domed ceiling. There, they merged together and began to pulse in time with the music like a huge ruby heart.

The heart began to descend slowly. The chatter of the room went silent, and everyone stood still watching it. I scanned the crowd, trying to pick out all the important players. Surprisingly, most of them seemed to be missing: I didn't see the Wizard, or Ozma, or Glinda, or Dorothy. The Scarecrow, the Lion, and the Tin Woodman were missing, too.

For now at least, it was just the B-list.

When the glass heart reached the floor, it exploded in a shower of red glitter. Something landed on my arm and I realized the flashing dots of red light thrown by the disco balls had magically solidified into rose petals. I brushed them off, trying to see through the haze of glitter, confetti, petals, and pink-hued smoke.

She really knew how to make an entrance, I'll give her that. There, in the center of the room where the glass heart had been just a moment ago, stood Dorothy. Her entourage appeared, too, fanning out behind her—the Scarecrow, the Tin Woodman, the Lion, and Glinda—but they dispersed quickly into the party.

Dorothy looked radiant and majestic, every inch a princess. Her lips were glossed but not with PermaSmile—her smile easy and relaxed, and somehow giving off physical warmth if you looked directly at it. Her nails were bedazzled with actual rubies; her hair was pulled up into a spiraling tower of curls, streaks of gold running through it, leading to an ornate emerald hair comb at the pinnacle—the road of yellow brick and the Emerald City, I realized.

She wore a long, formfitting, beaded gown that flared out at the bottom and was corseted so severely that I wondered how she could breathe. Her breasts weren't the only thing Dorothy was trying to show off: the fishtail was slit up the side, revealing her *most* important assets.

Her shoes, of course.

The crowd went wild at Dorothy's entrance. Their cheers and whoops resounded thunderously through the huge room. Dorothy batted her eyelashes and flicked her wrist, all fake-humble like *Aw, shucks.*

One of the servers scurried over to her and, without looking, she grabbed a cocktail, her lips pouting into a dainty sip. A long sip. Finally, the drink half finished, Dorothy blotted the corner of her lips with a napkin and raised her hand to silence her adoring subjects, as if everyone weren't already watching her.

"Thank you," she said, her voice all sugary sweet. "I'm so happy you could all make it here tonight to help me celebrate this wonderful occasion."

A Munchkin in a bright-orange tuxedo standing in front of

me turned to his companion, a squat, monkish man wearing a patterned kimono and a tentacle-like braid, and whispered, "What is the occasion anyway?"

"She just wanted to have a party," the other replied.

I'd assumed this was some Oz holiday I didn't know about. But all this work had just been for a whim.

Meanwhile, Dorothy draped a hand across her forehead.

"As many of you know, the last week has been a difficult one for me. One of my closest confidantes was revealed to be a wicked, nasty traitor, and as you can imagine, I was quite devastated. But I'm overjoyed to say that it's all been sorted out, and things are better than ever. Now, before we get back to our dancing, I'd like to introduce a *very* special guest who I'm so thrilled to have here."

The ballroom grew silent and we heard a rustling from the back of the room. A low murmur rippled through the crowd as it parted to make way for the new arrival. Who could Dorothy be talking about?

Then I saw her, lurching forward in jerky, awkward movements and barely balancing a serving tray full of drinks. Her face was bruised and swollen and her green maid's uniform was splattered with blood. Where her eyes should have been there were instead just two empty, blackened sockets. Her mouth was hanging open as if it had been frozen in mid-scream.

"Unfortunately there was a bit of a mishap during her interrogation," Dorothy said, "but luckily the Scarecrow was clever enough to reanimate her corpse so that she could be here tonight.

Deceased or not, I wouldn't want my favorite servant to miss the most fabulous party Oz has ever seen."

It was Jellia.

The Munchkin in front of me dropped his glass. It didn't shatter but was instead swallowed into the night sky beneath our feet. I assumed, around the room, other glasses were slipping soundlessly from other shocked hands.

I barely managed to steady my serving tray.

No one seemed to know what to do as Jellia limped forward—everyone's face seemed to bear the same look of horrified confusion. Even Sindra had stopped dead in her tracks to stare, tears reflecting in her eyes.

"Well, have a drink!" Dorothy urged us all. "Go on. It would disappoint me so much if you didn't." Her voice was cheery, but there was something in her eyes, something tantamount to a dare.

The giant frog in the three-piece suit looked hesitantly at Jellia, then back at Dorothy, and finally plucked a glass of pink champagne from the tray.

"Here's to loyalty," Dorothy said. Slowly turning in a circle so she could see everyone in the room, she raised an empty glass as if to toast. Everyone followed suit, raising their glasses, too.

"To loyalty!" they cried out. This time, it didn't sound so enthusiastic, but Dorothy didn't seem to care.

Suddenly the lights went out. For the briefest moment it was pitch-black. A flapping noise came from overhead, like bats soaring from a cave, and then the room lit back up, now bathed in a dim, warm glow. Several winged monkeys swooped slowly above us, each one with a sparkling chandelier harnessed to its midsection by a dangling chain.

"Now let's get this party started!" Dorothy howled. She let out a jubilant whoop, and dance music began to blast. Dorothy began to shimmy and shake, and soon the rest of the room was dancing, too.

Jellia continued her march around the room, tottering back and forth, stiff-legged, her empty eye sockets collecting stray pieces of glitter. Everyone she passed reluctantly helped themselves to a drink. It became a secondary sort of dance, watching guests anxiously shift around the room to keep clear of Jellia's path.

I tasted blood. I'd bitten down hard on the inside of my cheek to keep myself from screaming out loud. I couldn't believe I'd ever hesitated at the idea of killing Dorothy. Watching Jellia stagger around the room, a mockery of life, it took everything in me not to rush Dorothy right then.

"Ah, Astrid, long time no see."

The Scarecrow stood next to me, his scratchy hand coming to rest lightly on the small of my back. I'd been so distracted giving Dorothy murder-eyes, I hadn't noticed him approach. He plucked a flute of champagne from my tray, but didn't drink it. I wondered if it would soak right through him.

"Aren't these little gatherings just dreadful?" he asked me idly, his button eyes tracking a pair of fast-dancing Munchkins. "A tremendous waste of resources."

I didn't think I could look him in the face, knowing what he'd done to Maude and now Jellia, and not give everything away with my uncensored anger and disgust. I looked down at my feet and hoped it came off as demure.

"I think it's lovely," I replied through gritted teeth.

"Yes, well, you would," he sniffed. "I'll be ready to resume our nightly meetings soon, dear. I look forward to them."

I suppressed a shudder.

"I have to go," I said, and before he could reply, I shouldered my tray and started circulating through the party.

I noticed Glinda seated alone at one of the back tables. She wore a puffy, frilly gown, her red hair pulled into a tight bun and topped with a tall, cylindrical crown. Sindra approached her with a tray of drinks and the so-called good witch waved her off, not interested. Glinda never took her eyes off Dorothy, her expression mired in boredom, looking like one of those parents that begrudgingly attends a school play and then texts the entire way through it.

Meanwhile, Dorothy danced, hopping and shimmying and twirling. Some of the bolder guests—a fine-featured Winkie dignitary, a dashing-looking pirate with a wooden leg—attempted to dance with her, but she warded them off with wild glares, never breaking her motion. She was like a tornado, clearing her own space on the dance floor. It was manic and, in a way I didn't care to think about, sort of sad.

But then the Lion slunk through my field of vision—licking his chops and eyeing me, because apparently patrolling the outskirts and creeping people out was his preferred party activity—and I realized I'd been standing still for too long. I wished more than anything that Gert had managed to kill him that night in the woods.

I made another circuit of the room and ended up near where the Tin Woodman leaned. He'd stretched a tuxedo over his metallic frame, though it bulged at odd angles and didn't quite fit him. He wore a red corsage on the lapel, which had already begun to droop.

He looked miserable, staring at Dorothy with a combination of longing and self-pity. He turned something shiny over in his hands nervously and I inched a little closer to get a better look. It was a tin rose, delicately crafted, and shined to perfection. The way the Tin Woodman's fingers worried at it, clenching and twisting the fragile stem, I figured it would break at any moment.

As I watched, he seemed to come to some huge internal decision. He nodded and thrust his hands up and down, like he was giving a speech to himself, psyching himself up. Then, still clutching his rose, he marched across the dance floor toward Dorothy.

Someone plucked a tumbler of whiskey off my drink tray. I moved to keep circulating, but a hand grasped my elbow.

"It won't be long now."

Nox. His hair had changed back to its original color and was slicked back. He was wearing a sharply tailored suit with skinny-legged pants. Otherwise, he was entirely himself, like he wasn't afraid to be spotted.

"This should be good," he said to me.

Together, we watched as the Tin Woodman stood before Dorothy, presenting himself with a stiff bow. Dorothy stopped doing the twist to stare at him. He offered her the tin flower and, after a brief moment of consideration, Dorothy took it. Then, after barely looking at it, she placed it on a servant's passing drink tray.

"Ouch," I said. Next to me, Nox smirked.

Dorothy spun away from the Tin Woodman, returning to her feverish dancing. For a second, it looked like he would just skulk away. But then he reached out, attempting to pull Dorothy into an awkward embrace or maybe initiate a tango. He was so uncoordinated, it was hard to tell.

What he ended up doing was slicing the strap on Dorothy's dress.

"You lummox!" she shrieked, loud enough that the entire party stopped. "You rusty, empty-headed beast!"

This was an opportunity.

"Hold this," I said, my heart pounding, and shoved my drink tray at Nox. He took it, confused, and I pushed my way through the crush of gawking Munchkins, Nomes, talking animals, and other assorted Oz weirdos. I knew what I was doing was risky, but another opening as perfect as this one might not come along. I put myself right at Dorothy's side as she berated the Tin Woodman. Sindra was two steps behind me, her eyes narrowing into a glare as I spoke directly to Dorothy.

"Princess," I said, keeping my voice as servile as possible. "Isn't it time for a wardrobe change?"

Dorothy held up the front of her dress with one hand, the other jabbing a ruby-studded finger at the Tin Woodman, her glare like a death ray leveled on him. Slowly, with an almost physical effort on her part, she turned that gaze to me and forced a smile.

"Yes, Astrid," Dorothy said. "Wonderful idea."

So, she did know my name. The fact that it came out in the heat of anger made me realize that when she'd called me random *A* names in her chamber she had just been screwing with me.

Dorothy reached out and grasped my shoulder, effortlessly casting a travel spell. The swirling lights and thumping music of the party melted away, replaced by the relative serenity of the deserted hallway outside her quarters.

"Huh," Dorothy said to herself, looking down at her hands. "Must've had too much to drink."

She'd tried to teleport us directly into her chambers, I realized, but had failed. The witches' spell was working—they had cut off the palace's magic supply, just when I needed it. The magic must be leaking out of her. I felt it, too, a strange ebbing sensation; it was like lying in the sun, only to have a huge cloud pass slowly by overhead.

Dorothy flung open the door to her rooms and strode inside, already pulling her dress off. "Hurry up," she snapped over her shoulder. "I won't have buffoonery steal any more of this night."

I followed her, pulling my knife out.

I felt that same stretching and contorting I'd experienced when I was back in the Order's caves. I was Amy again now, I knew. I hadn't thought about the fact that the magical barriers the witches had cast would break my disguise. It didn't matter— there was no time to worry about that now.

And anyway, good. I wanted to be Amy when I did this. I wanted Dorothy to know.

She was still a few paces ahead of me, crossing toward her sprawling closet. I closed the distance.

"Something with sequins," Dorothy said. "Fancy, sequined, short—that's what I want, Astrid. Find it. The lower cut, the better."

"That's what you want to be buried in?"

Dorothy froze, turning slowly to face me.

"*Excuse* me?" she said, the words out just as she saw me— Amy, not Astrid—eyes widening, noticing my knife.

"This is for Jellia," I told her, and slashed my knife in a wide arc across her throat.

FORTY-TWO

Before I could connect, a black ball of snarling fur flew through the air, aiming straight for me.

Toto sunk his teeth into my wrist. I yelped in pain, unthinkingly loosening my grip on my knife, and watched in horror as it went clattering to the ground as if in slow motion.

Dorothy had stumbled backward when I first slashed at her, tangling her feet in the dress she'd just taken off and falling to the floor. Now she screamed, pulling the dress up, quickly covering herself.

"Get her, Toto! Kill her!"

I shoved Toto off me—he was little and his tiny bite had barely broken the skin—and scrambled for my knife. Stupid. I should've just stabbed her in the back, but I'd wanted to twist the knife figuratively, too.

Dorothy jabbed a finger at me, her eyes blazing with fury, probably trying to blast me with the same lightning bolt spell she'd slung at Jellia. But that fury changed to confusion and then fear as the spell sparked, sputtered, and died.

I grabbed my knife from the pink carpet but before I could charge Dorothy, Toto latched on to my arm again. He got my free forearm this time, so without really thinking about it, I stabbed at him with my knife. He let go just in time, yelping and barking, dancing around at my ankles. Fresh pinpricks of blood welled up on my arm, but I ignored them.

"Don't hurt my dog, you bitch!"

I glanced at Dorothy just in time to see the airborne plush, pink ottoman that she'd flung at my head. I ducked out of the way but lost my balance in the process, stumbling against the nearby vanity.

This was going great.

Dorothy, wearing the dress the Tin Woodman had ripped, now all wrinkled and not pulled on quite right, booked for the door.

Shit.

"Guards!" Dorothy screamed as she fled her room. Toto yipped once more at me, then went racing after Dorothy. I chased them, knowing I couldn't let Dorothy make it back to the party where she could rally her guards. I'd blown my perfect shot—I'd let Nox down, and the Order, and most importantly, Jellia.

As I sprinted into the hall, I heard alarms squealing from all around the palace. The screams of partygoers echoed all the way up here.

The halls were dim—the torches giving off less light than usual, as if even the flames here were augmented with magic. At first I didn't see Dorothy, but then I spotted the unmistakable dazzle of her shoes as she turned a corner.

I was faster than her. I'd been trained by the Order of the Wicked, and she was lazy, drunk, and used to relying on her magic to protect her.

Dorothy glanced over her shoulder and saw me gaining. Instead of heading for the ballroom, maybe knowing I would've caught her before she got there, she suddenly veered left, through a barred door normally forbidden to the maid staff, and up a narrow spiral staircase.

I took the steps two at a time. The spirals of the staircase were so tight that I lost sight of her, but I could hear her shoes clicking, her breath heavy and panicked. I pressed on, getting dizzy. How high was this tower? Where was Dorothy leading me?

Then I felt a breeze on my cheek. I was outside. For a second, the lights from the city below us blinded me and then I could see again. We were on a jacaranda-covered terrace and Dorothy was standing with her back pressed up against the edge of the balcony. Her psycho little dog was trembling in her arms. Not so brave anymore.

I had her trapped. There was nowhere for her to go.

Her shoes weren't going to help her.

I took a step forward.

With Dorothy helpless in front of me, basically just waiting to die, I hesitated. It was different this way—having time to think about it, not trying to kill her in the heat of the moment. I needed to be cold-blooded, to remember everything that she'd done, to remember that the girl standing in front of me was a monster.

And yet, I found my gaze pulled across the glittering panorama of the Emerald City, the place I'd read about in books my whole life. I was higher up than I'd ever thought it was even possible to go. I wondered what my mom would think if she could see me now, at the top of the tallest tower in the palace of a magical fairyland a million miles from the Dusty Acres trailer park.

About to stab the former heroine of the story.

For some reason, Dorothy didn't look afraid of me anymore. She just smiled sweetly at me, her eyes wide and glittering.

"Amy, right?" she asked calmly. "The one that got away."

I didn't reply. I knew she was buying time, a classic desperation maneuver. I inched closer.

"I suppose I'll never know what happened to the real Astrid," Dorothy said, sighing. "My sweet little maid."

"Like you care," I replied, not able to help myself.

Dorothy smiled sadly and half turned to gaze out over the skyline.

"It's pretty, isn't it?" she said. "I come up here when I want to think. Sometimes it's almost like I can see clear on back to Kansas. You know?"

There was a resigned, nostalgic tone in her voice.

This time, I didn't let her bait me. I wondered if this sudden change in her personality was all a big act, or if maybe, somehow cutting off the flow of magic from her shoes was bringing Dorothy back to her senses.

I took another step forward.

She didn't flinch. "I think my aunt Em would have liked

you," she said, still smiling, talking casually like I was an old friend. "She'd think you're awful pretty. She'd want me to give you a second chance. She'd say, 'Dorothy, there's no such thing as a bad apple.' She'd know you're no killer. That they tricked you. She'd say, 'You know, Dorothy, maybe you and that Amy have more in common than you realize.'"

I wasn't stupid—I knew I couldn't listen to her. But—what if she was right? What if we *were* alike? Dorothy hadn't been like this when she'd first gotten here. It wasn't until she killed the witches that she started to change.

If I killed her, did that bring me one step closer to *becoming* her?

No. I wasn't like her. I was stronger—strong enough to absorb all those years at Dusty Acres, all those years of being a nothing, of being a punching bag, and never letting them transform me into anything close to the cruel and twisted monster Dorothy had become. Killing Dorothy was the only thing that would make Oz great again. It would avenge everyone she had hurt. It was what I was here for. I didn't take it lightly—I knew I'd have to live with her blood on my hands for the rest of my life—but I wouldn't let it corrupt me.

They made us strong in Kansas. I could carry this.

So I raised my blade. As I did, Dorothy's unassuming, folksy smile widened, spreading into a twisted grin, her red lips grotesquely stretched with hate.

"Too late," she said, just as I heard a dull, clanking noise behind me. I spun around to see him burst through the door, his boutonniere long gone, his tuxedo ripped to shreds.

The Tin Woodman.

He moved quicker than a man his size had any right to, his ax a silvery arc as it sliced through the air. I ducked just in time to save my head from being chopped clean off, then dove to the side. The Tin Woodman put himself between me and Dorothy.

"My hero," I heard her say, and the Tin Woodman, so recently rejected, puffed out his chest. He sized me up, swinging his ax back and forth, and I saw in his eyes a homicidal devotion.

Could I win this fight? One-on-one with the Tin Woodman, with only my unenchanted knife?

He charged, swinging his ax overhead like he was chopping firewood. I danced aside, his blade drawing sparks from the stone rooftop. As he hefted his ax, I shot forward and stabbed for his eye, but he brought his hand up defensively and my dagger glanced off his gauntlet.

"Why do you fight for her?" I asked him, leaping backward from another brutal ax swing. "She doesn't give a shit about you!"

"Shut up," the Tin Woodman replied, all business.

I wasn't quick enough on that last swing and had a shallow slash across my abdomen to show for it. I backpedaled, trying to put more distance between us.

Then I heard footsteps thundering from the spiral staircase. Palace guards or Tin Soldiers or both. Dorothy's entire army. It sounded like *all* of them. All coming for me.

I caught my breath. There was no way I could take them all on like this: without magic, with just an ordinary dagger, and a psychotic, ax-wielding metal man already bearing down on me.

The Tin Woodman swung again. This time, I moved toward the blade. At the last moment, I dipped into a somersault and slid underneath him, between his legs.

A few strands of hair—the pink that I'd missed so badly when I looked in the mirror—floated down around me. He'd almost scalped me.

But he'd also made a mistake. Behind him now, I had a clear path to Dorothy.

This time I didn't hesitate. There was only one way to accomplish my mission.

"Kill her!" Dorothy screamed, so loudly I thought my eardrums would shatter. "Kill the bitch!"

"There must be some mistake," I said as I rushed toward her, my shoulder lowered. "*You're* the bitch. I'm the *witch*."

I barreled right into Dorothy, hugging her, our foreheads knocking together as we stumbled backward. She realized what was happening too late, slapping at my face when she should've been planting her feet. I shoved forward in a tackle, heard Dorothy cry out as her back struck the parapet, and then together we flipped over the edge.

We were suddenly weightless, tangled together, the blinking lights of the Emerald City stretched out beneath us. I heard the Tin Woodman bellow miserably and, just as we began to fall, I caught the briefest glimpse of Nox as he appeared on the balcony, a sword in his hand.

"Amy!" he shouted after me, his voice cracking in desperation.

It wasn't Dorothy's guards sprinting up the spiral staircase. It was the Order.

Too late. They couldn't help me now.

FORTY-THREE

It's funny how much time you have to think when you're plunging to your certain death from the top of a tower. You'd think it would be over in an instant, but it's actually just the opposite. It's like everything slows down.

At least, that's how it felt for me. I still had Dorothy in my grip, and she was clicking her heels together wildly as we fell. I knew it was a lost cause. Their magic was gone.

Unfortunately, so was mine.

Locked together in a crazy death spiral, my eyes met hers, and for a second—just for a second—it was like I understood her. It was like I forgot that she was her and that I was me. We were both from the same place, and we had both ended up here. We were both going to die together.

I think she felt it, too.

And then something happened. I felt something warm and tingly running through her body. I felt a burning sensation in my legs, coming from the vicinity of Dorothy's shoes. Her eyes lit up.

I wasn't sure whether it was because the spell the witches cast had been broken or because we had passed beyond its bounds, but Dorothy's magic was back. She was more alive than ever.

She knocked her heels together and was gone in a burst of swirling pink smoke.

And I was hurtling toward the ground.

But if Dorothy's magic worked now, that meant mine might, too. I could try to travel, but the way I was flipping and twisting, I was too disoriented—I would have just sent myself crashing headfirst into the ground even faster than I already was.

I closed my eyes, trying to concentrate. I knew that flight spells were some of the most complicated and difficult magic that there was, but if I could just come up with something to at least slow myself down, maybe I'd have a chance of survival. I tried to focus on everything Gert had taught me.

I pictured the energy running through my body, twisting and reshaping itself until it was pulling me upward, back into the sky.

And then I was floating.

Seriously. It had worked. I hadn't expected it to do anything and now I was actually flying.

My eyes sprung open.

That's when I realized I hadn't done it at all. Four furry hands had hooked themselves around me, a pair under each of my armpits.

Monkeys. The kind with wings. They were soaring up into the sky, and they were taking me with them. The buildings beneath us began to shrink. The lights receded.

"Amy," a familiar voice chirped. "We've come to save you."

It was Ollie. He was flying again.

"Ollie!" I exclaimed, still too confused from the last few minutes of insanity to form any coherent thought. "How . . ."

I craned my neck over my shoulder. It was Ollie all right—with one big difference. He'd been given wings.

"You can do a lot with magic," he said mischievously. "The problem is getting ahold of it."

Then I saw that his wings weren't your ordinary feathery white monkey wings. They appeared to be made from old newspaper and coat hangers, held together with little bits of tape.

"They could be more fashionable, but I was in a rush," the other monkey said. It was a girl's voice, smooth and soothing in contrast to Ollie's excitable chirp. Familiar, even though the last time I'd heard her speak, she'd been hoarse and half delirious. "Anyway, they do the trick, as you can see."

I craned my neck to look at Maude, a huge smile spreading across my face despite my confusion.

"Maude!" I shouted through the rushing air. "You're okay!"

"Thanks to you," she replied. "Figured I owed you a save."

"How did you find me? Where are we going?"

"Oh," Ollie replied. "It wasn't hard. The talisman I gave you when you rescued Maude—it doesn't just lead you to us. *We* can also use it to keep tabs on you."

"Looks like we came just in the nick of time," Maude said drily.

I let out a deep breath. We were sailing above the Emerald City, toward the western gates. The air was cool and refreshing against my face and the moon loomed huge above us. We were zipping along, the landscape sliding by. I hadn't realized monkeys could fly this fast.

Under different circumstances, it would have been fun. But once I'd had a chance to catch my breath, I was able to review the events of the evening. Also known as the complete disaster that had been entirely my fault.

The plan had gone into effect. The witches had done *their* part, but I'd botched mine in every possible way. I'd let Dorothy get away not once but twice tonight, and I'd come this close to getting myself killed in the process.

"Take me back to her," I said, having no doubt the monkeys would know who I meant. "I can't leave the job unfinished."

"Um, no," Maude said. "We didn't save you just so you could rush off and commit suicide."

"Yeah," Ollie added, "we've got a better plan."

I turned my head as much as I could, watching the palace disappear on the horizon. I'd failed. Dorothy was still breathing, which meant someone was still suffering.

"What is this plan?" I asked, resigning myself to the monkeys' clutches.

"We're off to see the Wizard," Ollie replied.

FORTY-FOUR

A few minutes later, Ollie, Maude, and I landed in a field just outside the city walls. A few paces off, a ramshackle building—maybe an old guard tower, the only structure in sight—looked like it might collapse in on itself at any moment.

The Wizard was waiting for us.

And so was Pete. They were standing in the field, side by side, the moon glowing on their faces. The Wizard tipped his hat at me as I stumbled out of Ollie's arms and onto the grass. Pete gave me an awkward little half wave.

There was a part of me that was so relieved to see him that I wanted to throw myself into his arms. But a bigger part of me was exhausted, wary, and above all *confused*. I reached down to gingerly press the cut on my stomach, but it wasn't so bad. Just a flesh wound.

"Amy," the Wizard said, all businesslike. "We have a lot to talk about and not much time."

"Hold up," I said. "How do you know . . . ?"

"I've been following your adventures closely since your arrival in Oz," the Wizard replied before I could even get the question out. "As best as I've been able to, at least. It's not every day that someone from the Other Place arrives here. When it happens, it has a way of shaking things up, For better or for worse. Of course I take an interest. I'm from there, too, you'll remember."

I looked at Pete. "And *you*? Have you been spying on me for the Wizard all this time?"

"Amy . . . ," he said. But, as usual, he didn't answer. The silence hung in the air.

"I assure you that everything will be answered in time," the Wizard said. "You've escaped for now, but Glinda is surely looking for you at this very moment. You may need to fight again before the night is through."

"Good," I replied, ignoring the ache from my abdomen and actually feeling a rush of energy. "I'm ready now. Send me back to Dorothy and let's finish this."

The Wizard shook his head emphatically. "The consequences of that would be disastrous," he said. "Dorothy cannot be killed yet. Not even by you."

I stared at him, remembering what Nox had said about him being a manipulator. Dorothy had seemed pretty scared when I was about to stab her, and even more so when I'd tackled her off the roof—not at all like some magical immortal.

"Okay, sure," I replied. "I'd still like to try it."

The Wizard guffawed, a twinkle in his eye. "I love the enthusiasm, but you still don't understand how Oz works. I wouldn't have expected the Order to teach you *everything*, but . . . surely they know that you're out of your league against Dorothy."

I folded my arms across my chest.

"Out of my league? They told me I was the only one who could kill her."

"That may be true," he said. "And, it may not. It's just a theory, and, after all, Mombi and her friends have been wrong before. But let's just say the witches' theory is correct. Just for the sake of argument. Do you suppose that Dorothy doesn't know about it? Do you suppose she hasn't gone to great lengths to protect herself?"

"Of course she has," I said. "That's why I had to spend all this time pretending to be a maid—so that I could get to her when she was weak."

"Her Highness has wrapped herself in intricate layers of protection, it's true. And with the Order's help, you've already managed to breach many of those walls. But the princess is not the only player in this game. She may not even be the most important player. There are things protecting Dorothy that she herself doesn't even know about. Just as you don't."

"She doesn't know about them. I don't know about them. The Order doesn't know about them. And *you* do?"

"Oh, Amy. I've learned a bit of magic, here and there, since I returned to Oz, but let's face it—I'll always be a bit of a hum-bug when it comes to that sort of thing. My real wizardry has nothing to do with *spells* at all. It has to do with knowledge. I knew about you the moment you arrived here, didn't I? Even the most unbreakable of spells are meant to be broken. You just need to know a thing or two. It's the *knowing things* part that just so happens to be my specialty."

This was getting very annoying. "Look. You obviously want to tell me something," I said, checking my imaginary wristwatch. "So just stop screwing around and let's hear it." I looked around nervously, knowing Glinda could come magicking around the corner at any second.

The Wizard sighed theatrically and rolled his head back and forth like he was really struggling to make up his mind.

"Killing Dorothy can only be done by a certain kind of person, and some people think that person is you. But what the Order seems to have missed is that it can only be done a certain *way*. Certain . . . *tools* are necessary. Certain items to which the princess has a special connection. You may have ascertained that several of Dorothy's *loyal companions* are not quite what they used to be. Am I correct?"

"How should I know what *anything* used to be?" I asked. "I'm new here, in case you didn't notice."

"Well, I hear there's a book," he said with a wry laugh. "Haven't you read it? I'm talking, of course, about the Scarecrow. The Tin Woodman. The Lion. Why do you suppose they're so different from the heroes you expected to meet?"

"Because of Dorothy," I said. "She changed them somehow."

"That would be the obvious answer. Maybe even the right one. But is anything ever that obvious? Haven't you learned by now that the *real* story is not always the whole story? Dorothy's friends didn't just change because they were her friends. They changed because of the things that they value most. Or . . . the things they value most have been changed."

"The Scarecrow's brains," I said, thinking out loud.

The Wizard twirled an index finger in the air.

"The Tin Man's heart . . ."

"I think she's getting it," he said.

"And the Lion's courage," I finished.

"Retrieve them and you'll be three steps closer to accomplishing your mission."

I shook my head. It didn't quite add up.

"*You're* the one who gave them those things. And you didn't even know magic. You were just messing with them. Giving them what they were asking for, whether it worked or not."

"Very true," he said. "Funny how even they never seemed to figure that out. You must admit, though, that my gifts *did* have a certain effect. Would you disagree?"

"How can I when I don't know what you're talking about? The only thing I know for sure is that I don't trust you. At all."

"As well you shouldn't," the Wizard said. "You shouldn't trust anyone. Yes, I could be lying to you. On the other hand, where's the risk in ripping out the Tin Woodman's heart? Just to see what happens. If you don't, he'll probably kill you anyway."

He had a point.

"Why don't you do it yourself?" I asked.

"Oh," he said, waving the idea away, "I could never stomach violence. And anyway, *you're* the one from Kansas. . . ."

The grass around us rustled, blown by a gentle wind. I glanced at Pete and found him staring up into the night sky. Suddenly he flinched, and put one hand on the Wizard's shoulder.

"She sees us," he said. "She knows where we are."

The Wizard nodded, as if he understood Pete's typically cryptic words. "We have to move. There's still a battle at the palace, but it won't last long. If she—"

"She *who*?" I interrupted, more than tired of being in the dark.

"Glinda," the Wizard said. "Gazing at us through the damn painting I should've destroyed years ago—"

The night flashed suddenly white, the air around us forcefully displaced and filling with the smell of motor oil. Startled, Maude and Ollie took to the air. I shielded my eyes from the bright light as the Tin Woodman materialized in front of me, still shimmering with a pale pink glow from the spell that had sent him here. Glinda. It had to be. I was beginning to see by now that she liked to rely on other people to do her dirty work for her. Instead of facing me on her own, she had sent someone else to deal with me.

His ax was raised, as if he'd just been plucked from the middle of a fight and transplanted here. He looked around, his eyes still adjusting to the darkness. He lowered the ax a fraction, but then spotted the Wizard. *"You!"* he snarled.

"Hello, old friend," the Wizard replied sadly. "I'm sorry to see that Glinda's using you as her little errand boy. It's really not very dignified, is it?"

"You," the Tin Woodman cried in outrage. I'd never heard so

much raw emotion in his hollow, metallic voice before. "I should have known you were part of this."

He rounded on me next, that all-too-familiar ax poised to strike.

"And you. What have you done with my princess? Where is she? If you've harmed even a hair on her head . . ."

"Whoa," I replied. Had Dorothy gone missing after she'd teleported away from me? "I don't have her."

Obviously, the Tin Woodman didn't believe me. He pulled his ax from his shoulder and took a lumbering swing at me, but I moved backward easily, feeling stronger and more confident than I had all night, and pulled my knife out. I felt my magic coursing through my body, charging the knife with energy.

The Tin Woodman was alone without his soldiers, without Dorothy and her magic. And he looked weakened: his metal body was battered; several of the frightening instruments that had once tipped his fingers had been snapped off. He had a huge dent in the side of his face, stretching from his cheek to his forehead.

The Order had only charged me with killing Dorothy—there'd been no discussion of the Tin Woodman or any of her other cohorts. But they were all just as evil, weren't they? I hadn't been able to kill Dorothy, but if I was able to do away with the Tin Woodman, that would at least weaken her ability to torture some innocent people, right?

I could do this.

"Kill him, Amy," the Wizard urged me. A wounded, betrayed look scrunched the Tin Woodman's features at the Wizard's words. "I've told you what you need to do."

I glanced over at the Wizard and saw him weaving his hands through the air—but not to help me. Instead, he was building what looked like a glowing green force field around himself and Pete. Thanks, guys. Very chivalrous.

The Tin Woodman, though, was focused only on me. He put his head down and charged, his ax extended in front of him. As he plowed forward, the ax transformed into a long, gleaming sword that almost seemed to be an extension of his body.

I was ready for him. Just before he reached me, I blinked myself behind him and he kept going, his momentum carrying him forward. He stumbled for a moment, almost falling, but then he recovered, pivoted, and—in one swift motion—hurled his sword straight for me. As it flew through the air, it transformed again: this time into a flurry of knives.

With a few lightning-fast flicks of my wrist, I was able to deflect most of them, but I felt one graze my cheek. Another plunged into my thigh.

Without slowing down, I pulled it out, feeling the warm blood seep down my leg, and tossed it aside. With that and the wound across my abdomen, I was steadily turning into a real mess. My whole body was shooting with a throbbing pain, but I didn't care.

I didn't feel weaker, I felt changed. Like I really had become something else—a warrior like Jellia had been when she'd confronted Dorothy—someone capable of taking the worst these assholes had to offer and then dishing it right back to them.

The Tin Woodman was unarmed now. From his posture, it

didn't look like he had much fight left in him.

I launched myself into the air and leaned into a spinning kick that connected with his midsection. The Tin Woodman toppled into the grass and I leapt on top of him.

"His heart, Amy!" the Wizard hissed. "That's the only way!"

I lifted my knife into the air, letting it fill with heat until the blade glowed white-hot. The magic was rich in this place—I felt supercharged, more powerful than I ever had before, Oz's natural, mercurial energy flowing like water from the grass and the air and the earth and into my body. Into my knife.

The pain from my injuries was still there, but it was easy to ignore.

"Please!" the Tin Woodman wheezed. He was powerless now—his weapons gone, his arms pinned to his sides. His metal face looked frightened and pathetic. "Please," he repeated. "I know what I've done. I know I've betrayed the people of Oz. I only did it for *her*."

A single tear rolled down his cheek.

I remembered what the Wizard said earlier. *Dorothy's loyal companions are not quite what they used to be.* Whether or not the rest of what he was telling me was a lie, that part was pretty obvious, and now, it seemed oddly relevant. The Tin Woodman's love had been twisted and perverted. It had turned into something ugly and evil.

That doesn't just happen. Something had done it to him. I'd assumed it was Dorothy.

But what if it was his heart itself?

Well, maybe it was and maybe it wasn't. It didn't matter whose fault it was. It didn't matter about the why of it all. Life isn't fair. And I wasn't doing this for myself. I was doing it for Indigo, and for Maude, and for Jellia, and for everyone else who had suffered because of Dorothy. People like Dorothy couldn't be allowed to run things. They didn't deserve a place like Oz.

My knife crackled with blue energy as I plunged it down. It sank into the Tin Woodman like a needle puncturing a balloon.

As I did it, his face collapsed in agony. He started to cry in earnest—sobbing really, his body heaving in pain. He began to look strangely human.

"Please," he managed to spit out. "Please take pity on me."

It was too late. I sliced diagonally across his chest and then drew the knife out only to plunge it right back in, drawing an *X* along his left side with the blade. It made a satisfying hissing noise, and met with almost no resistance. It was as simple as popping the top on a can of soda. In the end, he was only made of tin.

His jaw continued to open and close, but he wasn't speaking anymore.

I reached into the hole I'd just made and found his heart. It was soft and velvety but a little slimy, too. I yanked it, and there was a snapping sound as it came free of the threads of artificial muscle that had held it in place.

The Tin Woodman stopped moving entirely. His eyes were wide and bulging, his face frozen in place, now a record of his fear and pain. It reminded me of the statues in the sculpture garden in the palace.

I held the heart in front of me. I had done it. It was glowing and glittering, pulsing in my palm.

"Give it here, little dear," a voice said. "Don't you worry. Everything will be all right as long as you hand it over."

I spun my head around in surprise and saw Glinda standing right behind me in her frilly pink gown. The only thing that suggested everything was less than perfect was the smeared crimson around her mouth—it could've been messily applied lipstick, but it looked an awful lot like blood.

I jumped to my feet, still clutching the heart, and prepared to fight again. But before I could attack, a bolt of green lightning snapped through the air and hit Glinda right in the stomach. As she lurched backward, she pulled a wand tipped with a glowing star from her bodice.

"Amy!" the Wizard shouted. "I'll hold off Glinda. Take Ozma! Ollie and Maude will take you to the rest of the monkeys."

I whirled around. Ozma?

And then I saw. The green bubble that the Wizard had built around Pete to protect him was dissolving, and as it did, his body began to dissolve, too. Where the mysterious gardener who was my friend had been just a moment ago, Oz's One True Princess now stood. She blinked.

"Amy," she said. "Amy Amy Amy Amy."

Just like I'd been hiding behind Astrid's face, Ozma had been hiding behind Pete's.

"Duck!" the Wizard screamed, and I reflexively followed his instructions just as a neon-pink beam of magical energy crackled above my head.

"How . . . ," I started to say, staring at Ozma, but then the Wizard sent another one of his bolts shooting for Glinda just as Ollie swooped down from out of the sky and scooped me into his arms, carrying me up and away. I looked over my shoulder and saw Maude, carrying Ozma, right behind us. On the ground, the Wizard was locked in battle with Glinda.

In the distance, the Emerald Palace was burning, alight with flames.

I wondered if Nox was still in there. I wondered where Mombi and Glamora were.

But what I really wanted to know as we soared into the clouds, the jeweled city burning below us and the Tin Woodman's evil heart still pulsing in my hand, was where Dorothy was. I didn't know what was going on or where I was going, but I knew one thing: this wasn't over. Even if I had failed tonight, at least I was one step closer. No matter how long it took—no matter who I had to destroy first—Dorothy was going to die.

ACKNOWLEDGMENTS

Writing this book, stepping onto the Yellow Brick Road, has been the most incredible of journeys, and one that I could not have walked alone.

Special thanks to my beautiful family. My mom and dad and sister, Andrea, who have taken every step down every road with me, no matter what the color, with unwavering love and support. And who have always dreamed bigger for me than I have for myself. I share this and everything that comes after with them. Mom, you showed me how to love, to read, to write, and to try.

Thanks to my brilliant editor Bennett Madison, without whom Dorothy would not have been possible. His encyclopedic knowledge of all things Oz and his belief in Dorothy and me made him more than an editor—he's an invaluable creative resource and friend.

James Frey for his amazing support and faith in this book.

To my amazing team at Harper. I am so lucky to have

Tara Weikum, Jocelyn Davies, and Chris Hernandez, whose enthusiasm for Dorothy and support for me has made this all a dream, and whose fabulous editorial instincts and insights helped shape Dorothy and bring Oz into focus.

Ray Shappell for the gorgeous cover.

Sandee Roston and the terrific publicity team at Harper. Thanks for educating me and for giving Dorothy such an extraordinary amount of love and attention.

To my friends —

Lauren Dell, my forever friend, for being there from the beginning and still being here now. Annie Kojima Rolland, for saying you should really write a book before anyone else did, and for giving me a second family to love. Paloma Ramirez, for really becoming my friend a million years after we were floormates at Columbia. Leslie Dye, for understanding. Leslie Rider, for listening and for worshipping at the same altar of perseverance and loyalty. Carin Greenberg, for showing me how it's done and for fancy lunches and Great American ones. Jeanne Marie Hudson for advice and last minute photographers. And Bonnie Datt, for being on call, with empathy and humor, advice and heart . . . who knew that a Nanette Lepore dress could be the start of a beautiful and absolutely essential friendship.

To the rest of my girls' night girls, Lexi, Lisa, Sarah, Kristin, and Megan. My friends from the soap world, especially Jill Lorie Hurst, who was my very first mentor and is still a constant friend and cheerleader in my life. Claire Labine, Jim Brown, Barbara Esensten, Paul Rauch, and Tina Sloan, who always inspires and advises and shines.

And to the readers, thank you, thank you, thank you for picking up this book. I hope it has what I love in a book—takes you to another place, makes you think, makes you feel, and gives you a touch of magic.

To Josh Willis, Don and Sandy Goodman, Sue and Harry Kojima, Chris Rolland, Kerstin Conrad, Nancy Williams Watt, Jim and David Sarnoff, Josh Sabarra, Paul Ruditis, and to the many friends and family members not included here, but are so loved and appreciated!

And special thanks to Judy Goldschmidt who has been the most generous of friends and has opened countless doors for me. I am forever grateful.

To L. Frank Baum, for creating Dorothy and Oz. I hope he wouldn't mind too much that I borrowed her for a little while.

SEE HOW AMY GUMM'S MISSION TO
TAKE DOWN DOROTHY CONTINUES IN

THE WICKED WILL RISE

Full disclosure: I'm sort of a witch.

Fuller disclosure: I'm a pretty crappy witch.

Not like crappy as in wicked, although, hey maybe I'm that too. Who knows?

But really what I mean by *crappy* is, like—you know—not very good at it. Like, if there were a Witch Mall, Glamora would work at Witch Neiman Marcus, Mombi would work at Witch Talbot's, and I would work at the Witch Dollar Store, where people would only come to buy witch paper towels, six rolls for ninety-nine cents.

I just never really got the hang of the whole spell-casting thing. For awhile I thought it was because I'm from Kansas—not a place known for its enchantedness—but lately I've started thinking I just don't have a talent for magic, just like I don't have a talent for wiggling my ears or tying cherry stems in knots with my tongue.

Sure, I can do a few spells here and there. For instance, I can summon a tracking orb with not too much trouble. I've managed to teleport here and there without accidentally materializing inside a wall or leaving any body parts behind. I have a magic knife that I can call on at any time. I can finally throw a decent fireball. (It took forever to learn, but fire spells are now my specialty.) And I've actually gotten pretty good at casting a misdirection charm that makes people ignore me as long as I tiptoe and don't draw too much attention to myself.

It's not as good as being invisible, but hey, it's saved my ass on more than a couple of occasions. That's sort of how it goes: my magic is strictly the in-case-of-emergency kind. In nonemergencies, I prefer to do things the normal way. Call me old-fashioned. It's just easier.

But falling out of the sky from 5,000 feet probably qualifies as an emergency, right? If Maude, Ollie, Ozma, and I were going to land without becoming pancakes served Oz-style, it was going to take some serious witchcraft.

So as we plunged through the air, I just closed my eyes, tuned everything out, and concentrated, trying my best to ignore the fact that I probably had about fifteen seconds to get the job done. I couldn't think about that.

Instead, I focused on the energy that was all around me. I tuned into its frequency and focused on gathering it all up, channeling it through my body as the wind whipped fiercely past me.

Once, I'd seen Mombi do a spell where she reversed gravity, turning the whole world upside down and sending herself, along with her passengers, all shooting up into the sky. Like falling, but in the wrong direction. Or the right direction, depending on how you looked at it.

I wasn't so sure I'd be able to pull off that trick, but I hoped that even my bargain basement version of Mombi's designer magic would be good enough that my friends and I just might be able to walk away from this. Or at least crawl away. Or whatever.

And maybe it was because it was do-or-die or maybe it was something else, but for one of the first times ever, it came easily to me. I reached out with my mind and twisted the magic into something new; something that could help.

The first rule of magic is that it gets bored easily—it always wants to be something different than what it is. So I imagined it as an energy reforming itself into a parachute flying at our backs. I imagined it catching its sail in the wind, imagined it opening up and carrying us. It was like drawing a picture with my mind, or like molding a sculpture out of soft, slippery clay.

When I opened my eyes again, we were still falling, but our descent was slowing by the second. Soon we were floating like feathers, gliding easily toward the earth.

It had worked.

I can't say I wasn't surprised.

"Someone's been practicing her tricks," Ollie said. There was a hint of suspicion in his voice, but mostly it was just relief.

"I guess I just got lucky," I said. It was kind of a lie. It hadn't felt like luck at all. It hadn't felt like I had known what I was doing, either. Somehow I had just *done* it. But how?

I tried to put my insecurities aside. This wasn't the time for me to be doubting myself. It had been a gentler landing than I'd been planning on, but I felt as exhilarated and exhausted from the feat I'd just accomplished as if I'd run a marathon.

I picked myself up and brushed myself off, trying to collect myself. My body was aching, sore from the trip, and my mind raced as I sifted through everything that had just happened, knowing that I had to stay alert. I had a feeling that the Rocs hadn't attacked us by coincidence, which meant that, for now, we were still in danger.

And yet it was hard to be too worried when I saw where we had touched down: I was looking out over a sea of flowers, stretching far into the distance.

When I say a sea of flowers, I really mean that it was like an ocean, and not just because I couldn't see the limit to it. I mean, that was one thing, sure. More important, though, was the fact that it was moving.

The blossoms were undulating like waves, building themselves up and rolling toward us, petals spraying everywhere as they crashed at our feet, petering out into a normal, grassy meadow. If this was an ocean, we were standing right at the shore.

"I've heard of the Sea of Blossoms," Maude said. "I've heard of it but . . ."

Her voice trailed off as we all gazed out in something like amazement.

The Sea of Blossoms. It was beautiful. Not just beautiful: it was enchanted. Of everything I had seen since I had come to Oz, this felt the most like the magic that was supposed to be everywhere here. After our near-escape from the flying monsters, I knew I should be on edge, but there was something so joyful about the way the flowers were rippling in the breeze that I felt my heart filling with hope.

But then I turned around and saw what was behind us, and I remembered something Nox had once told me: that even in the best of circumstances, every bit of brightness in Oz was balanced out by something dark.

Here was that darkness, right on cue: At our backs, the way was blocked by a thick, black forest, with trees taller than I'd ever seen before, clustered together so closely that it was hard to see a way through. My body gave an involuntary shiver.

At least they didn't have faces. Still, there was something dangerous about it. Something that said *keep out*.

"Is this where the monkeys live?" I asked, hoping the answer was no.

Ollie gave a rueful little laugh. "Not quite. The Queendom of the Wingless Ones is deep in the forest, high above the trees. Flying would have been faster, but we still can make it there by nightfall, if we move quickly."

"And if the Fighting Trees decide to let us pass," Maude said darkly. "In the past, they have been friends to the monkeys, but nothing is certain these days. Things are changing quickly in Oz. The Sea of Blossoms was supposed to have dried up years ago. Ozma said the magic was returning. As foolish as she is, she is still deeply attuned to this land. I wonder if something your wicked friends did last night has awakened some of the magic Dorothy and Glinda have been stealing from it for all this time."

"It seems so," Ollie mused. "And what about the Rocs? They haven't been spotted in these parts in as long as I can remember. I had almost begun to wonder if they were just a legend."

"Do you think someone could have sent them for us?" I wondered aloud.

"Perhaps," Maude said thoughtfully. "But who?"

Ozma, who had been kneeling on the ground nearby, plucked a purple lily up and tucked it into her hair. She turned to us and spoke.

"He did it," she said, gathering up a bunch more of the flowers and pressing them to her face, inhaling the perfumed scent.

"Who?" I said, still not able to tell if this was just her usual babble or if she somehow knew what she was talking about. I studied her closely.

Ozma greeted my question with a blank stare and tossed the flowers to the ground. Instead of scattering, their stems burrowed right back into the dirt and then they were standing upright again—as if they'd never been picked in the first place.

"It's coming," she said. "He's coming too. Run and hide!"

Before I could question her further, there was a rustling in the trees and the soft, heavy thump of footsteps. A moment later, a hulking shadow emerged from the forest, and I knew instantly who Ozma had been sensing.

The Lion.

The air went out of everything. The chirping of the birds stopped; the sea of flowers was suddenly still and calm. Or, maybe calm was the wrong word. It looked more like it was afraid to move.

Even the sky seemed to know he was here. Just a second ago it had been bright and sunny, but in a flash the clouds had rolled across the sun, casting us in gray and gloomy shadows.

The Lion padded toward us. Where his feet met the earth, the flowers withered instantly into black and shriveled husks. Next to me, I felt Ollie and Maude freeze up with fear.

The Lion circled for a moment and then looked down at me, baring a grotesque mouthful of fangs in what was probably meant to be a smile. "Well, if it isn't little Miss Amy Gumm, Princess Ozma, and their two furry friends," he said. Maude and Ollie shrank back in terror. Ozma stood up and regarded the scene passively. The Lion glanced to my shoulder where Star was still perched, and he raised an eyebrow. "Make that *three* furry friends," he corrected himself.

My hand twitched as I instinctively summoned the magical knife that Nox had given me. The solid handle materialized in my hand and I took a step forward, feeling its heat burning against my palm.

"*You,*" I spat.

If the Lion was bothered by the threat in my voice, he didn't show it.

"I thought surely the fall would kill you, but I have to admit

I'm glad it didn't," he said, sinking back on his haunches and surveying us. "This way I get to enjoy you myself. It's been such a long time since I had a nice, square meal. And after that *terrible* brouhaha back in the Emerald City, I'm sure that Dorothy will forgive me if I don't take you back alive."

"Good luck with that, dude," I said. "I'm not as much of a pushover as you might think. I killed your pal the Tin Woodman last night, you know."

A look of surprise registered on the Lion's face, but it was gone as quickly as it had appeared. "The Tin Woodman is a lover, not a fighter," he said.

"Was," I corrected him. "Before I ripped his heart out."

The Lion narrowed his eyes and looked me up and down. He was used to people cowering before him, like Maude and Ollie, who were both quivering with fright, crouched on either side of me, their teeth chattering in terror.

This was the effect the Lion usually had. His courage had somehow been twisted into something dark and sick. Now it was a weapon. Wherever he went, he brought a cloud of terror with him. Just being around him was enough to make most people shrink in fear until it consumed them.

Then the Lion consumed it. He ate fear, literally. It made him stronger. I'd seen him do it—pick up a terrified Munchkin and suck the fright right out of him until the Munchkin was just a lifeless shell and the Lion was supercharged, bursting with power.

And yet, today, standing ten feet from him, I found that for the first time I wasn't afraid. I had already faced down everything that had ever frightened me, and I'd come out the other side.

Instead of fear, I felt my body fill with a deep rage. There was something about the anger that seemed to put everything into focus—it was like a pair of glasses I had put on, and I was finally seeing everything clearly.

The Tin Woodman's heart. The Lion's courage. The Scarecrow's brains. According to the Wizard, once I had all of them, Dorothy could finally die the death she deserved. I already had the first item in the bag strapped across my chest: the Tin Woodman's metal, clockwork heart. Now the second thing on my list was within reach—if only I could figure out where the Lion actually *kept* his courage.

No big deal, I thought. I could always figure that out after he was dead.

I wanted to wait for him to make the first move, though. I was counting on him underestimating me, but even on my best day the Lion still had ten times my physical strength.

"Now, let's see," the Lion was saying. "Who should I eat first?" He looked from me, to Ozma, to Ollie, to Maude, raising a gigantic claw and passing it around from one of us to the next.

"Bubblegum, bubblegum in a dish," he rumbled in a low, ominous croon. Maude. Ollie. Me. He paused as he reached Ozma. "You know," he mused, "I've never had much of a taste for bubblegum." The muscles in his hind legs twitched. "Fairies, on the other hand, are delicious."

"You're very bad," Ozma said scornfully. "You can't eat the queen."

I could have cheered, hearing her talking to him, totally unafraid, with such casual, careless haughtiness. You had to give it to her for nerve, even if it was just the kind of nerve that came from not really knowing any better. But the Lion didn't seem to think it was very funny.

I was ready for him when he growled and sprang for her. I moved before he did, slashing my knife through the air in a bright arc of red, searing flame, aiming right for him. Ozma clapped at the display. I was getting better at this magic thing.

But I was also overconfident: my blade barely grazed the Lion's flank. I drew blood, but not enough to slow him down. He simply twisted in annoyance and swiped for me with a powerful forearm. He hit me right in the gut and I went stumbling backward like a mosquito who had just been batted out of the way, landing on the ground on my butt in a burst of petals. I bounced up quickly only to see that Ozma, as it turned out, was perfectly capable of protecting herself.

She hadn't moved an inch, but a shimmering green bubble had somehow appeared up around her. The Lion clawed and poked at it, but wherever the force field had come from, it was impervious to his attacks. Ozma blinked innocently at him.

"Bad kitty!" she said. She scowled and wagged her finger at him. "Naughty cat!"

The Lion growled a low growl, apparently not amused at being called "kitty," and took another swipe at her. Again, though, his attack bounced right off of her protective bubble.

While the Lion was distracting himself with the princess, I

was stealthily circling toward him, positioning myself to strike again while charging up my knife with another magical flame.

"You've always been a stupid little thing," the Lion was saying to Ozma. "Nevertheless, I suppose you have your own *irritating* kind of power. It's a good thing there are other ways to teach a fairy a lesson."

He turned from Ozma and reached for Maude, who had curled herself into a ball on the ground, her teeth chattering with terror. She didn't even try to run. "No!" Ollie screamed, hurling himself in front of his sister.

This was my cue: I rushed him.

The Lion sensed me coming. He spun around and gave a furious roar, his jaw practically unhinging.

He lunged for me.

Fake out.

Just as he was about to grab me, I flipped myself backward into the air and blinked myself behind him, my teleportation spell reversing my momentum as I landed on his back. I grabbed a hunk of his mane in my fist and pulled hard, yanking his head backward.

"I've been wanting to do this for awhile," I said through gritted teeth, using every ounce of strength I had to slash my burning blade across his exposed throat. I cringed at the sound of his flesh hissing under my weapon's white-hot heat, but somewhere, deep down, I found myself surprised at how used to this kind of violence I had already gotten. At how easily it came to me.

As the Lion howled, I felt some small kind of pleasure in his pain. I pushed it aside, but it was there. I felt the tiniest glimmer of a smile at the corners of my lips.

The Lion bucked and shook wildly and I hung on to his mane for dear life, thinking of my mom's friend Bambi Plunkett, who had once won five hundred dollars riding the mechanical bull at the Raging Stallion on Halifax Avenue. Unfortunately, I quickly discovered that I wasn't going to be crowned queen of the rodeo anytime soon.

As the Lion desperately tried to shake me, I felt my hold on his mane begin to slip. He jumped into the air and we landed with a force that shook the ground, flowers flying everywhere. As he gave one last powerful shudder, I lost my grip and tumbled off of him, my head cracking against the ground.

My vision blurred. In a flurry of fur and fangs, the Lion pounced, the weight of his body crushing my legs as he pinned my arms with his paws.

"I see you're a courageous little one," he purred, pushing his face just inches from mine. "I must admit, I didn't expect it from you." He smacked his chops. "We'll just have to change that, won't we?"

A trickle of blood made its way from his throat, down his fur, and onto my shirt, and I saw that the cut across his throat was really just a surface wound. I'd barely hurt him.

This wasn't going as well as I'd thought it would. I tried to blink myself out from under him, but my head was still throbbing from the fall I'd just taken, and as hard as I tried, I found that I couldn't quite summon the magic for it.

Then, before I could decide what to do next, I heard a squeal. Out of the corner of my eye, I saw a white streak through the grass as Star scurried away, and felt the Lion's weight on my body lighten, as he leaned over and shot a paw out.

"No!" I screamed, suddenly realizing what was coming. But there was nothing I could do. He had grabbed my rat by the tail, and she wriggled and screeched as he held her over my face.

"Dorothy wants *you* alive, brave little Amy," he said. "And while I haven't decided yet whether to let her have her way this time, in the meantime, *this* one will make a nice appetizer."

The Lion snapped his jaw open. Star's final scream sounded almost human as he dangled her over his toothy, gaping maw.

First the fear left her. It went streaming from her trembling body into the Lion's open mouth in a wispy burst like a puff of smoke from a cigarette. Then she was still, looking down at me with wide, placid eyes.

There wasn't much left of her, but at least I knew that she wasn't afraid when she died. The Lion dropped her into his mouth and chomped hard. A trickle of blood made its way down his chin.

"Not very filling," he said with a laugh. "But I hear rats are actually a delicacy in some parts of Oz." He paused and licked a stray bit of my poor, dead rat's white fur from his lips. "Now, on to the main course."

"No," I said, as something strange came over me. I felt more lucid than ever, like my senses had been supercharged. I felt like I was looking down on myself, watching the scene unfold from somewhere far away. "Wrong. Fucking. Move." With that, I blinked myself out of his clutches.

The Lion lurched in surprise and twisted around to face me where I was now standing, a few yards away, my back to the trees. He pawed at the ground.

Somewhere in my peripheral vision—somewhere on the edge of my consciousness—I saw that Ollie and Maude were both clinging to Ozma under the protection of her bubble. They were safe, but I hardly cared anymore.

I didn't care about them, I didn't care about Oz. I didn't even care about myself. All I cared about was my dead rat.

That stupid little rat was the last connection I had to home. In some ways she was the only friend I had left. She had made it through Dorothy's dungeons with me. She had helped me survive. Now she was gone. The Lion had eaten her as easily as a marshmallow Easter Peep.

Now I was alone for real. But suddenly I knew that it was really no different from before. It was no different from Kansas, even.

I had always been alone and I would always be alone. It had just taken me this long to figure it out.

All I cared about now was revenge.

The Lion bounded for me with a thundering growl so loud it shook the trees. I didn't move to step aside. If the Lion thought eating my rat and creating a racket was going to make me afraid, he couldn't have been more wrong. I was less afraid than ever.

I was ready to kill, and I suddenly had no doubt what the outcome would be.

My heart opened up into an endless pit. I looked over the edge into the void, and then I jumped right in.

Brandishing my knife, I silently called out for more fire—for the white-hot flames of the sun. The Lion was going to burn.

The fire didn't come. Instead, like a glass filling with ink, my blade turned from polished, flashing silver to an obsidian so deep and dark that it seemed to be sucking the light right out of the sky.

It wasn't what I had been expecting, but that was how magic sometimes worked. Magic is tricky. It's not as simple as saying "abracadabra" and waving a wand. When you cast the spell, the magic becomes a part of you. Who you are can change it. And I was different now.

Once, I had been an angry, righteous little ball of fire. Now I was something else.

But what?